ALSO BY

CLEYVIS NATERA

Neruda on the Park

THE
GRAND PALOMA
RESORT

The GRAND PALOMA RESORT

A NOVEL

CLEYVIS NATERA

BALLANTINE BOOKS

NEW YORK

Ballantine Books
An imprint of Random House
A division of Penguin Random House LLC
1745 Broadway, New York, NY 10019
randomhousebooks.com
penguinrandomhouse.com

Copyright © 2025 by Cleyvis Natera Tucker

BALLANTINE BOOKS & colophon are registered
trademarks of Penguin Random House LLC.

Hardcover ISBN 978-0-593-87326-7
Ebook ISBN 978-0-593-87328-1

Printed in the United States of America on acid-free paper

1st Printing

FIRST EDITION

BOOK TEAM: PRODUCTION EDITOR: *Jennifer Rodriguez* •
MANAGING EDITOR: *Pamela Alders* • PRODUCTION MANAGER: *Nathalie Mairena* •
COPY EDITOR: *Taylor McGowan* • PROOFREADERS: *Amy Harned, Deb Bader,
Andrea Gordon*

Book design by *Barbara M. Bachman*

Title page image by Adobe Stock/Nikolay N. Antonov

The authorized representative in the EU for product safety and compliance
is Penguin Random House Ireland, Morrison Chambers, 32 Nassau Street,
Dublin D02 YH68, Ireland. https://eu-contact.penguin.ie

This book is dedicated to
the workers and laborers who keep
the Caribbean tourism industry thriving.

For my mother, Nicolasa "Fragancia" Lucas,
who taught me love is labor, and
labor should be grounded in love.

. . .

Este libro está dedicado a
los trabajadores y obreros que
mantienen viva la industria turística del Caribe.

Para mi madre, Nicolasa "Fragancia" Lucas,
quien me enseñó que el amor es trabajo,
y el trabajo debe estar fundamentado en el amor.

Because, after all, doesn't everyone behave badly given the opportunity?

—JAMAICA KINCAID,
A Small Place

And in Sylvie's eyes was a longing I knew very well, from the memory of it as it was once carved into my younger face: I will bear anything, carry any load, suffer any shame, walk with eyes to the ground, if only for the very small chance that one day our fates might come to being somewhat closer and I would be granted for all my years of travail and duty an honestly gained life that in some extremely modest way would begin to resemble hers.

—EDWIDGE DANTICAT,
The Farming of Bones

THE
GRAND PALOMA
RESORT

THE
GRAND PALOMA
RESORT

Paloma Falls,
DOMINICAN REPUBLIC

WELCOME TO THE GRAND PALOMA RESORT. OUR LUXURY, all-inclusive Four-Diamond-rated property rests on 2,500 acres of beachfront land located in Paloma Falls, Dominican Republic. Aside from our Four-Diamond-rated accommodations, we also house a Masters-approved golf course, a world-renowned spa with a composite score of five stars by Forbes, a suite of tennis courts designed by the Williams sisters, and eleven restaurants, including the only Michelin-starred restaurant in all of the Caribbean region, Mondongo. All areas of the resort are available to our Platinum and Executive Platinum members. Enjoy consciousness expansion workshops, yoga, meditation, mud baths, shaman-healing sessions, energy-shifting workshops, and a raw, farm-to-table diet (rated #1 for wedding readiness by *New Bride Magazine*) alongside our revolutionary back-to-nature walks guided by our conservationist team.

A map of the resort grounds can be found on the next page. A history of the Dominican Republic will be furnished upon request.

PALOMA'S SIGNATURE
PLATINUM BRACELETS

The Grand Paloma Resort's signature platinum bracelet is a collaboration between local artisans and our very own jewelers.

It sports a braided band made with locally sourced cotton fibers mixed with Egyptian silk and gold threads for durability. The signature platinum dove in flight is a symbol of the freedom and joy we hope you feel as we care for you. If you lose the bracelet, the replacement fee is $1,500 USD. *Bracelets must be worn at all times on and off the resort grounds.*

SAFETY

At the Grand Paloma Resort, our number-one priority is to keep you and your loved ones safe. A few tips:

1. Don't leave the resort grounds.
2. If you must leave the resort, do so accompanied by one of our resort's companions.
3. There are legal consequences and steep penalties for the consumption or sale of illicit drugs.
4. Kindly note that only registered guests are allowed on hotel premises.
5. Unregistered guests cannot be added to an existing reservation.

The U.S. Department of State has urged caution when traveling to Caribbean destinations and has recently issued a Level 4 advisory in the Dominican Republic. Claims of civil unrest, violent home invasions, armed robberies, sexual assault, and homicides are common. Our resort has never experienced a single incident of violence. There is no safer place to rest, play, and work than within the confines of the Grand Paloma Resort. But it is important to remember to be safe. Anything you wish for is within your reach on our resort's grounds. There is no request we will not fulfill. We offer a remarkable, elevated guest experience, every time.

We hope you have a lovely stay with us. Welcome, you Parasites!

YOUR TEAM AT THE GRAND PALOMA RESORT

THURSDAY

CHAPTER

1

THE TOURIST CHILD'S MUD-STREAKED BODY HAD BECOME heavy and sweat made her slippery in Elena's arms. As she made her way out from the tropical forest behind the Grand Paloma Resort, Elena headed not in the direction of the manicured grounds but into the water-starved, cracked dirt of the staff quarters. Looking down at the little girl's unconscious form, she whispered, "Please, please, please don't die on me."

She wove through row after row of beautiful casitas. Alternating between vibrant turquoise and the brightest yellow, with a flash of hot pink every fourth or fifth little house, each decorated with flower beds full of birds of paradise and lilac hibiscus bushes, it was the kind of sight that would make a visitor sigh in delight. Unless they happened to touch the plants and realize they were plastic. Nothing got watered in this part of the resort.

Once she was safely inside the casita she shared with her older sister, Laura, Elena took a breath and looked around, unsure whether to lay the child on her bed or her sister's. Relief washed over her. No one had seen her. It was as if the dusty ground of that forest had lifted and shrouded her.

She was paralyzed momentarily by the weight of the child's body. What was she? Sixty pounds? Two hundred? Elena was dizzy from the heat and humidity. She'd been hired to care for the now injured and unconscious child, looking after the girl by day and sleeping in a tiny cot-sized room in the back of the kitchen of the penthouse suite that the girl and her parents occupied. She hadn't been in the casita all week. Elena's side was as messy as she'd left it—unmade bed, strewn clothes, shoes everywhere. It was shocking. Her sister always cleaned up after her.

Elena laid the kid on Laura's neatly made bed. She called the girl's name and shook her gently. No response. The blond bouncy curls that had swayed when they'd tried the latest viral TikTok dance that morning, before their outing in the forest, were matted with mud and blood. The kid's flat chest seemed too still. Had it been a mistake, moving the girl?

Elena caught sight of herself in the full-length mirror. Her dark brown skin shone from the effort of carrying this kid. The bald head she'd shaved to celebrate her freedom from the global academy, from the confines of this place, appeared oversized. The big eyes that everyone always complimented her on were full of tears. The slender frame she worked hard at, swimming two, sometimes three times a day when she wasn't charged with full-time work as a babysitter, made her seem fragile, prepubescent. She was seventeen but looked like a fourteen-year-old. The pink scrubs that identified her immediately to all guests as a babysitter exaggerated that image, softening her. She'd worked hard to appear revolutionary, but now look at her: a terrified kid.

Elena sat on the bed to take a breath. She was comforted by the smell of her sister's woody perfume. Laura's row of white uniforms—which denoted her rank as part of the senior leadership team of the hotel's management—was rigid in the closet. On her sister's night table was Elena's final paper, the one she'd written just two months ago as a requirement for graduation from the international high school: "The Case Against Statelessness." Her teacher had said it was great writing but had predictable conclusions. *The questions you ask are important,* she'd said, *truly excellent, but what about resolutions? Is there a way through?* Still, she'd gotten an A. The walls were decorated with posters from the cities the sisters wished to one day visit together—London, New York, Milan, Paris.

Elena called her sister, who didn't answer her cellphone.

Elena called again and again and again.

Laura finally answered. "I'm busy, Elena," she said sharply, then hung up.

Elena knelt next to the bed. She kissed the girl's forehead, tasting the coppery mountain mud. There was a bit of sweetness in it. She remembered how warm the mud had been when she'd first suggested they should do mud masks. The kid's skin didn't feel warm anymore. It felt cold, clammy. Something was changing. The mud had dried and crusted on her skin. The girl's eyelids fluttered. Elena held her breath as it seemed she was on the cusp of opening her eyes. But then the kid seemed to grow more still, tiny red and blue veins becoming more pronounced beneath the soft, almost transparent skin of her eyelids.

Elena reached inside the pocket of her pants. She found the last yellow ecstasy pill she'd been holding on to, which she had planned to chew later when she took the kid to the beach. She had taken another pill just like it when they were deep in the forest, crunching it between her teeth, swallowing the grimy texture, tasting that bitterness that coated her tongue. When the kid fell, Elena had been outstretched on the dry dirt, glad that the feeling of hopelessness seemed galaxies away. As the CIELO brand seemed to promise, she'd felt like she was floating in the sky, but she'd also been fully present in her body, marveling at the beauty of the trees that canopied them in a warm glow, humming with the glorious vibration of interconnectedness. They were a part of everything. Harmony was within reach.

She was tempted to take this pill now, to escape this terrible situation. But she knew that was a bad idea. She was coming down from her high. She would take this pill later, save it as a reward for when she figured a way out of this circumstance. Holding the pill made her feel bold, brave. Time to act.

Elena called her friend Pablo, praying he'd pick up the phone on the first ring.

"Dimelo, loca," Pablo said, laughter lacing his tone. "What did you do now?"

Elena felt indignant at the way he stressed the word *now*.

She realized that calling Pablo for help was a bad idea. She needed Laura. "Do you have any more of the yellow pills?" she asked instead.

"Muchacha, what's wrong with you? Not on the phone. Swing by if you want, I'm descaling the fish."

Pablo hadn't mentioned it, so apparently, the parents of the unconscious girl hadn't yet rung an alarm, demanding to know what the hell had happened to their eight-year-old child. Elena supposed that, like most people who visited the Grand Paloma Resort to forget their boring, rich lives, to experience something shocking and surprising, maybe even transcendental, the unconscious girl's parents were sitting by the pool in the stifling August heat to burn their skin—to get that delicious, tingling feeling that eventually raised their body temperatures, that made them hungry for touching, licking; for feeling a rush of air-conditioned currents on their naked limbs so that when they went back home at the end of their vacation they could say to their friends, "Yes, Dominican Republic truly is paradise. I'm so happy I got away."

Snap out of it! The parents might call for their child any moment.

Elena redialed Laura, let the line ring again-again-again. She tried her office line instead.

"Laura Moreno," Laura said in a sophisticated tone.

"It's me," Elena said.

"What?!" Laura was annoyed.

"You've got to come to our room now!"

"Calm down, what happened?"

"There's been an accident with la muchachita from PH7."

CHAPTER

2

VIDA, THE TOWN'S CURANDERA, STOOD IN FRONT OF THE BED where the tourist child's body rested. She had yet to touch the girl. She looked so precious, so small. She might have been mistaken for sleeping if not for the crusted mud, the dried blood. Vida rubbed her hands against each other in small circles. Hopelessness was a magnet that pulled on her like an undertow. "What happened to this girl?"

Elena and her older sister, Laura, looked on, so hopeful, like Vida was a buoy. Vida made a noise in her throat.

"I only took my eye off her for a minute," Elena finally said. Elena pressed her tongue into the gap between her front teeth, a gap that stretched gigantic today, as if it might accommodate her entire tongue if she pressed hard enough. Neither Elena's wide, deep-set eyes nor her feet seemed able to settle. Noticing it, Elena tried to command her body to be still.

"Tell her what you told me," Laura commanded.

Laura, a decade older than Elena, had strikingly similar facial features. That wide forehead, the button nose, the wide, full mouth, the incandescent dark skin. But her body was that of a grown woman—she was wide in the hips with thick legs that seemed able to carry a great deal of weight. She also wore long, expensive extensions, acrylic fingernails, and a bracelet that dangled from her surprisingly small right wrist, all spikes and sharp edges. She cut her eyes at her younger sister.

Elena struggled to speak. Vida sensed the monumental way in which Elena's life was about to change. There was no way Elena could come back from the disaster in front of them unscathed. The little girl hadn't stirred in the minutes they'd been standing there.

"Tell me exactly what happened," Vida insisted.

"I just closed my eyes for a minute," Elena repeated.

"No," Vida said, gently, "when you found her. Tell me that part."

"We don't have time for this, Vida," Laura said.

"She fell in the forest, into a pit," Elena said. "She hit her head. I picked her up. Put her on my lap. I touched the back of her head."

Elena looked at her fingers as she spoke. Vida leaned in, listening carefully. Elena had not washed her hands. The gelatinous blood webbed her fingers to each other.

"She was bleeding from the nose," Elena said, words now gurgling out. "So much blood. I wiped the blood with my uniform shirt." Elena held that corner of the shirt now, shoved it toward the other two women. There was no way to tell the blood from the mud on the fabric. "I picked her up and ran here."

"Did she ever open her eyes? Respond in any way?" Vida asked.

Elena was almost sure the tourist girl's lids had fluttered when she'd laid her flat on Laura's bed. Elena inhaled, shook her head no.

"I told her to stay near me. I hadn't slept the night before. I swear to you, I closed my eyes for one minute. Maybe two."

"With children, it takes seconds for a tragedy to happen," Laura said. "You should've known better. Why would you take her into the forest?"

Elena remembered the colorful photo advertising the future water park. Kids playing, laughing, falling. But she knew Laura would be upset if she learned they'd been in that part of the forest. "Stupid girl. That's what she gets for not listening to me."

"I'm sorry," Vida said. "I want to help but I can't. Take her to the hospital? We've already wasted so much time."

Elena's eyes darted to Laura, who unbuttoned her suit jacket. The shirt underneath it was such a bright white that it stung her eyes. If Laura and Elena took the girl to the doctor, they would be in big trouble. The Grand Paloma Resort would kill to save its reputation as the safest resort in all of DR. The tension between the two sisters, all those silences and secrets, took what little oxygen there was in the room.

"No one's going to a hospital," Laura said.

"Maybe Vida is right. We should go to the hospital," Elena said, panicked.

"Now you want to do what's right?" Laura said. "Now you want to use common sense?"

Vida ignored the sisters. She brought her ear close to the unconscious girl's mouth. She pressed her thumb against her wrist. Her heart was beating. She was alive, still. "Where are the girl's parents?" Vida asked. "They must be going crazy looking for her."

"They're not that kind of parents," Elena said. "I've been babysitting for a week, and they rarely check on her. I send them photos all day long. They don't even heart the pics."

"This poor girl," Vida said.

"They booked a two-week stay in the presidential penthouse suite. Can you believe it, two weeks, that's how rich they are," Elena said.

"Vida, you have to help us," Laura said, shaking her head in irritation at Elena's nonsense talk. All the guests were obnoxiously rich. She walked away from them both. Standing by the window, she pulled the curtains closed, worried that someone might have noticed her coming to the staff quarters. She took a deep breath, grateful that for once all she inhaled was the salt-rich air. There was no denying that her little sister was at the bottom rung of a yearlong downward spiral. She felt panic rising inside her chest, threatening to choke her. Laura was responsible for her sister's recklessness, for her lack of grounding. Now, she had to pretend she was calm, otherwise Vida would leave. Vida was the only chance they had at getting out of this disaster. She didn't understand why Vida was hesitating—why she didn't just put her hands on the girl, perform her mysterious healing ritual.

"We should tell her parents," Vida urged.

"Vida, trust me," Elena said. "First day here, the couple left for the kind of bender no one has seen in years. Alcohol, drugs, prostitutes—Astrid from guest services had to be called to get them out of the Paloma Falls police station. This happened not once, not twice, but many times in the last week. From the moment I met them, I knew something was strange about them. They hired me to babysit twenty-four hours a day for fourteen days. Most guests ask for babysitting at night for a few hours so they can go dancing and the baby can sleep, but they just gave her to me."

Vida felt a growing sense of dread. Should she perform the ritual? Would it be safe?

"What are you waiting for?" Laura said. "Put your hands on her."

Vida felt inadequate in her cotton shift dress, her everyday chancletas. Laura was so elegant in her white kimono-inspired suit jacket and wide pant legs, even as her stilettos dug into the dirt floor. Laura's absurd weave fulfilled its intended purpose. She was polished, authoritative in the way only women who spent inordinate amounts of money on their grooming appeared to be. *Gerente,* her silver tag said beneath her name. The entire town had been so proud when she'd been selected as the head of personnel and Platinum member programs at the resort. She was the one who'd called Vida, sounding so desperate. Vida had been at her best friend's seaside beach bar. She had been tying intricate, colorful silk ribbons around Dulce's daughters' hair. But when her phone had rung and she'd ignored it, Laura's text had come through in all caps.

IT'S ALL ABOUT TO GO TO HELL.
PICK THE FUCKING PHONE UP.

Vida regretted taking the call, coming back to this place. Vida had performed miracles big and small. Laura and Elena needed a miracle, but now that Vida was pregnant, she had to prioritize her baby. Unsurprisingly, both sisters had been too distracted to notice Vida's body. Vida tried hard to remember if her mother had ever said anything about whether it was safe to heal someone when pregnant. The most pressing desire she'd had in her thirty-two years of life had been to have a baby. It had never occurred to her that she'd have to make a choice between a pregnancy and continuing her healing work. Since her mother had died so many years ago, she didn't have anyone to ask. There were no other curanderas in the local town of Pico Diablo. Too nervous to take a chance, she'd stopped all her healing ways. She'd done little more since she'd learned she was pregnant than sell her tinctures and remedios, refusing to touch another person. The resort had a doctor on staff who would see locals if they were related to someone who worked at the hotel. And at this point, Vida was the only person in their town who didn't work for, or was related to, a person who worked at the resort.

Laura made an impatient sound at the back of her throat, mimicking the noise Vida had made moments earlier. When Laura's acrylic nails tapped against the flat screen of her cellphone, Vida knew she had to move. Either decide to help the girl or leave.

Off in the distance, the crashing ocean became louder, alongside the sound of laughter and clapping hands. *¡Dale, Dale, Dale pa' bajo!* People were having lots of fun at the pool on this side of the resort. In the room, the silence grew thicker.

Vida studied the blood and dirt caked into the matted hair on the girl's head. The child still hadn't made a single sound. It might already be too late.

"I will not protect you this time," Laura said to Elena, fuming.

Vida remembered that from the time they were kids, after the sisters' mother had died, Laura had taken on the role of mother, shouldering a level of responsibility that had made everyone in the Pico Diablo Mountain town look at the girl with admiration, even if it had always been tinged with pity. Back then, Vida, four years older than Laura, had thanked her lucky stars that even though her father was a philandering deserter, at least he wasn't as big of a mess as Laura and Elena's father, Ezequiel Moreno. Everyone had known that E.Z. was a gambler, a drunk, a dreamer whose only life goal was getting to the United States. Laura had been sweet and hard-working, if a bit intense, but never this short, this impatient. There was a hardness about her, a toughness that hadn't existed before. Vida understood it had everything to do with this place where they worked. This was the kind of place that changed people, that changed priorities and values. Where else would someone not immediately call a doctor or an ambulance when a child fell and got injured?

"It's too late now," Laura said with finality. "It's up to us to save the girl. It's up to you, Vida. You know you will never be able to forgive yourself if you don't do everything possible to heal this girl."

Vida sighed and closed her eyes briefly, deciding. "I'm going to ask the two of you to leave so I can get to work," she said. It was always best she do the most dangerous part of her healing ritual alone.

VIDA HAD LEARNED TO use the heat from her mother when she'd been a child no bigger than this one. She went into her purse, moved the healing ointments she was known for out of the way, found the small pouch she needed, and began to rub bija seeds on her hands. The small red seeds filled the room with a coppery, bitter scent. When she was done, her hands were vibrantly red, as if they were wet with blood. Not brown, dried blood. Newborn blood.

Vida's mother had been so serious when she'd first taught her how to manipulate pain—to turn it into something else. "Listen carefully now," Vida's mother had said. "You have to be cautious when you do this because the heat is actually coming from inside the body, and it can burn your hands. That's why I put the bija on them. It protects the skin. But it's your mind that must be strong. Do you understand?"

Vida had nodded vigorously as her mother spoke, even though she hadn't understood. Small waves of heat emanated from this child's body now. Vida wished she'd asked Elena the child's name.

Her mother's words always swarmed in her head when she did this part. A litany. *What you're trying to do is catch the pain, wherever it is, and pull it out of the body. Take that pain into yourself and turn it into something else.*

Over at the Taíno-inspired wellness center a few hundred meters away, they offered what new-age folks called Reiki. When they'd first become serious, Pablo had talked Vida into coming onboard as an employee of the resort, so they could be together all the time. Vida had tried, but had ended up shaking her head at him after just one day at the job—this work she did, it was important. What the tourists wanted were massages with a little woo-woo thrown in. Her work was sacred, she'd explained. Not to be administered at the whim of a bored foreigner. She forced thoughts of Pablo out of her mind. She could hear her mother's words, clear, precise: *Pain either goes to your head or your heart. You change it to joy, or love, whatever you want.* But after practicing for over two decades, Vida had learned it wasn't always true. Sometimes, for days after she healed someone, she walked around with the stain of the bija on her hands, crying for no reason at all, a bigger stain slowly spreading inside her body.

Vida amassed the heat at a central point in the child's belly, then very slowly allowed it into herself. The girl's breath quickened; her body began to convulse. It was hardest working with children. But Vida relaxed as sacred knowledge flooded her being. Now that she and the child were completely open to each other, Vida felt flushed with competence, understanding. The pain entering Vida's body was something she recognized, knew what to do with. Neglect always felt a little cold. The danger, of course, was that she could transfer the burdens of her own mind to this fragile body. *Can't confront someone else's pain without facing your own,* her mother used to say.

The heat in her hands forced Vida to open her eyes. There was a resistance; this child didn't want to let all the pain go. Vida got it. There was comfort in embracing one's own misery. But with a bit of love, she persuaded the girl to let go. Drops of bija fell off Vida's hands onto the child, whose body glistened with a layer of sweat. The red drops shone brightly and did not dissolve or slide down the sides of her arms, neck, face. Instead, they adorned her body like jewels on a gold chain. Vida felt a growing coldness in her womb and felt the fetus inside her flutter.

"All three of us will be okay," she said aloud, feeling shaky.

She forged ahead, knowing deep down that what she had just said might be a lie.

CHAPTER
3

LAURA TOLD HER SISTER TO STAY PUT RIGHT OUTSIDE THE casita's door. She had to get back to work but would return as quickly as she could. Elena nodded, transfixed by her hands. They were trembling.

Laura felt her anger evaporate. She reached for her sister, wishing she could give her a hug. But Elena was filthy. She touched the side of her face instead.

"Why don't you use the hose to clean yourself up a bit?"

Elena nodded again. Then she looked up at Laura, her tears spilling over.

"Do you have to go?" she asked.

"I'll be back as soon as I can," Laura said.

Laura turned away. She took a few steps and turned back toward her sister. Elena was gazing through the window, attempting to get a glimpse of Vida's work, horror-struck. Laura thought Elena was scared enough to have finally learned her lesson. The staff quarters were at the foot of the Pico Diablo Mountain, inland and quite far from the guest section of the resort, which was spread over four miles of beachfront property. Turning back around, Laura climbed onto the golf cart and drove off, following a serpentine path. She would enter the resort via the lobby and reception. She did not want anyone to trace her movements back to the staff quarters. If Elena and Vida decided they needed to call the doctor after all, she'd catch hell if her boss learned that she had been around, had opted not to get medical help right away. Laura gripped the stiff steering wheel, willing herself to stop shaking.

Once she was meters away from the main entrance, she parked the golf cart to walk the rest of the way. She struggled to increase her pace on the cobblestone path, which, though picturesque, was illogical for walking. As she neared the circular entrance, she saw the four VPs who ran the resort alongside her climbing into their own golf cart. Where the hell were they headed? The staff meeting was set to start in a quarter of an hour. She noticed the golf clubs in the back of the cart as they drove off.

She paused by a shaded side of the path and searched her email inbox to see if the meeting had been canceled, feeling hopeful for a moment that her colleagues' departure to play golf meant she could also head back to keep an eye on the girl until she was out of danger. But no, the meeting was still on. Her boss had sent an agenda just a few minutes ago.

In front of her was the Grand Paloma Resort's main building. The twelve-story structure was made of glass and metal, sprawling with reflective glass so that all around her was the lush green forest and the clear, all-blue sky. She entered the lobby and felt the rush of frigid air—a monumental extravagance since all the doors were open, dispersing the conditioned air into the sticky, humid heat. A few steps ahead of her, a pair of thin Black women were making their way in, a bellboy pushing a cart with their expensive luggage. There was something stiff and proper about them. They were likely here for one of the scheduled business retreats. But they wore brightly colored print ensembles, had neatly box-braided hair that dropped all the way to the small curves of their backs. As Laura passed them, she said, "Welcome to the Grand Paloma Resort," at the same time that Pasofino, one of the greeters, approached them. The women exchanged appreciative glances as he extended a tray of welcome cocktails. If he was their type, the women would be in for nonstop eye candy. Pasofino wasn't even among the most handsome of the workers.

"Thank you," the women said in chorus. Laura was irritated by their American accents. How many more American tourists could this resort hold? They asked the server what was on the tray. He explained, pointing an orange-polished index finger at each option: Paloma Palomas, Mango Paradise, Cuba Libres. They each took a drink and sipped, then turned toward the view.

"Wow," one said.

"This is incredible," the other exclaimed.

In front of them, past the enormous tropical flower display, the lobby parted into an outdoor gallery with a handful of tables scattered on either side of a Santorini-white stairwell that led down to an infinity pool. Celadon tiles glistened prettily beneath the saltwater surface. On both sides of the pool, palm trees stretched sixty feet into the air, while at the bases of their trunks, stout dwarf bottle palms squatted, beckoning the touch of those who lounged nearby.

Beyond the pool, there was the sea, which stretched eternal. The view had been designed to be a showstopper, and these tourists weren't immune. They were glued in place, silenced in reverence, even as Pasofino nudged them slightly in the direction of registration. There was a big bus of arrivals coming, he said. They better hurry to beat the line.

The women remained fixed in place. They would not be rushed.

Laura's gaze didn't follow the tourists' as they admired the palatial ceilings or the inspiring views of water and sky. Her eyes remained locked on their expressions, then moved upward to the sculpture of a bird suspended two hundred feet above their heads by invisible, intricate wire. Today, the shards of black mirrored glass seemed even more regal, the bird's wings spanning almost the entirety of the lobby floor. Beyond it, a skylight that showed that perfect, cloudless sky made the fragmented bird appear to be in flight, a tapestry of all of them, workers and guests at once; of the structure of the interior of the hotel, including the expensive furniture and plants; of the sky above them; and even of the cold air, which frosted what could be seen and made it unseen. Laura acknowledged a momentary swelling in her chest.

On a less stressful day, she might have been comforted by the resort's tall columns and all-white décor; by the diffusers that sprayed one-of-a-kind scents, inspired by the local flora, into all public areas every ten minutes; and by the orderly way the employees went about their designated work. Truthfully, as of late, the resort had felt like a prison, an unbearable labor camp. In August, with the cycle of arrivals and departures, the often-ludicrous demands of these guests that she was required to bend to—no matter what—and the way her staff ballooned from the permanent to the temporary, Laura would be lucky if she got five hours of sleep a night until the last day of the month. Since last August, she'd consistently had less sleep than that.

Today, she reminded herself that they'd made it halfway through the month of August. In two more weeks, she'd learn if her request to be transferred had been granted. Everything had been marching toward a resounding yes. Now, with that small child barely conscious on her thin mattress, she was once again acutely aware of how tenuous her livelihood was, of how it could be snuffed through no fault of her own. She checked her phone, growing anxious that Elena hadn't sent her an update. She sent a text to Vida. How's it going?

She waited in vain for an immediate response. When her cellphone buzzed moments later, Laura hoped Vida had replied to her message. But no, it was just the ten-minute reminder for the upcoming meeting. She moved quickly, smiling in encouragement as she passed the two Black women, who remained dazed by the views. Just then, a blast of air-conditioned air swept through the lobby, and Laura's outrageous extensions lifted as if of their own volition, off her shoulders and back, the strands flowing as if she were the focal point in a photo shoot of a woman who possessed those things that most matter—if not power, then control over some; if not conventional beauty, then the accoutrements that told the world she was worthy of attention and respect. The kind of person for whom no door would remain closed for long.

Laura was being considered for a promotion that would include a transfer. If it went through, she and her sister would move to Portugal in just a matter of weeks—in Lisbon, they would make a brand-new life. But to leave this place, she had to ensure that the hotel thrived; it was the only way she'd get another chance somewhere else. With that child unconscious on the bed, she became ever more aware that it was all so close to falling apart. The silence from her sister and Vida made her fear it already had.

CHAPTER
4

OUTSIDE, THE DAY HAD BECOME BLAZINGLY HOT. WHEN VIDA
stepped into that heat, Elena was no longer standing there, not
waiting as Laura had instructed. Vida hadn't heard the exchange between the sisters. Now that she'd finished the more dangerous steps of
the ritual, she had to clean the girl up, dress her wounds. She reached
one of the hoses on the side of the casita and turned the knob. The
water spurted out—searing. She let it run until it was cool to the touch.
She took a few deep, calming breaths, made her way back with the wet
towels. She wiped the mud and blood off the girl's face, did her best to
do the same with the wound on her head. The girl immediately shuddered, moaned in pain.

Vida removed the tinctures from her bag. She applied pungent
balm to the wound, affixed it with a colorful fabric she'd inherited
from her mother. As she did so, she chanted the next part of the ritual
aloud, and for a moment, it felt as if her mother's voice were there
alongside her own, emerging as a chorus from her throat.

"Pain of hurt, amor. Pain of neglect, amor. Pain of broken bones,
blood flowing, flowing, turn to an abundance of health. Forgive the
body for being so frail, so easy to break, so easy to damage. Forgive the
spirit for its everlasting fear, for its tendency to hide, for its desire to
disappear. Choose courage, choose strength, choose the power to go
on. Come on, go on. When you cannot speak, sing. When you cannot
sing, dream of a better us."

Then it was done. She'd have to wait for the healing session to
work, for the injuries to respond to the spiritual intervention. Sometimes, with adults, it was only a matter of an hour or two. With kids, it

was difficult to anticipate. But already she saw the girl's cheeks flush with color, her breathing normalizing, growing steady.

Vida sat down on the hard ground to wait, resting her head on the shelf made by her bent knees. In just a moment, she'd catch her breath, gain some more strength, and stand, call them. Elena or Laura would come back, and she'd be able to head home to rest.

When a bit of wind blew into the room through the shutterless window, separating the curtains and lifting the edge of the yellow sheet off the dirt floor, Vida didn't lift her head. There followed, after the wind, the nauseating scent of human waste from the communal employee toilets, which were more often out-of-service than not. Some employees still used the toilets, even if they couldn't flush. Far-off, muted noises filtered in from the main resort grounds—the laughter of children, splashing from the pool, music interrupted by resort workers who were loudly encouraging their patrons to dance. *A bailar!* someone shouted into a microphone. Was that Pablo's voice she heard? When Vida snapped her head upright, her gaze became fixed on the sheet, which was stained brown along the hem, as it caught the movement of the wind. The sheet descended and settled on the fabric in perfect alignment with an already existing stain.

From the distance came the sound of the entertainment staff at the pool again. They were doing an aerobics routine.

> *La mano arriba*
> *Cintura sola*
> *De media vuelta*
> *Danza kuduro*

The women instructors in their tiny bikinis and the men, revealing even more skin in Speedos, were all on display for the tourists. Vida imagined that they were a menu of sorts that guests could pick from when a craving hit late at night. The staff at this resort did whatever they had to do to make the guests happy. Yet, Vida knew there were serious limits. She knew sex with guests was off the table for all employees at the resort. She was certain of this because early on, locals had lost their jobs, guests had been barred from coming back. Of late, she knew the mandates had stuck because of the frequency with which her best friend provided sex work off the resort to guests. She had to accept that it was the person she cared most deeply about who routinely took the risk of losing his job to please the guests in such a way. Vida felt the pull of her ex-boyfriend Pablo's presence meters away. Though Pablo wasn't one of the workers wearing tiny Speedos, he would be within touching distance of the ravenous tourists. Vida considered the way those tourist women would observe him, want him, have him.

In responding to Laura's summons, Vida could have made it to the casita without passing Pablo's workstation. But she hadn't been able to help herself. She had wanted to see him, had hoped she might do so without him noticing her. Vida had allowed her gaze to linger for a few seconds, watching him wield the blade as he descaled fish. One straight line and a rainbow of color spun down to the sand from each tiny scale, the sun reflecting beauty all the way down to his feet. He'd put the knife down and held out a hand. "I've missed you," he'd said, but she'd hurried away without responding, careful to cover the outline of her stomach with one arm.

Now, as she waited to learn if the tourist child would recover, she paid close attention to her body. Inside her belly, the fetus stirred in a jerky, rapid pattern, like a million butterfly wings. It made her think of a person struggling in deep water, trying to stay afloat.

CHAPTER

5

AURA'S PHONE BUZZED WITH AN EMAIL NOTIFICATION FROM Astrid, the VP of Guest Services and Media Relations. Someone had hacked into the welcome letter. Quickly, Laura scanned the letter, noticing the telltale signs of a prank by Elena. *Parasites!*

She walked down the hall to Astrid's office. But she wasn't there. Of course, Astrid was one of the VPs she'd seen climb into the golf cart on the way to play a round or two. Her computer was there, screen dark. She'd just scheduled the email to be sent at this time, to show activity even while she was away from her desk. Laura grabbed a sticky note, asked Astrid to come by or call when she got back to her desk.

Back at her own desk, Laura felt as if she were about to explode—they couldn't afford a public catastrophe when they were so close to getting what they'd wanted for so long. Laura's face flushed. She raised the blinds, stared out past the manicured lawn into the pool closest to the gym and spa. The aerobics team danced with the patrons. Everyone seemed to be having a grand ole time.

She had five minutes before it would be time for the staff meeting.

Laura took advantage of the lull to check her phone. Still no text from either Elena or Vida. She didn't understand why neither one of them had gotten back to her yet. She debated whether to have one of her staff check what was going on. The risk that word might spread about a sick tourist kid being in the staff quarters loomed large in her consciousness. But in reality, if the kid was dead, the idea of secrecy was a farce. All hell would break loose. She grabbed her walkie-talkie, switched to a sub-channel to ensure privacy, and called her head of grounds staff, whom she knew to be tight-lipped. She requested that Gustavo check her casita and inform her if Elena or anybody else was there. Within moments, he crackled in with a response. Vida was in the room watching over a little white girl.

"She doesn't look too good, boss," he said.

"Who? The girl?" Laura asked.

"The girl looks fine, sleeping. But Vida looks pale," he said. "Anything I should do?"

"Did you ask her if she's okay?"

After some moments of silence, he came back on.

"She says she's fine. Just needs to head home soon. Anything else I should do?"

"No, no," Laura said quickly. "Tell Vida I'll be right there just as soon as I'm done with this meeting. Thirty minutes, tops. And don't talk to anyone about this. Understand?"

"Copy that," Gustavo said.

Puzzled, she texted Elena.

> Elena! Call me back now!

When she raised her eyes, she saw Elena making her way to Pablo at his prep station, a short distance from the guests who were lounging by the pool.

Fucking Elena!

It was lunchtime and the resort was buzzing. On the bottom floor of the building that housed Laura's office, workers scurried around, balancing trays of fresh salads and colorful cocktails as they went in one direction, while others heaved armloads of fluffy, fragrant towels in another. All were careful not to linger, not to chat, not to waste any time acknowledging the brutality of wearing long-sleeved uniforms in the thirty-two-degrees-Celsius heat.

The circular infinity pool ahead soundlessly cascaded over its edge, peaceful and momentarily devoid of workers. The tourist women, with their asymmetrical white swimsuits and platform wedges, let the wind off the sea part their cover-ups.

———

PABLO BRACED HIMSELF. The Moreno sisters were both headed in his direction. Pablo's workstation was on a slope between the pool and the beach. It was a simple and tasteful wet bar. Guests liked watching him work. He'd been at it since before sunrise, first catching, then descaling the fish that the guests would devour as sushi later. Pablo slit open the mahi-mahi in his hands with his sharpest blade, exposing the soft white flesh and delicately removing the skin and entrails. He threw the tripas at a metal bucket that was a few feet away and missed. The fish guts and skin now littered the sand, and if not for the commercial-grade insect repellent, the place would have been swarming with flies. He would get in trouble if Laura saw the mess he'd made. But he couldn't stop what he was doing to clean up.

Was he already in trouble? Had Laura found out that he'd been giving Elena ecstasy pills? Did this have to do with Vida? He'd been wondering what had brought her to the hotel. It'd already been three months since their breakup, and his heartache refused to let up. In his thirty years of life, he'd never felt this way. He kept waiting to move on, for the pain to become less intense, but as the weeks had turned to months, his love for Vida had continued to creep through his body, finding new hollow spaces to fill, to calcify.

Elena made her way toward Pablo in a slow, zombielike trance. When she'd glanced through the window of the casita as her sister had left earlier, the little girl had been convulsing, seeming to struggle to find her breath. Elena had been horrified. It hadn't looked as if Vida could save the girl. She'd gone to the staff lockers to bathe and change, but had been too upset to do anything but sit in a bathroom stall, staring at her muddy, resort-mandated tennis shoes. Then she'd decided to find her way off the resort. She just needed to see Pablo real quick before she left. She didn't realize her sister was marching toward her until they were both in front of Pablo's workstation.

Frustration consumed Laura. Her body hot. Her mind hot. All she had wanted for more years than she could count was to find a way off this resort, away from her infernal country of birth. But Elena was ruining everything. She smacked Elena hard across the face. Elena didn't react, so Laura smacked her again, but used the back of her hand this time. Laura's bracelet reached Elena's face first, scratching her cheek. It reddened instantly.

Pablo, shocked, was momentarily speechless, and then, concerned guests had witnessed the incident, whispered, "Laura!"

Laura turned from Pablo, embarrassed. She brought her hand to her forehead, aghast.

"*Parasites?* Really? When are you going to grow up, Elena?" Laura hissed.

You hit me, Elena thought.

Laura couldn't believe she'd hit Elena, either. Of all the promises she'd made to herself as a child, to not raise a hand to hurt another human, most of all the person she loved most, was at the top.

If Pablo had not been there, had not whisper-shouted her name, she wasn't sure she would've stopped at a slap across Elena's face. It had been right there, underneath the surface, that impulse to punish the person she loved most. With disgust at herself, she feared she'd inherited the worst qualities of her dead father.

Laura quickly composed herself and smiled in the direction of the guests closest to them. But it was obvious that the handful within viewing distance hadn't caught the exchange. Without missing a beat, the guests squinted behind their aviator glasses and oversized frames into ultra-thin phones, or glared into laptops as they spoke into headsets about why the projections for this quarter had been this far off, solving work crises that had to be tended to right away, that required they work during their vacations. Laura exhaled, relieved that the incident had escaped notice. She had to get a grip.

Pablo gestured toward the scratch on Elena's cheek. "You all right?" he asked.

Elena touched her face absentmindedly. Didn't respond. Her sad, big eyes contained so much feeling. With her bravado, and her place among the young people as an organizer and all-around badass, she often seemed older, more serious, more put-together.

"If you only knew," Laura said, thinking about the child and Vida.

Maybe she had gone too far, but Elena's behavior warranted an extreme response. Even if that response filled Laura with shame.

Pablo kept cutting the fish and placing those petal-thin pieces of meat on a wooden board inside the cooler, because within a few moments, someone from the kitchen would come grab the freshly sliced catch. Soon after that, it would glide down someone's throat, soft enough that it didn't even need to be chewed.

"Take it easy," Pablo said. "Why are you always so hard on her?"

"If you're so worried about her, *you* take care of her," Laura said. "And clean up your workspace. This is unacceptable." Then she stormed off.

Pablo kept working, because at the Grand Paloma Resort, you could lose a foot and still have to deliver the drinks, serve the sushi. But after the spectacle that had just unfolded in front of him, it was a relief to have something to do with his hands.

"Do you have the pill?" Elena demanded, turning to face him.

The scratch on Elena's cheek was bleeding.

"Let me finish this," he said, as he gestured toward the three remaining fish he'd caught that morning.

"You all right?" he asked, again.

A manicured hand emerged from nowhere. It caressed Elena's bald head.

"You're so beautiful." The woman spoke with a British accent. "I noticed you earlier today, when you were swimming with the blond girl. I meant to tell you then. Just truly marvelous bone structure. And those eyes. You're like a doll. But what happened here?" She took a step back and away. "You've cut yourself. Did you know that? You need to go to the infirmary."

Elena's gaze fell to the sand. "Right away, ma'am."

The woman then stared knowingly at Pablo. "Maybe another massage this weekend?"

Pablo nodded, contorting his smile so his two dimples would be prominently displayed. When he'd buried his head between her thighs yesterday, he'd been surprised that her natural scent had leaned toward cinnamon, that she'd sported a clitoral piercing. The woman reached over the counter, pinched a slice of the fish. Had it halfway inside her mouth before she asked, "May I?"

He nodded again. She strutted away brazenly, toward the bar. Elena shuddered, not used to the touch of tourists. Pablo was the only male employee who, at times, actually slept with the guests, always careful to ensure that none of his colleagues knew, that management had no idea. Elena's hand trailed the same path that the woman's hand had followed on her head, cleaning it of her touch. The few workers who'd caught the exchange raised their eyebrows in acknowledgment, lips thinning into corrugated lines.

"Why is Laura so pissed off?" Pablo asked.

"She'll be fine," Elena said, her voice breaking a little as she turned her body away from him, suddenly enraptured by her phone. She slid through loud, seconds-long videos on one app before switching over to a different one. "Can you just give me the pills? I gotta go up to Pico Diablo."

"Now? Aren't you taking care of the little girl from PH7?"

Pablo, along with the others who had been born up on the Pico Diablo Mountain, like the Moreno sisters, was careful to not make routine trips back home during the workday. Pablo hadn't been up there in months. Not since he'd gone to Vida's house to beg her to take him back. Their town was six miles up the road from the Grand Paloma Resort, on a rocky, unpaved dirt path. Up there, it was like journeying back in time to a hundred years ago. There were wild boars, horses, cows, and chickens all over the place. The electricity was sketchy, with outages more routine than actual power. The running water had stopped months ago, after the last drought had forced officials to re-route all local waterways to the resort. Now, locals were forced to buy water by the botellon or truckful.

Meanwhile, the resort's 2,500 acres of land flourished. The flower bushes were watered daily, and the birdbaths were full of fresh water that was replaced even more often than that, lest the still water become a breeding ground for bacteria and other dangerous diseases. The golf course enjoyed thousands of gallons of water every night to keep the grass thick and full. The winds felt cleaner, fresher down here, the humidity nearly nonexistent thanks to the spritzers and the localized cooling centers.

Pablo wasn't sure why Elena would risk losing all of this by abandoning her charge. The risk Pablo willingly took ensured the guests were satisfied, almost guaranteed they'd return.

"You think that's a good idea?" he pressed. "It'll take you at least an hour to go there and back."

"I need to check and see if my dad came back. I haven't been up there in a week. Last time I found him, before his last trip, he'd been sitting in that hot house by himself for days. Brugal, agua, y pan, that's all he had."

Elena wasn't going to tell Pablo that she had screwed up so badly. That she needed to hide, to run away. The only safe place to go to was her and Laura's old house. Laura would never go there. Whatever happened to the young tourist girl next, Elena would at least get some time away from here. Maybe her father would have returned after being missing for so long, and she'd get to see him. He would know what to do.

Pablo glanced away from Elena, toward the ocean. It had shifted from a clear, nearly transparent blue to a stunning turquoise to this rich indigo.

"I can go up and check for you," Pablo said. "After I'm done with the Freedom Sunset Cruise, I'll be off until tomorrow. You shouldn't leave until you complete this job."

Finally done with the last fish, Pablo used the nearby sink to wash his hands.

"By the way," he asked, attempting to sound nonchalant. "Did you see Vida?"

Elena studied his features carefully.

"No," she said. "I haven't seen Vida."

Had he looked at her just then, he would have seen a quiver in her cheek. He would have known she was lying. Instead, disappointed, he dried off his palms and reached in his pocket, taking out a couple of pills and handing them, discreetly, to Elena.

"Why are you so stingy?" she asked.

"You've been taking these daily, El," he said. "You gotta cool it. Slow down."

"What are you, my dad?" Elena turned on her heels and left.

Pablo shouted after her. "Why don't you just come with me on the sunset cruise?"

She waved *no* at him with a hand as she hurried away.

"We're the only thing we've got," he yelled after her. He wasn't sure she heard him. But guests turned toward him, disturbed by his raised voice. He shrank into himself, ashamed to have momentarily forgotten his place.

It'd been up to the workers at the resort to keep an eye on Elena as her sister ascended in rank. Pablo had been the one she turned to more and more frequently, especially in the last few months. Since Elena had graduated from the global academy, she'd had a looser schedule, and Pablo had also had more free time after Vida had left him. They'd strolled down the two-mile path from the resort to the made-up town of Paloma Falls, wandering through the outrageous luxury stores, marveling at how in certain stores—Hermès, Prada, Gucci—a bag or a pair of shoes cost more than they made in a year. Even so, Elena moved through those places with ease and comfort. She never noticed how surprised the guests were that they were moving freely among them, as if their resort uniforms were a signal of trespass. But that was the thing about Elena. She'd moved here with Laura when she was only seven or eight years old. She'd never known hunger, thirst. She'd been an anomaly—a worker like them, sure, but also, because of her education, because of the manners she'd learned from the foreigners she'd spent so much time with, someone who had a fluidity none of them had. Not even her sister. Watching the drama unfold over the last year, Pablo had often wondered at the lousy place he'd been given when it came to the Moreno sisters' lives. Why had he been seated in the front row to every miserable thing that had happened to them?

Once he'd cleaned and sanitized the counter of his station, he bent to the ground, sifting from the sand the guts and coagulated blood he'd carelessly discarded, leaving the place so clean that it was as if he'd never worked there.

CHAPTER

6

I N THE CONFERENCE ROOM, LAURA PRESSED A BUTTON ON A handheld controller to close all the blinds, blocking out the guests who parasailed and rode Jet Skis far in the distance. She dialed into the video conference but kept the monitor's camera turned off. She was hoping to give her slacker colleagues time to arrive.

Moments later, there was still no sign of her colleagues as her boss, Miranda, said, "Is anyone on?"

Laura clicked her camera on.

"You're by yourself, right?" Miranda asked, passing a hand through her close-cropped blond hair. She was calling in from her cellphone, and the camera was so close up that Laura could see the flaking from swollen, sunburned skin. This summer, the French sun was as lethal as the Caribbean sun.

"I'm sure they'll be here soon," she said, but Miranda cut her off before she could try to make an excuse for her colleagues.

"We're at this very cool nighttime tour of the Château du Clos Lucé. Let me try to find a quiet place to talk to you. It is such a magical place."

Miranda was a tourist everywhere she went. But in a way, she owed her success to her ease with being persistently uprooted. She worked constantly, no matter where she was, efficiently booting up and getting shit done whether she was at an airport, a hotel, a beach, a spa. Because of her position, borders were as easy to cross as the screen of her device swiping the scanner at any gate.

Just as she'd done many times before, Miranda left her camera and microphone on as she made her way to a quiet place. She merely loosened her arm to carry Laura along with her. Laura saw the castle-like structure, softly lit, upside down, and heard the loud voice of a tour guide saying, "Due to the months-long drought, there will be no annual vintage in Bordeaux for the first time ever. But not to worry, dears, we've got plenty of wine on reserve for you to taste. Well, not you, little ones."

Laura was surprised that the woman wasn't speaking French. But maybe this was a tour conducted for American tourists. Miranda's phone was now facing the ground, and the jostling camera made Laura dizzy. She focused on the surface of the glass conference table to keep from growing nauseous. Miranda kept muttering—*just one more minute, Laura. Hold on, hold on*—with that American Southern drawl Laura had come to love.

Laura took advantage of the lull to check her phone. She began to text her sister. I shouldn't have hit you, she typed. But then she backtracked, erased that message. She started over. Have you checked on Vida? Where the hell are you? But her tone sounded harsh. She feared Elena would read her text, delete it, and go take more ecstasy pills in the fucking greenhouse. She erased the text and was typing again when Miranda's voice broke through the quiet.

"Thanks for being patient," Miranda said, out of breath.

Laura placed the phone facedown on the conference table.

"Sorry about that," Laura said.

"You're on mute," Miranda interrupted her.

Laura unmuted herself.

"Goddamn it," Miranda said. "Now I have to pee. Stay put."

Laura did as she was told. She stared, unmoving, at the ornate candelabra that shimmered with a fake flame on the screen. The walls were covered with antique frames that depicted bounties of grapes.

Elena. Go to our room right now.
Stop acting like a fucking child.

She hit send. Waited for a response. Under the conference table, her knee jerked up and down nervously.

The screen in front of her remained boss-less. When Laura had first met Miranda, she had been apprehensive. Laura harbored a deep-seated dislike for all Americans due to their treatment of the workers at the resort. But Miranda and Laura might as well have been separated at birth—from different parents, and from different countries, of course. Both were pretty short—neither came close to five feet tall and had what in these senior leadership spaces seemed to be a near-extinct full-figured, pear-shaped frame (neither would be caught dead dieting), but most of all, both proudly took themselves seriously in a workplace where it seemed that the more you bullshitted and treated the resort as your own personal networking happy hour, the faster you ascended the ranks.

Miranda was also the first and only boss who'd become Laura's champion. It was Miranda who had told her that, as the hardest-working person at the resort, she was being robbed of her rightful title in the senior leadership team. It was Miranda—with her blue eyes and blond hair and Wharton School of Business pedigree—who had dissuaded Laura from the idea that there was such a thing as a meritocracy and convinced her that when Miranda's predecessor had changed the rules and made Laura a senior director of staff management when the man she'd replaced had been a vice president of staff management, they'd had no real footing to do so. There was no such thing as an education requirement—she'd worked with the Sapphire Paloma in Singapore and the Dok Khun Paloma in Thailand, both places where locals had been promoted to vice president roles with no pedigreed education and with less experience than Laura. Miranda had been the one who'd shown by example that it was a waste of time to go on the golf outings or to hang out in gambling dens or strip joints so the men would think that they, as women, were just like them. When she'd taken over at the Grand Paloma just eighteen months ago, she'd told Laura that the way they'd get ahead was by making a few strategic moves that would yield high margins of short-term profit and glitter from the hemisphere. She'd asked Laura to come up with a big idea so she could raise her profile among the organization's decision-makers, and when Laura had delivered with the Platinum Member Companion Program, Miranda had quickly nominated Laura for—and influenced her winning of—the year's Soaring Paloma Employee Award.

Laura would do anything for Miranda because Miranda had shown her that, unlike the other people she'd worked for—read: *men*—who'd stolen her ideas and benefited from her hard work, who'd referred to the Grand Paloma as the place people cut their teeth at in order to make any subsequent move after it seem like a bigger deal, Miranda was trustworthy, loyal, and cared deeply about work. Laura, at twenty-seven, secretly thought of Miranda, who was in her midforties, as her work mom.

But that designation didn't mean Laura had fooled herself into thinking that Miranda's efforts meant she was special. Miranda encouraged and pushed all her subordinates—across the United States, Central and South America, and the Caribbean—to break through because she knew that their growth would accelerate her own ascension. *You grow, I climb* was her motto. But there was no doubt in Laura's mind that she held a place of honor in Miranda's estimation. Most of the people who came onto this team treated it like a vacation. The Caribbean was seen as an emerging market—a place that had the potential to attract the wealthiest people in the world but hadn't yet managed to do so. And so the one- to two-year stints were usually considered to be an opportunity for those with little experience to learn management skills and gain an understanding of the complexities of running a luxury resort that catered to the wealthy. *So easy a monkey could do it*, each of the new executives liked to say.

After just a couple of weeks at the resort, Miranda had looked at Laura and said, "You run this place almost entirely singlehandedly and yet you have the lowest rank in the team? Are you fucking kidding me?" and, without expecting a response, went on: "That's about to change."

Her boss had tried to open Laura's eyes up to the other inequalities she'd suffered. Miranda called the different pay scales criminal. Expats were paid in dollars because Paloma Enterprises was a United States–based company, yet the salary market data of their home countries was used to calculate their pay. Nationals were paid in local currency using local market data, which meant they were often paid significantly less than their counterparts. Miranda had turned her laptop toward Laura to show her that she made a tenth of what her lowest-paid expat peer made. But Laura had shaken her head at Miranda's outrage, feeling like she needed to talk to her boss the way she often spoke to her naïve little sister. She was grateful, Laura had explained to her new boss. How to explain that she'd been chosen, groomed? One needed to calculate the benefits of a job beyond a salary.

When she'd first started as a server, she'd sat through weeklong business summits where she'd learned the fundamentals of marketing, business forecasting, customer satisfaction, and strategic expansion. Over the many years that she'd been along for the ride as the same companies hired and then replaced executives, launched and then switched courses on strategic initiatives, Laura's business acumen had soared. She'd been trained among global chief executives on the subtle rules of negotiation, communication, how to lean in, stand out, become emotionally intelligent enough to manipulate employees to do exactly what the business required. She'd maneuvered, with her most recent promotion, to get her sister admission into the virtual global academy for her high school diploma, an institution respected and accredited in both the United States and Europe. The most senior members of Paloma Enterprises sent their kids there. Elena would have her choice of colleges, a future that would prevent her from ever having to work in a hotel, in any service job at all. Elena often joked that Laura had a PhD in capitalism because the education Laura had gotten here, all while picking up dirty napkins and discarded half-eaten shrimp tails and removing cold cups of ethically grown coffee and replacing them with happy-hour cocktails, was one that no one in the entire world could've paid for.

Miranda had responded by nodding, as if she agreed.

"You've been exploited and you're thankful for it," she'd said. "This is how they get us."

Laura had shrugged, confused at what Miranda could possibly mean by "they" or "us," but aware from the many meetings she'd sat through that the golden rule of being an up-and-coming star was to never correct a boss. She had also recognized that Miranda was limited by her own privilege. She looked upon Laura as if she were at the bottom of their senior team, neglecting to realize that Laura sat prettily at the very top of the nationals rank. But there was limited employee data on those numbers. If Miranda had bothered to learn what they paid the undocumented Haitian workers who cared for the grounds, she'd realize that Laura occupied a place that locals envied. Even if the work conditions favored others, exploitation hardly applied in Laura's situation. Didn't exploitation require a victim? Laura was no victim.

Now Miranda came back on the screen, face flushed from the hustle. She raised one finger and gulped down a bottle of water, closing her eyes as she swallowed. From somewhere in the distance, the voice of the tour guide returned, explaining that Leonardo da Vinci had taken his last breaths right there.

No one else had joined their meeting. If there was one thing Miranda had no patience for, it was people who didn't toe the line around requirements—she'd fired someone on the spot once when she'd learned that they'd decided to forgo the expected procedural forms for family stays and had finagled complimentary accommodations for their parents. Everyone knew that lateness was her biggest pet peeve, though. Laura was shocked that her colleagues had missed this meeting knowing they'd face Miranda's vexation later.

"This meeting is going to be short," Miranda said, face returning to its usual pale hue.

Laura nodded.

"All the feedback from our sister resorts where we've soft-launched the Platinum Member Companion Program has been raves. Increased productivity and competition right off the bat. Net promoter satisfaction through the roof. There are a few places that have been able to present a select number of their employees with the promotion."

Laura's brows furrowed. The point of the program was to incentivize employees to strive for high customer survey responses by keeping the guests company 24/7 or, as desired, by making their every wish come true in exchange for the promise of a tremendous set of perks—better accommodations; fewer working hours; educational reimbursement only directors and officers usually enjoyed—without ever promoting them.

"I know," Miranda said. "They screwed up."

"Should I talk to these people? I've managed to run the program here for a year and not one person has been promoted."

"I'm aware," Miranda said. Laura swallowed and straightened herself up, reminding herself to not cross hierarchy boundaries. *No seas igualada,* she told herself.

"The issue," Miranda continued, "is that at some of these other resorts, the employees saw through the bullshit quicker than they have at the Grand Paloma."

Laura had withheld details about how many of their own employees had withdrawn from the program. Laura hadn't been alarmed by that trend; as quickly as some had dropped, others had joined. But now that word would spread about some of the reps who'd gotten promoted ahead of those at their hotel, where the program had originated, she knew it might cause trouble.

"What do you want to do about it?" Miranda asked.

"We have several employees who are near the top. I've had those under review for some time."

"Promote someone," Miranda said with finality. "Send me a note by tomorrow EOB with the name of your choice. I don't have to approve it. I trust you."

Off camera, Laura heard Jacques's exaggerated sigh. Even from a distance, the sound was elegant and posh. Miranda was catching hell from her French husband because she'd once again refused to stop working, even while they were off in August. Miranda had committed that this year, she would be off for real. It was the reason Laura had volunteered to be on duty every weekend in August. With Miranda's controlling nature, she'd still carefully examine every decision made, and Laura counted that meticulousness to her advantage. Laura didn't make mistakes. Miranda would offer her support for the promotion and transfer once she saw firsthand all Laura could do—even now that she had more obligations and responsibilities than ever. When

Miranda had exclaimed that she'd forgo a review of the candidate for the promotion, Laura took it to mean she was kicking ass.

"We'll do it quietly, not make too big a deal of it, otherwise people will realize we've only promoted one person a year in."

"Yes," Laura said emphatically.

"Just two more weeks, Laura. I've already put in a request for your relocation to Portugal so you can be stationed with me. You'll oversee the Platinum Member Program internationally. It's going to be amazing."

Miranda glowed with pride. Laura felt her body swell. The statement meant that Miranda had been given her own promotion. That she now had oversight of the European hotels. This was what they had been waiting for. She felt flushed with emotion. This woman had seen her, recognized her, believed in her, and was on the cusp of changing her life.

"Anything going on over there that I should know about?" Miranda said, already reaching toward the phone to sign off.

A big bird crashed into the glass of the conference room where Laura sat, startling her with the deadening sound. Goose pimples formed on her skin, and she felt a chill run down her arms.

"Other than your team deciding to go golfing instead of attending this meeting, everything is copacetic."

Miranda pursed her lips distastefully. She hated gossip.

"I'm sorry that I forgot to include you in the email to them, Laura. I let them know I'd rather focus this time on a one-on-one with you."

Laura gulped.

"Anything else?"

Laura should have shaken her head and murmured that there was nothing worth mentioning, but she paused. If there was one thing Miranda hated more than lateness and gossip, it was surprises. She was almost certain that Vida would get them out of the woods with the injured tourist child. But what if the kid didn't recuperate? What if the parents found out and made noise?

"What is it, Laura?" Miranda asked.

At a loss for what to say, Laura vomited some more gossip.

"Not that I'm one to listen to nonsense, but you should know there's been talk that there might be some bigwig investors trying to buy out this resort from Paloma Enterprises."

Miranda narrowed her gaze, lifted the phone, and brought it closer to her face in a frustrated, exaggerated manner. "I'm glad you don't listen to nonsense," she said, then quickly made excuses to get off. Instead of ending the video conference, she only shut off the camera, and Laura stayed on, listening to her hurried steps, to her excusing herself to her husband and kids for missing most of the tour. Laura hadn't realized they were getting a private tour of the place.

She stayed on long enough to listen to the guide give an explanation as to why Leonardo's *The Last Supper* had been groundbreaking at the time. A painting that showcased a broader, all-encompassing view of the scene, rather than focusing on a single protagonist, felt truer to the way the real world worked.

"How did your meeting go?" Jacques asked.

"You know Laura, well-meaning but such a pussy. People are talking about the sale. That's not good."

Laura forced herself to press the button that ejected her from the virtual meeting. She was floored that the rumors of a sale were true. It made no difference to her, Laura told herself. Once the high season ended, she'd be on a plane to Portugal with her sister, ready to say goodbye to this country and to her past, both of which were too painful to bear.

Still, as she remained in the arctic conference room, she felt heat rising in her body despite the cool air being blasted everywhere. She wrote an email to Miranda naming Pablo as the employee who would get the promotion and scheduled it to be sent tomorrow morning. She couldn't risk forgetting this step. She then sent a request to get Pablo's ID upgraded, carefully establishing his new title as an encargado, a manager. It wouldn't mean anything to the expats on the payroll, but to Dominicans, it would clearly signify that Pablo was her second-in-command. Laura had no intention of promoting anyone else currently participating in the Platinum Member Companion Program. This would be done to pacify Miranda and to squash any discontent that might come up if word reached her staff that other hotels had promoted people in the program when they hadn't. Laura then scheduled Pablo's move from the staff quarters to a garden room for tomorrow evening. Checkout date: indefinite. She made a mental note to alert Pablo that he'd be promoted by the next morning. He deserved it. There was no one as dedicated as Pablo. Years ago, when Laura had been promoted to management, she'd had the opportunity to also move to the resort. But it would have meant leaving her sister behind to live by herself in the casita. Management had declined her request to have Elena move with her because they worried that if a babysitter moved to the resort, others would start pushing for it. Instead of risking that, Laura had declined the move altogether, knowing she'd never go anywhere without Elena.

Elena, who still hadn't responded to her last text.

Laura knew that she had to go check on the tourist girl, on Vida, on her sister, but she was unable to move. If anything happened and they didn't get to leave, if the place was sold to a new owner who didn't care for Laura's rags-to-riches story, what would she do? She'd tried to find a job elsewhere before. While Miranda believed that hard work should be the key that unlocked opportunities, the rest of the world didn't see it that way. Laura knew herself to be exceptionally capable. But she was also an unremarkable person from a place most people thought of as a third-world country. She didn't have a college degree. The education she'd gotten in Pico Diablo wasn't recognized as legitimate. She'd learned very quickly that experience went only so far, that her stellar annual employee evaluations, which routinely ranked her as far exceeding expectations, didn't mean much at all. No one was impressed that she'd somehow managed, against all odds, to reach heights no local had ever reached.

Laura didn't bat an eye over her boss calling her a pussy. The executive team thought she was a pushover. She had cultivated that impression intentionally. To her staff, she was a hard-ass, unrelenting in her demands. But with her colleagues and her boss, it didn't serve her, as the only Afro-Latina, to be anything but docile. Any form of an edge in her personality would too quickly be interpreted as aggression, hostility, and would lead to an assumption that she had an inability to lead, strategize, grow. She knew it'd do her no good to worry about this possibility of a takeover. She had to focus on the crisis at hand.

CHAPTER
7

Back at the staff quarters, Laura found Vida sitting on the ground, eyes closed, looking pale. The girl, on the other hand, looked rosy and peaceful.

"Are you okay?" Laura asked.

Vida's voice was hoarse. "It usually takes some time for me to recover. I need to go home."

"You don't seem to be in any condition to drive your Vespa. I need to find Elena. Why don't you rest here? Let me go grab Elena. Then I will take you home."

She helped Vida to her feet, laid her in Elena's messy bed.

"Dulce is expecting me back at her bar. We're supposed to spend the day together."

Laura nodded. Dulce, their childhood friend, was only a few miles away.

"I owe you a big one," Laura said, "and I hate having to ask you one more favor. But can you wait? Text me if anything happens with the girl? I'd hate to get anyone else involved here. Elena is out of control. I don't know what I'm going to do with her. It's like she's purposefully trying to sabotage our chances to leave this place."

Vida swallowed with difficulty.

"I'll stay," she said. "My body needs the rest. But if you want my advice, the longer you act like you're her mother, lying for her, ready to clean up her every mistake, the less likely she'll ever be to mature."

Laura began to protest. Didn't Vida see this room? She hadn't picked up after Elena, she'd been trying to help her grow up. But she decided against saying anything. What would that defensiveness serve?

"I'll be back as quickly as I can. Text me if anything happens."
She knew exactly where to find her sister.

LAURA HAD ALWAYS FEARED that this was how she'd lose her sister—
floating in the same pool of green water on the waterfall where they'd
both learned to swim. Her sister's body wasn't suspended in the water
faceup, as they had floated countless times while they were children.
She was facedown, completely naked, her limbs moving languidly
with the current from the force of the water pummeling down. It was
the same position they'd found their mother in when she'd drowned so
many years ago. Only both of their mother's arms had been encased in
casts.

It was deafening, that sound of the crashing water. It drowned out
her voice, the hysteria that bubbled as she glanced around, yelling for
someone to help. Halfway through a beautiful clear day, the sun a splat
of light yellow in the sky, there wasn't even one tourist in a ridiculous
sun hat and cargo shorts. Laura jumped into the water.

Without thinking twice about her sewn-in hairweave—the hair
that had cost most of a year's saved wages from both her and her sister's stash—or her phone snug in her pocket, Laura jumped in to save
her sister. She grabbed Elena's foot, pulled hard toward the water's
edge.

"Let me go," Elena said, twisting over, kicking her in the face with
the free foot. Maybe by mistake.

"Thought you were dead," Laura said, letting go of the other foot
immediately, touching the part of her head that had been struck—the
pain there for a moment and then immediately gone.

"What are you doing here?" Laura continued over the cascading
torrent. "You have to get back to work."

The two of them swam in synchrony, strokes elegant, a soft line
extending the full lengths of their bodies.

"I'm not going back to the hotel," Elena said. She emerged from
the water first and, turning away from Laura, put on her pink Medline
scrubs.

"Why would you decide to skinny-dip where any tourist could see you and post your photo to their Insta?" Laura asked Elena's back.

"I was just really hot," Elena said in a quiet voice.

Elena walked barefoot. Her wet feet made a soft sucking sound against the muddy ground. Laura noticed that there was a blood splatter on the uniform, all the way down her chest. For a moment, she again regretted her earlier burst of anger. Back at the staff quarters, looking at that child lying in bed, she'd been overwhelmed with a desire to find her sister, punch her in the mouth, shake her until she stopped acting like such an idiot. *You're seventeen years old,* she wanted to scream. *You know all I'd already done by the time I was your age to make sure we'd be okay?* Looking at her sister's face now, she understood she'd gone too far.

Elena bent down, and Laura was surprised at the small satchel she'd failed to notice. It was the bag Elena kept up in their old house in Pico Diablo. Where was her sister going? She almost laughed, thinking about her sister panicking about the young tourist girl—not even realizing that Vida had worked her magic, that the girl would likely be fine.

Elena headed away from the waterfall along an unmarked path in the forest. On the far end of the thicket to their right, there was an opening to the stalagmite caves.

"The girl didn't look good when I left," Elena said into the trees. It was her way of asking Laura what had happened after she'd fled the scene of the crime. Laura stopped walking. When her sister made to move on, she grabbed her forearm. A return to her constant need to apply necessary pressure.

"Vida did her best," Laura said. Then she shook her head somberly, implying that the girl hadn't made it. Laura let her hand fall off her sister's arm, thinking of what a dead American tourist child would have meant to her sister, to the resort, to all of them. Laura's face burned hot at the thought. The prospect alone made her vertiginous.

Elena gasped as she shook her head repeatedly. Her eyes filled with tears that fell fast. Her shoulders shook the way they had when she was a toddler. Back then, Laura would snuggle her in her lap, tell her that everything would be all right. Laura resisted that urge. It was the exact impulse that had brought them to this situation. She had to be tough.

"What are you planning to do next?" Laura asked.

Elena spoke in a whisper, not facing Laura. She told her that she thought it best for her to get out of town. She had her passport with a visa that enabled travel to the United States and Europe.

"You're going to leave the country?" Laura asked, incredulous.

Elena nodded.

"Where the hell do you think you're going to find the money?"

To find money for a same-day ticket would be impossible. The question shattered Elena's pretense of self-control.

"I'll figure something out," Elena managed to mumble between tears. "Just have to get a loan until I find work."

Laura told herself that this was an important moment. Her sister needed to learn a hard lesson. It was better for her to think that she had fucked up with this tourist child, that she'd made a mistake big enough to ruin her life forever. Laura had begged her sister to stay off the pills. Brown girls couldn't get away with doing drugs for fun, with experimenting just to see what it was like while young. Why couldn't Elena understand what was at stake?

When Laura had first seen that white child lying unconscious on her bed, she'd felt the floor give way; had felt herself at the center of a tiny tornado that sucked her down, stretching her taut, near her tearing point. This time, they had been lucky. What about the next time?

Elena, oblivious to her sister's agitated state, placed a hand on Laura's shoulder to gain some balance. She put her resort tennis shoes on. When she glanced back at her sister's face, Laura looked as bereft as Elena felt. It seemed like they were both shifting on uneven ground, about to fall. Seeing that raw fragility in her sister, who was usually so strong and capable, made Elena feel scared. So much so that Elena had to look elsewhere. Elena wished she could tell her sister the truth she held in her heart. She wanted to reach a place where she could find the words, to come to a meeting place. She didn't want her sister to constantly feel this stress brought about by the need to take care of her. But language failed her just then. If her sister didn't take care of her, where would she end up?

Above, in one of the trees, Elena noticed a huge kite. She pointed up so her sister would see it, too. It was shaped like a giant butterfly, and its colors—purple and the pale yellow of the sun, bordered with thick black lines—made sense in a strange way, surrounded by so much green. She smiled at her sister, and Laura gave her a small smile back. Some pendejo tourist had likely tried to fly a kite in the middle of the forest, and the sisters wordlessly shared that visual. They were surprised that no one had texted PALOMA an SOS for immediate assistance to bring the kite down.

Laura reached for her sister's hand and squeezed.

"Why were you at the waterfall?" she asked, knowing the answer.

"I figured I'd try to sink, one last time," Elena said instead of the truth. The truth would have her speak of how she'd wanted to say goodbye to their mom's spirit.

The sisters were quiet for a moment, thinking of the same moment when they'd come upon the floating figure of their mother, how pretty all her hair had been, slithering because of the pressure of the water, like elegant snakes. How neither of them had jumped in, too terrified. But it had been Laura who had bent down and held her then-four-year-old sister. It had been Laura who had understood, as a fourteen-year-old, that now it was her duty to take care of her sister from that point forward.

"If you think leaving is the right move, go," Laura said.

Elena stared at her sister, surprised. It was Laura's turn to shrug.

"I'll drive you to the edge," Laura said.

CHAPTER

8

THIRTY MINUTES LATER, THE SISTERS WERE AT THE LIP OF THE resort's ending acreage. Laura pulled the car over and parked. Neither of them moved or spoke. When Laura pressed the button that switched the engine off, Elena understood that her sister had to go. Laura exited the car first, slamming the door. Elena removed her fingers from the AC vent once she felt the cold air finally die. On the silver handle of the car's door, the cold imprint of her fingerprints slowly disappeared. Outside, the heat of the day stunned them into a deeper momentary silence.

They were surrounded by ocean cliffs, fluffy, pretty clouds, and some lazy goats that roamed, fed and left to wander solely for the startled delight of tourist children. Elena had often taken the kids in her charge down this hill when the activities in the kids' club became so unbearable that she had to get away.

The block of light that hovered over the ocean was gorgeous, even on this day. Elena noticed a single dark cloud among all the fluffy ones and felt a seed she recognized as dread in her body.

"Who will you ask for help?" Laura said.

"I just kept remembering," Elena said, reaching to touch her sister's knotted hair, "how much time we wasted as kids, trying to sink."

Elena's hand lingered in the sewn-in hair. Laura's eyes softened the way they did whenever Elena brought up their mother. But Elena wasn't thinking of their dead mother just then. She was thinking about how the deepest part of the waterfall's pool went at least thirty feet down. Because of the force of the water descending from such an enormous height, it was impossible to sink, no matter what tricks they'd tried: jumping in with a huge rock; pushing each other down with all their strength. The last pill, the one she'd taken hours ago when she and the little tourist girl had first gone into the forest, was still having a bit of an effect on her. That was why she could focus on a thought for so long, shut out the worry about that little girl, about the blood on the back of her head like JELL-O spooned out before it had fully set. The little tourist girl had confessed, just that morning, that every time she ate JELL-O, she pooped in colors. At that thought, Elena giggled a little.

Laura's jaw hardened at the sound. A vein on the side of her neck swelled, about to pop. She could probably tell that Elena was still high. Elena tried on a serious expression, but her face went slack. For many years after their mother had died, Laura had been sweet, caring, a better mother than the one gone. But lately, this was what was left of her sister. A cold efficiency, a swiftness like the blade of a machete. Elena could tell that Laura wanted something else from her. What? Maybe an apology? A promise that she'd be more careful? But Laura always covered for her. Fixed her mistakes. Elena turned her face so her sister would see the wound on her cheek. Laura needed a reminder that she'd hurt her.

Laura knew it'd be utterly impossible for Elena to get a flight. With what money? But the anguish as she searched for a solution would be enough to sober her—to remind her to consider every step.

Elena, just like Laura, often thought of the resort as a prison. But she wasn't stupid enough to believe for one moment that she'd survive real prison. Elena remembered the one time their father had managed to make it into the United States, how he'd told her that he'd ended up at a detention center in Texas, caged like a stray dog. At times, when she grew bored of the monotony of their lives, Elena imagined herself next to her father in that cage long ago, curled like a caracol, her father the shell. It was the way she'd tried to fill in the many silences in their past, silences her sister refused to fill but with the grimmest of warnings about what they'd inherited as a legacy—a suicidal mother and a neglectful, absent father.

Elena didn't believe they'd been abandoned. When their father had disappeared last year, she'd concluded that he had been arrested again for attempting to enter the United States illegally—that this time, they might have figured out that he would never give up and had decided to keep him locked up indefinitely. When Elena tried to speak to Laura about their father, Laura abruptly left the room. She wouldn't so much as entertain a conversation about what they might do to find him.

Elena had grown convinced that it was an escape from this place that both she and Laura needed to become the best versions of themselves. It must've been the job, the relentless catering to others, that had changed them both so much. Once, Elena had lost a toddler, and it'd taken much effort to find her in Pablo's fishing boat, scared and knotted up in his nets. Another time, she'd lost track of a pair of toddler twins at the cafeteria, and of course, they'd both gone directly for the absurd display of sushi, shrimp scampi, crabs, and lobsters. One had snatched a giant purple octopus, placed it on his head like a hat, and pulled a puckered tentacle toward his face as a mustache, slipping the tip toward his mouth. Elena had reached him just in time to prevent a catastrophe. The kid had been allergic to mollusks. Each time, she'd turned things around, turned up the fun and the adventures. Every year, returning families requested her. The children adored her.

Laura had often told her that one of these days, if she didn't stop the fuckery with the pills, she'd make a mistake that would turn out to be too big for her to fix. Her sister had warned her that after the next infraction, no matter how small, she'd be transferred to housekeeping. So, if she didn't end up in jail—if somehow, some way, her sister figured out how to get her off—she'd end up cleaning up after dirty, crazy guests.

Though her sister liked to yell at times, she'd never hit her. But what Elena had done was unforgivable. The horror of the young tourist girl being dead was unfathomable. She recalled her sister's fury as she'd slapped her once, then again, spinning incoherently to protect this life. A life neither of them wanted.

Elena convinced herself it was a minor inconvenience, that throbbing cheek. She'd been careful not to catch her reflection in the rearview mirror as they drove—no use worrying about her face on top of everything else. She focused on her sister's appearance. Her hair was a disaster. The difference in texture was visible between the kinky roots of Laura's natural hair and the smooth, plastic-like straightness of the extensions, knotting from the swimming. Her sister had been robbed. There was no way that cheap-looking, quick-to-knot hair was the same as Rihanna's. She'd have to get conditioner on it fast, comb it through before it dried, or it would be ruined, irredeemable.

"Maybe I should turn myself in?" Elena said. "Maybe you can convince Miranda to give me another chance, like you did before?"

Laura's shoulders stiffened. "After everything you've done to piss everybody off? You staged that ridiculous walkout."

The walkout had happened six months ago. Elena had had no choice but to protest the inhumane conditions against the undocumented Haitian workers. Every week, there were immigration sweeps, separating families and sending people born in DR who'd never set foot in Haiti, who didn't so much as speak Creole, back to "their" country on the other side of the border. If the parents were unable to show proof of legal status, their offspring, even those who'd been born here, were considered illegal. No birthright citizenship. Their parents suspended in indefinite transit. Months before Elena had staged the walkout, the situation had worsened. Even those who had official records were being hauled away. Documents thrown away. It was almost impossible for a Dominican of Haitian descent to replace such instruments once lost, the racism was so severe. Elena had had to do something. If not her, then who? How else would they—and there were plenty of Dominicans who believed there should be a path to citizenship—make their voices heard?

"It would have worked if we'd kept protesting," Elena said. "People showed up, walked out. I wasn't alone."

"You only made their conditions worse, Elena. Nothing changed for them, and it never will. You live in the clouds. It was because of your stupid protest that they stopped the construction of the water park. Less work for them. Did you even consider that?"

Her sister was right. Today, when Elena had made her way to the forest with the tourist girl, she had wanted to check to see if there was anything else she might be able to do to help. She'd found that the families who'd decided to stay, who'd somehow managed to avoid deportation, had created a tent city on the grounds that had been cleared for the water park. Two miles into the tropical forest, in a place meant for the amusement of the tourists, they had created a temporary home. She suspected that someone had noticed that she and the girl were making their way toward them, because when she'd gotten there, there had been no one around, the tents completely empty. She'd been flushed with shame and helplessness. She'd taken the pill to make herself feel better then, figuring that if she couldn't find harmony in real life, she'd settle for the synthetic kind.

"There are no more chances for you," Laura said. "Not here."

Elena nodded. She blinked away the sting in her eyes.

"That hair was expensive," she said, forcing her voice to sound strong. "Real expensive. I'm going to get in touch as soon as I find a place to land. Don't worry about me."

Laura had been so happy when she'd had the hair put in. Elena had nearly cried when Laura had said she'd never felt more beautiful, not once. It was one of the few times Elena remembered thinking of her sister as being young, vain enough to care about being pretty.

Laura nodded in agreement, abandoned her with her eyes. Elena followed her line of sight all the way to the ocean. Waves crashed against sharp rocks, not altogether different from what foamed from the waterfall, which became mist, dispersing into nothing.

Did Laura get that they might never see each other again? The way she got inside the car, turned on the ignition, and roughly made a broken U-turn said no, said that her sister thought this was just another stunt Elena was pulling. That she didn't think her little sister was capable of finding a way to save herself. The SUV bent a corner out of sight.

Laura was right. She was always right. There was nothing left for Elena here. She had to focus on leaving. The fact that she hadn't yet seen an ambulance or the police told her she had only a couple of hours to get away. Un gran lío like the one she'd made could only be fixed by making an example out of the help. She'd be damned if she'd willingly become the subject of anyone's lesson on neglect.

There was only one place where she could get money fast, and so she headed over to the Beyond Proof Bar, sure that one way or another, the way ahead would surface.

CHAPTER

9

Us, the Workers

WHEN LA JEFA LAURA SNAKED HER WAY THROUGH THE doorway marked STAFF ONLY at the Grand Paloma Resort, she didn't make eye contact with any of us. As often happened when she walked into any space, we all stood at attention—attempting to anticipate what she might need, what we might be able to do to ensure we didn't land on her bad side. Within moments, there were some gasps from those of us paying close attention. No one had ever seen Laura Moreno look like that.

It's important to understand that as much as Elena and Laura thought they were being slick, sneaking around causing havoc that Thursday afternoon, we saw what was going on. One of us had been cleaning a hallway when we noticed Elena running like a maniac with that little tourist girl. We spotted Vida la Curandera as she made her way to their casita. We gasped when Laura slapped Elena right in front of the guests by the infinity pool.

What those two had been through! First the mother drowned, a year after Laura first got her period. Most of us didn't believe that the drowning had been accidental. E.Z. Moreno had had a mean side, especially when it came to his wife. Usually when he was on a losing streak. Had we ever seen him have a winning streak? No. When E.Z. Moreno went missing last year, most of us thought the girls were better off. No one blamed their mother for choosing a way out.

It's important to say that at the beginning, even though everything that was happening was a man-made—*ahem,* rather an *Elena-*

made disaster—we were rooting for the sisters. We were hoping that Vida's hands would cure the child, and that things would go back to normal.

We're not rewriting history here. Laura walked in looking pale, as if she'd just seen a ghost, and we snapped into action. One of us jetted ahead to iron one of the spare uniforms she kept in the employee locker room. Another one of us encouraged Miosotis to undo the pretty headscarf she'd worn to work, even though staff weren't supposed to wear any kind of cultural fabrics on their hair. We got worried when Laura didn't tell Miosotis off for violating the strict dress code.

Without a word, Laura lowered her body so her head hovered at Miosotis's chest level. Without a word between the women, the fabric was made taut, twisted, knotted, fanned, and flared until it resembled a crown on Laura's head. She managed a distracted nod of appreciation, grabbing the ironed uniform from one of us and hurrying into a changing room to make the switch of clothes. There was movement in PH7. The tourist wife had stepped onto the balcony to sunbathe. Wasn't it only a matter of time before the couple realized their child had been gone for hours without so much as a picture from Elena? We'd been paying close attention to the Moreno sisters' casita. That little child hadn't moved off that bed.

Once dressed, Laura fastened her walkie-talkie to her waistband. Her shaky fingers troubled her name plate as she pinned it to the fabric of her uniform. She grabbed her phone, seeming relieved that even though it was wet, it was still working.

She slipped on her wet stiletto-heeled pumps, visibly shuddering, probably at the nasty feel of the sodden faux-leather insoles. Nothing worse than wearing soggy shoes. She bent down, sliding a finger into the back of each shoe to glide the insoles into place. Absentmindedly, she wiped at an itch on her cheek.

When Laura left the employee locker room, heading with determination toward the staff quarters, we parted for her as she hurried past. Not one of us was brave enough to mention that she had something white on the side of her face. We were relieved that her familiar steel of determination was safely back in place. Who would risk embarrassing her over a booger-like bulge she'd accidentally placed on that cheek? She would likely wipe it away in due time, catch her reflection, and neaten herself up.

CHAPTER
10

THE TOURIST GIRL COUGHED. SAT UP SLOWLY, AND REACHED FOR Vida's tinted hands. That insistent and impatient touch brought Vida out of rest. When the girl spoke some words to Vida, smiling wide, showing her those not-yet-perfect American teeth, Vida's eyes grazed the room.

Neither Elena nor Laura had returned.

The girl made to leave and Vida shook her head, hurriedly rising from Elena's bed, holding the girl by the arm through a rush of dizziness. The girl shrugged her off, forcibly trying to step back, but Vida didn't loosen her grip. Vida couldn't get past the disgust in the child's posture, most notable in the upturned nose. She was glad that she was fluent in English, that she understood when the girl said, "Where is Ellie?"

"Your babysitter will be right back," Vida said. "Just hold on for a few minutes."

The girl consented, sitting back down on the bed where she'd been lying unconscious for hours. She touched her head, removed the fabric that Vida had fastened to it to ensure that the salve was absorbed into the wound. She tossed it aside.

"How do you feel?" Vida asked, still holding the girl's arm.

"Good," the girl said. "Really good."

Vida released her. The girl immediately stood up—and ran out of the room.

"Wait," Vida called out weakly after her. "Come back."

There was no way Vida could chase the girl. She felt too ill, too weak. In just a moment, she'd catch her breath, gain some more strength, and stand. She would call Laura and Elena. Someone should double-check that the girl made it to her parents fine. She reminded herself that the girl had been at the resort for an entire week—that by now she'd know the property grounds like the back of her hand.

When the door flew open fifteen minutes later, slamming against the wooden wall, Vida lifted her head with effort, her gaze fixed on Laura. She was wearing a bright, colorful headpiece. She'd changed clothes.

"What happened?" Laura asked. "Where's the girl?"

"She left," Vida said.

"Left?" Laura asked. "What do you mean, *left*?"

Vida's lips were dry and chapped. She looked like she was about to vomit.

"Shit! Are you all right? Do I need to find you a doctor?"

"No, no. It's always bad the first day. Go, go find the girl."

Laura hesitated. She squatted on the ground next to Vida, put a hand on her forehead.

"You feel as clammy as the kid did when I first got here," she said.

"I'll be fine," Vida said. "Go! We've got no time."

Laura knew Vida was right. They'd done everything to make sure that the girl would be all right, and now that she was, they could still be discovered by her parents. Face a lawsuit, a public relations nightmare.

"I can take you home, right after I'm done with her parents?"

"I won't be here," Vida said. "I need my own bed."

"I don't think you should drive your Vespa. Let me give you a ride? I can take you back to Pico Diablo."

"Why are you still here?" Vida snapped. "Just fucking go."

Laura didn't have time to argue. She moved out of the casita fast to try to intercept the girl. Vida was left with a sinking feeling. In her belly, the fetus was no longer jerky. There were no butterflies' wings fluttering. Her baby had grown completely still.

TOURISTS WEREN'T USED TO WHOREHOUSES QUITE LIKE Beyond Proof, or at least, that's what they always said to Elena. She'd been making a commission on the side by bringing in men—hardworking, dedicated fathers who always cautiously asked her, within a day of meeting her, if she might know where, *ahem*, they could meet a nice local girl, a clean girl, who'd be discreet, for a fun afternoon. *Claro que si*, Elena would say, she had a best friend who fit that exact description, who she may or may not be able to get to meet them on account of how busy she was with studying at a university, on the cusp of becoming a teacher, or a nurse, or an attorney. But! This friend, she did have a side hustle working as a snorkeling instructor, if the dad was interested in taking a class. Elena couldn't make any promises, because there had to be genuine chemistry, true attraction, but if there was, a good time would be had by all. Okay?

Dads were always surprised, so surprised, especially because Beyond Proof (known as "the Gringo Trap" to locals) seemed so unassuming. It was a beachside bar decorated with seashells and colorful bar stools that boasted a pay-as-you-wish menu inclusive of the freshest catch of the day, cooked simply with lime, salt and pepper, and homemade mamajuana rum potent beyond proof, made all the more so by the tree bark that Dulce—the owner—shaved off her own trees, grown in her own finca five miles away on the Pico Diablo Mountain. The same Dulce who provided the local rum to the Grand Paloma Resort.

Elena was always careful to explain that no money was to change hands, not directly between the man and her close friend, who would be so offended to think that an amorous afternoon with a private snorkeling client had been a transaction. But a payment had to be made. *Put what you wish in the tip jar,* Elena would say, absentmindedly pointing in the direction of an old tin can. The fathers happily agreed. The Grand Paloma Resort—at least the one on this side of the island— had a strict rule against sex work for the protection of the staff. Pablo was the only person she knew who routinely crossed that line, but he was so careful that Laura and the rest of the management team did not know.

After Laura dropped her off on the side of the road, Elena walked a couple of miles, then descended to the white-sand beach that housed the bar. She paused to touch her throbbing cheek, remembering the tourist girl with her matted hair, those translucent eyelids. The girl's last day alive had consisted of swimming in the ocean, mud masks, and chasing bumblebees, the girl rapt as Elena told her the story of Pico Diablo. An entire town founded by fleeing enslaved people from the little girl's own country who'd survived terrible lives and been rewarded with this beautiful land, a promise of freedom forever.

When Elena reached the slanted, receding shore, she stared into the horizon. It was a sweltering day, and after walking to get to Dulce's bar, she felt a coat of sweat all over her body. She moved farther onto the beach until the lapping waves touched her calves. She bent at the waist, made a bowl with her hands, filled it with salt water, and dropped her face into that limpidity. The salt water was refreshing for a moment before it stung her face. Then it felt lukewarm, as if it had been swished around inside someone's mouth. It was a repulsive feeling. She wished she could transport herself to the coldest place in the world and be enveloped in an arctic chill until goose pimples formed on her skin, the way she'd only ever witnessed in TikToks and YouTube videos.

Dulce hollered at her from the bar. "Elena! Is that you?"

Reluctantly, she turned to face Dulce. Dulce's giant frame—she stood at almost six feet tall—was obscured by the bar. But her pretty brown skin and dimpled cheeks were visible, and her brilliant brown eyes swam in merriment.

The bar had been recently renovated. It now sported couches for lounging and a natural caoba bar with the curves and knots from the original tree. It had been sealed with a thick, glossy coat of lacquer. The ten or so stools were made of the same material, only the legs had been painted over with colorful, festive Caribbean flags from Trinidad and Tobago, Jamaica, Nevis, Puerto Rico, and Cuba.

"Jesus sent you," she yelled as she gestured for Elena to get closer, not taking in her sad expression or her small traveling bag. Elena thought about Jesus sending her to a quiet bar when she had no time to spare. She looked out onto the road, expecting a police car, or her sister, to drag her back to the resort to pay for her mistake.

"Can you stay here for a bit?" Dulce said. "Watch the girls? Keep an eye on the bar?"

She explained that she had to rush to find out what had happened to a college-student-turned-snorkeling-instructor who'd been gone for way more than the two hours allotted for the tour. The girls Dulce had mentioned were her daughters, a ten-year-old and a nine-year-old whose golden skin and pale-green eyes said that they had been products of snorkeling adventures for Dulce, back when she'd conducted tours herself.

"Don't let my girls swim," Dulce said over her shoulder, jumping on a Jet Ski. "Vida just did their hair. It has to last until church on Sunday."

Elena was grateful for the quiet, empty bar as she saw Dulce splash away through the waves. She had to ask herself some hard questions before deciding her next move. Would today be the day she'd sleep with a man for money? Or could she persuade Dulce to lend her the money to get away? She checked her cellphone, opened Insta. She scrolled through the posts of a handful of women she'd helped along the way. These were the women who had seen the gringos as a way out of a life of servitude, who had said, *Yes, I will sleep with you, visitor, I will take your money and make my own life.* Elena had never been tempted to do so.

She'd been convinced that she was happy with her simple life, with her sister watching out for her while she lived out her life as a chaos agent. If she was completely honest, she'd childishly thought that she couldn't leave this plot of land without first defeating the waterfall—

without first figuring out the trick to sinking—thought it might help her understand something about her drowned mother. Maybe the mysterious depths could reveal something about her father's obsession with flight.

She took a damp rag and wiped the already spotless bar. She rearranged the few souvenirs that Dulce had placed within arm's reach so that the dedicated fathers would have a token of thoughtfulness to take back to the resort—there a coral necklace; there a faceless ceramic doll; there a T-shirt with the words *Paradise is the Dominican Republic* above a sunset, a tiny island floating with sea, sun, and sand. She served herself a shot of the dark rum and set it on the bar. A few flakes of tree bark rested on the surface of the liquid, and she stuck her index finger in it, hooked them up, licked them off.

Elena told herself that the mystery of her absent father no longer mattered, just as the circumstances that had led to her mother's drowning were beyond her grasp—this was yet another topic that Laura refused to speak about. When she was younger, Elena had hoped that her mother would visit her in dreams. But she'd never had a dream that featured her mother. No matter how hard she'd tried to conjure it otherwise, her mother stayed dead.

As Elena's graduation from the global academy had neared, Laura had grown frustrated by the uncertainty of their future. She was confident that she'd get the promotion that would enable them to travel abroad. The plan then would be for Elena to apply to college, preferably wherever they landed. Laura had been pushing Elena to apply for an au pair company that had offices in Lisbon, London, and New York City. Even though Elena had told Laura that she hated being a babysitter. That she didn't want to take care of kids anymore.

Now she considered who she might be able to hit up to house her if she were able to make an escape. There were her friends from the global academy, a group she'd been friendly with who'd all planned to meet up and backpack through Europe. When they'd offered to pay for her trip so she could join them, Laura had been livid. *We're not charity cases,* she'd shouted. But maybe Elena could link up with them? She checked her friends' socials and saw that they were now in London.

There was a photo of the group with their goofy grins saluting next to the Queen's Guard at the Tower of London. Elena reminded herself that she was now a fugitive. How embarrassing it would be to be with her friends if she ultimately had to be captured, arrested, and sent back.

Maybe she could rely on some of the women who'd left Pico Diablo to help. There was Socorro, aka La Gata, who had been one of her closest friends. If she could get herself to London, she'd crash with La Gata, then figure out if it was safe enough for her to meet up with her friends. She texted La Gata now.

I'm on my way to London, she wrote. Any chance I can stay with you for a few days? Just until I find some work. The Au Pair agency should be quick to find me a placement.

Within seconds, La Gata wrote back. Send me your flight info and I'll pick you up from Heathrow. Fuck the au pair agency. There's a home and work waiting for you with me.

Elena went into the bathroom, a tiny room that Dulce didn't allow anyone else to use, and changed into a light dress she found hanging on a rusty nail. It had huge pockets, and she imagined Dulce, at the end of each shift, giving money to each girl, keeping most of it for herself. It would be better if anyone who wandered over didn't see the bloodstained uniform, so she pushed it down into the small garbage bin. She craved another shot but decided against it. It would be better for her to come to a decision sober—before a choice was forced under duress. She confronted her reflection, pleased by how the wooden boards of the walls allowed blocks of sunlight to make vertical lines across her face. The scratch on her cheek didn't look as bad as she'd feared. It was reddish but not raw. Swimming in the waterfall had helped clean and then seal it. If she was diligent over many months, putting coconut oil and aloe on it, it might eventually disappear.

As she moisturized her face with a good-smelling cream Dulce had on the window ledge, she heard Dulce's girls running and laughing somewhere upstairs in the beach apartment above the bar. She leaned against the wall. Yes, today would be the day she would have sex for the first time. And she would do so for money. She'd somehow kept that secret from everyone but her sister. She was embarrassed to be seventeen and still a virgin. Her friends at the academy, everyone whose relationships had been forged over video conference calls and Slack groups, had long ago had sex. Maybe, if she admitted to a would-be Juan that it was her first time, they'd be willing to pay more? But how many times would she have to go through that to earn the thousands of dollars—tens of thousands of pesos—she'd need for a same-day plane ticket? The entire prospect seemed impossible.

CHAPTER
12

THE FABRIC MIOSOTIS HAD FASTENED AROUND LAURA'S TEM-
ples was tight, so as she exited the service elevator, she stuck a finger
by her ear to loosen its grip. In that spot was a terrible headache's initial pulsing. Laura was worried about Vida, who'd looked pale and
shaky, who'd refused to wait until Laura had solved the issue with the
tourist girl. What if she fainted off her Vespa? Making it all the way
up the six miles to Pico Diablo over rough terrain was difficult even
when one was feeling their best. She paused, holding on to the modern
metal banisters. Ahead of her, in the enormous cavern that plunged
twelve floors to the lobby, the suspended glass sculpture of a paloma in
flight showed her fractured reflection staring back at her. She looked
terrified.

Ahead of her, on the penthouse-level guest elevator landing, she
found a set of muddy, child-sized footprints that marked the path she
was meant to follow. Every few steps, there were a few drops of blood.
When the girl had woken up, she'd told Vida that she felt very well.
But the sight of the perfectly circular blood drops ahead of her made
Laura dizzy with concern over the child. It dissolved the worry she'd
felt for Vida moments earlier.

There was no reason to be afraid, she reminded herself. The little
girl had fallen. *It was an unfortunate but blameless accident,* she practiced saying aloud.

Laura turned on her walkie-talkie. She requested that a cleaning
crew come upstairs to clean up the muddy prints on the penthouse
floor.

"Make sure to leave the floor spotless," she commanded. What she didn't say: *There should be no sign of blood anywhere.*

THE TOURIST GIRL ANSWERED the door, no trace of mud or blood to be seen. Laura took special note of the girl. Showered and changed, she held a tablet flush against her chest. There was no noticeable sign of injury or fright. In the all-white living room, there was no adult. But Laura could hear the beeping sounds of the safe from the master bedroom—and yes, through the flowing sheer curtains on the wide balcony, she caught a glimpse of the mother on her stomach, topless. The parents were now up.

"Where's my Ellie?" the tourist girl asked, glancing behind Laura as if half-expecting that Elena would suddenly appear. This was the part that Laura had never understood. As often as Elena screwed up, one would think that the children would want nothing to do with her. But they always adored her. Requested her time and time again.

"She's not feeling well," Laura said. "I've arranged for another girl to come up a bit later. May I speak to your parents?"

The girl shook her head. Laura's brows knit in confusion.

"You want to tell them what happened to me?" the girl said in an accusatory tone.

"Was thinking about doing that," Laura said. "Unless you have another idea?"

The girl smiled. She turned the tablet's thin, flat screen in Laura's direction, showing her the fully realized Water Park Extravaganza at the Yellow Paloma. The girl must've already imagined herself racing down the two-story twisty slide and dancing bachata with dolphins in the children's aquarium. Laura was relieved that the little girl was acting just like any savvy eight-year-old would act. She was trying to negotiate her way into a better vacation. In her excitement, the tablet slid down, showing the part of her chest that had been hidden. There was a big, angry bruise there.

"Do you feel okay?" Laura asked, alarmed.

The girl nodded. "My nose started bleeding again on the way here, but it stopped when I showered. Nothing hurts. I just want to go to the water park."

At this utterance, drops of water fell from her coiled hair. Laura took even more careful stock of the girl. Elena had been just like this as an eight-year-old child—cunning, strategic.

"Your parents will go along with changing hotels?" Laura asked. "The Yellow Paloma is far away from here, in another part of the country. It's almost a six-hour drive away. It's also landlocked. You know what that means? No beach."

The little girl bit her lip. "You can convince them," she said.

Just then, the father stepped out from the master bedroom, shirtless. He had a designer cross-body bag, its zipper straining against whatever he'd overstuffed it with. He held one of the arms of his aviator sunglasses tight between his impossibly straight white teeth.

"Where are you going, Daddy?" the girl asked.

"To explore real life outside the resort," he said.

Laura was startled by the brightness of his green eyes. There was something at once electric and dead about them.

"Sir," Laura said. "May I have a quick word?"

"There is something wrong with the sink in the master bathroom," he said, ignoring her question. "Can you go see what's happening?"

"I'm really sorry about that," Laura said. "I'll make sure one of our plumbers comes right away."

"Go see," he demanded.

Laura wasn't surprised by his tone. Americans were consistently, unnecessarily blunt.

She made her way to the master bedroom. It had a fishbowl effect—three quarters of the wall were all glass. The California king–sized bed faced the ocean. The windows had automatic shades programmed to open at dawn, allowing sunlight to brighten the room incrementally and wake guests naturally, with tenderness. Laura avoided looking at the sky. She moved directly to the bathroom. This room alone was larger than the casita where she slept every night. At its center, an oversized Japanese tub sat at hip-height—deep and wide enough to submerge several adults at once. Feeling weary from so many months with little sleep—or only restless sleep from the prescription pills she'd gotten her hands on from the resort's doctor—Laura imagined what it would feel like to discard her clothes the way her sister had to jump into the waterfall, slipping into this tub. If she were a guest and not an employee, she would extend her hand toward the aperture on its side as it soundlessly spouted warm water that would hug her body as it filled the tub, shutting off automatically when sensors detected that it was three-quarters full. She would remain in the warm bath for hours, until her entire body pruned. If only.

Laura stepped over discarded items of clothing and wet towels as she made her way into yet another space, this one with the twin basins, where she found the offensive leaky faucet. The mechanism on the wall adjacent to the sinks had been turned on and left on, so the water would continue to run all day unless it was switched off. She yawned as she deactivated it with a simple press of the right button. The water stopped running at once.

She looked at her fingernails for a few seconds, waiting for a bit of time to pass. On the counter of a vanity off to the side, there was an array of perfumes, a fancy bag full of makeup. She sniffed the expensive-smelling sunblock. When she lifted Dior's L'Or de Vie La Crème, she had to smile. In June, right as Elena and her peers had been getting ready to graduate, they'd started to compare beauty regimens in their group chat. One of Elena's friends, whose mother was an executive at Mumbai's Arabian Paloma, had written in disdain that her grandmother had gifted her this same anti-aging crème. I'm eighteen years old the girl's message had read. Elena had turned the phone's screen in Laura's direction, showing her that the price tag was over a thousand bucks. *You know how many people could be fed with what that family spends on cosmetics?* she'd asked.

Laura had nodded in agreement. Rich people were, admittedly, insane. But also, if you had enough money that gifting that face crème to an eighteen-year-old seemed like a good idea, you must have made some right decisions in your life. Or your ancestors had.

She almost snapped a picture to send to Elena, wondering if the fact that her sister hadn't sent one to her first meant that she hadn't sneaked into this couple's room to snoop. If this had been a normal day, she'd have dipped her third-world fingers into the lotion, slathered it all over her face, and sent a text to her sister: Do I look younger yet? But she reminded herself that this wasn't the time to joke around with her sister. The most terrible possibility had been averted, but they weren't out of hot water just yet.

Laura decided that enough time had passed.

She wandered back to the oversized Japanese tub and found at its center a strange-looking cylindrical object, made of various-sized marbles that grew bigger until the bottom one was the width of Laura's forearm. It shone sea green with spots of gold. She reached into the tub and held the strange object in her hand; the plastic was harder than she'd expected. Instinctively, she brought it to her nose—and immediately gagged. It wasn't gold—it was shit.

She dropped the enormous anal beads back into the tub. She couldn't believe she'd touched it. It served her right. She washed her hands repeatedly, adding more and more eucalyptus-scented soap until foam covered her hands. She had a feeling that sickening stench would remain nestled in her nostrils all day. She pretended to call plumbing services on her walkie-talkie, speaking in exaggeratedly loud English so the man would know she had taken care of his request. These people had no shame. To send a stranger into the bathroom, knowing they'd be seeing that. But then again, guests never really thought of staff as people who would surely pass judgment on them— she was just a worker.

"Could I have a word with you, sir?" she asked again when she re-entered the living room. Taking note of the man's slender hips, she wondered if he was the one who liked to have that absurdly large phallic object in his anal cavity.

He placed a hand around his ear, as if to ensure that the running water was off. "See, you fixed it."

"Yes, sir," Laura said. "I came up here because there's an important matter I need to discuss with you."

"Sophie," he called onto the balcony. "Come deal with this. I gotta go."

He slipped on the season's most popular Gucci sandals, then turned on his heels. No mention of when he'd be back. No kiss on the forehead for the tourist girl, who was now standing closer to the balcony doors. No inquiries from the mother.

"Text me if you want me to bring you anything from the town," the father said as he made his way down the hallway.

When the door to the outside opened, a rush of wind rustled the sheer curtains. The air smelled salty and fresh. The mother had the glassy-eyed gaze of someone who'd started on the cocktails at breakfast and by this time in the afternoon was in need of a nap. She wore a tiny thong bikini.

"We wondered where you'd gone," Sophie said. She grabbed an oversized cotton button-down shirt and covered her reddening skin. She perched herself on the arm of the L-shaped oat-colored bouclé sofa, finishing the last few buttons. The shirt fit her like a large dress.

"No," Laura said, unable to hide her annoyance. It was still shocking how often tourists—and truthfully, her foreign colleagues—mistook her for others. And not just her sister, which would make sense, since there was an obvious resemblance. She'd been mistaken for women who were three times her age, who had different skin tones, who were a foot taller or inches shorter. She'd been mistaken for pretty women, old women, even, once, for a man. The tourist wife raised an eyebrow at Laura's tone.

"No," she repeated, softer, correcting herself. "I'm not your sitter. She had a personal emergency. I will make sure a new sitter comes shortly."

"I'm sorry," Sophie said. "I didn't put my contacts in. I can't see anything unless it's directly in front of my face."

Sophie shifted her gaze from Laura's blurry shape, staring at the eighteen-foot gallery wall that sported images of still lifes she remembered but couldn't see—a mango, a bird of paradise among some bushes, a pyramid of stones on the beach that seemed ready to topple over. She'd seen a show by this photographer at the Guggenheim last year. The hotel must have paid a fortune for these photographs.

"We're planning to stay in the room today. The service really hasn't been the best at this Paloma. First, no one comes all day to fix the leaky faucet. Second, we need to deal with a new sitter halfway through the trip. We've only got a week left, you know?"

Laura nodded, transfixed by the woman's mannerisms. She used her index finger to touch the digits on her other hand, counting the hotel's infractions. Laura wondered if she was the one who liked to have that huge anal bead monstrosity stuck into her butt. She shook her head, newly revolted at the memory of the stench on the object. Laura explained that to make amends for the issues they'd been dealing with, she wanted to get the family out to their sister resort, the Yellow Paloma, a six-hour drive away. She explained about the water park and how it'd been voted the best family resort in the Caribbean by *Condé Nast Traveler* just earlier this year. The mother seemed turned off by that. Laura felt the child take her hand, loosely tugging at it, as if to make her feel supported. Was this child encouraging her to make a better case? She almost laughed. Laura explained to the mother that the Yellow Paloma also had a very exclusive adults-only area called La Paloma Negra, which would provide an ideal way to close out their trip.

"I've heard the parties there are legendary," she added, remembering the way Elena had described the couple hours ago. The woman's interest seemed piqued. When Laura had last visited the resort a couple of years ago as part of the Paloma's Leadership Team, to celebrate the grand opening, it had been an adventurer's dream, meant to attract the zip-lining and bird-watching enthusiasts who were drawn to Costa Rica, one of the few countries where Paloma Enterprises had been unable to open a resort. But since then, the resort's reputation as a haven for the libertine had become well-known.

"Can we get back to you?" Sophie said.

That was definitely not a yes.

"We have a gorgeous spa there," Laura went on. "I'd love to give you and your husband a couple's treatments on us? And we can assign a sitter to take your daughter to a separate bedroom for the night, so you can have some time to truly enjoy a bit of adult fun without this lovely one"—here, Laura did a boop on the girl's nose that she'd hate herself for later—"who could have her own adventure?"

The mother shifted her weight from one ass cheek to the other, tucking her foot beneath her hip. She bit her lip in concentration. Laura wondered if it was her butt that was sore.

"If you don't like it, you can come right back?" Laura said. "No bother at all. We'll provide transportation there and back."

The mother turned her attention to the girl, who had let out a loud whine.

"Please, Mommy," the girl said. "It's so boring here."

After a few uncomfortable moments, Sophie said, "Of course. We can try it. If we don't like it, we can just come right back."

As Laura listened to the mother, she felt a strain in her face where Elena had struck her with her foot. Was it possible that her sister had lied about the couple's partying ways? This woman didn't strike her as the type. But then again, she'd been fooled by more than one innocent-looking guest. Without thought, she brought her hand to her head, only to find the fabric she'd forgotten was wrapped around it. Laura imagined the mass of hair under the fabric continuing to knot.

The tourist girl let go of her hand and moved onto the oceanfront balcony. Laura felt a vague echo of alarm that neither of the parents had noticed the bruise on the girl's chest, nor the fact that she'd obviously been covered in mud and blood when she'd made it back to the suite. Laura felt a tug at the sight, recalling when Elena had been a few years younger than this girl. They'd gone out seeking help during the last major hurricane on the island and had been turned away by every neighbor. It still haunted her, the way every adult in Pico Diablo had ignored the knocking, their need for help. Later, they all said it wasn't true. That none of them had heard their frantic calls for help.

What if there was a lingering injury that was hidden in this child? What if the girl needed to see a doctor? But the little girl had been well enough to shower, change, and blackmail her for a water park reservation.

Now, as the girl stood in that doorway with a salty breeze lifting her wet curls, she seemed perfectly undisturbed. Laura made her way to the little girl. The ocean ahead of her was incredibly still, all turquoise slashes in that navy-blue infinity. The dark silhouettes of flying ospreys were the only movement that disrupted what would otherwise have been a perfect picture. The birds glided close to the shore, dipping in and out of the ocean as they hunted for their next meal.

"Mommy," the girl said. "Are those birds killing the fish?"

The mother returned to the chaise longue and lay on her side. She placed her sunglasses on her face and strained against the bright day as she pressed different buttons on her tablet. She didn't bother looking toward the water.

"Yes, sweetheart," she said. "Just the cycle of life."

"We'll let you know the best time to leave, then?" she said without looking at Laura, either.

"I'll send someone to clean the floors. Looks like your daughter brought a bit of mud in from outside."

The mother didn't react to that. Laura thought she might regret what she did next, but she couldn't leave things be.

"I think your daughter might have hurt herself," Laura said. Sophie sat up immediately.

"What do you mean?" she asked.

"I just noticed she has a slight bruise on her chest," Laura said, pointing.

"Come here," the mother said. She raised her sunglasses so they were suspended on the crown of her head, taking a close look at the girl's chest. "This looks awful, Peanut. Does it hurt?"

The mother touched the girl's skin lightly, right at the tender spot. The girl shook her head, even as she winced. She widened her eyes at Laura, as if she'd messed things up for them both.

"What happened?" Sophie asked.

"I don't know," the girl said. "We were at the pool and then Ellie and I gave each other mud masks. With real mud. I didn't fall or nothing."

The mother breathed out. Placed her sunglasses back on her face.

"I'll just have the doctor come by," Laura said. "That'll be on us, too. Better make sure she's okay."

"I'd appreciate that," the mother said, leaning back on the chaise longue. She picked up a pair of wireless headphones and put them on. She hit play on her thin tablet, and Laura heard the theme of a show popular among the guests, about guests at a fictional luxury resort. Laura had taken one look at the show's first episode and turned it off. She found the idea that the most interesting thing at any resort could ever possibly be the guests absurd.

The little girl got up from her mother's side and, after making sure that her mother was completely absorbed by the screen, picked up the hem of her dress and brought it over her head. She sprayed herself with sunscreen, then moved to the chaise longue next to her mother. She brought the thick ivory towel that was draped on the lounge chair above her head, which required her to scoot-scoot-scoot her small tush, each time checking to see if the released fabric would give her enough shade for her tablet. By the end, the towel formed a tent held up by her outstretched legs.

The girl uncovered her head, giving Laura a wide, toothy smile and a big thumbs-up, then made some silly gestures of swimming with her legs and arms before fading into the cave of her enormous towel.

Laura faced down the long stretch of beach. Below, Pablo rushed to the Freedom Sunset Cruise. He moved fast, tiptoeing on the sand as if it hurt. The sun was searing, producing a heat so intense that she wondered how the mother and daughter could stand it. This unrelenting weather reminded her of the many days she'd spent on this beach holding hands with her mother. Those had been the days when her father had been fixated on making his way to the United States. Every time he could find someone willing to loan him some money—in exchange for land, always a piece of land—he'd try again and then be gone for weeks or months at a time. Every time, he'd come back irreparably harmed—an eye injury that robbed him of half his sight, an injured finger that had to be amputated. The severity of his injuries never hampered his attempts—every time he got enough money to try, he'd be at it again, full of hope that this would be the time he'd make it. That he'd send for them shortly after. That they'd have a life of luxury and freedom unlike any they'd ever known. That in America, they would be safe.

In his absence, Laura and her mother had spent most of their days trying to sell food to beachgoers. Of course, back then, there had been no hotel on this beach, and those who'd frequented the place had been other Dominicans, who'd come from faraway towns for the supposedly medicinal powers of Paloma Falls. They often ended up on this beach after their visits and would buy pastelitos, quipes, yaniqueques, or fried fish plates complete with rice and beans and a side of spaghetti from her mother. Laura remembered how long those days had been, how hot the sand on the beach, how the things that always went first had been the cold Presidentes. On some days, they'd sell nothing at all, and would walk the ten-mile stretch until Laura would fall over, pretending to faint from exhaustion. Her mother's laughter would make her peek out of one eye. *We didn't come this far to give up, did we?* she'd ask, and Laura would rise, hands outstretched, pretending to be a zombie. It was rare that she remembered the sweetness of her mother without thinking of all the ugly parts that went along with her childhood— death, violence, secrets. Why had she remembered that day of all days? Then she recalled her mother taking her zombie hand and putting it on the softness of her protruding belly. *You're going to have a sister in a few months,* she'd said. *As soon as she arrives, you'll have a big job to keep her safe.*

Laura was grateful to the tourist mother-and-daughter duo for evoking within her such a tender moment. She turned her attention to them both now.

"If you need anything, just let me know," Laura said.

"Hi," the mother said over the sharp blade of a shoulder. It was as if she'd forgotten what Laura was doing in her suite. "On your way out, can you ask them to bring me another bottle of Moët and a few Coca-Colas for Peanut? No plastic bottles, only glass."

Laura nodded and reentered the suite's living room, grateful for the reprieve from the burning sun. She should be relieved. She should be ecstatic that it had all gone so well. But her rapid heartbeat kept her from leaving this entire unpleasant scene behind. The loose insole of her right shoe was stuck to the bottom of her foot, and as she walked to the telephone and ordered their drinks, she felt a rising helplessness. Her heart continued to pound at her temples. That slimy, disgusting feeling from her foot echoed the base of her hairline where the fabric that covered her hair had grown damp above her neck and had begun to release moisture down her spine. The unsettled feeling was there, trapped on the surface of her skin from foot to neck, pounding at her temples. Something was wrong.

Elena's eyes, wide and frightened, came to mind. She'd been devastated at the thought that she'd harmed the child. She should call her sister and tell her the girl was okay. She looked at her phone and saw that the screen had gone black. *Damn it.*

She wasn't going to call anyway. She remembered her sister's giggle at the sight of the kite and how quickly she'd seemed to self-transport to lunaland, floating away without a care, unaffected by the seriousness of the situation. One way or another, she'd push her sister to become a grown-up.

She placed the order for the champagne and soda, hung up the phone, and left the suite. She welcomed the much-cooler air-conditioned hallway. Maybe this bad feeling was just a case of sunstroke. When she'd driven her sister to the outskirts of the resort grounds, she'd felt as if she were about to faint. But once she'd dropped her off, she'd felt lighter, better. Maybe the feeling of dread would slip away as soon as she got herself settled, took care of her hair. She wondered what Elena was doing at this moment. She wondered if she had experienced enough stress to understand the severity of the situation.

She shook her cellphone, hoping any excess water would come out of it, and it turned on. It worked. She texted her sister. Time is running out, she said. Can't hold things off here. What have you figured out? Time to move!

Let Elena stew in fear. Let her get so stressed out that she would realize goofing off at work could derail her entire future.

The cleaning cart ahead of Laura had turned the footprints into two distinct muddy tracks. She stepped over to the doorway of the next suite to find Arely, an older worker, on her knees, scrubbing red wine from the white porcelain floors. Sharply, Laura asked if Arely hadn't heard her earlier command.

"Clean the fucking floors," she said. "Don't you see you've made an even bigger mess?"

Arely grabbed a few soiled towels from the cart. On all fours, she sprayed and wiped until the floor was pristine. Clean enough that someone could eat off it.

Inside the descending glass guest elevator, Laura admired the sculpture of that bird in flight. From this angle, the small pieces of reflective glass suspended in the air reflected everything around them in diminutive, reversed detail. As Laura went down in the elevator, the reflection showed her traveling upward until she was lost in the vastness of the skylights above. There was a version of her somewhere else that was traveling elsewhere, that was free.

CHAPTER
13

ELENA HAD SPENT THE BETTER PART OF THE LAST HOUR UP-stairs in the apartment above the Beyond Proof Bar. Niña and Perfecta, Dulce's girls, with their perfectly golden skin and pretty green eyes, were splayed on an oversized couch. They wore adult-sized Leverkusen shirts over their swimsuits—Niña's was a black tank top, while Perfecta's was a red T-shirt with the team's twin lion emblem. The girls had been attempting to talk Elena into letting them swim. She told them it wasn't worth it. They wouldn't want to ruin their pretty hairdos.

They sported identical gorgeous hair puffs decorated with long, extravagant silk ribbons. Such unusual ribbons—a rainbow dominated by red. She had assumed they might have been a gift from Fabien, the girls' foreigner father, who loved to send his daughters lavish presents. But the girls had told her that these were from Vida, who had left a while ago. Who had said she would be right back. Their hair was styled in exactly the way Elena and Laura's mother had once done the sisters' hair, to Laura's consternation. Laura, who'd always complained that she was too old for that little-kid style. Elena recalled the hurt she'd felt, even as a four-year-old, that her big sister didn't want to look like her.

Elena raided the cabinets and found chips, candy, soda. She and the girls stuffed their faces while watching funny videos on TikTok. No one had come searching for her yet. She began to think that her sister had exaggerated what had happened back at the resort. There was no way that if something terrible had happened to that little girl, people wouldn't be searching for her.

"You should come take care of us more often," Perfecta said.

"I'd rather take care of you than be in the resort. Believe me. Maybe your mom will give me a job!"

"Aren't you going to college?" Niña asked.

Elena thought about college. The plan was that she would rest over the next year and apply to college so she'd start in a year's time. She wanted to attend a school in the United States because she'd always imagined that by the time she went to college, her father would have made a home there and they could be near each other. She planned to study social justice. Laura thought that sounded like a poor person's profession and that it would be better for her to study law or become a doctor in Europe. She didn't think the United States was a great place for immigrants, and she often fantasized about the day when Elena would sport a stethoscope around her neck or a gavel in her hand. But Elena didn't want those jobs. She figured that it would just be a matter of time before she convinced Laura to allow her to choose her own future. That once they ended up somewhere else, she might be able to make the right decision for herself. But her tuition reimbursement was based on Laura's job. So, Laura would get to call the shots on where she went, what she did.

Dulce texted Elena. She told her that she'd found Toqui, who wasn't in good shape. They were heading to the hospital. She should be back soon, though, as soon as one of her other workers came to stay with Toqui. Elena wrote her back. No biggie, she said. No rush!

She snapped a live picture of the girls making silly faces. Sent it to Dulce.

Dulce hearted the photo immediately.

When her phone buzzed a few minutes later with a text from Laura, Elena stood up. Laura said she couldn't hold things off any longer. Elena had to move!

"You both stay here," she said. "I have something to figure out."

A WHITE MAN STOOD with his back to Elena, staring at the beach. Much in the way she'd done when she'd first stepped up to the shore, he bent down, cupped his hands, and splashed his face with the salt water. Then, as if sensing her presence, he turned and smiled at her. *Oh.* The father of the girl she'd left dead back at the resort. He was shirtless, his blond hair shining white in the sunlight. She couldn't say a word, couldn't move. He advanced toward her slowly, like he was in no big rush. She glanced furtively up the incline back toward the road, trying to locate his grieving wife, or Laura with the police at her heels.

"Hi," he said. "What an awesome bar!"

He clearly did not recognize her. She'd been caring for his child for the last seven days. He'd never asked her for an intro to a local girl. He and his wife seemed to know exactly where to go to get what they wanted.

Snapping out of it, she forced the words out, mimicking the way Dulce greeted everyone who sat at the bar. "What can I do you for, guapo?"

He turned and gazed at the shelves full of liquor. "What's with that red-label bottle?" he asked.

Elena turned to see. It was the oversized bottle of Mama Juana's Beyond Proof.

"That's just for decoration," she said. "You might have heard about it in the news a few years ago? A bunch of tourists that were at the resorts in Punta Cana and Boca Chica got so sick they had to be airlifted out? That was the culprit. The drink is so potent that everyone started calling it Beyond Proof. Now it's been outlawed."

"I'll take a shot of that," he said.

One of the insights Elena had gained into wealthy people, those who'd inherited their money and not worked hard to earn it, was that they had this sense of invincibility, of all-encompassing power. As if money meant that they weren't bound by the rules that other people followed. Hadn't she just said the drink was poison?

"It's not liquor in it," she lied. "It's just honey and water. Happy to serve it to you if you'd like?"

"Three shots of regular Mama Juana on ice, then," he said. He turned back to face the ocean. He sighed deeply, the way they all did—a way that said, *Look at all this paradise.* "This is paradise," he said.

She followed his gaze. The same gorgeous sky, the same turquoise waters. Birds swooped in and out of the sea, grasping fish with sharp talons. She was exhausted from looking at the same thing every day of her life. She'd worked so hard to make a difference, to improve the lives of those who deserved to be treated better, but all her labor had come to nothing. She remembered when she'd staged that walkout to protest the mass deportations of Haitians, how disastrous the aftermath had been. When hopelessness had gutted her soul, her sister had told her that trying to stop injustices in a place like this was like trying to stop a tsunami with a bucket. *Good luck making a fucking difference.* Or the way Elena herself had begun to think of it—in quicksand, the more of an effort you made, the quicker you sank. This was home: a beautiful paradise with a rotten core.

"No place like it," she said in the bright tone reserved for the guests of the resort. "It's a true blessing to live in a beautiful place."

He gazed at her intensely. "Your English is very good," he said. "You don't even sound Dominican."

He had said this exact thing to her on the first day they'd met. She remembered him looking away, losing interest as soon as she smiled. She stared back at him just as intensely, wanting to see if he was pulling her leg. The first time he'd made this remark, she'd explained that children in the local town of Pico Diablo learned English before they learned Spanish, and he'd immediately pursed his lips in distaste. *That seems so unnatural,* he'd said—as if they were taught the language to serve tourists. She'd been unwilling to explain the truth to him. It was a matter of legacy—they spoke English because it was theirs from their ancestors, not because their parents were anticipating a lifetime of servitude.

"I was born in Boston," she said now, lying easily. "My dad is there still."

Elena wasn't sure why she'd brought her father into this conversation. Her face burned as she thought of what he would make of what she was about to do.

"No wonder you left that shit show for this," he said.

She served the man his drink quickly just to get him to shut up.

She picked up her empty shot glass and refilled it, and they both said cheers. She sipped while he took a huge gulp. His hands were so big. She wondered if he would be rough, violent. She wondered if she should initiate the transaction, then quickly realized that she had no idea how she'd navigate such a conversation. She'd always been puzzled that Dulce didn't name a specific price for the services her prostitutes rendered. If a price tag wasn't placed on this kind of service, the amount of money a man gave as a tip said everything there was to know about what he thought their bodies were worth. What would this man think her body was worth? But she wouldn't be foolish and take such a risk. She would name her price. Once, Elena had marveled out loud that women would have sex as part of a transaction, and Dulce had told her that it wasn't always unpleasant, this work. That it could afford a certain kind of freedom. The entire time, she'd been looking at her girls with the tenderness of someone with no regrets.

A single dark cloud reached the sky over the beach, and though the sun could be seen through it, a localized rainstorm started quickly right above the bar. Dulce's girls rushed down the stairs and into the rain shower. Elena was glad that they hadn't removed their father's German soccer team's shirts. Maybe that meant they wouldn't try to rush into the water. They ran back and forth on the sand, first to the part where it was raining and then to the part where it was sunny.

She was caught off guard by the girls' joy. She took her phone out, snapped a few images of the girls as they ran away and made their way back. But the camera did a poor job of capturing the truth. There was no way to tell from the pictures how gorgeous the sight was, how happy they were.

"No swimming," Elena said to the girls in Spanish when she noticed that they were getting closer to the shoreline. She posted one of the pictures of the girls running away from her to her social media feed—the one that best showed the silk ribbons floating in the wind. Immediately, some likes, some hearts, some comments of *pero que lindas y grandes esas niñas de Dulce* appeared, and those responses made her feel alive, real.

The man finished his drink and placed the glass loudly on the bar.

Elena was startled. She'd gotten lost in her social media feed for a moment. His expression was indecipherable. He asked her for a double shot. She reminded herself that she needed to stay present. He waited until her back was turned and then spoke softly.

"I heard there are special snorkeling tours," he said.

"Yes," Elena said. There was something grainy on the inside of her throat. "I can take care of you."

"If I wanted something a bit more unusual . . ." the man started, then, turning his attention pointedly back to the girls as they ran back and forth, he let his words trail off.

"Which one?" Elena asked, as if this was no big deal. As if men came and asked to have sex with little girls all the time. She rubbed her fingertips silently against each other under the bar where he couldn't see, remembering the sticky, gel-like moisture on the back of his daughter's head.

"Both," he said.

"I'm afraid it's very expensive," she said. She remembered the tenderness with which Dulce had looked at her daughters, one ten years old, the other nine years old, reminders that sometimes a mistake didn't turn into regret. "Neither has ever been touched."

The man took his fancy cross-body bag, unzipped it, removed his American passport and rental car keys, and, placing both on the side of the bar, went on to count out ten thousand dollars in hundred-dollar bills. "Would that be enough?"

There was something mocking in his tone, as if he realized that the amount of money was preposterous. Elena looked at the stacks of dollars, then at the man. She'd never seen that much money. His eyes were glazed over in a familiar, feverish way that reminded her of her own reflection. She wondered what drugs he was on. Maybe he was high enough that he'd fall asleep the minute he laid his head down. Out in the ocean, there was no sign of Dulce's Jet Ski. Behind the bar, on the road, there were no police sirens, no Laura wagging a finger at her, telling her that she'd pulled the last stunt of her life with the tourist girl. That now, she was off to a jail cell.

For a moment, she thought of her friend Pablo, of the sobering concern he'd shown her earlier in the day. It was as if his voice floated to her from inside her own head, but also from outside it, from somewhere nearby. *Any risk is too big a risk with our girls,* he would say if he were here. He'd remind her that it was okay not to care so much for these fucking gringos, but that for the locals, there ought to be nothing but care. *We're the only thing we've got,* he'd said as she walked away from him.

Maybe she should have gone with him on the Freedom Sunset Cruise.

On the beach, the rain finally stopped. The girls came over to the bar and sat on stools on either side of the man. These girls were used to compliments. They sat next to this stranger, smiling, unimpressed by his money. Elena imagined they'd seen piles of cash around their rich dad and their pimp of a mom.

Elena noticed how the hair puffs on both girls had remained dry—maybe because of the back-and-forth on the beach. Several drops of rain rested perfectly undisturbed in their strands of kinky hair, reflecting the glow from a block of sunlight that bent from the wooden slats of the bathroom into the bar. Those drops of rain, with the light shining on and through them, were as bright as jewels on the girls' heads. She reminded herself, just as Laura had insisted she understand, that she wasn't responsible for anyone but herself, no matter how precious they were. The clouds, those fluffy, pretty ones, moved across the sky quickly. Off in the distance, she heard the sound of goats bleating. *Meehhh. Meeeh. Meeeh.* She'd always loved the sound of their songs. But that love had never made her pause before taking a bite of their delicious meat.

She topped off the man's drink. Served herself a double shot of rum. This time, neither said cheers. The man's heavy eyelids seemed ready to drop. He would pass out soon. There would be absolutely no danger to the girls. None-none-none-none. These girls were safe. Of course, any minute now their mother would return. And if Dulce was delayed at the hospital, then surely Vida would be back, because she was supposed to come back here after she dropped by the resort. She was probably now finishing her statement to the police, telling them how hard she'd tried to save the tourist girl. Vida would climb on her Vespa and be here in a matter of minutes. Or one of the prostitutes who worked for Dulce would drop by in search of some unscheduled work.

Elena grabbed the money, put it into the big pockets of the dress she wore. She told the man he'd find the stairs next to the bath-room. She told him to wait in the apartment, in the big bedroom on the left. She would bring the girls up to him in a few moments. He left. He didn't bother taking the fanny pack or the car keys with him. There was such arrogance in that trust. She wasn't sure why she placed his passport in the lost and found. She pocketed the car keys and zippered up his fanny pack.

"Mami doesn't like strangers upstairs," one of the girls said in per-fectly unaccented English. "It's a resting place. Family only," she added, parroting her mother's words.

Elena nodded. "I know that," she said.

Elena spoke some words to the girls. Later, she'd try to remember precisely what she'd stated. Maybe it had been about how their mother had asked for their help, and it was important that they do exactly as she said. She would have reminded them that as long as they were together, nothing bad would happen. Did they believe her? Both girls had responded yes, because they'd known Elena their entire lives, be-cause they were still giddy from running on the beach—from this in-credible miracle they'd just lived through, flowing through rain and sunlight within a single breath. What she'd recall, without a doubt, is that when she'd told the girls what to do next, she'd been certain no harm would come to them. The girls had a pampered life. Their father was part of the group of investors who had financed the creation of Paloma Falls, with its cobblestone colonial-inspired streets and all-white luxury stores. She reassured herself, again, that it was only a matter of a few minutes before someone wandered to the bar. Tonight was Locals' Night, and people would start heading over as soon as their shifts were done at the resort.

"I need you to run away from here," she said. "You hear me? Far, far away. I'm going to send someone to find you. Got it?"

The girls nodded, and as they moved their heads, all those gems fell, glittering all the way down until they were absorbed by the sand.

"I gotta pee," the smaller one, Perfecta, said.

And off they went, into the bathroom.

"Everything all right down there?" the tourist man's voice boomed from upstairs. ·

"Be right up," Elena responded.

For the longest moment of her life, she considered what to do next. She knew she likely should wait for the girls, but she couldn't afford to take them with her and drop them off before she left. The airport was in the opposite direction of the resort, too far away from Pico Diablo for her to take them up there without risking getting caught.

She went over to the tin can, which still held hundreds of dollars in tips. Dulce had been arrogant in her trust, too. Dulce had likely never known a moment of real desperation. Elena took all the money from the tin can. She went to the white man's rental car just as the girls came out onto the beach. But instead of walking up the hill, away from danger, they slipped out of their shirts and ran to the water. Elena's heart quickened with worry. She opened the door to go get them, but then they returned and put on their shirts. The girls lingered there, as if deciding what to do next.

Elena's heart hammered. She stared at Laura's last text on her cellphone. You better move!

With hands trembling, she sent a text to Pablo. She looked at the beach. The tourist man hadn't come down from the upstairs apartment. Porfa, come to Dulce's FAST, she wrote. It's an emergency.

As she turned on the ignition and expertly reversed up the hill, she couldn't stop thinking about the drops of rain in the girls' hair. Nothing bad could happen to those girls. She was certain. They would do exactly as she'd told them. She glanced at them as they took a few steps. Before she could tell which direction they were headed in, she stepped hard on the gas, pushing-pushing-pushing down all the feelings that bubbled up. But there was no denying them today, so she tried to recall the kite on top of the almond tree. Had it been the same pale yellow as the sun? On the day they'd found their mother's body floating in the water, she'd forced her eyes away. The trees had seemed to grow taller, leaves glowing a verdant shade that she'd never seen since. Laura had grabbed her hand, then lifted her into her arms. Her sister had tenderly shielded her face, buried her vision in the folds of an embrace. Her cheek pulsed with the memory now, and she felt the scratch Laura had inflicted palpitating. Just before Laura had showed up and pulled on her leg, she'd asked herself what it might take for her body to grow heavy, to plummet through the density of the cold water. Was it an inherited trait, their odd difficulty? How their bodies failed to sink?

She checked to see if Pablo had responded to her text. The message remained unread. But he would read it, hurry over, help. Pablo was always good like that.

THE
GRAND PALOMA
RESORT

*Cordially Invites You to
the Freedom Sunset Cruise*

PALOMA FALLS WAS FOUNDED TO HONOR THE SURROUND-ing land's remarkable history. Join our Freedom Sunset Cruise every Thursday to raise a glass of champagne in honor of this rich legacy.

A GLORIOUS PAST

During the Haitian invasion of the Dominican Republic in the 1820s and the subsequent twenty-two-year occupation, Jean-Pierre Boyer, then Haiti's leader, extended an invitation to abolitionists in Philadelphia: He would finance passage and re-settlement of as many enslaved people as the abolitionists could muster. The result? Six thousand Black Americans fled to the Dominican Republic, and more than two thousand ended up staying, surviving, and thriving. It is estimated that of those, a small number of families settled on the Pico Diablo Mountain.

HISTORY IS ALIVE TO THIS DAY!

The locals celebrate Freedom Day with a delightful annual scavenger hunt every October 2! Tracing the footsteps of their ancestors, locals go from the beach, to the stalagmite caves, through the forest, and finally end up hiking to the peak of the mountain, which houses a rock formation that resembles a dev-il's profile, pointy chin and all! It is because of this rock formation that the local villagers nicknamed the mountain Pico Diablo. Children are introduced to their rich history every year. The children chant the community's mantra: *I'm a freedom-seeking warrior. In the face of injustice and greed, I stand tall, like my ancestors.*

As each part of the journey is completed, the elders of the community teach their youngest members how to forage for food in the forest and the medicinal purpose of plants. The children also search for hidden spots where locals can hide food, water, and treats throughout the year. This generosity ensures that tired visitors can always find a treat in unexpected places. What hospitality! What warmth!

CELEBRATING FREEDOM
THE GRAND PALOMA WAY!

- Lobster, bluefin tuna, and caviar entrées pay homage to the naval journeys of the ancestors of this idyllic land.
- With its various spicy rim options, the Diablo rum flight reminds us that even the devil likes to have some fun. Caliente! Sugarcane rum fermented and distilled locally.

We hope you love this history as much as we do!

YOUR TEAM AT
THE GRAND PALOMA RESORT

CHAPTER
14

AMBER AND IDA VARGAS SHOUTED AT LAURA AS SHE ATTEMPTED to make her way past the lobby of the hotel on her way to the beauty parlor without being noticed.

"Where are you rushing to?" the older woman, Amber, said. "Stop rushing everywhere. Look at this glorious sunset."

Laura stilled her breathing, stopped the trembling of her legs. The interaction with the parents of the injured child had gone better than she'd anticipated. Now she needed to take care of her hair immediately. But maybe it was for the best that she take a moment to calm down, slow her racing heart.

Laura stepped up to the table where the sisters were sitting. These two old women were her favorite guests at the hotel. Maybe they were her favorite people in the entire world. They were expats who lived in Cabarete, running a quaint bed-and-breakfast for ten months of the year. In July, the widows headed back to Mallorca, Spain, where they had a small hotel managed by their children and grandchildren, and then came back for the last two weeks of August to enjoy the scorching end of summer at the Grand Paloma. They'd started coming here at the hotel's inauguration, the same summer Laura had begun to work at the resort as a server. They'd had their ten-year anniversary together, the three of them, this summer. She was shocked that after decades of living on the island, the sisters were still moved by the shifting colors in the sky.

She had so much to thank these women for. She felt a rush of affection for them, even as irritation threatened to blind her to it.

Oye, it must be said. Laura had long ago stopped seeing the sky. After all, a sunset's stunning impact stopped being awe-inspiring after the hundredth time. She'd been living on this island, crushed under this sky, for every single day of her twenty-seven years of life. But there was more to it than that. Anytime she took the sky in, it would bring with it such painful memories that she'd be forced to fake a migraine, go into her bedroom, and hide in the shadows for a day or two.

Now, under the duress of her patrons' demand that she be attentive to the transitory beauty of the sunset, Laura attempted to appreciate the view, which was undoubtedly magnificent. There were deep purples on one side of the sky and a vibrant magenta-pink on the other. The center was a throbbing blood red, which dispersed into gradations of burgundies and oranges until it became the sweetest, calmest yellow. Despite her wish to slow down, to be in the moment, her heartbeat raced a bit faster as she glanced at the sky. The colors tugged at something that she didn't want to think about, that she'd rather keep buried.

"I've never seen anything so beautiful," she lied as she pivoted to leave them. "Truly, God, stop being such a show-off"—here, she raised her gaze toward the heavens, which happened to be blocked by the ceiling of the Grand Paloma lobby, and for a moment, it seemed as though she were praying to the building itself—"aren't you tired of such improvisation? The sky more spectacular each day? We're awed, breathless, yeah, impressed, sure. Tone it down a bit."

The women were delighted.

Then Ida, the younger of the two sisters, reached over with a warm, meaty hand. Her gaze overflowed with love. "Sit with us, mi'ja. Have a glass of champagne. You work too hard."

"I wish I could," Laura said.

"I won't take no for an answer, Laura. What's your motto? *A remarkable, elevated guest experience every time?* I need you to sit for this to be remarkable."

Laura shook her head in resignation, feeling again the damp headpiece as Rio, the violinist, came out of nowhere and pulled a chair out so Laura could plump her ample ass on it. It was important she get to the salon fast—soon, the knots would be unsalvageable, and she'd be worse for wear. But there was no way around it—she would have to spend a few minutes with the Vargas sisters.

Her walkie-talkie made a series of annoying, alerting sounds. She lowered the volume of the staticky, popping dings. There was a weather advisory. Tropical Storm Consuelo was set to make landfall on the western coast of Puerto Rico. Although the Grand Paloma wasn't on the trajectory, since they were on the farthest point east on the coast closest to Puerto Rico, they'd get rain and winds. Laura stepped away from the women momentarily. Through the walkie-talkie, she spoke to her head of grounds staff, commanding Gustavo to make sure that all umbrellas, lounge chairs, and pieces of water-sport equipment were moved into storage tonight and that anything that could become airborne was secured. It was better to be overly cautious—just in case the storm took a turn and rough winds headed their way. She prayed for good weather the next day. Nothing more annoying than a hotel full of restless guests.

"Mi'ja," Amber said. "You really are a workaholic. Ven, siéntate!"

Laura nodded obediently, turned off the walkie-talkie.

Off to the side, Rio began to play a repertoire of Juan Luis Guerra's merengues on his violin. The guests around Laura glanced toward him with appreciation, clinking their glasses. The Vargas sisters also clinked their glasses, shouting *bravo, bravo* to Rio. They'd been drinking for a while. Laura thought of her sister again, wondering what Elena was doing at this moment. Wondering if she, or this fucking hair, could ever be forced to straighten out. She felt the damp headpiece and tapped at it with her hand. Her scalp was getting itchy.

Amber noticed. "Were you swimming? I don't think we've ever seen you swimming."

Laura murmured agreement because it was easier than telling the truth. How would she explain that she'd jumped into a lake to save her sister, who she thought had drowned, just like their mother had thirteen years ago?

"Where's Sammy?" Ida said. "We need to get you a glass."

"You know I can't drink while I'm on the clock," Laura said, glancing at the bottles of champagne they had on ice. One was nearly finished. The sisters' daily ritual included holding court by the majestic open-floor-plan gallery that faced the ocean, admiring the beautiful sky, and drinking and reminiscing until they were both tipsy. The two women weren't obsessed with swimming with dolphins or kissing stingrays, and they couldn't care less about zip-lining through the forest or taking selfies with the amazing, world-famous Paloma Falls as their backdrop. They came here to drink, talk shit, and eat until their buttons didn't button. And they were unapologetic about all of it. It made all the workers at the resort adore them.

Laura had a lot to thank the sisters for. They had included her name in every glowing evaluation, often encouraging other guests to do the same. Five years ago, they'd demanded a meeting with the hotel's CEO, using their clout after a racist incident—a moment where the most-senior executives of the hotel had mistaken them for cleaning staff, never mind that they were wearing sparkly gowns and heels to the weekly gala—went viral. They'd leveraged the embarrassing situation to bring about Laura's first significant promotion. It had been the Vargas sisters who had somehow known how to work the system, who had pulled the right lever at the appropriate time to catapult Laura into a part of the organization that no local had ever occupied in DR—not at the Grand Paloma and not at its sister hotel on the other side of the island, the Yellow Paloma.

"Sammy," Amber called out, but the sound of crashing waves, growing louder as evening neared, drowned out her voice.

Sammy, the server, was over at the end of the gallery, exposing her clavicles as she threw her head back in laughter, a hand on the shoulder of a guy who seemed no older than a college freshman. Scanning the space, Laura noticed a number of guests throwing concerned looks in Sammy's direction—guests didn't like it when the staff seemed to be having too good of a time. She caught Patrick, the VP for interiors, with a tight line in the place where his mouth should've been as he observed the guests observing Sammy. Somehow feeling Laura's gaze, Patrick made eye contact with her, his lips turning into a smirk; they'd been having this ongoing fight for several weeks at staff meetings. He kept insisting that they needed to fire Sammy, who was working here just to find herself a gringo and a green card, he always said in his obnoxious gringo accent.

This would give him even more ammunition. Patrick's smugness rested on the soft line of his rounded chin. And to think she'd slept with him, Laura thought, mortified.

She picked up the bell from the middle of the table. Rang it. Following the sound, Sammy found her and immediately straightened up, withdrawing her hand as if it'd suddenly touched a flame. When Sammy reached them, Laura asked for a glass for the champagne. Then, as Sammy began to walk away, she leaned toward her and whispered, "How many times have I told you to settle down? Get your shit together."

Sammy's gaze dripped hatred—after all, she wasn't older than the boy she'd been flirting with, a teenager herself at eighteen—but then she quickly gathered her composure. "I'm sorry, jefa. I'll do better."

Before the Vargas sisters had taken another sip, Sammy was back with the glass. Laura held it to the light, inspecting it. Satisfied with its sparkle, she held the glass out to Sammy to be filled.

"Take it easy," she said to Sammy so all guests nearby would hear. "You're doing such a great job."

The sip of champagne was exactly what she needed. There was too much carbonation in this brand, and the bubbles always made her mouth come alive in a way that was disturbing, yet pleasurable. The effect was almost instantaneous. She felt her shoulders drop away from her ears.

"Aren't you glad we made you sit down?" Ida said.

"I am," Laura said, pushing her worries about her hair aside for the moment.

When the sisters had first taken a liking to Laura, she had welcomed it. The women, Black and Spanish, were a blueprint that she hoped was prophetic of what her future relationship with her own sister could be. They had married young and lived next to each other for most of their lives. Though their husbands hadn't gotten along at first, they'd managed to make them best friends, vacationing together every year. That was how they'd ended up in DR, falling hard for the sunsets, they often said. It only made sense that they'd buy a piece of land in one of the less developed parts of the island. And when their husbands had passed away within months of each other, one in a terrible train derailment and the other from cardiac arrest, the sisters had decided they were ready to call it. Their children would have to figure out babysitting, Sunday dinners, and who to contact when they ended up in a last-minute jam. The guilt had fallen away quickly, the sisters used to say, because they each had been forced to understand that life was fragile, that it could end at any moment. They deserved to spend as much of the time they had left as possible doing what they loved, which included staring at the ocean as it receded and crashed onto the shore.

The sisters said the only reason they were still alive was because they had been born with two soulmates—one a lover, the other a sister.

The widows were closer in age than she and Elena were, and she wondered sometimes if it was the fact that she'd inherited her sister's caretaking when their mother died that had soured their relationship. It had been terrifying that at fourteen years old, when her sister was only four, she'd had to scramble to figure out how to help her father take care of herself and her younger sister. A father who was more interested in drinking and gambling than child-rearing.

Sometimes, she thought about how different her life would be if their mother hadn't drowned, if they'd had a different kind of father— one who hadn't been crushed by his shortcomings and failures, who'd had good fortune—and if she hadn't had to grow up so fast. Other times, she blamed this place. Had she been born in a country where her skin color wasn't seen as a liability, she wouldn't have spent most of her life in survival mode. She might have thrived if she'd been part of a community that didn't neglect its most vulnerable members, where Black pride meant holding on to a myth of the past and not arming each other with what the present moment required. One thing she knew for sure was that she wouldn't be working this miserable job and she wouldn't be living on this miserable island. She would find a way to leave this place, to have a shot at making a new life with her sister.

"Here it comes," Amber said, her voice hardly above a whisper.

Laura clicked her tongue with practiced gratitude, expecting to turn and find the sky the same as it had been moments earlier. But today, she couldn't deny what was in front of her. The sky had become even more intense. It was the most striking expression of itself she had ever seen. She closed her eyes for a moment, knowing that what the blood-red sky concocted for her were the myriad injuries on her mother's face—blooming burgundies bordered by the most delicate plums, the unfathomable swelling after a kick, a slap, a closed-fist punch, each making of her mother's skin a debilitating canvas.

Que linda mi mami como una pintura, she used to say, touching her mother's tender skin. Back then, she had been too young to understand that there was a connection between her parents' fights and the bruising that appeared the next day and, if a limb had been broken, could last many weeks. Too young to understand that her father's swollen hands had anything to do with it. Laura had instead seen the connection between her mother's skin and the sky, awed that the colors that bloomed and changed on her mother's body were a gift from God.

Next to her, the sisters *ooh*'ed and *aah*'ed in the universal language of tourists.

When Laura raised her eyelids, the sun had dropped into the horizon. What had been vibrant a moment ago had now vanished.

She kissed the sisters on each cheek and hurried away before they could protest.

Looking at the clock, she knew that Carmen was likely sweeping up, ready to call it a night.

CARMEN'S LIMP WAS PAINFUL to watch. As she swept the salon, she stopped every few steps, a finger digging into the hip socket of her slightly shorter leg. Laura observed her through the clear glass of the hotel's salon. She felt dread weigh her down as she considered leaving things be—letting Carmen finish her day and head home. She undid the headscarf and touched the hair, trying to assess whether she'd be able to handle it on her own. There was a knot at the crown of her head, and she knew, instinctively, that it would be impossible to do it by herself. She took a deep breath, pushed open the swinging door.

Carmen looked up, startled.

"What in the world," she said, meeting her halfway and reaching immediately for the hair. "Sit down."

Laura sat in the swivel chair. She took in the fragrances of hairspray, finishing cream, eucalyptus-scented shampoo.

"Why? How?"

Laura didn't respond. She reached in her pocket for her phone. Found its screen dark. The water damage had caught up to it. She used her walkie-talkie to ask one of her kitchen people to bring her a bowl full of rice. She'd have to let her phone sit in it. She hoped it would be sufficient to get the phone to turn back on.

Carmen sighed. "This is going to take hours," she said.

Laura felt a rising heat on her neck. But it would do her no good to show remorse, or mortification. The times when she'd tried to do that, to be a decent and thoughtful boss, had all blown up in her face. She set her jaw, hard.

"It's a good thing you don't get paid by the hour," she said.

Carmen was overcome with a sense of helplessness and frustration. She had young children she needed to get home to. A hot husband who worked on the farmland owned by the Grand Paloma, who would come home expecting dinner. Carmen carefully and very slowly applied deep conditioner, using a wet brush to untangle the hair. Sometimes, she was overcome with pity for Laura. She understood that this woman was terribly lonely, that most people didn't trust her and were forced to tolerate her because of the power she had. At some level, Carmen imagined Laura knew that. After the tragic loss of her mother and the disappearance of her father, everyone admired how much she loved and cared for her sister. Still, she was a bully.

Carmen slowly worked the front and back of the hair, making her way in a roundabout tornado shape until she came to the crown of Laura's head. That knot was still impenetrable by comb or finger, no matter how much conditioner and detangler she used. A worker delivered the bowl full of white rice. Laura stood and stretched her neck, dropped the phone into the bowl. Then she sat back down and crossed one leg over the other, waiting for Carmen to get back to work.

AFTER AN HOUR, CARMEN had made very little progress. She picked up the fabric that had fallen on the ground.

"It's a pretty print," she said.

Laura didn't respond.

"Miosotis lent it to you?" Carmen asked.

Laura nodded.

"She's always been so sweet," Carmen said.

"What is it you want to say?" Laura asked, exasperated.

"Can I cut some of it?" Carmen asked.

Laura stared at her own profile in the mirror. Her round face wouldn't look good with a bob or a pixie cut. Her own hair, corn-rolled in a swirl around her head, was nappy and sparse—wearing it natural was out of the question. Because she was a bigger woman, she could never get away with a bald head like Elena. Maybe she could put both herself and Carmen out of their misery, take the weave off. There must be someone in the staff who'd let her borrow a wig. But she thought of all the money she'd spent—thousands of dollars, the majority of both her and her sister's secret stash. All because Rihanna's hairstylist had leaked where the Caribbean superstar got her hairweave from, had said that if looked after carefully, this hair could last a person an entire lifetime. Was it okay to give it up as a loss, to accept the deficit and move on? If it'd been a personal loss, she would have taken it. But there was so much at stake. There was always too much at stake: She was responsible for hundreds of people's livelihoods. Very few of them understood the kind of pressure she was constantly under, including Carmen, who just then tugged at her hair with force.

"Ouch," Laura said.

Carmen let go of her hair, took a step back from the styling chair. Her face was tight.

Laura bit the inside of her cheek. She knew that big decisions had to be made every day, and whether she liked to admit it or not, her ability to get support, influence her peers, and maintain the air of authority that had been so hard to come by often hinged on what she looked like just as much as it did on what she said. Sometimes it felt like her appearance was the single most critical element of who she was. Competence went only so far in a place like the Grand Paloma Resort. She thought about Astrid, the VP of Guest Services and Media Relations, a Colombiana raised in New York City who had a curly, gorgeous mane of hair. At the beginning of the peak season, she'd bleached her hair to disastrous effect and had spent a week wearing a turban. Maybe Laura could borrow that headpiece. She didn't remember anyone making mention of it—religious exceptions were the only reason anyone could get away with headwear. Astrid wasn't someone she trusted, someone she felt she could go to for help in a difficult moment. The early attempts she'd made to befriend the only other Latina on the senior team had been met with polite indifference, and Laura just couldn't get over how much of a man's woman Astrid was. She hadn't even bothered to text or call her, as Laura had requested on that sticky note hours ago. Laura wouldn't be surprised if it'd been Astrid's idea to go golfing today when she and the other VPs had learned that they weren't required to attend the staff meeting.

Looking intently at her reflection, she noticed a pale little clump stuck by her mouth. She wasn't surprised that Vida had missed it. She'd been totally out of it. The Vargas sisters hadn't noticed, either but the older women's eyesight was suspect. But she'd spoken to and walked past dozens of workers, and not one of them had told her she had something on her face—a simple hand gesturing where to wipe. Even Carmen, who'd been working on her hair for over an hour, hadn't bothered to alert her that she had what looked like a quarter-sized booger on her face, that she resembled a disgusting clown.

She licked her thumb, wiped the stupid white mark off her face.

"Don't cut one single fucking hair," Laura said. "Just do your work."

Carmen stopped. Slowly, she extended a calloused hand toward the phone that had been vibrating on the counter. Fastidiously, she wrote, erased, and then finally settled on the right words to explain why she wouldn't be home on time. When she turned back to Laura, her hands itched to wrap themselves around her boss's neck, to strangle her until her face turned the same dull plum as the sky outside.

Knowing she couldn't afford to get fired, Carmen turned away from Laura. But in the salon's multifaceted mirrors, Laura could clearly see Carmen's face. Carmen caught Laura's intense stare. The women looked at each other through the duplicative reflections. Carmen was thinking, *Laura doesn't care what anyone thinks about her. She doesn't care about anyone but herself.* Laura was thinking, *Carmen despises me.*

With practiced gentleness, Carmen untangled the hair, one strand at a time. The painstaking work allowed for the fire in her stomach to spread upward into her chest, settling in her heart. Carmen had never hated another human being so much.

Carmen's expression was familiar. The curl of the lip, the narrowed gaze, the shallow breaths. Laura was used to the way her presence affected those around her. It didn't bother her as much anymore. Not really. The quiver of the eyelid that moved downward and rested on her cheek was just a sign of exhaustion. Laura couldn't care less that everyone hated her guts.

Years ago, she'd cared. The isolation had felt crushing. She'd never bothered her sister with any real problems of the job, first because Elena's success at the global academy was too important and distractions wouldn't be of any use, but also because she feared that her sister would connect Laura's struggles to the workplace dynamics that capitalism thrived on. Elena had said time and time again that the workers needed to unionize, that unfair wages and unjust conditions didn't just affect the construction laborers who were getting deported and abused on a weekly basis. Her sister insisted that individual suffering always translated into collective suffering.

In moments when she hit a dead end and hopelessness at her situation seemed nearer than ever, Laura liked to daydream. She wondered what it would be like to live abroad—not to go to Portugal for work, but to go to Spain on vacation with the Vargas sisters. The first summer they'd spent here, they'd invited Laura to see their suite and snapped open an old-school laptop. The glare from the sunlight had made the screen pitch-black, impossible to see into. Las viejitas had asked her to lift it, to carry it around to the shaded side of the suite.

It had been so heavy that Laura almost dropped it.

Feels like a dead body inside, she'd said.

It has many dead bodies inside, one of the sisters said. The two women had laughed. Laura hadn't understood what was so funny.

The sisters began with pictures of their children and grandchildren, all of them beautiful Black people who seemed so genuinely happy that it took Laura's breath away. Had she ever been that happy? No, never. Then the women started showing off pictures of what they called their *pequeño hotel*—which turned out to not be quite so small. The pictures of Mallorca were gorgeous. There was the ocean off in the distance, crystalline water so blue-green and clean that it was as if no one had set a foot in it. There was even a garden where the sisters grew beautiful olive trees.

Maybe one day you'll join us there, Amber said. *Spain has its pockets of racism, don't get me wrong. You can't escape certain things no matter where you go. But once you have your own piece of land and you make a home somewhere, it's easier to live in peace. You make your own peace.*

They held fast to the belief that no matter how horrible the world they inhabited was, they still had the ability to create bubbles—to only allow in whom they wanted. *You can be* in *a place and not of it,* they insisted. It was a sentiment that Laura's old teacher, Doña Fella, had shared from time to time back in Pico Diablo.

Part of her job was to agree with whatever the guests said. To nod along with their worldviews, even when they were obviously flawed. In that way, every guest at the hotel was her boss. But she wasn't dumb. She knew that no local was meant to truly access class mobility through work. It was merely an exercise in treading water for survival. Most employees barely did that. It felt at times like working at the resort was actually an exercise in frantically thrashing around until finally, exhausted, they gave up, allowing themselves to figuratively plummet into the depths of a crystalline ocean, with swaying palm trees bearing witness.

Except for Laura. She and her sister would climb up, out. With that global academy education, her sister would be able to attend an elite college, and that would be Elena's way out. Laura's ticket to real freedom was trickier. It hinged on her relationship to Paloma Enterprises, to the mentorship of someone like Miranda. With the success of her new Platinum Member Companion Program, she'd write her ticket and do what had ultimately doomed her father—leave this place for good.

Carmen's expression hadn't changed. Her lips were pursed, her forehead scrunched. But her hands were gentle, her touch the softest. Laura forced herself to remember the blue-green water of Mallorca. It would be nice to go away with the Vargas sisters. How good would it feel to live inside their bubble, where she didn't have to worry about her sister or this hotel or the history of the town she'd grown up in? To be able to part with all the pain of her childhood and each loss inflicted after that?

WHEN CARMEN TAPPED HER on the shoulder, Laura startled awake to find a miracle. The hair cascaded down her shoulders, knotless and luminous, reflecting the fluorescent lights above them. She touched her scalp. The familiar tightness of the thread Carmen had used pulled at her temples, giving her usually round eyes an almond shape. She let her gaze fall, not sure what to say.

"You can take tomorrow off," she said in a small voice, flushing with shame when she realized night had fallen.

Carmen's eyes were bloodshot, but she managed to mumble a thank you as she stood back, favoring her shorter leg. Laura lingered in front of the mirror and turned from side to side, admiring her hair, until she caught a glimpse of Carmen, who was waiting with arms crossed for her to get the hell out.

Laura grabbed her phone from the bowl of rice and slipped it into a pocket to turn on in a few moments, once she'd made her way out of the glass doors. Carmen called her name. The hairstylist handed her the pretty, African-inspired headscarf that Laura had been wearing earlier. As Laura held it in her hands, she saw how damaged the fabric was. She decided she'd go into town the next day, find a finer piece of material to replace it. Maybe she'd get enough that Miosotis could make herself a matching shift dress. She crumpled the ruined fabric and threw it in the garbage.

Carmen gasped. She inhaled what she hoped was a steadying, calming breath but found herself unable to hold it in. "The way you treat people," she said. "Your parents would be ashamed."

Laura stared at her reflection. She flipped her hair over one of her shoulders and stood taller.

"No," she said. "My parents wouldn't be ashamed, Carmen. The dead feel no shame."

She turned away. Her heartbeat galloped as she realized that she shouldn't have been so careless. She hoped Carmen hadn't caught that she'd referred to both of her parents as dead. Everyone was under the impression that her father was missing, not dead.

As she moved past the lobby, several guests waited in line to check in. A few asked if they could take a picture with her. She smiled, a smile that was wooden, but good enough for the guests.

"Is it okay to post?" they asked.

She nodded enthusiastically, even as she wished that the earth would open and swallow them all.

"Please don't forget to tag the resort," she said brightly.

Back at the staff bathroom and lockers, she pressed the power button on her phone and waited a few moments, so happy when the screen came alive. She opened the texting app and found several messages from Dulce, each one shorter than the last, more frenzied. The first was an invitation to come over later—it had been ages since she'd last taken part in Locals' Night. They could enjoy some grilled fish on the beach. Elena was watching her daughters. A few hours later, a series of questions. Have you heard from Elena? Where has she gone with the girls? PLEASE call me back. CALL ME BACK NOW!!!

Laura lifted the phone to her ear, called Elena. Her voicemail hadn't been set up. She texted Elena. Where are you? What's going on? Her texts weren't marked as delivered. Was Elena's phone turned off?

She called Dulce, who picked up immediately.

"Do you know where Elena is? Where my daughters are?" Dulce's voice was strained, as if she was trying hard not to seem worried.

"No," Laura said. "I've been at the salon. But I'll make sure we check everywhere here. Let me get back to you."

With her walkie-talkie, she mobilized her entire grounds staff. If Elena was anywhere on the 2,500 acres of resort land, they'd find her. She made her way to their casita, thinking it'd be just like Elena to be there, dique hiding. But when she walked in, she found that the bed remained unmade, no sign of Elena anywhere. She removed her high-heeled shoes but kept her uniform on. She decided to check the beach barefoot. She'd be able to move faster. Elena loved to swim—maybe she'd brought the girls there and had foolishly lost track of time. But Elena wasn't at the beach. And after what had happened with the tourist girl, Laura doubted she would come back to the resort.

Her walkie-talkie began to go off, the voices of men and women tallying where they'd looked: No Elena at the gym. No Elena at the tennis courts. No Elena at the spa or the Taíno Wellness Center. No Elena at the greenhouse, where they were currently growing peonies for a special corporate event that would take place at the end of October. No Elena in the Olympic-sized pool. No Elena in the business center. No Elena in any of their dozens of kitchens, or the few unoccupied guest rooms. No Elena wandering the two-mile path to Paloma Falls. No Elena in Ciudad Paloma Falls.

Then from the shore there emerged a dark-skinned figure, and Laura's heart jumped until she noticed the long braids. A guest of the resort, adjusting her swimsuit. She winked at Laura as she walked past her. Laura offered her a warm greeting. Moments later, another guest of the resort, a tall white man, moved past her, bumping into her, oblivious.

Her walkie-talkie made its usual noisy popping sounds.

"Dimelo?" she asked into the tiny holes of the speaker, a burst of optimism breaking through. Maybe they'd found her?

"Sorry to bother, boss. There's been a small fire in the Mondongo kitchen. No damage, but Fernando burned his arm and had to go to the infirmary. No one else working tonight knows how to make the shrimp risotto."

"I do. I'll come over. Go check on Fernando and let me know how he's doing."

She'd have to take over the dinner service. She'd be stuck in the kitchen for several hours. She wouldn't be able to go meet Dulce and find out what happened as she'd hoped.

Laura dug her toes into the fresh, spiky seaweed, wished for a clear sky that might turn the moon into a spotlight that would illuminate her way. Somewhere deep down she felt a terror spreading, the kind she'd felt the last time her father had left to attempt to enter the United States. Back then, just like now, Laura had felt the wind from the cold sea fastening around her, like the fabric of a straitjacket before it's pulled shut. As Laura stared into the absolute darkness, she imagined an enormous whale swimming close to the surface of the sea, furiously distancing itself from the shore. She imagined all the other sea creatures swimming beside and below that whale, keeping pace. The thought chilled her. Somewhere deep inside, she knew it was true: There was something ominous in the air.

CHAPTER
15

GUESTS RETURNING FROM THE FREEDOM SUNSET CRUISE teetered across the beach toward the resort on the hill. Pablo knew most of them by the drinks he'd served them during his second shift— spicy diablo flights, rum punch, margaritas-no-salt, and bourbon, neat. Now, long after the sun had set, he still wasn't done. Management required that he wait on the beach until the last guest exited the boat.

His eyes rested on the ocean's inky blackness as it retreated, then pushed hard against the shore. There were sharp pebbles where there had been only sand and seaweed that morning, though the seaweed would come relentlessly back. If they'd been consulted, the locals could have given advice about how to deter the aggressive seaweed. Pablo's father, a lifelong fisherman before he died, would have known the answer. His grandfather, who'd also worked the sea, would have known, and Pablo thought that, if asked, he himself would remember what he'd been taught as a child.

In his back pocket, his cellphone vibrated, and he heard several pings that signaled text messages. None of them were from his exgirlfriend, Vida. The Wi-Fi had gone down on the boat, and the guests had been annoyed. The main reason to do the damn cruise was to post it, several of them had said. Pablo knew that anytime the guests began to act annoyed, it was time to double-shot the drinks, turn up the charm, and gently guide their attention to their surroundings. This place was paradise. But most of them acted as if the surroundings were insignificant unless they were able to take a pic to show off immediately. It had been an exhausting afternoon.

Elena had left him an odd message. She'd asked him to come to their friend Dulce's beachside bar around 3 P.M. Porfa, come to Dulce's FAST! she'd written. It's an emergency. That had been over five hours ago.

But El had known that he was on the Freedom Sunset Cruise. He'd invited her to come along when she'd dropped by to get more pills. There were no follow-up messages, no *never mind got it*, none of the things she often added moments after she'd texted him looking for pills. Surely she would have reached out to someone else if it was truly an emergency. He had just begun to text her, to ask what was up, when one of the last two tourists leaving the boat interrupted.

"Bartender," the woman slurred. "Are you free tonight? Want to meet us at the disco?"

When she stumbled, the brightly colored beads at the ends of her cornrows made the sound of young children playing. Pablo caught her before she could fall and carried her to safety, beyond the sharp stones. It was ridiculous that she'd gotten this hairstyle when only little girls wore their hair in such a way. Her clothes and makeup and hair had none of the elegant effortlessness of the wealthier guests'; maybe she'd won the trip. Still, he was just two starred reviews away from becoming a Platinum Member Companion, and even if this woman couldn't afford an en suite massage (with or without fucking), her reviews were as valuable as those of the rich guests who frequented the resort.

He figured it would only take a few moments to show this woman kindness, and in return, who knew? If she completed a review, he would be one review away from gaining a new world. He'd no longer have to slip his fingers into the waiting mouths of women who'd been drinking since breakfast, whose tongues were slimy as they squirmed. He expected that being a Platinum Member Companion would change all of that. He wouldn't be at a bar where the guests (no matter how rich or refined they started out as) got sloppy and horny within a few hours. Instead, he'd live in the main hotel, with his own room and his own magnetic key. He'd get to entertain guests during meals with his light banter and extensive knowledge of Dominican history, make light conversation as he offered to fetch drinks for and was declined by guests who were truly there to enjoy orchestra seats in the hotel audi-

torium. He'd have the kind of stability that might win Vida back, and
if that happened, when they had children, they'd get to go to the global
academy that Elena had graduated from, where the hotel's most senior
staff had their children educated. Their kids, like the children of the
most privileged, would never know scarcity or loss.

A few steps behind them, another woman snorted, then hacked a
smoker's dry cough.

"Don't hurt yourself," she said to Pablo. "That's a heavy load."

Her voice was thick, deep; there was something sexy in it.

The woman in his arms leaned her head against his shoulder and
sighed. The breeze carried the reek of her recent vomit elsewhere. They
reached the wooden pathway, lit by in-ground lights that made it easier to see their way to the resort. He set her on her feet.

"God, Christine," her sexy-voiced friend said, catching up to them,
"why are you so embarrassing? It's our last night. Sober up."

"Why are you such a sourpuss?" Christine's braids swung from side
to side as she bent down to slip on plastic flip-flops. "It's so beautiful
here. Why can't you just be happy?"

At the top of the hill, the resort was majestic. At night, the all-glass
structure was a slick black. It was built like a crown up top, and each
peak was spectacular with dazzling lights. The three of them continued
to walk quietly, and in their silence, the nature around them came to
life. There were cicadas, night frogs, the strange fluttering of a small
animal among some bushes ahead.

Sexy-voiced Sourpuss took a cigarette out of her bag and lit it. He
could see in the low light that her eyes were set too close together.
Nose too big, forehead too small, a sneer set in her mouth. She met
Pablo's eyes as she inhaled from her cigarette, leaving the lighter on
even when she no longer needed it. *Have a good look,* she seemed to say.

Christine tugged at Pablo's sleeve and left her hand on his arm.

"So, will you?" she asked when she had caught her breath. "Will you
come to the disco later? Maybe teach me the merenga?"

"Sounds fun," Pablo said, still thinking of Vida.

During Pablo's father's last living days, Vida had spent nearly all
her time in their small shack, from time to time encouraging his father

to stand, to dance merengue with her—to keep his strength up, she'd said. By that point, there had been no need for her to prepare and apply the healing ointments she was known for. It'd been clear to all three of them that his father wouldn't last very long, that he was by then beyond the healing powers of a curandera. But when his father had asked Vida if she wanted to learn to fish, she'd eagerly consented. That day, his father's last on the ocean, they'd hooked a mahi-mahi, his father's favorite. Vida, delighted to have caught it, had asked him to throw the fish back. His father had laughed, and, to Pablo's surprise, he'd agreed.

Christine's attention turned to the weekly fireworks display that had begun. The booming explosions cracked the dark sky into wild, bright veins. She moved her hand down to meet his.

Pablo's phone vibrated. He reached for it with his free hand. Pasofino, his best friend, had sent a text: Come to Dulce's STAT. We need you here pronto, Loco. What the hell was going on at the bar? First Elena, now Pasofino.

Back before he'd met Vida, he, Elena, and Pasofino would sneak out of the resort and hang out at the Gringo Trap, shit-talking the job until Dulce kicked them out. After things had gotten more serious with Vida, he would still go, sometimes with her, but less frequently. These days, he preferred staying at the resort, putting all his effort into his goal. But something was up, and who knew? Maybe Vida would be there. On my way, he texted back.

Christine squeezed his hand and smiled widely at him. "We're home! What do you say? Disco date?"

"Sure, sure," he said, hoping she'd stop asking. It worked. Christine finally let go of his hand and began to make her way into the lobby.

Pablo remained outside and stared up at the face of the building's twelve stories. Small shadows moved on every floor. Some leaned lazily on balconies, sipping from wineglasses, smoking cigarettes, their gazes falling into the darkness. Others, uniformed, hurried from room to room as they shoved carts topped with room-service trays, cleaning supplies, towels, sheets. On the outdoor patio of the lobby floor, white fabric swayed in the breeze while patrons in tuxedos and sparkly gowns stood around Rio, the violinist, who played a lovely melody, soft and romantic. Underneath that music, reggaeton vibrated, coming from the sunset pool party that always carried on far past sunset, and Christine and her friend stopped to do a little dance.

"I'll be waiting for you," Christine yelled at him, upsetting the other patrons, whose shoulders stiffened. The two friends high-fived and stumbled on toward the entrance.

Pablo shook his head and turned to go—the last thing he needed was to be associated with those women. He focused on the music coming from the pool. It was a song he and Vida had danced to often. *La mano arriba, cintura sola, da media vuelta . . .*

He went in his pocket, pulled out his phone, swiped through old photos of Vida. There, the image he was looking for. The last time they'd been at the Beyond Proof Bar. Pasofino had taken the picture— Vida's ass ground against Pablo, and his eyes were fixed on her neck. He'd been shocked when Pasofino had sent him the image because the lust was so clear. But clearer still was what hadn't been captured in the photo—how much he adored her. They'd been dating for a few months short of a year. Had spent all their free time together once his father died. He'd often thought that it was the gift his father had left him, that invitation to take her out to sea—a way to ensure that he wouldn't be alone. La curandera who'd tried but failed to save his father could maybe rescue him from all his despair. He'd felt they'd met at the exact right moment—Vida, in her early thirties, preferred a quiet life spent mostly outdoors. When he reached thirty, they were a couple, and he'd known he wanted the stability of his own family.

The last time Vida had slept over, he'd been working the pool party. She'd sat at the bar, amused at the crude music, at all the Dominican workers making sure the tourists had a good time. *This is work?* she'd asked him as she made complicated hair ribbons. The scrunchy she'd created was flexible, and he saw how some of the fabric hanging off it was silky and straight, while other sections were braided and so bright. Resort work seemed easy in her eyes because her own work was so physical. As a curandera, she used her hands, her entire body to cure people of ailments big and small. A few weeks after their fishing trip, when Pablo's father had died, Vida had decided abruptly to stop the healing work. She'd refused to drink, saying she must have a weird stomach bug because she'd also been feeling nauseous.

He'd had a strange feeling that she was keeping something important from him. When he'd asked her if she was pregnant, she'd immediately said no. He'd wanted to show her that he was ready for it, if not now, then soon. Because she was two years older than he was, he'd worried that she saw him as immature. It had seemed to him like it was as good a time as any to start a family. Had she been ready to give up the work that was so tough on her body because she wanted their relationship to be the center of her life? He hadn't known how to ask that question, so instead, he'd asked, in the dirt-floored staff room, why she had decided to stop working. But she'd avoided the question, focusing instead on his ambition to be a Platinum Member Companion. What could possibly be appealing about being tethered to another human being, a stranger, for days at a time? Following their every whim like the lapdogs those women loved to travel with? He'd explained the perks: It would be as close to a guarantee of lifetime employment at the resort as he could get as long as the survey scores showed high satisfaction. He'd told her how he'd be able to work a quarter of his current hours and have his own room in the same building where paying guests stayed.

"Eventually, maybe, I'll be able to stop with these women," he'd blurted out.

"Stop what with them?" she'd asked carefully.

His silence had brought everything between them into stillness. She'd gotten up very slowly and left.

Pablo had beaten himself up for his carelessness. How had he allowed himself to say such a thing to Vida, who he knew valued loyalty above all else? Sometimes, he feared he was lying to himself by pretending it had been a mistake. There was a part of him that had hoped to never have to keep anything from Vida. He'd wanted Vida to accept his behavior as an unpleasant, but bearable part of his obligations. Days later, when he'd mustered the courage to show up at her house on the cliff at the edge of the Pico Diablo Mountain, she'd asked him straight up: *Are you ready to give them up?* But could he? There were so many people waiting for a job like his, who'd be willing to do anything. Didn't she understand that focusing on the only useful skill he had, fishing, was impossible to do now that the resort had its own fishing boats? That it didn't matter whether he loved the sea when it provided no lifeline? She'd pushed him hard out the front door, yelled that it wasn't true, that there were plenty of ways to make a living. She'd called his goal *porquerías,* told him it was clear that what he desired was the life afforded only to those who lived at the resort. Startled, he'd left without saying what he'd gone there to tell her—about the schools, about their future children. He'd been shocked that she didn't seem to want the same.

Ahead of him, Rio's violin conquered all other sound. The music was no longer soothing, no longer romantic. He played masterfully, with an intensity that captured what most of the workers must've been feeling at that moment. Pablo wondered if Rio and Pasofino were in a fight. For a while, it had seemed as though their romance would be the stuff of legend, but now, the song Rio played dripped with loneliness and sadness. Or was it just Pablo? Sometimes, this entire place was exhaustingly difficult to understand.

CHAPTER
16

U P ON THE PICO DIABLO MOUNTAIN, VIDA ROSE FROM HER BED for the umpteenth time. She made it to the bathroom, where she had been throwing up since she'd made it home. As soon as she was finished, she would call Dulce, ask her to come get her. She should not spend the night alone. She had never been this sick after healing someone. She might need to go to the hospital. She placed her hand on her belly.

"Hold on," she whispered. "Be strong."

But this time, as soon as she made it to the bathroom, she collapsed. She tried to rise off the floor but found she had no strength. The last conscious thought she had before she passed out was to ask her dead mother for help.

CHAPTER 17

THE HAND-PAINTED SIGN SAID THURSDAY NIGHTS LOCALS ONLY in English, to make it plain for those who were unwelcome. At Dulce's Beyond Proof, the live music was in full swing and every staff member from the resort who had a night off was there, letting go. There were drums, a güira, a bass guitar, and a singer who gave his heart a jolt—in profile, she had Vida's pointy, dimpled chin. Pasofino sat at the bar, nursing a bottle of Presidente. They'd known each other since they were as small as Dulce's girls.

Pablo glanced around, searching for Elena, but she was nowhere to be found.

Behind the bar, Dulce's brow furrowed as she stared at her phone.

"I know," Pasofino was saying in a low tone, "but if they're with Elena, they're fine. She probably just lost track of time. Bet you they're at the waterfall, her phone battery dead."

Pablo took the empty stool next to Pasofino, who gave him a loud smack on the back in greeting.

"What's going on?" Pablo asked.

"I left the girls with Elena this afternoon," Dulce said. "But when I got here they were all gone. She's not picking up her phone. Hasn't responded to texts. Anything happens to my girls . . ."

"Why don't I try her?" Pablo said and dialed. He wasn't sure why he hesitated to tell Dulce and Pasofino that Elena had texted him earlier that day, and that even earlier than that, she'd found him and asked him for more pills with an urgency bordering on dependency. Dulce stared at him expectantly. In his ear, Elena's phone rang. She hadn't even set up her voicemail.

"Fuck this," Dulce said, and asked Pasofino to take over the bar. She'd go to her house a short distance away, where she could hear herself think, and call the police.

"Is that why you texted?" Pablo asked as they watched her weave through the bodies around them. Pasofino nodded.

"Are you worried?"

Pasofino nodded again.

Pablo wasn't terribly close to Dulce. She was in her early forties, and the decade between them meant they flowed in different circles. But she and Vida were very close, so he had naturally grown closer to her during the time he'd been with Vida. Plus, they were all from Pico Diablo. They were a community. Dulce's two girls, Niña and Perfecta, were ten and nine years old, and were often out of sight from the goings-on in the bar. He tried to remember the last time he'd seen them and could not.

Down the bar, the women who worked for Dulce huddled together, and he assumed one must be telling a joke or sharing the latest outrageous story of a client's kinky desires. Young or old, soft or hard, everyone had a story to share. Often, there was something in their eyes—a vacancy, a toughness that set them apart. Sometimes, he wished he could ask them what it was like for them to sleep with strangers. He wanted to ask the older ones if it ever got easier. He'd often thought it was the fact that he was fucking these women for free that made it worse. Would reaping the benefits of the labor make it less of an infraction?

"You all right?" Pasofino asked him.

"Hell yeah," he said, "just hungry."

Off to the side, someone was roasting sweet plantains on sticks in an open fire. There was a lot of smoke, but underneath it was sweetness. He stood and went over to the food. He grabbed what was ready and ate, searching among the newcomers that arrived every few minutes. There were so many employees here from the resort, dozens who were part of the temporary staff only hired during the summer peak season. Some were freshly showered, dressed up. He became aware of how bad he smelled—fish guts and spilled alcohol, a lethal combination. Why hadn't he gone to his room to change? Surely Vida would arrive any moment now.

He took his phone out and called Vida first, then, after that failed, tried Elena again.

The phone rang, rang.

"A round of shots on me," Pasofino said, calling him over. "Twenty American dollars says Elena arrives in the next hour with the girls."

Pasofino reached into the cooler beneath the bar and handed Pablo a beer. Then, grabbing a container filled with a bright-yellow liquid, he served shots to everyone at the bar. Inside the cooler, several blocks of ice cracked loudly, a sound exaggerated by the lull in the live music. Passion fruit seeds floated in the glass Pasofino handed Pablo. Pablo felt them slide down his throat when he took the shot. Instantly, he felt better, that warmth spreading.

"You and Rio had a fight?" Pablo asked.

Pasofino knit his brows. "No, not a fight. It's the same conversation. He wants to head back to New York and I don't. I don't believe we'll be better off there."

Their small community in Pico Diablo was supportive of gay couples, despite the conservative nature of most Dominicans. Many people had lived there as same-sex couples openly, without harassment or chisme. At the Grand Paloma Resort, though, gay couples weren't as common as cis-straight ones, and there was a general indifference among the guests that Pablo took to be cultivated open-mindedness. But it was dangerous to be openly gay men beyond these parts—there was always some unspeakable violence that happened every few months elsewhere. Pablo had heard Rio speak of New York, where you could live your whole life openly without fear of violence. Pablo supposed it had more to do with a certain lifestyle, too—Rio had come to DR to reconnect with the land of his parents' birth after he lost his mother to cancer. He had a successful life as a Juilliard-trained musician that he wanted to get back to.

Pablo was glad that his friend was standing his ground. He liked having Pasofino around. Even though they didn't spend as much time together as they used to, he was still Pablo's best friend.

Pablo swiveled around. His eyes searched the crowd.

Soon Dulce returned. "The police said the girls aren't missing unless they've been gone for twenty-four hours," she said as she took the stool next to Pablo. She cradled her face in both hands, laid her forehead against the bar. "Twenty-four hours."

"What do you want to do?" Pasofino asked.

The moon emerged from behind the clouds, casting a brilliant white light over the blackness of the ocean. The light rippled, then ridged. It extended over the bodies of those on the beach. Most were in their late teens, early twenties. All those bodies moved as one, arms and legs bare. Pablo felt like an asshole. He knew Dulce was terribly worried. But he enjoyed the motion, so easy, as if he'd wandered into a shaded area in the middle of a bright day, and the drums and the güira made him want to dance.

"I'm going to lose my mind if I have to wait an entire day," Dulce said.

"How long has it been?" Pablo asked.

"I left them a bit before three o'clock."

"It's just after nine. That doesn't seem long enough to be worried."

"It's past their bedtime," Dulce said.

"It isn't long enough to be worried," Pablo insisted.

Dulce gave him a hard stare. "You know what these fucking tourists can get away with, Pablo."

The huddled group of women parted and turned at Dulce's tone. Several murmured agreements. Out on the sand, the group quieted as Dulce's tone rose. Soon, she was shouting.

"Toqui didn't get back on time . . . If I hadn't caught the bastard and gotten her to the hospital, she would be dead. He shot her full of so many drugs that it's a miracle she's still breathing. Ask me if the police went to pick him up?"

Pablo didn't know what to say. He'd been wrapped up in Vida's absence, but now he realized that among the women, there was an empty space that belonged to Toqui. Dulce, visibly annoyed by his silence, went down the length of the bar, and after a brief exchange, many of the women left, murmuring where they would be heading to look for Elena and the girls.

"Do you want to go look for them?" Pasofino asked Dulce.

Pablo decided to try Vida one last time. If she didn't pick up, he'd call it a night. Go back to his dirt-floored room in the staff quarters of the resort. The phone rang and rang. When her voicemail picked up, he listened to it, savoring her voice. He hung up before it ended.

"What if Elena turns up?"

"We can go," Pasofino said, motioning to Pablo.

"Yes," she said. "You can get a head start. Then we'll all go. Laura should get here soon."

Pablo sent Elena a text alerting her that Dulce was freaking out and asked where she was. Then he turned his attention back to his carousel of Vida pictures. The ones he'd taken of her at the beach, her mouth full of spaghetti and white rice. Then one of her running off into the crashing waves, wearing nothing but a bikini bottom. The words she'd said over her shoulder came to him softly, forcing him to put the phone away. *You gonna keep taking pictures, Pablo, or do something worth filming?*

"Wait," he said, turning to Dulce and Pasofino. "What about the cameras? Aren't there cameras here that should be filming what's going on? Just look at the tape and we should see if there's anything to worry about."

Dulce shook her head. "We had a tech issue months ago. I never got it fixed."

Pablo nodded in understanding and turned his attention back to the pictures, remembering what was missing from this carousel. Vida's mouth against his, the salty taste of the ocean as her legs circled his hips. The feeling of her, a warmth and wetness so different from that of the sea. It was as if she was within touching distance right now, the surge of arousal was so potent.

"Look at this one," Pasofino said, slapping the bar near Pablo's arm. "Still heartbroken that Vida won't take you back? Listening to her voicemail again?"

Dulce extended a hand over Pablo's. "Laura texted her that some kid was sick at the resort, you know? Around noon. She texted me late in the afternoon to say she wouldn't come back today. And you're here waiting como un pendejo? Why don't you go to her house?"

"Just what we need," Pasofino said, interrupting Dulce and jabbing Pablo's ribs with an elbow. "The gringos have infiltrated the trap."

When Pablo looked up, he was surprised to see the two women from the Freedom Sunset Cruise. He had assumed that they would pass out in their rooms and forget all about their dancing plans, but now here they were. Christine, the one with the beaded cornrows, wore a sparkly blue halter-top dress. Sourpuss hadn't bothered changing. They both lit up as soon as they saw him.

"Hell no," Dulce said. "*Locals only* means *locals only*."

"They're not like the others," Pablo said to Dulce quietly. If Vida really wasn't coming, maybe the night could be salvaged. He would make sure the gringas had such a great time that they'd give him the last two starred reviews he needed.

"Bartender!" Christine said.

"Elena wouldn't let anything bad happen to them," Dulce said to Pasofino, eyes lingering on the newcomers. "Right?"

"Of course not," he said, and Pablo felt a rush of guilt, wondering if Pasofino really had no idea about the pills. He almost brought it up now, but, sensing how worried Dulce was about the girls, he thought better of it. He would likely only make things worse.

"Let's go," Pasofino said. "We should start at the tent city. Never know what those Haitianos might be up to."

Pablo knew many of the Haitian laborers. Those who had remained after the construction was shut down were often terrified of migration raids. They kept their heads down and just worked hard, took care of their families. He doubted they would cause any harm. But he didn't correct Pasofino. With what time? The tourists were upon him. With exaggerated familiarity, he folded them both into a big hug. They smelled nauseatingly sweet—of perfume, or maybe lotion, that was meant to smell like tropical flowers but barely covered up a day of sweat. Christine did a little curtsy, and he gave her a thumbs-up, figuring that her and Sourpuss's glassy eyes meant that they had hit up the minibar during their free time.

"The violinist told us we might find you here," Sourpuss said with a smirk.

"You ready to teach us to dance?" Christine asked him.

Pablo leaned toward Pasofino's ear, said quickly that he wasn't going to go with him right now. He'd catch up when Dulce joined him a bit later. Pasofino raised an eyebrow, then nodded tersely as he left. All the locals from Pico Diablo headed out with Pasofino. Several of the temporary staff members from the resort, on hearing that a couple of girls were missing, left, too. Pablo thought that everyone was exaggerating with their reactions. Elena was seventeen years old. A dead battery and a lapse in judgment didn't mean that anything bad had happened.

Pablo took the two women by the hand, went into the smaller crowd, didn't stop until they were right in the heart of it. There was a funk that waited for them there, sure, but it wasn't anything to be ashamed of. Under that malodor, everyone smelled like what they did for a living—detergent from laundry, Fabuloso from mopping, dirt from gardening. His own smell was familiar to all, a stronger stink. The act of sex, the promise of sex, the regret of sex. He couldn't deny it. He loved the way every body touched every other body. They were sweaty, drunk. He felt happy and free. He danced and drank. Danced and drank, for a long time.

A COUPLE OF HOURS later, through the remaining bodies, he saw the startling white suit and knew immediately that it was Laura. He saw her hug Dulce, cup her ear to hear all she had to say. With relief, he put Elena out of his mind. Laura was here. She must know all that had happened where her sister was concerned. And if not, she had influence, power. She could get things done.

Pasofino tugged at his arm, having left to search and come back again. When he motioned to the bar, Pablo saw Dulce holding Elena's dirty pink scrubs. She was crying.

"There's blood on Elena's uniform," Pasofino said, alarmed.

Pablo shook his head, walked the short distance to Dulce.

"Laura hit her earlier. It was by mistake, the scratch on her cheek from the bracelet. That's old blood."

Laura shot him a look that said it wasn't really necessary to put her business out on the street like that. But Dulce and Pasofino breathed a sigh of relief.

"Let's go," Laura said.

Pablo didn't move.

"No sign of them at the tent city," Pasofino said, taking a step away. "Any idea where we should look next? You know Elena."

Pasofino glanced behind him, seeming surprised that Pablo hadn't budged.

"I don't know where she is," Pablo said. "Call me if you need me," he added, then turned toward the tourists. He refused to confront Pasofino's expression, which he was sure would show his disappointment.

Moments after the group left, an alert made his phone vibrate. He glanced at it absentmindedly, numb from so many drinks that he wasn't even thinking of Vida anymore. The text came from Elena. I had to go, she'd written.

This time, when he tried her, her phone didn't even ring. He found a dead, empty space where sound belonged. He looked for her on social media, found that she'd updated her status. The picture was unmistakable. Out of an airplane's window, a wing—and beyond the wing, an endless carpet of fluffy white clouds. He scrolled down, and sure enough, there was a post from earlier in the day, an image of the girls running on the beach, colorful ribbons trailing behind them. When he scrolled up again, the image of the clouds was gone. Deleted.

Had she taken the girls out of the country? What the hell had she done?

Pablo stumbled out of the crowd. His thoughts were hazy. He'd never wanted to go. Not to New York City with all its green dollars, or to Spain with its euros, or to Argentina, where one of his clients had once told him that he'd never have to work another day in his life, that he could feast on the juiciest steaks until his arteries exploded. He'd had no desire, ever, to leave this land, this heat, these people he'd grown up with. He imagined Elena finally finding a place where she could settle, take root, give up the pills. But she was so young, not even eighteen. He wished she'd reached out to him before she'd gotten on the plane. He would have explained. She'd be exchanging one set of humiliations for another.

Pablo went toward the beach, thinking to wash his face, to sober up. Laura's presence had ended the party. Most people had either joined the search or left.

He smashed his phone's keypad. Where are the girls? he texted to Elena.

Elena is typing, his phone said. Then she stopped. No words came through.

He thought about calling Dulce and Pasofino, who had yet to return. But how would his phone call help? He didn't know anything.

The tourists had disappeared by the time he returned to the bar. He searched for them and saw their figures some distance away, walking down the beach. He went back to the bar to charge his phone and wait for them. He'd take them back to the resort and then join up with the search group. He fumbled until he found a bottle of water. When he stood up, a white man was sitting there. He looked familiar, and Pablo tried to place him. Maybe he'd been on the Freedom Sunset Cruise earlier.

"I left my passport here today," he said to Pablo. The man didn't blink as he spoke, and his tone commanded quick action.

Pablo found it quickly enough in the lost-and-found bin on the other side of the bar. "You can trust us locals," he said. When he held it out, he noticed the man's wrinkled fingertips. The marks of a person who'd spent hours at sea. He held the man's surprisingly bright green eyes and was struck by the amount of coldness he found in them. Not one note of gratitude or relief. Pablo felt a chill down his spine.

"Fun at the beach today?" Pablo asked.

The man stood and walked away, didn't bother to respond.

On the beach, Sourpuss was yelling at Christine that they would miss their flight if they didn't go back immediately, pack their shit up, and leave for the airport. Christine was yelling back, saying to chill the fuck out, that they still had close to four hours. Their flight would leave at 3 A.M. They would be fine if they checked their luggage curbside.

When Pablo tried to find the man's retreating figure, he'd vanished. Pablo drank from his bottle of water, reminded himself to snap out of his stupor. He'd had too much to drink, that was all. Why in the world would he think that the man had anything to do with the missing girls?

"Not to worry," he said to Christine and Sourpuss. "I know a shortcut to the airport that cuts the trip from two hours to one."

"We already arranged for a shuttle," Sourpuss said.

As Pablo went to leave, Pasofino came back with Dulce, who was crying again. Laura was no longer with them. They'd seen Elena's post on social media and turned around to get Dulce's car. They were going to head to the airport—try to find out if anyone had seen Elena leave with Dulce's girls.

"Laura went back to the hotel," Dulce said to Pablo. "She wanted to check again if anyone knows anything there. Can you find her? Call me back?"

"We have to go," Sourpuss said.

"I'll go straight to Laura," Pablo said. "I'll find out whatever there is to know."

Christine and Sourpuss buckled up in the back of the resort SUV that Pablo had borrowed. Neither sat up front with him. Momentarily, he felt humiliated. He sat up a little straighter, sped up the car, reminded himself to smile. He'd feel much better once he got a shower and some coffee, sobered up.

The women chatted about what waited for them back home— *wiping dirty old ass,* they both said. *Wait until we tell the girls at work,* they said. *Who had the last laugh about our too-good-to-be-true Costco last-minute vacation package? Not bad for two old broads, huh, Pablo?*

They knew his name. That was worth something. He glanced at

them in the rearview mirror, smiling as wide as they were. How long would this happiness last? They both were as red as skinless tomatoes. They'd be in pain for weeks, skin sore, layers peeling. Would it all seem worth it to them? Pablo felt an impulse to make sure they understood this land was about more than sun and parties.

"Not only a beautiful place," Pablo said. "But also founded by fugitive slaves. This land is about freedom every way you look at it."

"We heard the spiel during the cruise," Christine said, yawning.

"Don't you think it's messed up that this town celebrates Freedom Day on the same day that the Parsley Massacre began?" Sourpuss said.

"Don't pay any attention to Abigail," Christine said. "She loves history. Spent way too much time learning about your country. She's been a show-off and teacher's pet since we were in second grade."

But Pablo saw true curiosity in Abigail's gaze.

"Two unrelated things can happen in the same country on the same day hundreds of years apart," he said, parroting what Doña Fella used to say whenever the issue came up in the classroom. "You can be *in* a place and not *of* it," he concluded.

"What does that even mean?" Abigail asked.

"What can we do for you?" Christine asked suggestively, interrupting her friend.

He was glad to get off the topic. The ugly parts of history were in the past. They had no impact on the present, really. He told them about the reviews, about how close he was to getting to spend more time entertaining guests. "Next time you come, I'll be able to spend the entire day with you," he said, eyeing the women in the rearview.

"Starred review numero uno done," Abigail said within a couple of minutes, her face still illuminated by her phone.

Christine laughed in a strange way. "Anything for you, mi amor. Could you give me a hand with my luggage? I'll do it after that."

Pablo felt the world spin. Of course Christine would want him to go to her room. Of course he wouldn't be making any immediate attempts to speak to Laura.

"It would be my pleasure," he said. "I just have to go by my room to freshen up, if you don't mind."

Pablo thought of the long hours he had worked to make it here. How each moment of pleasure he'd give her would make all the hardship insignificant if it led to a better life.

"I'd prefer if you don't shower," she said, giggling. Abigail whistled, then loudly, so loudly, said, "You're a fucking pervert."

FRIDAY

CHAPTER
18

LAURA SAT ON THE FLOOR IN THE CASITA SHE SHARED WITH her sister. On the wall, posters of cities from all over the world loomed above her. She'd turned the small space upside down. She'd searched through Elena's drawers, rummaged through her pockets, leafed through her many books. She'd found nothing that could give her a clue.

She didn't believe that her sister had left. She didn't believe that her sister had done anything to put two little girls whom they'd known since birth in any kind of danger. Simply said, she believed that something unexpected had happened to her sister. That Elena, just like Niña and Perfecta, was missing.

But how to explain that picture out of a plane's window? How to make sense of the quickness with which Elena had deleted the post? Laura hesitated to call the police, to get anyone in the hotel involved.

Laura stood up, her entire body aching. It had been a long day. Now it was past midnight. She began to pick up the mess she'd made. She cleaned up after her sister, too. She lined up the flat, ugly shoes the babysitters were required to wear. She picked up the pink uniforms strewn among the many books that were splayed open on the floor like birds who had just landed for a moment, wings wide.

Yesterday, when they'd been on the side of the road and Elena had talked about turning herself in, Laura had felt her entire body tense as if she were a fist. She'd felt an incredible, overwhelming resentment toward Elena. How had she survived this wretched life they'd both had to live but ended up so different from Laura? Elena had a beautiful, childlike sense of optimism. Her little sister always believed things would work out, no matter what. Laura knew that this was, at least partly, her own doing. That she'd decided to spare her sister the heartbreaking truth of their reality to protect her innocence.

A year ago, Laura had been summoned to the police station in her father's name. She had chosen to ask Pablo to come along with her before she had any clue of the horror that lay ahead.

IN PALOMA FALLS, the police station and the tourist info center had once shared the same space.

Even after the tourist center had moved to its own building, the police station had retained a degree of cheerful levity, with murals on the entry wall highlighting local attractions—Ciudad Paloma Falls with its cobblestoned, colonially inspired resplendent glory; the Paloma Waterfalls with their rushing, crashing endlessness of white vapor, framed by those dark rocks, a serene blue-green lake at their base; the tropical forest with its lush caoba trees and a happily soaring emerald Hispaniolan amazon; the stalagmite caves with their dramatic glass-like spears. Other walls depicted pristine white-sand beaches.

Inside that brightly lit waiting room, with her back to the painted waterfall, Laura had observed a familiar scene, and she'd hit Pablo with an elbow so he'd look up from his phone. An arrested couple followed a predetermined path: After booking, the Dominican prostitute was roughly taken to the back and placed in an unseen cell while the tourist she'd been caught with had his handcuffs removed, then was politely told to sit in a section of the waiting area labeled HOLDING ROOM. Laura checked out the man's wrist and found many beaded bracelets. Thankfully, none of them were the woven guest bracelet from the Grand Paloma Resort. She noticed the cheap plastic bracelet of one of the hotels in Cabarete. This man had traveled quite some way to come here. Why?

The undocumented Haitian migrants who'd been arrested in surprise sweeps at the resort construction grounds earlier that day never came indoors. They were kept in vans outside, in the heat of the day, armed guards standing at attention until they'd gathered enough of them to make the five-hour drive to Centro de Retencion Dajabon worth it; there they would await processing, then swiftly be deported en masse. Unless they happened to come in when certain officers were manning the process and happened to have someone willing to pay obscene bribes, in which case they would be granted freedom. Those bribes never protected the migrants willing to pay them from being harassed again, arrested again, processed again, deported again. The shouts of the Haitianos in the vans reached Laura as if they sat next to her in one of those plastic chairs. They were calling out for water, and someone needed to use the bathroom. An alarmingly young voice, that of a child no older than six years old, said she was hungry. None of the officers at the police station reacted in any way whatsoever to their calls.

The drunken gringo stumbled to the desk.

"That's not right," he slurred in British-accented Spanish. "You should let those people get some food, water, go to the bathroom. They have human rights."

The woman at the front desk reassured him that the migrants were given breaks at intervals throughout the day. "We feed them," she said, "give them water. Some of them are better off here than on that construction site at the resort, take it from me."

With that she nodded, swiftly dismissing him, and the man went back to his seat. After a few moments, he stretched his body across several of the plastic chairs and dozed off.

In the waiting room, Laura sighed in exasperation. First off, that woman had never set foot on the resort, so she had no idea what she was talking about. Second, this man, who'd been arrested for fucking a prostitute, who had probably traveled here primarily for that activity, who in a few moments would walk out of here with no trace that he'd ever committed a crime, was lecturing them on human rights?

Pablo, sitting next to her, swung a knee against her leg. "These gringos are putting in some real effort now. Is it Rosetta Stone? Duolingo?"

Laura couldn't smile because she was irritated. When the country-wide sweeps had reached the resort weeks ago, Elena had organized all the resort employees against the unjust conditions of the Haitians. Unsurprisingly, it had only been the youngest of the workers who'd joined forces, who'd gone on strike and demanded that the hotel use its influence to stop the deportations. The pressure hadn't aided in stopping the deportations, but it *had* stopped the work on the construction site. Then a group of Haitian workers had spoken to Elena. They didn't need the Dominican workers to protest in solidarity and take away their work. They needed work. When Elena had asked what she could do instead, those migrants had walked away, pissed off.

Laura had told her sister, "See, no good deed goes unpunished."

It was just like her sister to lead with her heart and not her mind. Even the elders in their town had been quick to warn the younger people against getting mixed up in the situation. They were supposed to be above it all, avoiding racist Dominicans as much as they avoided Haitians at all costs.

Many of the Dominican workers, those who'd been born away from the Pico Diablo Mountain, acted as if Haitians didn't exist, looking past and through them with the same easy disregard that the tourists had for Haitians and Dominicans alike. But there was a vocal minority who actively denigrated the migrants, who repeated the vitriol often heard from the conservative far-right movement about how the Haitians were an infestation, vermin, violent and ready to do the most vile things if given the chance. It was that opinion that fueled the current governmental atmosphere, that had forced such definitive and abrupt action to mass-deport Haitians who couldn't show proof of legal residence.

"These are our neighbors!" Elena had exclaimed. "They deserve work. They deserve our solidarity."

Laura had grown used to her sister's emotional responses. Elena had grown inconsolable in the aftermath of the group of Haitian migrants storming away from her, playing Sia's "Snowman" on repeat, refusing to babysit or leave their casita. She'd looked at the many books she'd read for school—Audre Lorde's *Sister Outsider,* Angela Davis's *Women, Race and Class,* Nelson Mandela's *Long Walk to Freedom*—as if they'd all misled her.

Laura had hoped that the failed strike would be the experience that taught her sister there was a big difference between abstract ideologies of justice and freedom and real-world applications. She needed to learn to mind her own business.

Even though their father was a loser, Elena had held on to hopes of his redemption with a childlike obstinance. She used to routinely go up to their mountain town on her days off, to their old house in Pico Diablo that overlooked the sea, to bring him food and clean clothes and give him whatever money she could spare for his next attempt at freedom. Since he'd left in June for his latest attempt to get into the United States, Elena had been getting a text every few weeks from some random number. Laura had told Elena that she didn't want to hear any updates. Elena had insisted on telling her anyway, not without admonishing Laura. *What happened in your chest? What in that cavity calcified your organ and made it into such a pebble of a heart? Gambling is an addiction, you know. Alcoholism is an addiction, you know. People deserve the right to start again. To make themselves brand-new.*

When Laura had been summoned to the police station on her father's behalf that day, she'd thought he had some nerve giving the police her name. But then she realized Elena hadn't told her that their father was back in town, which meant she didn't know. Since they hadn't heard from their father in weeks, Elena had turned to magical thinking. Out of the blue, she'd say, *I have a good feeling that this coyote is the one who'll get him across and in.* Laura hadn't responded.

As the gringo began to snore, Laura was glad that she was the one who'd been called to present herself for their father instead of her sister. She'd get him out of whatever embarrassing situation he'd put himself into. Their father often journeyed down criminally adjacent spirals. Her sister didn't deserve to have her heart broken by him—again.

An unfamiliar cadet with light skin, a flat ass, and the swagger of someone who has suddenly come into the tiniest bit of power asked Laura to follow him. He wasn't local. Laura was led away from the warm murals and the drooling gringo, past a red-white-and-blue Dominican flag where someone had painted over *Dios, Patria,* and *Libertad* with the words *Please Come Again.* The paint used to cover the original words was thin, nearly transparent, so *God* could be seen as the shadow of *Please. Homeland* as the shadow of *Come. Freedom* as the shadow of *Again.* Pablo mumbled something unintelligible. Laura turned to him, surprised that he was walking behind her. She'd assumed he'd stay behind in the waiting room.

"What did you say?" Laura asked.

"These lambones," he said. "They turned the police station into another tourist attraction. It's like Tinder here."

Laura nodded, forced a smile. She hadn't noticed what was happening in the cells they'd walked past. Bored police officers meandered down the halls and lingered by the holding cells. The cadet led her through a door she'd never walked through before, down a narrow labyrinthine path with a steep decline. The sunlight stayed on the other side of the door. They plummeted into a thick, suffocating darkness. She smelled rancid, days-old garbage, the sweetness of spoiled meat.

When they finally arrived at the end of the dark hallway, the cadet opened yet another door, and on a metallic table at the room's center was a plastic body bag.

"Will you need any help disposing of the remains? Have you called the morgue?"

Laura took a step back, bumping into Pablo. She noticed the additional body bags, haphazardly placed on top of one another on the ground surrounding the table. She'd had no idea that they kept dead people down here. The smell was revolting; it stung her eyes. She suppressed the urge to gag.

"There must be a mistake," Pablo said, stepping around her. "She was called about her father. Maybe he's in one of the cells?"

The cadet lifted an oversized tag on the black bag. Laura didn't understand what was happening. The bag was too flat, too small. It couldn't possibly contain her father's body.

"Ezequiel Moreno?" the cadet said, turning the tag over so that Pablo could see it.

Who knew what possessed Laura in that moment? She went to the bag, unzipped it halfway. In it, there was no recognizable human body. It looked like whoever this person was had been hit by a truck, then run through a meat grinder. The smell was unlike anything she'd smelled before—pungent, acidic. It became a halo that blinded her.

She unzipped the bag the rest of the way. There was her father's hand—it was whole except for the pinky, which had been lost in a previous attempt to enter America. And so Laura was able identify her father not by what was there, but by what was missing.

"What happened to him?" she asked in a small voice, her eyes closed, her body all chills.

"Recovered after a failed attempt to cross the Rio Grande," the cadet read robotically from a form. "Cause of death: drowning."

He read on as if he were looking through a list of office supplies.

"He was recovered after his body got stuck in some buoys," he said. "Extraction was a bitch, which accounts for the hamburger-meat look of the body."

"Barbaro," Pablo said. "You're talking about her fucking father. Have some respect."

The cadet looked stricken, seemed to finally take stock of Laura. In front of her, he transformed into a young boy, hardly older than a child. Her fingers had a strange electricity to them before they grew completely numb. An odd hum emerged from somewhere deep inside her body—too many memories rushing at once. Not of the terrible times. No. Him, dancing with her mother on the back porch of their house. Her mother's laughter, her voice saying *not so fast, E.Z., not so fast.* The moon taking up the entire sky, reflected in the ocean beneath it. Elena, only a baby, clapping her hands in glee, drool falling from her toothless gums to Laura's bare thighs. Elena gazing adoringly at Laura, touching her chin with wet, chubby fingers. The sound of the rocking chair as Laura planted her small feet against the hard earth and pushed. In all the years she'd wished for her father's death, she'd never considered this reaction. The grief that engulfed her was crushing, absolute.

IN THE CASITA, LAURA finished cleaning their room. It was now pristine. It seemed impossible that her sister would have done anything that truly put the girls' lives in danger. With tears running down her face, she kept asking herself: *What have I done?*

CHAPTER 19

THE FISHNET, STUCK IN THE WATER, JERKED AGAINST PABLO'S
pull. He'd had no sleep, but a new day had begun. The boat's motion
made nausea rise in his throat. He thought he'd learned long ago never
to drink as much as he had last night. He'd be paying for it all day. He
didn't have the strength to pull hard against whatever was holding the
net in place. He put a hat over his face as he leaned back onto the deck.
Seawater soaked through his shirt, cool in the early morning chill. He
closed his eyes.

He'd gone to Elena and Laura's casita, the largest in the staff quarters, as soon as he'd helped the gringas into the airport shuttle. He'd
figured it was the right thing to do. Outside, the morning air had carried
the rancid smell of the toilets that had yet to be fixed. It had reminded
him of his house up in Pico Diablo, of the many days he'd spent squatting above a hole in the ground to relieve himself. He feared after the
last day of work, his own body odor wasn't far off the stench that permeated the air. On top of the fish guts and spilled liquor, he now had the
unmistakable funk of sex. Poised to knock, he'd been momentarily struck
by the sound of Laura's singing voice, so different from her shrill speaking voice. It had been clear and melodic. He'd imagined how quickly
Laura would fire him as soon as she caught one whiff.

He'd texted her instead. You got a few moments to chat? Want to plan
what to do about El? The girls?

On the other side of the door, he'd heard the alerts on Laura's
phone as she stopped singing. "Fuck all of this," she'd said loudly.

No response to the text had come through. He'd turned around,
glad he hadn't knocked. He'd gone back to his boat to sleep.

Now Pasofino was kicking him awake. "Time for last haul," he said. "We were looking for the girls for hours and you were too busy drinking with some tourists to help?"

"You need to leave me the fuck alone," Pablo said.

"Gladly," Pasofino said, stepping back onto his own boat.

The sun had burned through the fog. The air around him was charged. The heat of the sun warmed his body as the boat tilted this way, then that. There was an ache behind his eyes.

Pablo pulled at the net again, and this time, it came up with no resistance. He was met with hundreds of squirming shrimp and an octopus with radiant skin that shone pink, purple, neon blue as its tentacles narrowed and enlarged. He took his catch and placed it in one of the coolers that lined one side of the boat. Then he saw a beautiful silk hair ribbon. There was no mistaking that it was the complicated type that Vida had learned to make. He grabbed his phone and confirmed his suspicions. It matched the ones in the girls' hair shown in the picture that Elena had posted the day before.

He cast his eyes every which way, scared that he would see the bodies of the girls floating in the ocean. But there was no sign of them. Pablo leaned over the side of the boat, suddenly overcome with the need to vomit. After he was done, he felt a numbness spreading.

"What have you got there?" Pasofino shouted at him. He made his way over to Pablo's boat again and grabbed the hair ribbon from his hand.

"It could be anybody's," Pablo said.

"You wouldn't have found it if it wasn't theirs," Pasofino said. What Pasofino said didn't make any sense.

Pasofino jumped quickly, with surprising grace, onto his boat, not bothering to explain what he was about to do or where he was headed. He turned on the outboard motor and sped away in the direction of Beyond Proof. Pablo didn't consider following him. Instead, he slowly threw the net back into the ocean, hoping to miss the vomit that had attracted a school of tiny, sparkling fish—too small, too precious to eat, keeping vigil in case the bodies of Dulce's girls surfaced.

CHAPTER
20

US, THE WORKERS

THE THING ABOUT LOCALS' NIGHT AT BEYOND PROOF WAS that the beach was often a total dump the next day. Those of us who spent all our waking hours caring for other people—catering to their every need, feeding them and cleaning up after them, rubbing aloe on their sunburned skin, straightening their hair just so they could turn around and plunge into the sea, carrying their fat babies on aching hips—couldn't be bothered to lift one limb to clean up after ourselves. But we cleaned the morning after the girls went missing. There were no empty beer bottles, no food wrappers of any kind. Even the place on the sand where the firepit's flames had risen five feet into the air was devoid of any evidence of charcoal or ash. We lingered into the early morning hours on Friday.

Laura had been there alongside us for several hours before sunlight broke the sky. She'd given a curt nod when we said we were too sick to go in. We'd searched all through the night—countless miles of beach; the surrounding roads and forests; a group of us had even headed to the waterfall right as dawn was about to break. Before that group had split from the others, Laura had come up to each of us, zooming in on the shirts the girls had been wearing as they ran on the beach. The German futbol team's name would be impossible for us to remember, but we memorized the important details: a sleeveless black shirt on Niña, a bright red T-shirt on Perfecta. When we'd arrived at the still- ness of the trees, where the only sound was the deafening crash of the water on the surface of the waiting pool, we'd had to pause in awe. The bioluminescent water had flung sparkles of bluish-greenish light that dissipated almost as quickly as they'd appeared, a glowing display more marvelous than any firework show that had ever lit up the sky. It had distracted us for a bit, reminded us that beauty existed even in the most terrible circumstances.

Bueno. No one had time for navel-gazing. Not with the girls missing and Pasofino dropping by Beyond Proof just as the sun strained against that dark inverted bowl of gray sky. Pasofino brought the once-crimped silk ribbon, limp and stained from the sea, and handed it to Dulce, who'd been in a daze, looking off into the flat, mirrorlike surface of the sea. At the sight of the ribbon, she gave a bloodcurdling scream.

The way Dulce held on to that hair ribbon, the way she seemed to intuit that its discovery meant the worst had happened, it broke us open. How many of us, during the years we'd worked in resorts all over—in Punta Cana, Samana, Cap Cana, Cabarete, Puerto Plata, Pedernales, Barahona, Boca Chica, Juan Dolio, La Romana, Bonao, Constanza, Santiago, La Vega, Montecristi, and beyond our own country, across every island: Turks and Caicos, Saint Lucia, the Cayman Islands, Barbados, the Bahamas, St. Barts, St. Kitts and Nevis, Antigua, Curaçao, St. Martin and St. Maarten, Aruba, Guadeloupe, Jamaica, Cuba, Puerto Rico, Trinidad and Tobago, in the cities, on the beaches—had witnessed firsthand, time and time again, our women and girls going missing and never being found?

A few of us went with Dulce to the police station after sunrise. The night before, they'd dismissed her out of hand. It hadn't been twenty-four hours, they said. But all of us agreed that it wasn't reasonable to wait for the evening. Not after Pasofino showed up with the hair ribbon. A search had to be called for the one place we hadn't thought to look: the sea.

There was a darkening overhead. The wind had grown violent. We were expecting bad weather because of our nearness to Puerto Rico, where the hurricane was supposed to land. It could very well be a matter of life or death, getting a search team out on boats. We pushed a few men forward to stand beside Dulce and Pasofino. The man in charge was immediately hostile, ostentatiously rude, informing her that the regulations hadn't changed just because she was "worried."

The guy was a jerk, admittedly, but it was because of him that we learned the storm had changed course. Headed right for us, its eye was no longer in Puerto Rico but set to pass over Canal de la Mona, just sixty-one miles away. They had expedited shipments because the storm would affect all traffic in and out of the Panama Canal. In other words, a case of missing girls wasn't going to derail storm preparations, no matter how rich their father was.

Dulce seemed betrayed, confused. When she'd hit the jackpot with Fabien, that rich German tourist, the one who'd built her a mansion, who before then had built a beautiful town and called it Ciudad Paloma Falls, worthy of the sharpest luxury shopping skills of the wealthiest people in the world, putting us on the map, she'd assumed it meant that she would be safe. That her children would always be protected.

But that morning, as she tried to remain calm, to appeal to this policeman's sense of justice and order, reminding him that there were helicopters available, that this might be as simple as the girls and Elena having lost their way on the mountain, she realized that he couldn't see past her skin or her Dominican Spanish, and that if she'd been with Fabien with his German accent or one of the league of rich men who'd decided a decade ago to build themselves an entire paradise on the other side of a swamp—or at the very least had Fabien's last name—this comemierda policeman wouldn't be looking down his nose at her.

Dulce wilted before our eyes. Some of us had felt a pressure on the back of our necks and recognized it was on hers, too, by the way her gaze stayed fixed on the ground. Most of us knew the feeling of that invisible foot on our necks. Had any of us ever wished her harm? Of course. Up until now, she'd lived a life we envied. When we saw her deflate, it was as if she finally understood what it meant to be helpless, to begin to grow hopeless. But not one of us wished her harm if it'd come by way of her girls. She'd been the one who'd intentionally created a subcategory of women and men who fit neither in decent circles nor in the prostitution rings many of us knew (some of us intimately) and were from different parts of our country, from other places in the Caribbean. This is all to say that there had been a time when we felt nothing but love for Dulce in Paloma Falls. But that time wasn't now. When her girls had gone missing, it had been quite a while since most of us had felt anything other than resentment toward Dulce. As we watched her crumble, helpless, it became clear that a relationship with a rich foreigner could only do so much by way of protection, especially when the man was nowhere to be found.

We made our way back from Paloma Falls to Dulce's mansion. Even during the calamity, that place took our breath away. We had to walk down a steep slope to arrive at the beachfront, four-story house made mostly of glass, with a rooftop pool that dripped water down the entire back wall. Not many of us had ever been invited inside. We noticed the similarities with the architecture of the Grand Paloma Resort.

We wondered why she didn't just pick up the phone and call her man. She could have used his influence to get this policeman asshole to do what was right. And so, many of us left to take care of our own families, or to ensure that we made it back to the resort and secured our position. No one could predict the level of damage that the storm would bring. What we knew was that it took years and years for some resorts to recover after a devastating natural disaster. Say what you will about tourists, but we needed the money they brought, and we knew that they'd only be back if they weren't confronted with what had happened to people outside the secure walls of their vacation escape. They'd remember there was a hurricane somewhere and just remove that island from their travel list. There were so many other islands to choose from. Could they tell the difference? Did they care to?

We took one last look at Dulce's private beach, at the pristine white sand. Already, the waves were higher than usual, numerous and relentless. The palm trees were erect, hardly swaying in the wind. We admired the mansion, where she might be safer than most of our families, and saw her looking out but not seeing those of us who had begun to ascend away.

CHAPTER
21

ULCE HAD OFTEN HEARD THE WOMEN OF PICO DIABLO TALK about the pressure they felt from time to time on the skin where the curve of their spines tracked up into their hairlines. It was a soreness she'd heard her mother talk about, and her grandmother before that. Dulce had never experienced it until Pasofino had handed her the silk remnants of Perfecta's hair ribbon and she'd rushed to the police station—until the police station chief had looked down his nose at her and told her that they would, in fact, be of no help in trying to find her daughters.

Back home, she watched through her floor-to-ceiling windows, stared as her employees, friends, and neighbors hurried away. A storm was heading for the island. Her daughters were out there somewhere.

They'd searched for the girls overnight without stopping. She'd gone up to Pico Diablo, straight to Elena and Laura's old wooden home, thinking maybe they were there. The house had been empty, and the next-door neighbor hadn't seen her girls, but she *had* seen Elena come by alone earlier in the day, had seen her take a small satchel full of clothes. That must have been before Elena had come to her bar.

Dulce's feet were swollen, bruised. She tried to snap herself out of her stupor. To think strategically of what she should do next. She needed Fabien, the girls' father, to exercise the influence he had over the police. She understood that time was slipping away. Fabien hadn't responded to her phone calls or texts. His oldest daughter was getting married this weekend, and when they had last spoken on Thursday morning, they'd agreed he'd be in touch as soon as he could. If he knew what was happening, he'd be on a plane here. She was certain of that.

Outside of her enormous house, the ocean crashed and crashed and crashed; there was no retreat. In front of her was a closet full of frilly dresses. Lace, tulle, cotton, even silk. The task ahead stretched gargantuan. There was a suitcase on the floor, half-full but still deflated. She kicked it out of the way. Yesterday, she'd begun to empty out the closet of dresses that the girls had outgrown. She'd been meaning to do this for the last few months, to take them up to Pico Diablo—there were always children who had so little, who could use the beautiful dresses. She just hadn't gotten around to it.

She touched the fabric, separated the hangers. There was a pair of sparkly chiffon dresses in an obnoxious shade of yellow. Niña had begged her to let her wear one of them yesterday.

Where you going? Dulce had asked.

Colmado, the girl had said, the wind through the gap left by her missing front teeth giving her a lisp.

It's a special dress, Dulce had reminded the girl.

That's why I mean to wear it, Ma, the girl had responded with the haughty tone she'd learned to mimic from her dad.

The dresses are too small, too fancy. Just wear regular clothes, Dulce had told her.

She thought of the many missteps she'd made as a mother. The many times she'd been absent when she should have been there. Times when she'd grown annoyed at her girls instead of offering comfort and love. Was it possible something horrible had happened to her daughters?

Her eyes were like the hands of a clock, marking what had been. A series of drawings; liquid markers mostly left without caps; two cups with congealed bright-red circles at their bases; half-eaten Cheetos (Perfecta's favorite) and some chocolate-covered pretzels (Niña's favorite) that had bled brown on the surface of the white coffee table; and a single purple Croc with the charms that the girls had been obsessively collecting: a stethoscope, Poppy from *Trolls*, a soccer ball because their father had played semiprofessionally after college. That had been before the corporate job, and the wife, and before he'd become one of those rich men who spent their time in the Caribbean finding a way to make other rich men even richer.

She grabbed the dresses, one after another, and frantically placed them inside the suitcase until it was full, zipper teeth straining against the pressure. Fabien had bought the girls these dresses, and they loved their father—despite his almost-never-ending absences—for the way he often spoiled them when he finally came back, for his white skin and golden eyes (speckles of which he'd put in their own green eyes). Dulce would come home from work in the middle of the night and find them both in a sea of fabric, arms and legs intertwined, wearing dresses that didn't fit. Now she made room in the closet for the bigger clothes she'd have to buy to accommodate their growing bodies. The girls would be back, unharmed. They would grow. She went over to her home office down the hall. Frenzied, she shopped for the next hour from online stores in the United States, sending all the packages to a special address in Miami. She'd hired a service that would take the packages and send them on to her via courier. She sent an email to her contact there. She would need these clothes ASAP, she wrote. When the girls were found, the clothes would be here, waiting for them.

Clearly, the police would be of no help in finding her girls unless she could get her rich lover to exercise his influence. He could get to the police who understood how to search for missing people, who would put helicopters in the sky, boats out to sea. How many times had Fabien warned her, told her that she was playing with fire? That running a business where local women fucked men for money was a bad idea when she herself was the mother of two girls? She had purposefully never spoken to her girls about the real dangers that men posed, had chosen to preserve their innocence by withholding horrors that she'd been confident would never affect them. Explaining the truth would likely traumatize them, she'd reasoned. Done more harm than good. Fabien wouldn't be wrong to blame her. He'd warned her many times about what could happen—but he would be as worried as she was, and he could do more to find them than she could do on her own.

She called him over and over again. But just as had happened last night, there was no answer. She'd texted him last night when she'd first called the police, then again every couple of hours. She tried texting him again now. The texts remained unread. Spiraling, she convinced herself he was deleting them without reading them. Or maybe he had blocked her number for a few days to avoid the danger of his wife catching her name in a text alert. If that was the case, he would be unreachable for days.

Desperate, she texted Fabien's best friend, who had been to DR a few times with him. She wrote in all caps: PLEASE HAVE FABIEN CALL ME RIGHT AWAY. OUR GIRLS ARE MISSING. That message also remained unread.

Dulce left her office to walk along the wraparound balcony that surrounded this entire floor. Her body ached, most prominently her feet. She was sure that if something terrible had happened, her body would know. It would know. Her stomach, which had housed them both so long ago. Her arms, where she'd held them as they suckled from her breasts, as they contentedly dozed off. Her legs, which had run after them when they'd first begun to walk—worried, so worried, that they might crash into a sharp corner. Her eyes, which had cried alongside them when they had begun to teethe, tiny, serrated speckles cutting from the insides of their tender gums, finding room in their small mouths—so much pain in the act of growing. Was it her heart that would know? A heart that had expanded when she'd first given birth, then again the second time. She'd anticipated terrible things happening to them as babies. Her body had been in a near-constant state of anxiety, always expecting the worst.

There was no message inside her body telling her anything about her missing girls.

The tiles of the balcony were hot. The humidity enveloped her tightly. Although it was barely ten A.M., there was almost no oxygen left to breathe.

Somewhere, muffled by the sliding glass doors, her cellphone rang. She ran, but by the time she found it, it had gone silent. Fabien's name appeared on the screen as a missed call. She called him back immediately, worried she'd missed him. The screen of her phone lit up with the last picture he'd taken with the girls.

"Mujer," he said. The background was muffled and quiet. He had, once again, snuck into a remote bathroom, or perhaps an oversized linen closet. "What's going on? You know I can't talk."

"The girls are gone," she shouted. "Why haven't you responded? Why haven't you called?"

It took some time for Fabien to understand what she was saying. And then it was rapid-fire: What had the police said? They wouldn't help. Had she reached out to his friend, the mayor of the municipality? He hadn't called her back. Where exactly had she looked? She listed the places where she'd been, where her friends had gone. There was nowhere left to look.

She sobbed into the phone.

Finally, he said, "Would this have happened if you'd been there?"

Dulce heard the spit fly out of his mouth. The venom in his voice was so thick it made all his words sound wet. "It wouldn't have happened if *you'd* been here," she spat back.

"I'll be on the next flight out," he said. There was a sigh of relief. Hers? His? She wasn't sure.

"Oh, thank God you'll come. You'll come anyway?"

Then, as if he'd just remembered that it was Friday, and the next day was his grown daughter's wedding, where he was expected to give her away, he groaned.

"I'll figure something out after the wedding," he mumbled, pained. "In the meantime, I'll make some calls."

She'd made so many bad decisions.

"You understand that I can't leave here. Not today. Not tomorrow. Probably, the earliest I can come is Monday."

They were both quiet on the phone for a while. When the girls had been babies, Fabien had tried to convince her to move to Germany. He'd thought it would be better for the girls to be closer to him, and for the two of them, too. Her heart had raced at the possibility that they'd be together, a real family. But she'd been met with this same silence when she'd asked him if things would be different. *So you're offering me this same situation, just in a country where I don't speak the language, don't have any friends, and will probably be treated like a piece of shit because I have Black skin?* He'd watched her so carefully when she'd said that, as if he was noticing a birthmark he'd never seen before smack in the middle of her mouth. Maybe that had been the first true rift between them. Her inability to accept that their situation was permanent, unchangeable.

Fabien's temper had flared from time to time during the years they had been together. When he'd gotten word about what had happened in his absence, about how the parties he'd encouraged and initiated between his colleagues and her gorgeous friends had morphed into something else entirely, he'd been furious. There was no convincing him that the girls weren't in any danger. The women she hired met the tourists in front of their beach, yes, but they left on boats immediately and traveled half a mile away from the bar. It only happened during the daytime, when their girls were away at school or at swimming camp or at piano lessons. She had sworn to him, on her life, that nothing bad would ever happen to them. It was important to her to give the women of her town the ability to do things their own way. Not to be exploited for their bodies, but to make choices that would help them build a better life. So many of them had. So many.

"What about the cameras at the bar?" he asked now. At her silence, he must have assumed she was crying. But she wasn't crying.

She was exhausted. "I never got them fixed."

"I installed new cameras. They're recording around the clock. There should be a seventy-two-hour loop before they're erased."

"What's the app name? Send me your credentials."

Fabien was quiet.

"Oh, for fuck's sake," she said.

"Whatever happened at the bar," he said, "you have it in the computer upstairs."

She didn't have time to be mad. He'd maneuvered the installation intentionally to withhold this from her—so that he would have access to their lives, so he could spy on them without her knowing. In the split second before she snapped into action, she glanced around her luxurious house. Wondered how many cameras he'd hidden in their home. Then she hung up the phone without saying goodbye, ran.

———

THE BAR WAS ONLY a half-mile walk down the beach. Dulce wasn't sure how she'd made it there, but she found herself sitting at the bar, her laptop screen opaque because of the brightness of the day. But soon enough, the laptop self-adjusted, and she was viewing the feed from the recording. There was a dial she could use to rewind to Thursday morning, to show Vida braiding the ribbons, parting the girls' hair into perfect halves. Dulce stopped the video, zoomed in. Hit play. She was out of frame for the entire time that Vida was doing her girls' hair. Though there was no audio, she knew she'd been chatting, joking, agreeing with Vida that she was better off not telling Pablo about the pregnancy just yet. The girls stared at their tablets, swiping upward, giggling at some ridiculous YouTuber. Dulce sobbed. She didn't understand how yesterday morning, everything had been fine, perfect.

Eventually, she got ahold of herself. The most relevant portion of the video ran for only a few minutes. The man, with his woven Grand Paloma bracelet, platinum dove sparkling in the slanted sunlight, drank shots and talked silently at Elena. She paused the video. *How do I recover the audio?* she asked Fabien. He responded that there was no audio. It was just video.

She felt herself seethe. Hit play. Watched the entire period that the girls had spent running around the beach. Then the girls came over and sat at the bar. Elena took all that money and placed it in her pockets. The man had left the area, heading in the direction of the bathroom, or maybe he'd gone upstairs? Then Elena moved out of the frame, possibly leaving. The girls went to the bathroom, then went to the beach and swam for a while. Several minutes went by before the girls came back into frame. They spoke to each other, lingering on the beach. When they began to move back in the direction of the bar, they held hands, walking in the opposite direction from where Elena had gone. They seemed to be responding to someone's call. From that point forward, there was no more sign of the girls. The tourist man, also, never came back on screen. Dulce rewound the video. Carefully zoomed into the girls' faces during the last moments they were captured on screen. They didn't appear scared at all.

Dulce rushed home, got into her roofless Jeep. She had to find that man with the Grand Paloma bracelet. When she tried to think of Elena, the hurt was so big she couldn't even fathom it. She hoped her eyes lied—that Elena hadn't sold her girls to that tourist man.

CHAPTER 22

PABLO CUT THE HEAD OFF THE OCTOPUS'S BODY, TURNED IT inside out, and carefully detached the entrails with a sharp blade. Its luminous black ink spread in his hands, creating mucous gloves. When drops fell from his fingers, they blotched the counter of his station. He turned on the faucet, rinsed the head. The world spun. The bile was a constant in his throat, threatening to project out of his body. He let the cold water run through his fingers. Even though the ink slid off his skin, the slimy texture remained. The octopus's multicolored skin had faded to pearl white now that it was dead. It was soft, squishy. He moved to the tentacles, located the beak, hard as that of a bird, and tried to remove it with his bare hands. But the beak was stubborn, so he had to use the blade. Pablo considered how many crabs, snails, clams, and small fish this one octopus had consumed with the help of that hard beak.

Once, he'd seen an octopus eat a sea star. It had pulled it into an embrace, and then, in a flash, the star was dead. But that hadn't been as astonishing as the time he'd seen a large adult octopus eat a smaller baby octopus. Pablo had been a child, tiny enough that the fear of the hungry octopus turning toward him, hugging him with its many arms, and making him disappear in a big, powdery cloud of ink had forced him to swim to the surface and find his father mid-motion on top of the boat, unspooling the fishing line. He remembered his father reassuring him that octopi didn't eat humans. Humans ate octopi. To calm him, his father had explained that an octopus could squeeze its entire body into any space that its beak fit into. *They may look big,* his father had said, *but they are only as big as the hardest part of their body. Let's catch the one that scared you.* And they had. He'd swum with his father under the surface of the sea, the sun above them an indistinct strobe that had made the underwater world slow, magical. Pablo had seen his father hold the slippery animal in both his hands. The octopus had easily escaped his grasp, danced, twirled, and shot its ink in dusty mushrooms that expanded as they dispersed and disappeared. Later, they'd caught the octopus with a net.

He was transported from that moment back to his own boat, to the feeling of the silk hair ribbon. He couldn't believe he was still here, at the hotel, standing in the same spot, holding the exact posture he'd held yesterday when he'd last seen Elena. Quickly, he completed the steps of slicing the tentacles apart from one another. He placed everything in the waiting cooler and was just wiping away the ink with a bleach-soaked rag when he glanced up to find Laura studying him. She wore the skirt suit today. Her hair was wavy and perfect. Her makeup immaculate.

They were both quiet, looking at each other.

She seemed to be on the verge of tears. He didn't have to ask to know that Elena hadn't called, hadn't responded to Laura's attempts to reach her. Pablo was reminded that his boss was also a girl he'd grown up with. That she was three years younger than he was. Pablo wiped his hands dry and came around to where she stood.

"What can I do?" he asked. "I was thinking of taking the day off? Going to help with the search. With the storm coming, we have to find them, wherever they are. Elena was out of it yesterday when she came by. Had mud and blood on her uniform."

His words snapped Laura out of her sorry state. She stood erect.

"I have good news for you," she said in her boss tone.

He was disoriented. One minute, she was about to break down, and the next, her eyes were clear and alert. But at her next announcement, a surge of happiness shot its way through his entire body, an orb that sparkled, illuminated him from within. When she gave him a new name tag with his full name, Pablo Frost, and the word ENCARGADO indented into the metal, he felt himself grow tall, strong. She needed him to head out of town, to the Yellow Paloma, with an American family as their resort companion. He'd have to leave right away to beat the storm, since the sister hotel was in Jarabacoa, inland, a six-hour drive from here.

"The family will be waiting for you in the lobby in half an hour," she said. "Better hurry."

The magnetic key to his new garden-view room eclipsed all concerns about hair ribbons and lost girls. There were many people on that task. Half the resort's local employees had called out sick to help. What more could he do?

LAURA USHERED A FRESHLY showered Pablo, wearing a baby-blue uniform, to meet the family he'd be accompanying to the Yellow Paloma. His heart jolted when he recognized the man as the same one who had come by Dulce's bar late last night in search of his passport. But the man looked through him as if he'd never seen him before, and Pablo was relieved. Happy to pretend they'd never met, Pablo explained that he'd grab their vehicle and they'd be on the road in no time.

As Pablo made his way to the security office where he would claim the keys to the resort SUV, he slowed his pace. He had to walk about half a mile away from the main building, past towering bougainvillea, their colors so bright: yellow, pink, and purple. He was doing his best to keep his mind blank. A few days away from here would serve him well. He hoped the couple would get rid of him as soon as they arrived at the Yellow Paloma, and he would be able to relax with the other workers until it was time to drive them back.

When he arrived, he found Guillermo Taveras waiting for him. The short man, who had an oddly square head, treated his job as head of security at the Grand Paloma Resort as the most important thing in his life. He had always been hostile to the employees from Pico Diablo, acting as if those who had grown up nearby were inferior. Pablo had always dismissed him and his sense of superiority as out of touch— just as he did all the other Dominicans who somehow subscribed to such outdated and obvious racism. *Enjoy your light skin and light eyes,* he thought, unwilling to directly confront the unease he felt around Guillermo and his like.

Guillermo handed Pablo a loaded gun and the keys to a large seven-passenger Escalade. The car was so massive that it seemed to be four feet off the ground. With nonchalance, Pablo checked to make sure the safety on the weapon was on, then tucked it in the back of his pants. The cold metal felt good on his lower back.

"There has been a series of robberies on the road," Guillermo said in a gruff voice. "We think they know our cars and assume that the people we transport have a lot of money. Just last month, there were two people who got shot during an encounter. Juan Jose lost an eye. Whatever you do, don't make any stops. You need to get them to the Yellow Paloma safely. That's your job."

Pablo nodded, understanding that this man's job was to make everyone paranoid about their safety. Of course everyone was on the verge of being robbed and murdered. Otherwise, who would need him? It was ridiculous to think they'd drive six hours inland without stopping.

He got into the car and headed to the curved driveway that led to the main lobby, where the family was waiting. He opened the door for the little girl and, holding her by the armpits, helped her into the car. He was surprised not so much that the husband let himself into the car, but that he chose the front passenger seat. The man, wearing aviator glasses and a fedora that sat low on his forehead, settled into the seat and immediately turned his attention to his phone. In the light of day, Pablo could see that the man's face sported fresh scratches. He tried to remember if those marks had been there the night before. He felt nauseous again. He might not be able to make it through this drive without getting sick. Pablo went around to the other side of the car to open the door for the wife, who waited for him to do so. He put out his hand to give her a boost. She seemed a bit jittery, as if panicked about touching him. He gave her his biggest smile, understanding that some women, even though he was slim and unimposing, found him intimidating. He tried to make himself small, to fold into himself as if he were an octopus fitting through a slot. After an awkward pause, she took his hand, climbed in. She didn't return his smile, not even with a small one. And with that, they were off.

CHAPTER
23

As she made the drive to the Grand Paloma Resort, Dulce wished she had a portal that allowed her to see Fabien in France right now, pacing back and forth, dealing with a sorrow he couldn't share with anyone in his real life. There was silence on the road, a strange thing. Not one bird was in the sky or scavenging for the garbage that beachgoers left behind all the time. In the back seat, there was no sound of her girls, who never stopped making noise, even while using tablets and headphones; who were always singing, laughing, speaking way too loudly, mimicking the horrible croak of the birds as they circled; who rushed outside the minute one of those birds slammed into their clear glass windows. It had been a design flaw as serious as the energy consumption required to keep the glass house cool. Birds often died because when they flew toward the house, all they could see in its façade was the sky's reflection. Her girls cried every time it happened.

She imagined them together now, somewhere near, holding hands.

On the radio, there was talk of the storm.

Would it cause terror or havoc? Or would it pass them without even one drop of rain, like the last one?

When she neared the hotel, she saw one of the resort's SUVs, with its tinted windows, driving cautiously in the windy weather. The car slowed to a stop when they were just about to pass. Dulce did the same. Pablo's face came into view as the window lowered. He was driving for a white man, who didn't glance up from his device, aviator sunglasses on even inside the shaded vehicle.

"Any word?" Pablo asked.

Dulce shook her head.

She craned her neck to peer inside the vehicle, to see the face of the man who sat up front. But his face turned from his device toward the ocean. There was no way she could see it. Dulce heard a girl's voice and thought it was Niña's. She bolted against her seatbelt, trying to see through the tinted windows into the back seats.

"Who's back there?" she screamed at Pablo, sounding unhinged to her own ears.

"They're guests of the hotel," he said in a low tone, beginning to raise the window. "We're headed to the Yellow Paloma. We have to try to beat this storm. I will call you later, okay?"

Dulce unbuckled her seat belt, ready to make her way to the car, yank open the back door, and demand to see who was back there. But just then a little girl stuck her body between the front seats. "We're going to the water park," she was saying excitedly. "I want to ride in a Jeep, Mommy," she added, addressing a mom that Dulce couldn't see. Dulce gave the girl a pained smile. A few fat drops of rain fell on her windshield. Pablo gave her a curt nod as the window closed, as if he couldn't get the hell away from her fast enough. Dulce stared at her own reflection on the glass, speeding away from her. She continued on her way to the resort.

AT THE GUARD POST for the hotel, she showed her liquor distributor ID. They checked an electronic tablet and said she wasn't on the schedule for the day. She shrugged.

"I can leave," she said. "The last thing I need is to be out here with the coming weather."

The guards looked at one another, wordlessly remembering what happened at hotel bars during long stretches of bad weather. They raised the gate. Dulce drove in.

THE LOBBY OF THE hotel was madness. Guests were trying to check out, leave before the storm hit. The representatives acted unruffled. Dulce tried to spot Laura in the mayhem.

"It is too late," she heard one of the representatives say calmly. "All air traffic has been suspended. No one is setting one foot off the island until it's over."

People wanted to know how long the storm would last.

"It's hard to predict," another representative said. "But we promise to keep you updated via the hotel's television channel, our website, and our social media pages, or, if you prefer a direct text, I can sign you up right now?"

The guests wanted to know how bad this storm was predicted to be.

"They're saying it looks like a category five," the representative said.

The guests wanted to know how many categories there were.

"Five," the representative said.

The guests wanted to know if they'd be safe.

"We expect flying debris, floods, and winds upward of 160 miles per hour. As long as you stay indoors, you'll be fine. This hotel was constructed using state-of-the-art materials. It can withstand winds up to two hundred miles per hour."

Dulce cut through the crowd, twisting past the many bodies until she had made her way to the outdoor gallery where, just a day ago, unbeknownst to her, the Vargas sisters had drunk an astonishing amount of champagne. Set a record. Dulce felt as if she were the wind, gaining strength, spinning out of control. Her daughters, out in a category five storm? But she had a clue—that man with the Grand Paloma bracelet—and Laura would tell her where to find him. If she so much as hesitated to speak truthfully, Dulce would kill her, then find Elena and do the same to her. No exaggeration or hyperbole.

Laura was nowhere to be found. Dulce cut through the crowd, pushing people out of the way.

CHAPTER
24

ELENA ANTICIPATED POLICE SIRENS AND VESTED AND ARMED officers waiting to lift her off her feet and slam her to the ground, fastening handcuffs on her wrists. But when she made her way to immigration at Heathrow Airport, there was nothing but admiring glances from tired passengers in line—hoping to be released into the late afternoon air, shuffling along one by one as their documents were examined and questions she couldn't quite hear were asked and answered—who mistook her for one of those study-abroad students that they themselves had once been, long ago. Elena was momentarily transported to the Grand Paloma Resort—to the surreal reality that just that morning (*no, that was yesterday morning*), she'd been walking barefoot on the cushiony carpeted floors of a presidential suite, holding hands with an eight-year-old tourist girl who kept asking to be helicoptered around the room. *Faster, higher, faster, higher.*

In the queue for customs and immigration, everything moved mechanically, so frictionless in fact that she became convinced that the man she would eventually reach—for all the workers inside the glass encasements checking passports and visas for visitors were men— would be the one to turn her around, and send her home to Paloma Falls to get locked up.

To her right, beyond the rope that kept her and the other visitors in an organized line, various futuristic-looking screens stood erect, and some lucky travelers—including the big-bellied man who had been her seatmate—stepped into some giant footprints on the worn carpet, staring stoically into a miniature green light before proceeding. There was no need for them to speak to another human being as they made their way out of the customs and immigration area. She believed that in another few years, the men inside the glass encasements who spoke to, smiled at, and welcomed visitors would be a nostalgic memory. Elena, suspended inside that thought as she grasped the cold metallic clasp that held the rope barrier in place, considered what it meant to be alive during a time of such great transition. She was thankful for the person who motioned for her to step forward. She had some hope a human might miss the fact that she was a wanted criminal, a mistake a computer was unlikely to make.

In her distracted state, she missed the hand gestures of the man who was calling to her from inside the glass encasement, and the person behind her stepped past her aggressively, taking her place in front of the available immigration inspector.

Almost immediately, another man called her forward. When she stepped up to the dark-skinned man with glossy hair and wet eyes, he seemed startled to see her. He fumbled her passport, and there was a bit of a scene as he tried to retrieve it in the much-too-small space.

After he managed to get ahold of himself, he began to type rapidly into the computer. Then he raised his eyes, staring with a burning gaze, going back and forth between her real-life face and the image on the computer's monitor. Elena held her breath. She found herself slightly mesmerized by his eyebrows, how softly they met in the center, a few rebellious follicles shooting the tiny hairs in a spiral.

"Elena Moreno?" he asked in a thick British accent.

"My friends call me Lena," she said through a dry throat.

He held her gaze for what seemed like a long time. She wondered if he could tell this was her first time uttering this name when referring to herself. During her layover in New York City's JFK, she had rushed into the bathroom to examine her face, worried that the scratch on her cheek might have started bleeding from all the crying she'd been doing. She had been unnerved to find that it had all but disappeared. In its place, there was a tiny red dot that could have been a birthmark, could have been a trick of makeup to call attention to the indentation of the dimple that would be in that exact spot if she smiled.

"What's the purpose of your visit?" he asked in a businesslike tone that seemed at odds with his love-filled countenance.

"I'm here to work," she croaked. "As an au pair," she added, an image of the blond tourist girl—who'd gone from a rigid blade to a limp rag doll in a matter of a few moments—intruding into her mental résumé. Elena's hands were as clammy as her face.

He asked for some work documents. She produced them. He pretended to read the papers carefully, but she suspected that his gaze was fixed on her photograph. She'd had long, straight hair when she'd taken that photograph six months ago. She'd worn the tiny pearl earrings that Laura had said would make her seem more presentable to whoever would judge whether she should be allowed entry into another country as hired help.

He scribbled something on a piece of paper that he slipped between the pages of her passport, but not without first covering the gesture with an open palm. He didn't look at her as he did it. *Type, type, type.* He typed with only two digits—his pointer fingers. Unlike Laura, who typed furiously, all fingers engaged, and might have used her nose and lips to type faster if she could've managed it. Laura, who always bit down on her lip as her fingers flew over the keyboard. Finally, the man produced a stamp. Pressed it with a loud noise into her brand-new passport. Imprinted on the page was a rectangle with a bright-red set of numbers, granting her entry into this new country—permission to stay for a year before her visa must be renewed. She let out the breath she'd been holding. He smiled at her in a shy way, parting his lips to show her his teeth. His left front tooth was jagged, broken off in a perfect forward slant.

"Hope you enjoy your stay," he said. Then he released a lever, and the glass door ahead of her swung open. Her new life was just a few steps away.

As she moved away from him, she sensed that if he could've, he would've turned to look at her, but already, someone else had taken her place in front of him. She stopped, looking at the piece of paper he'd slipped into her passport, noting his name—Michaelangelo—and the way the numbers he had written down seemed to palpitate. She felt a warmth rising from her stomach. This piece of paper, she decided, would be her lucky charm. She placed it in the exact same position where he had left it for her.

Elena advanced with confidence down the long moving walkway, as if she knew where she was headed. Back at home, she'd been straddling ways of being that never matched up. She'd always been good at motivating people to change their lives, to push against racist, colonialist thinking. She knew that without her, her sister wouldn't have worked as hard for the resort's workers' rights. She would have just bent her neck, grateful for the paycheck, for the migañas that were extended to them both. When their father had disappeared, Laura had begun to lose steam. Elena had suspected something bad might have happened to their father. And that constant worry that he was suffering somewhere, lonely, hungry, and cold, had suffocated Elena, pushing her to reach toward one more pill, just one more pill, so that she could feel light and good. When Laura had asked her to act her age, she'd meant for Elena to act like seventeen-year-old Laura, who'd been a grown, tired adult from the time she was fourteen. Elena didn't think there was anything wrong with taking some pills. All her global academy friends had done much more—they used coke and mushrooms, and some of the wilder kids had tried heroin, meth. She *was* acting her age. Of course, Laura wouldn't know anything about that. She thought having a drink during work hours was wild behavior.

Elena found it difficult to let go of the strain of the past day, even as her body took those big, long strides. There was a heaviness choking at her throat, wrapping itself around her neck, settling at the bottom of her hairline; she wasn't sure that she'd ever be rid of it. She'd been careful not to think about Dulce's girls, but their faces kept intruding on her. What had they done when they'd stepped off the beach? In which direction had they gone? Had the tourist man caught up to them? If he had, had the girls managed to get away from him? During the first leg of her trip, Elena had promised God that she would stop her partying ways, that she would quit drugs in exchange for the girls' safety. If she pushed herself to be a better person, perhaps that would be enough to prevent another catastrophe like the one she'd brought about with the young tourist girl.

Focused on each step, she navigated her way through the airport. Just like at the hotel, there were people from all over the world here. They spoke languages she didn't understand, were determined to arrive at their destinations. She tried to channel that vibe. There was no luggage to retrieve since all she'd brought with her was the small satchel. During the entirety of her journey, she'd kept her phone's Wi-Fi off, worried that if she turned it on, her sister (and maybe the authorities) would be able to track her down. She'd given in only once, when she'd taken a picture of the fluffy clouds from the window seat of the plane. What had possessed her to post the pic? She had deleted it within five minutes. Had taken the last pill she still had in her pocket, deciding to float away in bliss until she arrived in London.

As she'd thought ahead to her plan upon arrival, she'd worried that she'd have to turn her phone's Wi-Fi on to find her friend Socorro. They'd agreed that she'd leave the airport via the baggage claim area, where Socorro would wait for her. But baggage claim was downstairs— with no exit from that floor. To exit the airport, she had to ride an escalator up the equivalent of at least two floors. Her heart began to drum with panic as she made her way up the escalator. What if she didn't find her friend? She'd emailed the agency she'd been in talks with last year to say that she had arrived in London and needed work. They'd responded within a half a blink: Demands for au pairs were at an "all time HIGH." They'd agreed that she would go in on Monday morning. She commanded herself to take a deep breath and calm down. She'd never imagined that it would be this easy to make a new life. And yet, here she was. After starting with nothing, she'd managed to get herself to Europe. She had hidden all her money in an interior compartment of her satchel. She'd never claimed it as she made her way through the various customs procedures and filled out so many forms. Now she held it close to her chest. If worse came to worst, she'd just exchange dollars for pounds and find a hostel to stay at for the night. Maybe she'd have to buy a burner phone, or some other such absurd thing to make sure that no one found her.

Her worries evaporated as soon as she stepped out through the exit.

"Elena!" Socorro screamed from way down the road, exhaling smoke, stepping fast on the cigarette, and ignoring the disapproval of the many people who seemed unprepared for the volume of her voice. Her friend rushed toward her, and when she was close enough to touch, Elena noticed that Socorro had managed to maintain the scent of home—of a wide ocean, of a blue sky, of a breeze that swept most bad things away—after all these years. When that breeze settled, there was the scent of something less pleasant, a gritty funk, a bitter scent that was *also* home. Socorro was taller than Elena had remembered. Her hair, also voluminous, gave her extra height, with perfectly kinky curls that framed her heart-shaped face. She had bright-red lipstick on lips that had obviously been augmented with fillers, nails that glittered in the dim light of the airport's thruway, a button nose, and the wide, unmistakably feline eyes that had earned her the nickname "La Gata."

Elena allowed herself to be folded inside her friend's embrace. It was late afternoon in London on Friday. Despite the many people who were making their way through the exit, the air lacked any scent. But when she nervously wet her lips, Elena tasted something chalky.

"I can't believe you're here, Elena," Socorro said.

"It's Lena, now, I think," Elena said, sounding unsure.

Socorro gave her shoulder a tight squeeze. "See you're wasting no time kicking off the reinvention! Me encanta," she said.

Socorro reached for Lena's small satchel. Lena reluctantly let it go.

"And I thought *I* traveled light," Socorro murmured.

They walked some ways, crossed a road, and entered a building that turned out to be a parking garage. Something seemed off about Lena's friend. She was walking too fast, speaking without pausing to take a breath. In a crowded area where people waited for their rideshares, they wove through suitcases and crying children until they reached a two-door car so small that the front seat had to be folded so they could fit in the back. Socorro entered first. Lena had to enter the car backward, squatting with her ass out. She couldn't quite look at her friend's face. Socorro's long-winded speech had now brought her to the weather in London—how one moment it was warm, then windy, then raining, then cold. But always humid, so you couldn't forget that here, they were also on an island.

"A place with the volatile temperament of a woman," the driver said in English.

The driver had large dreadlocks, but he was fair-skinned. His face was partly obstructed by his hair, though his profile was illuminated by his phone. There was a map on his screen. He murmured something about *el puto trafico,* and Elena heard in his voice that he wasn't Dominican. He was Argentinian. He didn't speak to or acknowledge Elena. *Lena,* she told herself, *you're now Lena.* She flipped through her passport. Maybe she could choose a new name for real? Change herself completely? She fingered the phone number of the immigration inspector, Michaelangelo.

Socorro grabbed the piece of paper out of her hands. "That beautiful smile never fails you," she said. "Whose number is this?"

Lena said something quick about the immigration inspector.

Socorro crumpled the paper and pressed a button on the driver's side of the car door. The glass slid down, disappearing inside the door. Socorro threw the crumpled piece of paper out of the window.

"You didn't come to London to hang out with a broke-ass government worker," she said. "Did you?"

No. She hadn't come to London to hang out with broke men. She'd come to get away from a mistake the size of her life. She wanted to be rid of the infernal heat, of the nagging sound of waves, of the suffocating feeling of Laura's constant disappointment and her insistence that all she wanted was for Elena to get her shit together, to grow the fuck up. She'd come to London to be free.

She thought about Dulce's girls. Imagined the tourist man, with his large hands, hovering over the girls, ripping their clothes off, hurting them. She pushed those terrible thoughts out of her mind. The girls had to be fine. They had to be. She wished that she could open the car door, pick up the piece of paper. What if the girls' survival depended on her having that piece of paper, holding on to a bit of good luck?

"Did you?" Socorro insisted. "Are you here to hook up with broke men?"

"No!" Lena said, telling herself that she didn't need to be superstitious, didn't need a good-luck charm. She would make her own good luck. Yes. She. Would.

"I can't believe you're here. Papi Chulo," Socorro said, speaking to the driver, "when we were girls, we dreamed of moving to Europe. We said, *We're going to leave this damn campo and we're going to be sophisticated and rich women in London.*"

Lena didn't correct her friend. Their plans had never included London. They had spoken of New York, Ibiza, Rio de Janeiro, Paris, Singapore. Never London.

"We're going to have so much fucking fun," Socorro said. "You believe me?"

Lena nodded. Socorro had always been the queen of fun. Lena had never met another person who cared less about what others thought, who truly danced only to her own tune. As if in response, Socorro slipped her hand through the driver's headrest in front of her, caressing his neck. "Put some good music on," she said. "Stop obsessing about traffic. Let's go!"

The man started the car. Maluma's "COCO LOCO" blared from the speakers, starting mid-song. The passengers who were still waiting for their cars hurled annoyed looks. Socorro acted oblivious as she began to sing along, hooking an arm around Lena's neck. Chulo laughed a throaty laugh, and Lena wasn't sure what he found to be so funny. He joined Socorro, singing. He had a great voice. It made her think of Laura, of how much she loved listening to her sister sing.

Lena pretended that it didn't make her feel strange that the driver hadn't yet acknowledged her. She ignored the creeping feeling that maybe the reason he hadn't turned around was because he was greatly disfigured, a lurking, childish fear that insisted that maybe in place of a face he had nothing but taut skin shaped firmly around the bones of his skull.

"Take the long way, Chulo," Socorro said.

The car reversed out of the parking spot and rushed away. Lena finally gave in, singing along to push away scary thoughts of Socorro and her faceless man. She was very tired. Who cared if he was disfigured? It was more likely that the man was just ugly. She was exactly where she wanted to be, and nothing was about to change that. Socorro's arm tightened around her neck, making it hard for her to sing.

Socorro asked her man to give Lena a tour. The long way turned out to be a drive through Piccadilly Circus. The small car curved with agility around the statue that stood small in the grim sky, weaving dangerously in and out of traffic to get as close as possible so Lena could observe it. With its bow and arrow and spread-out wings, a leg off the ground as if it was ready for battle, it gave Lena the sensation that this city understood her. She, like the statue, had taken flight. Lena asked Socorro what the small statue represented.

"Who gives a fuck," Socorro responded, then, as if reconsidering, popped open her smartphone and typed with her left hand while her right arm remained hooked around Lena's neck.

"Anteros is the god of selfless love."

"Just like you, baby," Chulo said.

Socorro grew quiet at that. Unhooked her arm from Lena's neck.

On they went, leaving behind the bright, flashing lights of the giant monitors on the sides of the tall buildings in Piccadilly Circus—a vision that evoked for Lena the image she had of Times Square in New York City from watching way too many YouTube videos. Afterwards, they drove within kissing distance of Westminster Bridge, and Lena was genuinely wide-eyed. This city was jaw-droppingly beautiful, a truly majestic place. Every building stood regal, stained the color of wet sand. There was a soft light that hovered over all things and a grandiosity to the scale of each block that ushered her into a new state. Lena squeezed Socorro's hand in gratitude. Socorro squeezed back, began singing again.

Lena had done nothing wrong. The blond girl had woken up, was right now being entertained by some other babysitter. Niña and Perfecta had gotten away from the pedo, who had never even laid a hand on them. Everybody was fine. Everything was fine. In what world would she have been rewarded with this miracle of a place if she'd actually done something terrible? She'd arrived in a land of queens and kings, princes and princesses.

She felt her stomach grumble. "Can we find something to eat?" she asked Socorro over the loud music.

Socorro continued to sing loudly, ignoring Lena's request. She slipped a hand through the headrest once again, held a thick dreadlock, and wrapped it around her wrist.

CHAPTER
25

THE TWO WOMEN FACED EACH OTHER IN PH7, THE SUITE vacated by the family that Pablo had driven away. When Dulce had demanded that Laura view the video in the lobby, Laura had hit pause immediately. She knew exactly who the guest on that video was. She had told Dulce they could go to the family's room; watch the video up there; look around, even.

Dulce studied Laura as she watched the video. Laura felt the intensity of her glare as she tried to make sense of what she was seeing. As soon as the two-minute clip was over, she hit play again.

The first time she'd watched, she'd been floored, horrified. There was a conversation they couldn't hear that resulted in money changing hands. Then the tourist man left the frame in the direction of the bathroom or the stairs that led to the upstairs apartment. When he left, Elena was still at the bar, speaking to the girls, and everyone was fine. The girls went to the bathroom, swam, returned to the beach, and lingered there for a few moments, then seemed to go off into the distance in response to being called. But they went in the opposite direction from the one in which Elena had gone.

The second time Laura watched the video, she was thinking about liability. God forbid something terrible had happened to the girls, but her sister hadn't been anywhere near them. The video didn't show the guest of the hotel so much as touching the girls. So the hotel, too, was off the hook. Then, reeling at her own coldness, she stared at the girls on the screen. Running, happy. This may have been the last time they were captured alive.

"Can you turn the audio on?" Laura asked.

"No," Dulce said, taking her phone back. "There is no audio."

"I don't know what this video means," Laura said. "That man, he's the father of the kid Elena has been watching at the resort. Maybe he gave her money to buy something? To get him something?"

Laura knew why her sister had taken the money from the man—to run away. Had Elena arranged to meet the man at Dulce's bar? It made no sense. She thought she was responsible for the death of his daughter. Why would she call him? Unless she knew the girl was fine. But there was no recognition in his eyes, no indication that they were talking to each other as if they knew each other. Could it be as simple as the man not knowing it was her, and Elena going along with it? For once, Laura was relieved that these fucking tourists never truly looked at any of them; instead, they looked through them, past them, as if they were just pieces of furniture. Her sister wouldn't have been too surprised that this man, whom she'd been around for a full week, hadn't been able to tell who she was without the context of her uniform, her job. It happened all the time.

"So where is he?" Dulce said, sounding frantic, pacing back and forth.

"Pablo just took them to the Yellow Paloma."

"So why did you bring me up here? If you knew it was him? Why are you wasting time?" Dulce couldn't help the trembling of her hands, how it spread until her entire body was shaking.

"Because the girls weren't in the car with them, Dulce. I figured we might as well start up here, since they're gone."

"I saw them on the road. Maybe we can catch them?" Dulce unlocked her phone, called Pablo.

He didn't answer.

"Call Pablo, ask him to turn back around."

"Sit down," Laura said.

"No, I don't want to sit the fuck down. Call Pablo now, tell him to turn around. If you don't, I'm going to call the police. I'm going to tell Fabien to call the CEO of the hotel."

Laura dialed her own office landline, pretending she was calling

Pablo. She was worried about what the man might say about her sister. She wanted to get to him, but not with Dulce around. When the voicemail picked up, she spoke with authority into the phone.

"Pablo, please call me back as soon as you hear this message. We need you to turn around, come back to the hotel. That's an order."

"Get the man's phone number. Call him directly."

"I have to go to my office for that, log in to the system."

Laura went over to the bar area. She took four sleeping pills and, with a glass, pressed them into powder. She dropped the powder into a glass, poured an ice-cold Presidente into it. She poured the rest of the beer into another glass.

She then placed two pills in the palm of her hand, extended them to Dulce. "Why don't you take these?"

Dulce didn't take the pills. "What? What are they?"

"Sleeping pills. You obviously need some rest."

Dulce threw the phone at Laura, striking her on the chest. It hurt. Surprised, she dropped the sleeping pills on the carpeted floor. The phone slid underneath the couch. Neither woman bothered to pick it up.

"Have you lost your fucking mind?" Dulce shouted. "There's a hurricane coming. My children are out there. You think I'm going to sleep? The man left with Pablo; he didn't take the girls with him. So, they must be here. Somewhere."

Dulce made her way down the hall to the master bedroom. She opened the enormous walk-in closet doors, threw all their clothes on the floor. She moved into the bathroom, slammed open the shower doors. She went back out into the hallway, went into the little girl's room. Dresses had been folded and arranged on top of the dresser by the cleaning staff. Her small sandals had been lined up by the balcony's double doors.

The storm's first lightning bolt lit up outside, illuminating the profile of a palm tree and bringing Dulce's frantic movements to a stop. Half a breath later, the palm tree broke under the force of the wind and rain. There was the sound of water hitting the windowpanes, of the howling wind. For a moment, it was as if a wave had splashed the windows, but they knew the ocean wouldn't reach this floor. It was only rain.

Laura touched the sore spot where the phone hit her with one hand, pointed outside with the other.

"We can't go anywhere right now. Try and get some sleep, and by the time you wake up, the storm will be over. That man will be back. We'll get the police."

Dulce scoffed. "I'm going downstairs. I'll get his number myself."

Laura nodded. "We'll go together," she said. "Let me just get something to drink."

Back in the living room, she grabbed the glass of Presidente she'd poured for herself, drank it. She didn't turn around for several moments. When she finally did, Dulce had drunk the beer she'd served her all in one gulp, as Laura had expected.

"This beer tastes like shit," Dulce said.

"I just need to pee," Laura said, heading down the hallway in the direction of the little girl's bathroom. She took as long as possible before she headed back to the living room.

"There has to be an explanation," Laura said. "Have you spoken to Vida?"

"No," Dulce said. She was sitting on the white couch, her face in her palms. She was crying. "Vida is pregnant. I didn't want to bother her with this."

"Vida would want to help us," Laura said as her eyebrows went up. "I know you're worried sick. But I swear we're going to find the girls. This has to be a big misunderstanding. They're safe and happy somewhere."

Dulce imagined her daughters in a safe place. She envisioned them happy, joyful, even, the way they had been as they'd danced in the rain in the video. Dulce felt her eyelids grow heavy. "If anyone hurt my girls, I will hurt them," she tried to say.

Laura had no idea what the slurred, mumbled words meant. Outside, the noise grew louder and louder. But the pills were so strong that no noise would wake Dulce. At least she would get a bit of rest. Laura held her hand, watched her fall into a deep slumber.

Laura kept wondering if it was possible that the lesson she'd tried to teach her little sister had ended up creating this disastrous situation. If it was true, then that meant Laura was responsible for whatever happened to those girls.

She called her sister again. Then again. There was no voicemail to leave her a message. She wrote her a text. She told her sister that she'd seen the video, that Dulce was at the hotel. Please call me, Elena. You have to tell me where you are. At least let me know that you're OK?

She tried Pablo, this time for real. But he also didn't pick up the phone. The call went directly to voicemail.

Her sister had posted a picture from an airplane. She didn't have many friends abroad. Laura tried La Gata, Elena's old friend who'd moved to London. The call went to voicemail. A moment later, a text came through.

What's up, Laura, La Gata wrote. Can't talk right now.

Is Elena with you? Laura texted back.

No, Elena isn't here, La Gata replied immediately. What's going on?

Laura closed the text box.

On Laura's cellphone, a message lit up from one of her workers: EMERGENCY! EMERGENCY! SOME TOURISTS ARE HEADING TO THE BEACH WITH SURFBOARDS.

Laura covered the sleeping Dulce with a warm blanket. At least she'd be able to get through this day, make some headway, without worrying about Dulce's manic state.

She went downstairs. Out on the beach, she faced the crashing, massive waves and the hurling winds. Farther down the beach, she saw Pasofino motioning for the tourists to come to shore. His voice was lost in the wind. Thoughtlessly, she stepped into the ocean— her hair, lifted all around her in strands frenzied by the wind, lashed her over and over again. The water only reached her knees, but the undertow was strong, pulling her with such force that she lost her footing. When she grabbed at the sand to find equilibrium, she came away with a handful of what she at first thought was seaweed. But it wasn't seaweed. It was an adult-sized red T-shirt sporting the logo of the German soccer team that Fabien loved. It was the T-shirt that

Perfecta had been wearing yesterday. She threw the shirt back in the sea.

She struggled to her feet. Stupefied, she motioned to the surfers to *get off the fucking beach,* screamed at them. But they stayed where they were, ignoring her as if she wasn't there. She made bigger and bigger motions with her arms; it wasn't safe out there. They had to come back ashore. Eventually, Pasofino pulled her out of the water, wrenching her toward the shore. But she refused, held her ground.

"It isn't safe," he said. "They aren't worth it."

She looked back at the tourists, worried. They had selfie sticks, were recording their idiocy. She thought about the T-shirt. Were the girls dead? The girls must be dead. But where were their bodies? What had she done?

"Come on," Pasofino said, gently turning her face, pulling her body. She gave in and let him drag her inside, where one of her team members waited for them both with dry, warm towels.

CHAPTER
26

A S HER HUSBAND SAT NEXT TO THEIR DRIVER, EYES GLUED
to his phone, and their daughter dozed off—an expected crash
after the excitement of preparing for the visit to the other resort—
Sophie was thankful that they'd picked the Grand Paloma as their
destination. She hadn't been there for nine years, not since she'd
worked there the first year it had been open, and found it hard to believe that the Grand Paloma Resort remained so posh and crystalline
after a decade, the period after which most resorts began to show their
seams. But the leadership had doubled down on replacing furniture
and upgrading materials; even the manicured lawns and trees were
maintained with a level of care she'd hardly seen at any of the dozens
of Paloma resorts she'd visited. She couldn't understand how it made a
profit. Of course, the company paid no rent and no taxes for the real
estate. The government had kicked the locals off the land without paying them a cent, telling them that there would be so much work available that they'd never even miss that land. They paid the local workers
a pittance. No surprise there. If they remained open, it was because
they were making money.

That first year, they'd practically given away reservations. It had
been a strategy designed to create the buzz they needed among the
very wealthy. And it had worked. As a client satisfaction associate,
she'd spent very little time outside of the resort grounds. It had only
been an eighteen-month stint in the Caribbean region—her territory
had included Jamaica, Turks and Caicos, and the Dominican Republic.
Back then, she'd been focused on ensuring that whatever their guests
needed, she provided. From Oscar de la Renta gowns with a day's no-

tice to helicoptering a couple around waterfalls, mountains, or insert any other beautiful setting for an impromptu birthday surprise, she'd learned that there was pretty much nothing a rich person couldn't get if they wanted it. Back then, Sophie had gotten such a rush from solving any problem and meeting any desire, no matter how outrageous. It had filled her with pride, knowing she was able to get shit done.

When the Oscar de la Renta–clad woman had decided she wasn't quite ready to say yes to a lifetime of marriage, the would-be fiancé had been left in a presidential suite by himself. Sophie had decided to bring him some drinks, to listen to what she'd anticipated to be the laments of a heartbroken man. Instead, she'd found him calm, unfazed. She'd been alarmed, then pleased. He had become her husband.

Though the roads they drove on were wide and smooth, the asphalt still pitch-black, with electronic road signs that blinked in English about safety hazards, the land they drove past seemed like something out of *Condé Nast Traveler*. It stretched everlasting, uninhabited, desolate, and peaceful in a way that defied the present year.

Pablo drove fast. He maneuvered through the sharp, treacherous turns with an agility that was thrilling to watch, nerve-racking to experience. Next to her, Peanut slept hard, a little bit of drool dripping onto her chin. She had won. They'd reach the water park with plenty of daylight to spare, and she'd plummet down slides as tall as the fifth-story window she looked out of at home on Central Park East in New York City.

Sophie's husband seemed to be elsewhere, staring out the window for the many hours they'd been on the road. Even when they'd made a quick bathroom stop some time ago, he'd remained distracted. By this point in their trips, he was usually calm, satisfied. But whatever he wanted, he hadn't yet gotten. She could tell by how tense and perturbed he remained. She was determined to get him a good time. These trips calmed him, made him happy in a way nothing else did. It used to be other women that did it for him, until she'd discovered his infidelities. He'd anticipated outrage, an expensive divorce, but Sophie had been relieved. She'd never believed in monogamy, had often grown bored in relationships. What others saw as a clear ending, she'd seen as the beginning of their real life. Released from the need to hide and lie, they'd become free to be their true selves. Of course, it had been difficult to make it work. They'd tried bringing in a third—Sophie also enjoyed sex with women. But it had always ended in some sort of drama. It had taken a while for them to figure out that it was a matter of getting on a plane. Living wild and free for a couple of weeks until they could do it again.

Sophie felt billowed with tranquility by the changing landscape—from the blur of the ocean to that lush mountain to canopies of trees that made everything darker, cooler. It was almost as if she were alone in the car—well, alone in a way where the only two people who mattered were her and the driver who would get her to their destination. And to think her mother had warned her not to travel to the Dominican Republic. *There are robberies every day, kidnappings. People get shot in the head for used sneakers,* her mother had said. She'd reminded her mother that the same had been true when she'd lived here. Nothing bad had ever happened to her. Still, her mother's warnings had played and replayed in her mind during the early part of their trip, mainly because of Peanut. Though she was meant to stay on the resort grounds with the nanny, Sophie had worried that something terrible would happen to them during one of their adventures. She had locked away the obscene amount of cash they'd snuck into the country, unscrewed her diamond-studded earrings, and removed her engagement ring and her wedding bands—she wore three of them on her ring finger, as was the trend on the Upper East Side. She'd taken her husband's Hublot watch—a gift for their most recent anniversary—and had folded it among his socks, then locked it away in the safe.

He'd reminded her why they traveled when they did. There was a restlessness that would make them both miserable if they didn't let it out here. They had booked the twenty-four-hour babysitter, determined to leave the resort. She'd been surprised that he hadn't given the pretty girl a second look—but she had a bald head, that gap between her teeth. Not his type.

On their first trip off the resort, they'd gone to a local cantina (*bayou,* corrected the bartender, a British expat who reminded her she wasn't in Mexico) at the recommendation of her husband's best friend, who'd been coming to the region for the past five years. They'd fucked the most beautiful Black woman Sophie had ever seen in her life. A woman who'd spread Sophie's legs with a playfulness that seemed genuine and planted a soft kiss through her underwear right on that magic spot, then used her teeth to pull Sophie's lacy thong down, off.

There had been many adventures over the last week, all centered around more beautiful women with deep cacao skin tones. And not once had they faced an unpleasant moment. Even the arrests had proved to be a minor inconvenience.

Sophie pressed the button to lower the window, her diamond rings glittering in the sunlight as she pushed against the pressure of the wind. Her earrings were fastened in place. Her purse was on the floor by her French-manicured feet. She wasn't scared to travel through this alluring land. Outside, beyond her splayed fingers, the vibrant forest thickened. The canopy obscured the sky. She began to say something to her husband, but just then, he made small sounds in his throat. Someone at work was getting on his nerves. Better to leave him alone for now.

Next, they drove through a flat, arid, desertlike land, where the torched grass, nearly as blond as her hair, remained stiff and unmoving. The dust lifted off the ground in swaths the width of bedsheets, moving with delicacy. She felt the gritty sensation of dirt on her hands. Within moments, Pablo cleared his throat.

"You have to close the window," he said. The humidity outside had made all the windows foggy.

"Oh, oops," she said, closing the window.

She asked Pablo why this part of the country was so different. He responded that the scorched land was a result of the drought, the increase in temperatures, the relentless sun. He explained that during the pandemic, many farmers had died, and much of the land had been abandoned.

"But the grass at our hotel is so green," she said.

"It takes an ocean's worth of water to keep it that way," he said, then looked at her, as if worried he'd said the wrong thing.

Off in the distance, there were clusters of trees that remained verdant by some miracle of the land. She took her phone and snapped pictures of them, learned from Pablo that the most resilient of the trees were the species that bore mangoes and oranges. She couldn't catch a glimpse of her husband, who had moved his body forward and to the side at an angle that made it impossible for her to reach him. His body posture told her he was irked at how much she was speaking to the driver.

They drove on in silence for a long time. Through the years that they'd been taking their *pleasure vacations,* as they referred to them, she had wondered if maybe when he insisted on taking a day or two to explore the exotic locales they visited on his own, he went away to fuck other men. Though he'd never showed any interest in men, he really enjoyed ass play and was unapologetic about asking her to penetrate him with various-sized toys. But when she'd asked him if he wanted them to bring a man home the last time they'd been in Curaçao, he'd shaken his head.

About an hour later, she typed the name of the Yellow Paloma into her phone's GPS app, just to make sure they weren't being kidnapped. It would be just like her to be so taken and distracted by the tropical landscape that she'd lose sight of the situation and only figure out what was going on when it was too late.

The app made an obnoxious sound, alerting her that they were an hour away.

Sophie gasped, embarrassed. Her husband chuckled. Even Pablo smiled, and his entire face was so warm that she got a sudden yearning to touch him. He threw her a knowing glance, and she wondered whether it was because he was used to his passengers double-checking that he wasn't abducting them or if the smile was meant to be a signal between them, while her husband's nose remained buried in his phone.

They neared some brightly painted homes that were right up against the road. She wondered why people would choose to place their houses so close to the noise and pollution of a busy street like this one, especially when they had the option to be seaside, or up in the mountains.

"Where are we now?" she asked Pablo.

"Close. We're about an hour from La Línea Fronteriza, the border between Haiti and DR. We should arrive at the hotel in less than an hour."

He didn't say anything about the 224-mile border being divided by the Massacre River. She appreciated that he didn't get political. Even as they'd passed through cities where various sweeps were gathering and forcefully pushing Black people who didn't look that different from him, he'd acted as if nothing alarming was happening. As if it was no big deal that children were being roughly thrown into the backs of immigration vans, that the cries of their mothers were met with closed fists to the face. She appreciated Pablo's commitment to their peaceful transit.

She'd googled all of it once, asking her handheld device to explain what was happening in the Dominican Republic. Quickly, she'd learned about the collapse of the government in Haiti after the president had been assassinated a couple of years ago. About the mass exodus from Haiti to its neighbor, to other nearby islands, to the United States. She'd turned off her phone. It was a terrible shame to be a spectator of so much suffering, but they had yet to visit an island where they weren't bystanders to some tragic display of poverty. Who was she kidding? Even back home in the United States, Haitians were mass-deported regularly. She recalled some barbaric image of a man on horseback, a lash loose in the air, and a terrified Black man running for his life. What had been happening on the other side of Hispaniola was a humanitarian crisis so large, so seemingly without end, that there was little to do but look the other way.

But as she watched the passing scenery, it was easy to pretend that nothing ugly had occurred there. What dominated the landscape was red soil and a completely clear sky. On the radio, the announcer spoke of the approaching hurricane, which was headed east. Her husband had been uneasy that morning, had said that maybe they should try to beat the storm and head home.

But we've got six days left, she'd reminded him.

We've had our fun, he'd said.

No, she'd said, staring blatantly at all those scratches on his face, the scratches he'd not explained, *you've had your fun. I'm owed some real fun before we go.*

As you wish, he'd said. He had been cold and removed with her since. She knew their unspoken agreement required that she look the other way, not ask questions, acquiesce to whatever he did without her by never peeking too hard. By tipping the right people when the situation required it. In return, he protected her, took care of her, made sure her needs were always met.

She imagined that this was why he'd requested a male companion. Maybe he just wanted her to get her fill and then head home. Or maybe she could persuade him that she would feel no shame if he wanted to have sex with a man. They had never had sex with a man before.

"Aren't we lucky we left today?" she said. "It's supposed to be bad back by Paloma Falls."

Her husband sped up his thumb-typing, as if making the point that he didn't have time for her small-talk nonsense.

Sophie stretched out a hand and squeezed his shoulder. She was sure that if he just told her who was responsible for his scratched face, he'd be less irritated. Honoring their yearslong agreement, Sophie didn't push, didn't ask. She'd just stay out of his way. When she'd told him that he might as well stay behind at the Grand Paloma while she and Peanut went to the Yellow Paloma, he'd seemed uneasy. She imagined that all her mother's nagging about crime had gotten to him, too.

Pablo waited for Sophie's husband to respond to the comment that had so clearly been meant for him. When he didn't, Pablo shot Sophie a pitying look and then, because of her clear displeasure, quickly refocused on the road.

Sophie felt her skin burn.

Are you going to tell me what the fuck is going on with you? she texted her husband.

He sent her a thumbs-down emoji.

"Might have been cool to see the hurricane," her daughter said. Sophie jumped. She hadn't realized that the child was awake.

"How much longer?" her daughter asked in the direction of the driver as she stretched her arms over her head.

Pablo craned his neck backward. "We're close. Should be there in half an hour or less if we don't find donkeys on the road."

Her daughter laughed. "I want to see a donkey."

"Then we'll find a donkey," her husband said.

"I'm thirsty," her daughter said.

"We need to get her something to drink," her husband said to Pablo.

Sophie pulled her daughter into her arms, where she sighed dramatically and tried to whisper but ended up shouting, "WE'VE BEEN IN THIS CAR FOREVER, MAMA."

Sophie nodded, then turned her attention back outside. They were driving past a small village. There were zinc-roofed wooden shacks and children walking in small groups, wearing blue shirts and khaki skirts and short pants, their hair neatly braided and their knees ashy. On the side of the road that they rounded as they turned, skinny cows lingered near crowds of men—so many men—who leaned on motorcycles as they sucked on cigarettes, blaring bachata from someone's portable speaker. This didn't seem like a scene out of a third-world country. The men had strong, lean bodies, long necks, thick lips. They wore bulky gold jewelry on their necks and chunky rings on their fingers. Some of them had grills on their teeth with jewels that rivaled the glitter of the diamonds on her rings.

The men outside all wore flashy luxury-brand shirts—Gucci, Prada, YSL. The ones who had buttons had left most of them undone to show hairless, muscled chests. Pablo stopped the car, blared the horn. Ahead of them, a group of small boys was playing baseball in the middle of the road. They weren't dressed in school uniforms.

"I'm dying of thirst," her daughter whined.

"It's probably best that we go directly to the resort," Pablo said, pushing down on the horn with more insistence. "We're very close."

"I'm going to die," her daughter said.

Some of the boys turned toward them. They yelled, made obscene gestures. Sophie noticed that they sported the aggressive expressions usually seen on old men.

"We need to get her something to drink," her husband repeated, irritated that he'd had to repeat himself.

Pablo explained that they had water in a cooler in the back, that he'd be happy to pull over once they were past this village. There was an obvious strain on his features.

"She doesn't want water," her husband said. "Get her a Coke. There's a grocery store right at that corner." He pointed behind them, where less than half a block away the group of men leaned on motorcycles.

"No problem," Pablo said. "Please don't come out of the car," he added as he left them and locked the door behind him.

"MAMAGUEVO," one of the kids yelled at him as he made his way to the store.

The next few moments moved very slowly, and then alarmingly fast.

Out of nowhere, a donkey attempted to cross the road, right by the group of boys. The donkey had an enormous belly. Her husband, on seeing the donkey, told their daughter, "Oh, look, your donkey."

Her daughter, on seeing the donkey, let out an excited yelp.

"Can we go pet it, Daddy?"

"Sure," he said. "Let's just wait for the driver to come back."

"We probably shouldn't pet animals out in the wild like that," Sophie said.

One of the boys took his bat and held it overhead, but struck the donkey right in the belly with his foot. The donkey let out a painful screeching sound before it collapsed. Her daughter was out of the car and running toward the boy with the bat before Sophie knew what had happened. The car had no child lock. The door had opened as soon as she'd pulled the handle.

Sophie called out her husband's name in panic.

He was slow to react, so she jetted out of the car. Her husband then followed her as she ran toward her daughter.

The sun brightened, and Sophie felt outside of herself. All the boys stood very still, watching them with their old-man eyes. The men from the corner, with their gauche clothes and sparkling jeweled teeth, began to walk toward them. There were some women who looked out of windows from homes that were close to the road. The women looked at the family with a mix of anger and annoyance, yelling at the children. Sophie hoped that they were telling the boys to leave the donkey alone.

Her daughter had reached the boy and was yelling at him through tears to stop it, to leave the donkey alone. Her husband had somehow maneuvered around Sophie, reached their daughter, and pulled her away from the donkey, who was on the ground braying, and away from the boy, who still held the bat above his head, ready to strike. The boy turned his entire body in the direction of her husband and daughter, slowly. Her husband then quickly overpowered the boy, took the bat from him, and held it ready—as if to hit him.

Some shit was about to go down and Sophie knew it would end terribly. But then Pablo stuck his fingers in his mouth and whistled—a piercing, high-pitched sound. When she turned toward him, she saw that he had a gun in his hand, which he held casually with the same arm under which two bottles of Coca-Cola were nestled.

He walked over to them and handed Sophie the sodas. "Please, go back to the car," he said, not taking his eyes off the boys.

Her husband seemed unable to move, frozen in place with the bat overhead. Sophie moved with trembling legs until she reached them, took her daughter's hand. She tried not to run, even though that was all her body wanted to do. As she passed her husband, she gave him a little nudge to get him moving. They needed to get inside the car.

Some of the men from the corner were suddenly advancing toward them, right arms folding toward their lower backs. Pablo reached for the bat as he asked her husband to go back to the car. From the car, Peanut screamed in the direction of the boys.

"Please, don't hurt the donkey," she said.

Pablo didn't turn toward the men, or Peanut's screeching voice. He raised the gun toward the sky. There were scars that roped his fingers and forearm, a toughness to his body that she hadn't noticed before. The donkey managed to get on her feet. She made her way back the way she'd come, sluggishly, down a small alleyway between two wooden houses.

"No estamos buscando problemas," Pablo said. "Yo solo necesito depositar estas personas extrangeras al Yellow Paloma."

Drawing on the little Spanish she knew, Sophie hurriedly translated. "'We don't want any trouble,'" she whispered. "'I'm taking these foreigners to the resort.'"

The men looked Pablo up and down, and then, as if recognizing something familiar in his features, one of the men made a quick motion with his wrist to the boys. They ran off the road in the direction the donkey had gone. Some of the men crossed their arms at chest level; others headed back to their corner. The women who had been looking out of their windows turned away.

Back in the car, Pablo pulled off the curve smoothly. His hands didn't tremble, not in the slightest. Sophie was certain that had it come to it, he would have taken the shot to keep them safe. Whereas her husband would have escalated things in a manner that would have likely gotten them all killed. He'd plopped himself in the seat next to her, as if too ashamed to continue to ride up front with Pablo. There was a tremor on his cheekbone that he quickly hid with his sunglasses. For the remainder of their married life, Sophie knew she would never forget that her husband had hesitated to leave the car to protect their daughter.

"Will those boys hurt the donkey?" her daughter asked Pablo, weeping.

"No," Pablo said, his voice as smooth as his hands on the steering wheel. "The boys kicked the donkey to get her off the road. Some farm animals get killed by drivers because they don't know better. Sometimes what looks like cruelty is care."

"There has to be a better way than kicking her," Peanut insisted.

Pablo didn't respond to that. Instead, he bit his lip as he concentrated on accelerating the car. Sophie noticed that Pablo had a nice mouth. Full, meaty lips. Her daughter leaned back, unsure. The weeping became sniffles. She twisted the cap off her soda, and the satisfying pop of the released fizz filled the interior of the car.

Thank God for Pablo, she texted her husband. He read the text, then stared blatantly at Pablo with such intensity that Pablo eventually turned his attention to him, a look of confusion mixed with dread on his face. When her husband wouldn't break the eye contact, Pablo refocused on the road. He stepped hard on the gas and the engine revved. He fidgeted with the screen, hit some buttons to bring up a playlist. The sounds of "Hotel California" by the Eagles boomed before he lowered the volume. *Some dance to remember, some dance to forget.*

I think you might be right, Sophie wrote to her husband after he still didn't respond to her text. We should probably try to head back home early.

Her husband turned his attention back to his phone, and she felt his body relax against hers as he read and began responding to emails from work. Pablo met her eyes in the rearview mirror and offered her a small smile, as if saying, *Everything will be fine.* An unfamiliar current of desire wove its way from her rapidly beating heart down to the center of her body. Sophie smiled back.

CHAPTER
27

THERE WERE THRASHING BRANCHES HITTING THE DIRT OF HER
garden. There were incoming then retreating sheets of rain splashing the windowpanes. Vida's eyelids parted slowly. She struggled to see
in the darkness around her. It took several moments to place herself in
her living room, facing the door to her backyard, which had somehow
flown open and kept banging against the wall. It was that frightening
sound that had pulled her from unconsciousness. How had she made
it back from the bathroom?

Outside, beyond the rain and wind, there was a faint white illumination. *The moon must be full, no clouds on the way,* she thought. Which
was illogical in a storm of this magnitude.

She attempted to push herself up and found that the couch cush-
ions she pressed against were wet, just as wet as the front of her dress.
Puzzled, she felt chunky bits, and the scent of vomit filled her mouth.
In between her legs, a rush of moisture. She reached down, brought it
to her nose, hoping it was urine, pero no, immediately she recognized
the sweet scent of iron-loaded blood. *Oh, no.*

She stood up and had to sit back down immediately. The dizziness
knocked her over.

"Robot," she shouted into the void. "Turn on all the lights."

The robot did its work, and her entire house became bright, turning
the outside into the throat of a cave.

She saw the mess she'd made when she first came home. She'd
stumbled, and several of her house plants had tipped over, dirt and
roots now displayed. She remembered taking some food out of the

refrigerator, food that was now rancid as it sat on the island of her kitchen. How long had she been out?

"What's the day and time?" she asked aloud, but the speaker-robot wouldn't answer unless she called its name.

"Robot, what's the day and time?" she repeated.

"It's Friday, 5:25 P.M.," the computer said.

She'd been out of it for the better part of a day.

From outside, the sound of padding feet got closer and then was swallowed again by the turbulent wind.

Vida's dead mother appeared in the doorway. Vida brought her wet fingers to her eyelids, rubbed. Her mother came over and squatted right by her face, overwhelming her with the scents that were only hers: nutmeg and the sweetness of sugarcane.

"Ta fea pa la foto," her mother said, her breath a gust of bitter coffee and wet earth.

Vida tried to speak but couldn't. Was she already dead? Her mother turned from her, told her she needed to sleep. "I'm going to make a remedy for you, to cure you," her mother said.

Her mother spoke aloud to herself, the way she used to when she was alive. She mentioned all the ingredients she needed, the sequence that needed to be followed for the remedy to work. This was how her mother had instructed her, by doing exactly what she would normally do while articulating her every step. Vida wanted to ask her mother to slow down. She needed to remember this.

"Do you know these plants? Will you be able to find them in the dark?" her mother asked in that same abrupt tone.

Vida didn't think she could stand up and follow these instructions. Then there was a blur of motion. Her mother wasn't speaking to her. Dulce tried to focus her vision, understand what she was seeing. There was a girl, a small girl who resembled Dulce's oldest. But what was she doing here? And why would she be by herself?

The girl said yes, she knew the plants, how to pull them from the earth without disturbing the roots, at what stage of budding they needed to behead the flowers. Back when she'd been alive, Vida's mother had spent countless Freedom Days teaching all the children about plants, about how one could survive in the wild if it ever came to that. She remembered bringing Dulce's girls with her. It was the legacy of their people, who had traveled so far in boats to be free. *It would have been terrible to have escaped death at the hands of the enslavers only to die because of mosquito bites or other complications to do with their very frail bodies*, Doña Fella, their teacher, used to say, walking alongside Vida's mother.

Her mother bent down to Vida, kissed her on her forehead with those tough lips, then walked right out through the back door, pulling it shut behind her.

Vida attempted to stand again and again felt the rush of nausea pin her down.

A chill ran from the bottoms of her feet to her forehead, made her break out in a cold sweat. She felt very small, as if she were a child, shivering and feverish, hoping everything would be okay. As if concocted by this last thought, she heard the sounds of children outside, muffled yet somehow unmistakable—running bare feet on the muddy road.

She closed her eyes. She wished that Pablo was here with her, that he'd appear to her in this dream-hallucination. Why didn't her mind give her what she really wanted? Maybe because things never quite worked out according to what she wanted. After all, she didn't think it had been too much to ask Pablo to give up his whoring ways. Such a simple desire. Just the two of them, making a small life, taking care of the land around them, lovingly raising half a dozen children. Her mother had once told her that dreams were powerful. That sometimes, the solution you sorted out in a dream remained the solution when you woke up.

Speaking to that faraway place, she asked her mother if her baby would be okay. Bodiless, her mother responded.

"My grandson will be just fine. But you came close to losing him. Don't be that stupid again."

Leave it to her mother to be firm and direct, even in death.

CHAPTER
28

FOR THE FIRST TIME IN MANY DAYS, VIDA WAS THE FURTHEST thing from Pablo's thoughts. When he and the tourist family reached the presidential suite at the Yellow Paloma, Pablo pretended familiarity with the babysitter as he made introductions to put the nerve-racked family at ease. He understood his job in a deeper way. At the Grand Paloma Resort, they'd been trained how to go about rescuing someone's stay—and he'd often assumed that would be necessary after someone had fallen ill due to undercooked or contaminated food or had had an unpleasant encounter with a local outside the resort. But as the babysitter rushed to get the girl into a swimming suit and they headed out to the water park, the parents didn't move off the couch. Neither had taken a step toward the balcony to stare at the approaching pink sunset, nor had they inquired about their spa credits or asked him to schedule their treatments. They both sat on the couch, not speaking, not moving, obviously waiting for him to leave them alone. He understood that it would be disastrous for them to speak to each other about what had just happened without him there to help them reframe. Rescuing their stay meant rescuing the resort.

Unbeknownst to Pablo, this was the closest he'd ever come to understanding his bosses' mentality. Because it wasn't just *this* couple that would likely never return to the Grand Paloma Resort or this island, but everyone in their circle. Each time the experience was revisited, it would become more grotesque, incalculably scarier. Soon enough, the mere mention of this island, of the Caribbean as a whole, would evoke in this family and their friends a vision of gunslinging children ready to City-of-God any tourists who dared set foot on their land straight to hell. Pablo understood that he had a small window in which to act, influence, correct their narrative. Thank God that just then, they were too shocked to tell him to go.

Pablo felt a momentary respite from his loneliness, from the heartbreak he'd been battling. He, an ambassador, was responsible for safeguarding the sanctity of his homeland. What did he have at his disposal? Only a Diamond-rated playground called a resort, and his body.

Pablo called downstairs, asked for two pitchers of Paloma Palomas to be brought to the room—along with an extra bottle of mezcal on a serving tray with all the ingredients to keep the party going. The drinks came insanely fast. He'd just turned on some Maluma and, hoping for some subliminal messages, played "Borro Cassette." He unbuttoned his shirt and served them all shots—pa'bajo, pa'arriba, pa'fuera, pa'dentro. Without pressuring the couple in any way, he began to dance, moving his hips, and with the infectious energy of a good beat, he actually began to feel better.

The drinks did their work. The wife's face flushed red. The husband removed his Gucci loafers. Her shoulders started moving from side to side with surprisingly spot-on rhythm. Pablo gestured to the husband, asking if it was okay for him to ask the lady to dance. By way of a response, the husband leaned his athletic body backward and spread his arms on the oyster bouclé couch to watch.

Pablo kept a respectable distance from the woman, who kept breaching it. She turned away from him and dug her ass into his groin. Coughing, Pablo moved away from her, extended a hand toward the husband to join. The husband narrowed his gaze, a soft, surprised smile playing on his features as he stared at his drunk wife. He shook his head at Pablo, made some motion with his arms to indicate that they should keep dancing, and stood.

"How about another round of shots?" the husband said.

The wife removed her oversized cotton button-down shirt after she took that shot. Underneath it, she wore a delicate silk chemise the color of the inner curve of a seashell, the color of her tongue as it wetted her lips. She wasn't wearing a bra. Her nipples were erect—maybe from dancing, maybe from desire. Pablo was astonished when she leaned close enough to him that he could feel those hard buds through the soft fabric. He was even more stunned when she leaned up and kissed him full on the lips. It happened so unexpectedly that he kissed her back without thought. It was a few seconds before he came to himself, stepping away from her, bracing himself for the husband rising off the couch and punching him on the jaw. But when he looked at the white couch, the husband was gone. The wife pulled Pablo to her once again, biting his bottom lip, taking his hand in hers and slipping it under that soft chemise to touch her soft, barely there breasts. He let his body do what it knew to do, easily discarding the shirt, pinching her, returning the bite on her shoulder, leaving a trail of spit as his tongue took that little bud and flicked it. That trail raised delicious goosebumps on her skin. Sophie moaned. From down the hall, Pablo heard the husband's voice call out to them both.

"Come to bed," the husband said.

The wife walked ahead, leading the way. She threw her arm back, the pinky of her left hand a hook, all those diamond rings on her ring finger sparkling under the overhead lights. The move was so coordinated that it seemed like she'd done it many times before. Pablo instinctively let his pinky strike hers. From somewhere far in the past, he heard the ocean lapping against his old boat. He ignored it.

This night would prove to be the worst and most painful sexual experience of his life. But just then, Pablo didn't know it. He merely thought, *I can't believe I get paid for this. I can't believe this is my job.*

CHAPTER
29

ENA FIGURED THAT THEY WERE IN A DIFFERENT PART OF London because the streets narrowed and curved under fluorescent lighting. There was nothing soft about this place. The colors were all wrong, too vulgar. Storefronts alternated yellow awnings with red letters, blue awnings with white writings, white awnings with yellow words. All of it incoherent and loud. The buildings themselves were just as abhorrent. White brick next to red stone next to a brown building. Chulo pulled into a narrow alleyway, and they exited the car to find themselves in complete darkness. Lena grabbed her satchel and held on to it with a fierce grip, careful to not touch the car or the walls of the building around it. It all had a damp, slimy look to it.

When they reached upstairs, a giant pair of wooden doors gave way to a massive room. Everywhere Lena looked there were pairs of people—sitting on giant pillows, dancing close, drinking, laughing. Farther away, smaller groups hung around a foosball table; next to them were a few people with bent heads, snorting powder from mirrors. But the place smelled sweet, heavy with cinnamon and spices. There were some mattresses off in a corner, and under sets of sheets, there were a few couples fucking. Men with men. Women with women. Men with women.

"This is where you live?" Lena asked, dazed.

Socorro nodded, pulled her the other way. Chulo had disappeared.

"Do all these people live here?" Lena asked.

"Some stay, some go," Socorro said. "Everyone here is from somewhere else," she added. "Some documented, some not. Most don't have anyone else in the world. We're not blood family but something stronger than family. People who earn each other through hardship and loyalty, know what I mean? Way deeper than those assholes most of us inherit at birth. These are my true gifts. Familia de hueso. Chulo and I have an open-door policy. Those who stay find a way to contribute. Those who only need a place to crash are always welcome."

Lena's face broke into a smile, a genuine one, for the first time. This sounded like the corniest, cheesiest thing she'd ever heard. But when she focused on Socorro and saw how her big brown eyes were about to spill real tears, she understood that it wasn't a joke.

Lena knew that Socorro had been estranged from her family for a long time. When she'd come to work at the Grand Paloma Resort, she'd confessed to Lena that she was only fifteen, even though she'd somehow managed to get papers that said she was twenty-one. They'd bonded immediately, not just because they were the same age but because they had similar dispositions. They wanted to have fun and enjoy life to the fullest, but they also had a strong conviction about being agents of change. It was clear that Socorro and Chulo had created a truly safe place for people who needed it. Socorro had lived up to her destiny, to be the change she wanted to see in the world, like Mandela had said. At least, Lena thought it was Mandela who had said it.

"This is beautiful," Lena said.

Socorro introduced her to people, dozens of people, and Lena knew that she would retain not a single name. By the time they went through another set of wet wooden doors, Lena was wondering how she'd ever get any sleep in a place like this. On the other side of the slimy walls was a large industrial kitchen with many ovens on one wall, and there was a sour smell of yeast in the air. But the source of the scent was actually just ahead. A pretty, slender guy, maybe fifteen or sixteen years old, was flipping donuts in a big cast-iron pan. His fingernails were the same glittering gold as Socorro's.

"Perfect timing," he said in Portuguese. He had a pierced septum with a thin chain that hooked onto his bottom lip. He took a still-steaming malassada that he had already started eating from a nearby plate and pushed it toward Socorro. Chocolate or Nutella spilled out as soon as she took a bite.

Socorro swallowed, closed her eyes, moaned in pleasure.

"Padre eterno," she said. She blew on the donut, then brought it to Lena's mouth. Lena didn't like eating things that other people had bitten into, but she understood that Socorro would be insulted if she rejected the offering. She opened her mouth, took a small bite, and murmured her compliments, even as she felt the delicious fried dough burn her tongue.

Lena noticed a couple in a corner. The woman was wearing a skirt, but it was obvious she was riding the man, that they were having sex.

"Is that hygienic? People having sex so close to where you're cooking?" she asked.

"Who thinks sex is dirty in this day and age?" Gold Nails said, flipping another malassada in the pan.

Socorro studied Lena carefully. "Someone who still hasn't done it. Still pining for Pablo? Waiting to see if he'll give in to your crush?"

Lena's face burned red. When you'd lost enough in a lifetime, it got easier to travel light. Lena remembered Pablo's left clavicle, how the place where the bone protruded was also where he had a birthmark—a perfectly round dot. When he had gently pushed her away a few months ago, right after Vida had broken up with him, she'd noticed the birthmark for first time. *El, you're a girl. I'm a grown man. You're like a sister to me.* She had noticed the finality of that shape, had understood why that mark had been chosen as the symbol for a full stop. The circular outline might have gone on indefinitely except for the absolute silence of the blackness that consumed its heart.

"Don't be ridiculous," Lena said, laughing as she saw the woman in the corner throw her head back in ecstasy. "I'm so over Pablo."

After her stomach was about to burst from the half a dozen giant malassadas full of Nutella, Lena grew drowsy. Socorro offered her a cocktail, and she quickly gulped it down. Through wireless speakers, someone began to play "People" by Libianca. She didn't want to cry today, the first day of her real independence, but she felt disoriented and on the cusp of tears. That song made her feel lonely.

"You're just jet-lagged," Socorro said, then offered her some edibles; she chewed a bunch and picked the elastic residue from between her teeth.

Lena asked Socorro for ecstasy and Socorro went to find some.

It seemed like it was only seconds later that Socorro shook her roughly, pulled her from the couch. She'd drifted off to sleep.

They walked far away from everyone else to a place with a coffee table that was low to the ground. There was a mirror with lines of coke. Socorro bent her head. When she raised it, a couple of lines had disappeared.

She pulled Lena toward her so she could go next. Lena had never done coke. She stared at the snowy substance, which was not so different-looking from the sugar that had coated the malassadas. She bowed her head and took a deep inhale with each nostril, first one, then the other, noticing that the drug had no real smell. A nasty bitterness coasted down her throat, settling on her tongue.

Lena's drowsiness left her.

The warehouse was now packed with people, and some of those she'd met earlier in the night kept coming by, chatting with her. People wore crop tops and short-shorts, ass cheeks hanging out of the shredded denim, their skin luminous with sweat. They had beautiful smiles, even the ones who had rotten or crooked teeth. From far in the past, the image of her mother smiling came to her. Her mother, who had had the same gap-toothed smile that Lena had inherited.

Someone pulled her to dance. They were now playing Bob Marley songs in honor of her, their Caribbean newcomer. Socorro had disappeared. Lena danced a little, for a long time, and then with a start realized that she didn't see her satchel. She rushed back to her chair and was relieved to find it there. When someone else came to ask her to dance, she said no, clutching her bag.

Lena became worried that if she fell asleep again, someone might take her satchel. She had to find a safe place to hide her money.

She slid down from her chair to the floor. She treated the satchel as a pillow and put her head on it. She stared at the illuminated time on her phone, trying to calculate the hours and minutes. She'd left home and now she was here and it was five hours ahead in London. It would be just after ten P.M. at home.

Socorro appeared with the slender, pierced cook. She looked terribly pleased with herself. They each took one of Lena's arms, sat her up as if she were a rag doll. Socorro gave her a pill.

"I'm so tired," Elena said.

"You'll sleep when you're dead," Socorro said, and laughed.

Lena laughed, too, even though she thought that the dead probably had no need for sleep. She tried to remember her dead mother's smile again, but the face that kept coming was Laura's. No matter how hard she tried, she couldn't concoct the image of her mother. Lena allowed herself to feel her feelings. She was sad. She was scared. She reached inside her bag, took her phone out, turned the Wi-Fi on. Socorro shared the password that enabled her connection to the world. Lena didn't care if it was used to track her down. Laura had been texting her nonstop. There were dozens of missed calls. Lena swallowed the pill Socorro had given her.

Lena read the last text. Just let me know you're OK, Laura had written.

I'm OK, she wrote her sister back. Immediately, Laura called her, but she declined the call. What could she possibly say?

Pablo had been texting her, too, asking her so many questions. Dulce's girls were missing. Dulce was freaking out. Everything wasn't fine. Everyone wasn't okay.

She dialed Pablo. His voice greeted her. He sounded as if she'd woken him. But that was strange. It was only around 10 P.M. back in DR.

"I feel really bad about that little girl," Elena confessed. "From PH7."

"Why?" Pablo said. "That girl is fine. I'm with her parents at the Yellow Paloma. It's Dulce's girls you need to be worried about. They're missing."

The tourist girl was alive! The knowledge brought Elena to tears. She couldn't help herself, couldn't stop crying. She wasn't sure if it was from the happiness and relief that she wasn't responsible for the girl's death or from her frustration and anger that Laura had lied to her, tricked her into leaving DR.

"Where are you?" Pablo asked. "Are you at a party?"

She was quiet as the noise around her boomed. "I'm in London."

"London? Why? How?" Pablo said sternly.

Lena hummed some unintelligible sounds. Socorro, next to her, was listening attentively.

"What happened with Dulce's girls?" he demanded.

"Nothing happened to them," she said. "They were fine when I left them on the beach."

"Do you know what could have happened to the girls?" Pablo asked seriously. "Any idea where they might have gone?"

"They were fine," she said. "They were swimming in the ocean when I left them. They were fine."

But she wasn't sure. She remembered sitting in the driver's seat, reversing, being filled with dread that if she left, the worst might happen.

As if sensing her concern, Pablo said, "Are you sure, El? Are you sure the girls were all right when you last saw them?"

Fuck. She wasn't sure at all. She told Pablo about the green-eyed man, the father of the girl she had taken care of. He had been around the girls when she'd left them.

"What do you mean, *around* them?" Pablo asked. "Were you partying with that guy in front of the girls?" He sounded disgusted.

"We had a few drinks together," she said. "But no, nothing like that."

"And what? You left him there with the girls? Why?"

She'd thought that the tourist girl was dead! And she'd texted Pablo. She'd told him to hurry up and get to the bar *stat*.

"You can't blame me for this, El," Pablo said.

"I just needed enough cash to book a flight," Elena said.

He said something about the pills that he'd given her that same day, said that when she was high she probably had no concept of reality, no common sense. She might not even know who the man really was.

"Ecstasy doesn't screw up my ability to see faces, jeez," she finally managed to say defensively.

"Are you one hundred percent positive that there's no way you might be wrong?" he asked.

She wasn't sure why Pablo was so invested in making her say that it wasn't the guy. She knew it was him. But who could be 100 percent positive about anything? In her fancy private school that the Grand Paloma Resort had paid for, they had spent an entire quarter discussing the unreliability of eyewitnesses. At virtual model congress, she'd once argued that government-sponsored AI surveillance was worth losing personal privacy for in order to combat human prejudice in the carceral state. She had won. So no, she would never say she was 100 percent sure of anything she had seen with her flawed human eyes.

"Do you think the girls are dead?" Lena asked.

Pablo was quiet. When he finally spoke, it sounded as if he was in pain. "I don't think the girls are dead. They are smart. They know the land, where to go to be safe. But there's a big difference between alive and okay. You should have done everything to make sure they'd be safe."

Elena sat with the seriousness of that statement. He was right. Pablo was so often right.

"Will you please call me when you find out the girls are fine?" she asked. But there was only silence on the line. The call had dropped. Or Pablo had hung up on her.

Her sister had lied to get rid of her, but now, the joke was on her. Thanks to Laura's lies, Lena had pulled off an impossibility, arriving in a new place ready to be a new person and have the absolute best time of her life.

It only took a few more minutes for the pill to do its work. Everything around her turned bright, gorgeous; time moved in languid waves, and her body felt electric. She said the word aloud and just saying it felt harmonious. Language had been created to express feelings and that was such a beautiful thing. Right now, this was the feeling she had been chasing, the one she'd had no language for before. To be young and to be among people who didn't judge her or want anything from her. Not Laura, who had always felt shackled to her.

"*Freedom*," she whispered, closing her eyes, feeling her body become slippery and loose. She was one with the universe.

When she felt the tug of small, wet fingers on the pinky of each hand, her eyes flew open. Dulce's girls were already walking away from her. She called to them, but they didn't turn around. She outstretched her arms, begging them to come back. Those enormous hair puffs, glistening with rainwater that glittered like jewels, reflecting an endless rainbow, twisted through a crowd of bodies. Lena closed her eyes, convincing herself that they weren't really there. It would be over in a matter of minutes. But as if to show off, the girls turned back and were suddenly on her—tugging, pulling, multiplying, crowding the space around her until she could no longer breathe.

She'd wake up on Saturday morning to the bright light of day stinging her eyes and an empty, silent warehouse. No music, no drugs, no malassadas, no satchel. No Socorro. She would feel a chill engulf her unlike anything she'd ever known. Pablo's words from the night before would echo. She should have done everything to make sure the girls were safe. Elena would rise off the ground, determined to find her way back home. To right what she had so royally screwed up.

But just then, as she felt herself crowded by phantom girls, Socorro came to her rescue. Rubbed her arms. "It's just a bad trip," she assured Lena.

Socorro brought the mirror with more lines and Lena bent her head. Inhaled.

SATURDAY

CHAPTER
30

WHEN ELENA CALLED, PABLO HAD CAREFULLY EXTRACTED himself from the nude tourist couple, who were passed out on the bed. Sophie was the little spoon; the husband was the big spoon. Pablo had been in the middle. He slipped on his uniform and left the master bedroom, soundlessly closing the door behind him. There was the heavy scent of Pablo's semen, Pablo's shit in the air, even out in the hallway. Or maybe it was on his fingers, staining his skin. Pablo moved through the living room to the service bedroom. It was tiny, devoid of windows, and lacked a closet, or any breathing room. In a four-thousand-square-foot suite, the staff were supposed to feel lucky to have been given a bedroom that barely fit a twin bed. When he sat down on the thin mattress to better hear Elena's insistence that Dulce's girls had been *fine-fine-fine* when she'd left them by the beach, he reeled at the sharp pain in his anus. Maybe he needed to put ice on it. When the call dropped, he quietly left the presidential penthouse at the Yellow Paloma. He tried the service elevator, but it took too long to come. He headed for the stairwell, taking two steps at a time despite the pain, leaning heavily on the railing as he descended all twelve flights of stairs.

He redialed Elena. He texted her.

Call me back!

Waited for a response. None came.

How unforgivable that Elena had taken a man's money—whoever that man was—in exchange for Dulce's girls. He shook his head in frustration at both Elena and himself. As Pablo landed on the ground floor of the Yellow Paloma, weaving past good-smelling, smartly dressed guests, he didn't want to believe that the same man whose bed he had just left had harmed Dulce's girls. Pablo recalled the man's care for his own child. The way he had insisted on the colas to satiate her thirst; the way he'd run smack into danger to protect her, holding the bat above his head, ready to strike anyone to keep her safe.

And in bed, the tourist had encouraged Pablo, guiding his fingers with his own hands into Sophie's swollenness, never taking his eyes off her moaning mouth. The tourist had held the anal beads, turned them this way and that, so that Pablo could get a good look. When he'd asked and Pablo had shakily nodded, unsure that he wanted to go through with it, the man had asked again, making it clear that he needed verbal consent. That he was aware that Pablo was uncomfortable. There would be no confusion among the three of them about whether he had asked for and received permission. They all had plummeted into the artificial darkness of blackout curtains, the wife heaving, everyone still waiting for Pablo's response. Pablo had been scared. He'd hated the strange impulse that bound him to say yes, feeling an eerie presence, an invisible mass made up of the souls of the countless people who'd be willing to do anything for this job. The more disposable he knew himself to be, the stronger the urge to give everything of himself away to become valuable. He had felt the tourist man's self-control. Had Pablo said no, the tourist man would have stopped. But even as Pablo had known that what would follow would be terrible, he had hoped for the pleasure that could be found in subjugation.

A man like that, careful and exacting, wealthy and powerful, had no need to do something as atrocious as hurting two little girls. It was possible that Elena was wrong about the identity of the man she'd left with the girls. But within that same breath, Pablo contemplated the man who had come back for his passport at Dulce's bar, a man whose cold disregard said control and precision plus wealth and power always led to the same result: He'd have what he wanted no matter the cost.

That he'd likely never had to pay for what he was willing to take, what he knew he'd get away with.

It was past midnight. He texted Laura anyway.

> Spoke to Elena.
> Have new info.

Within seconds, Laura called him. It was loud on her side. He couldn't make out what she was saying. She kept saying, *hold on, hold on, just give me a sec,* until eventually, she was in a quiet place.

"Tell me everything," she demanded.

He did.

"She's in London?" Laura shouted.

She was.

"She told you she took money from the man and left the girls for him to do as he pleased?"

Not so much, no. "She took the money because she was sure one of us would go to the bar before anything bad happened. She thought the tourist kid was dead."

Laura considered Pablo's words silently before replying.

"But she's far from here. That's good news. Dulce is demanding that we get the man back. She woke up furious and lodged a formal complaint against the tourist man and Elena. The only reason the police aren't here right now is because of the storm."

It was a clear, bright night at the Yellow Paloma. Six hours away, there was a category-five storm. Dulce had formally accused Elena of wrongdoing.

"You have to bring them back tomorrow," Laura said.

"Laura," Pablo said. "The man is here. But the girls aren't."

There was a silence.

"Where are the girls?" Pablo asked.

"I don't know."

Another silence. Pablo felt like he would vomit.

"The police will find out when you get him back here."

"How am I supposed to do that?" Pablo asked. "The little kid is so excited about the water park, she won't want to leave after one day."

"Just be honest," she said, sounding exhausted. "Tell him there's video that places him at a bar that's the last known location of two missing local girls. Tell him their father is just as powerful and rich as he is. That it's in his best interest to comply. If the wife and kid want to stay behind, they can."

"This sounds like a message *you* should be delivering to these people," Pablo said.

"I'm grooming you for my job," Laura said. "Don't you get that? In less than two weeks, I'll be out of here, and I plan to recommend you."

He was quiet, unconvinced. But if that was true, it would be a huge promotion.

"If you only knew what I'm dealing with here," she said. "Pure nightmare-level of chaos. Just tell him you're delivering the message on my behalf. Management wants to handle things as discreetly as possible. We want to clear him with as little fuss as possible, so we're hoping not to go through official channels. Your manager can't speak to him directly because she's dealing with the storm. She trusts you to convey the message. If he puts up any fuss, tell me and I'll call him. Got it?"

"What's going to happen to Elena?" Pablo asked.

"Nothing, long as she stays the hell away from home. But bring that man back tomorrow. Your job depends on it."

With that, she hung up.

Pablo found himself in the gallery off the lobby, above the illuminated rectangular pool that was the exact replica of the pool at the Grand Paloma. There was a Rio here, too, playing a lovely melody on the violin. Palm trees lined the sides of the pool, casting beautiful, elongated shadows across the water. Around him, guests spoke German, French, Russian, Italian, Polish, English, Serbian, Danish, Swedish, Czech. Doña Fella, his old teacher, had always said that borders were in place to control the flow of poor people, because rich people could glide through any gate, stand on any land. Elena's visa application had been approved so fast solely because of her resort work. She had managed to glide through, too. She would be free as long as she stayed away from home. Laura was right about that. He glanced up and located the suite where the couple and their child were staying, noticed the slender figures of the adults moving about. The jets from the pool came on, pulling his gaze away. From up here, the rapid movement of the forced air on the surface of the pool made it look like hundreds of wings flapping, liquid birds escaping confinement, soaring.

He wouldn't go back up there tonight. He'd have to excuse himself in the morning. Laura would have her way, but only after daybreak.

From out of nowhere, a pair of soft but strong arms pushed him. He craned his neck to see who they belonged to. He saw a young woman who'd been wearing nanny scrubs when he'd noticed her earlier that day as they drove onto the property. She was now wearing a black bustier, leather shorts, and gladiator sandals that came up to her knees.

"You're bleeding," she said.

Pablo placed his hand on the back of his pants, felt the heavy wetness there. He made to turn from her, embarrassed.

"No es nada," she said and continued to push him forward. They went up a curved Santorini stairwell that spiraled above them and along a softly lit pathway until they reached a doorway. They ended up walking down a bright hall with a colorful tropical forest painted on the walls. They walked so fast that Pablo didn't have a chance to ask a question; he just let himself be led by the arms that pushed him down the hall. Most of the doors were ajar, and Pablo saw attractive young people getting ready for the night. There were the smells of strong, bitter coffee and sweet marijuana, the sounds of beer bottles clinking and loud bossa nova coming from one room, while dembow played in another. Someone spoke with the lilt of St. Kitts and Nevis, and another responded in a commanding Jamaican accent. Here, there were workers from all over the Caribbean. Near the end of the corridor, the young woman turned the knob of an unlocked door. She quickly went to a drawer, shuffled around in it. Pablo noted the spacious room, the half-opened door that led to a private bathroom. A gust of air cooled down his sweaty frame.

"This is your room? I thought you were a worker here," Pablo said.

"I am," she said, turning to him.

"They dock your pay to stay in a regular guest room?" he asked.

She laughed. "No, tonto," she said. "These are the staff quarters. We each get our own room. Isn't it the same at the Grand Paloma? *Aja!*" she said triumphantly and handed him a green-tinted pomade jar.

Management at the Grand Paloma had insisted the casitas were temporary, that eventually they would build better quarters for the employees, but they had stopped investing in the Grand Paloma Resort. He saw that here, the hotel leadership had made the place comfortable enough that no one would want to leave. The workers' rooms even had AC! How had Laura and others at the Grand Paloma managed to keep this news from the workers back home?

"Apply it generously to the affected area," she said, reaching into a mini fridge that was in the corner of the room and taking out a couple of beers. "I'll grab you a uniform. You're Pablo Frost, right?"

He nodded, confused, but took a long swig. How did she know who he was?

"And you are?" he asked.

"Pilar Santos," she said. She winked at him, left the room.

When he came out of the shower, he toweled himself dry and used Pilar's lotion. When he applied it, he felt a sharp sting, followed by a cool, comforting numbness. The sore, tender skin immediately began to shrink. The bleeding stopped.

The door to the bathroom opened, and Pilar handed him a plain black uniform. He put it on and came out. Pilar was applying sparkly blue lipstick.

"Better?" she asked.

He nodded.

"If I told you how many times these tourist assholes plunge into me too roughly," she said, and gave a little laugh. Pablo thought it was bizarre, the way Pilar spoke so easily about being assaulted. "Son animales. But this medicine will make it all better—heals and numbs it. I make it myself. Keep it."

"Thank you," Pablo said, after taking a long sip of his beer.

Pilar's watch went off. "Time for third shift," she said, standing up and throwing her unfinished beer in the trash bin. "We're down a pair of hands at the bar. Do you mind helping? Just for a couple of hours?"

He didn't have a chance to say no. Before he knew it, her surprisingly strong hands were pushing him down the same hallway they had come from. He could have stopped her. He could have said no. But he figured it might be best for him to have a few drinks, to numb the pain he felt in the rest of his body, the parts no pomade could reach.

PILAR LED PABLO TO a beautiful lounge. Sheer, soft curtains draped chaises longues, and a handful of tables surrounded a stage where a handsome Dominican man with a sculpted, muscular body played the saxophone. Next to him, a slender Guyanese played the trumpet. Next to him, a lithe white man played the piano. They were riffing with one another, smiling from time to time when someone did something daring or unexpected. It seemed like they were playing for each other, not for the audience of rapt middle-aged tourists that watched them. There was an absurdity to the bar—at one end, there was a classy, upscale feel, but at the end where he and Pilar were making drinks, there was a boisterous vibe.

But who was he to try to make sense of the resort's social spaces? Work was work, regardless of whether it made any sense to him. It was easy to fall into place. He made drinks, served them, smiled, and joked around with Pilar, who told him that after spending her first shift at the omelets station and her second shift nannying, she was happy to serve drinks to the ethically nonmonogamous. She hit him with an elbow to make him look at the white woman at the end of the bar. *Esta aqui solita,* Pilar mouthed.

"The single ladies are the biggest freaks," she confided in English. "Also, big tippers," she added, rubbing her fingers together in the universal sign for money.

Pablo thought it was funny that Pilar was constantly mouthing words. But he imagined that the management here likely frowned upon the workers speaking Spanish, since she only mouthed words in their native tongue. There was something about Pilar, a buoyancy that reminded him of Elena. He felt that same weight of disappointment he'd felt when he'd been unable to get Elena back on the phone, only now it was paired with a sense of his own responsibility. How had they all failed her to such an extent that she would think leaving two young girls with a stranger was acceptable? He found himself closing his eyes, silently praying that Dulce's girls were okay. But he had to be honest—he was beginning to feel hopeless that they would ever be found.

"No sad face," Pilar shouted at him.

He nodded. This wasn't a place for sadness. He made a big show of doing shots with Pilar, and a few of the couples who had been standing off to the side shyly came over for drinks. He felt lighter as he served them. He hardly felt the pain in his body, no longer worried that he might bleed through his clothes.

Eventually, he made his way to the woman at the end of the bar. She was small, with big green eyes and voluminous, doll-like, wavy blond hair. When she turned to him fully, he noticed that part of her face was disfigured. The scar looked like a big, bad burn that had healed long ago. But she was still a stunning woman. Her skin sported the taut, golden rosiness of someone who'd spent much of the day in the sun.

"I'm celebrating my fortieth birthday," she said.

"Feliz cumple," Pablo said, thinking that she didn't look old enough to be forty. "I'm going to make you a special birthday drink."

She nodded, observed him with astute eyes. He allowed his gaze to linger as he mixed her drink. She wore expensive designer clothing. Had nice, tasteful jewelry. He decided to make her something tart. When he returned with her drink, he watched her as she took the first sip. She closed her eyes as she swallowed, making small, pleasurable noises.

"Perfecto," she said in accented Spanish.

He nodded in appreciation. He took pride in giving women pleasure.

"Raenna," she said, extending her hand. It felt soft, like warm candlewax.

"Nice to meet you, Reyna," he said.

She laughed at his pronunciation.

"Where are you from?" he asked.

"That's a complicated question," she said.

"I'm in no rush," he said, eyeing Pilar, who nodded at him to indicate that she could handle the other patrons at the bar.

Raenna was a big-time lawyer from New York City who had grown up in Chicago. Though she could obviously pass for a white person, she had been brought up to believe she was a Black woman. Except, to celebrate her upcoming milestone birthday, she'd recently taken a DNA test and learned that she was half-white, half-Dominican. She was laughing, like the whole thing was crazy.

"No way," Pablo said, examining her features. She had no trace of Dominican anywhere.

"I have some kink in my hair," she said.

He closed the distance between them by extending his torso over the bar, took a whiff of her delicious-smelling perfume, gently touched her hairline. He was careful not to graze the folded-over sections where hair extensions had been sewn into her scalp. Was cautious not to stroke any of the scar tissue.

"There's no kink in your hair," he said.

"Not that hair," she said, reddening.

He tugged at her earlobe playfully. "And you came to DR, why?"

"To get in touch with my roots," she said, then covered her face at the bad pun.

"You came to a luxury resort founded by an American company to get in touch with your Dominican heritage?"

She shrugged. "I needed a soft landing. I have a very stressful job."

He laughed.

"The DNA test includes an app that allows you to connect with relatives, if you choose to. I'm going to meet some primos before I leave the country," she said. "I'm not here to exploit the homeland. I'm here to be one with it."

He felt such tenderness for this stranger. He remembered feeling this same rush for Christine two days ago, then pushed away the memory of how that had ended.

"Want another drink?" he asked.

She nodded. "I thought the Paloma Negra was supposed to be a wild place. It's been pretty tame."

Pilar overheard the statement. Leaned into Raenna as she pointed to a shelf full of books. "If you pull on either Edwidge Danticat's *The Farming of Bones* or Julia Alvarez's *In the Time of the Butterflies*, a secret door will release. You have to be accompanied by one of the workers if you're not part of a couple. But I have to warn you," she said, furrowing her eyebrows. "It is an unbelievably decadent place. Every sexual fantasy, fulfilled. Every desire, satisfied."

"That's pretty dark," Raenna said.

Pilar and Pablo both stared at her, befuddled.

"The unlatching books?" she said. "One about the 1937 Parsley Massacre and the other about the assassination of the Mirabal sisters?"

Raenna had done some serious reading as she was getting ready to come to the homeland, Pablo noted. In all the time he'd been working at the resort, he'd never met anyone who took time to learn about their country. Now, in the space of a couple of days, he'd met two.

"No, you don't understand. The designers did it as a way to pay homage to the history of the country. It's a way of acknowledging the terrible past in a meaningful way."

"As the way to unlatch the door to a sex dungeon?" Raenna retorted.

"Because some people go down there and don't see the light of day again until it's time to go back home."

At Raenna's horrified expression, Pilar relented.

"I mean, they did their best. It's a resort, not the Holocaust Memorial."

Pilar walked away, shrugging, as if she had done her job. Raenna was quiet for a few moments. She swiveled in her bar chair, glancing around as if she wasn't sure how the hell she'd ended up here. Pablo knew he should lighten up the mood, should turn on the charm. But at that moment, he felt too exhausted and sad to do anything other than finish making her a second drink.

"What's your story?" she asked when he returned with her cocktail.

An hour later, Raenna was on her fifth drink and resolutely drunk, listening attentively as Pablo confessed his heartbreak over Vida. Raenna seemed disappointed at first, but quickly recovered. "What would you say to her? If she were here?"

"That I've never loved anyone the way I love her. And that I never will," he said.

"Wow. That was right there, huh? You also have to tell her how you plan to be different. Deep down, you know what she wants from you. Give her that. Never lie again unless you want to lose her for good."

His phone vibrated. It was Laura. He excused himself from Raenna.

"Where the hell are you?" Laura shouted. "The wife called downstairs, saying you've been gone for hours. No one has your phone number, so they called me. You can't let that man out of your sight. Are you partying?"

Pablo felt the sobering effect of her words. He turned back to look at Raenna, but already the big, muscular saxophone player was talking to her. He caught a glimpse of her touching his flexed arm as he led her toward the wall with the heavy velvet curtains, every thought of massacres and social injustice out of her mind.

Just as well, Pablo thought.

In his ear, Laura was mid-sentence. Her voice was all static.

"It's a bad connection," Pablo said.

"Of course it's a bad connection. The hurricane hit."

Pablo motioned to Pilar that he had to step outside. He made his way out of the lounge and found the night was humid, dark. But there was still no sign of a tropical storm here. Not even one drop of rain.

Laura went on, unaware that Pablo's attention had been split.

"Go back and do your job, Pablo. That man is the key to us learning what happened to the girls. He can tell us where they are."

Pablo was quiet. They both were wondering the same thing. Whether the girls were alive or not.

"Got it," he said. Pablo hung up and stared at the black screen of his phone, catching his reflection, cast in dark shadows. He remembered holding that gun up to the sky, those Black boys just a few feet away— how quickly he'd assumed that the kids, and the men who were quick to protect them, were capable of doing unspeakable harm. How immediately judgmental he'd been of Elena's actions. How much he had resisted believing that the tourist man was guilty of causing any harm. He went back inside the bar, thanked Pilar for everything, told her he had to go. He made his way toward the tourist family's suite, ready to do whatever was required.

THE
GRAND PALOMA
RESORT

Paloma Falls,
DOMINICAN REPUBLIC

*ADVERSE WEATHER ALERT
IN EFFECT!*

HURRICANE CONSUELO, NOW A CATEGORY-FIVE STORM, is barreling its way through our beaches. We are fully prepared for a direct hit. We expect to emerge from this storm unscathed, but the situation is serious. For your safety, it is very important that all guests remain in their rooms. We've provided water, snacks, and two bottles of our best Malbec to make the time in your suites as pleasant as possible. Our hotel staff is available to meet your every need. We are thankful for their commitment and focus even at a time when their own families are at risk.

Thanks in advance for your cooperation and collaboration,

YOUR TEAM AT
THE GRAND PALOMA RESORT

CHAPTER
31

NONE OF THE GUESTS AT THE GRAND PALOMA RESORT HEEDED the request that they remain in their rooms. The lobby had been transformed in the space of a few hours. Laura had commandeered the band members—güira-playing Angie, accordion whiz Caro, maracas-playing Lilliam, and tambora-drumming Jaquira—to keep the atmosphere lively and fun. She told those present that it was tradition, when truly catastrophic bad weather struck the island, to throw #HURRICANEPARTIES! She'd made that up on the spot. But it was based on truth—for some people. It was a thing of beauty, the way Laura described how families hunkered down together in whoever's homes had the strongest foundations, shared meals, sang songs, passed down the legacies of oral storytelling. Children stayed up until all hours of the night.

"Together, we can overcome anything," she finished. "This country is all about community."

She didn't bother telling her guests that the one time her family had desperately needed shelter during a storm much like this one, the good folks of Pico Diablo had turned their backs, played deaf.

Laura asked the bartenders to take Dulce's rum and offer shots to the guests. She wanted them happy and drunk. It worked so well that they hardly seemed aware of the storm raging outside. She overheard one of the guests say that it would be so cool if they had a disco ball. Immediately, Laura ordered one of the workers to make their way across the resort to the disco, to grab colored strobe lights and some of the disco balls that spun from the ceiling. The worker had looked at her as if she'd lost her mind, then turned to do as he was told.

Even the Vargas sisters were having fun, pointing from the vantage of their bar stools at the young people who were thrusting their bodies this way and that and had no idea how to dance tipico. No one was concerned about the hurricane, about the winds that hurled outside at eighty miles per hour at the very outset of the storm. They still had a few hours before the storm reached its full power. They could not see the wind battering the palm trees or how the chaises longues, beach umbrellas, kayaks, canoes, and paddleboards that hadn't been secured became weapons as they were flung hundreds of feet in the air, crashing down with such force that anyone in their path would have been injured or killed. Laura had no time to find out who had neglected to place the outdoor furniture and all their water sports equipment in the storage unit. She would take care of that the next day. She felt a restlessness in the crowd and noticed how many people had turned their attention to their phones, how a few people were attempting to open the locked doors to the gallery that led to the infinity pool. She knew they had to switch things up. After a few songs, she motioned for the band to cut it, for the DJ to go next.

With the disco ball suspended from the magnificent signature bird in flight high above them, it turned into a real party. And shortly after that, it became a rager. Young women were dancing on top of the bar and coffee tables, everyone posing for their phone cameras, many streaming live on their social media platforms. She had tried to get these people to stay in their rooms, but there was no controlling this crowd. She looked around helplessly for the rest of the management team—the people who should've been helping her, keeping things under control. When they'd had an emergency meeting with Miranda, who'd joined the video conference with her camera turned off, she'd let Laura know that she was allowing those in management who had families to travel to parts of the island less likely to be affected by the storm. The only ones who stayed ended up being Laura and Astrid. But she hadn't seen Astrid since the meeting.

She searched social media on her cellphone, hoping to see if Elena had posted anything. She searched La Gata's posts, too, trying to see if she'd lied. But there was nothing. She went back to her sister's Insta and quickly scanned the list of her followers, trying to jolt her memory to recall the name of a single one of those friends she'd made at the global academy. But it was no use. Her sister had hundreds of followers; it would take hours to go through them all. She'd hoped school would be a portal for her sister to enter another life. And it had been.

Laura was still fixed in place, feeling alone and desolate, when Ida Vargas came over.

"Mi'ja," she said. "You look like you need a hug."

Laura shook her head, feigning a smile. There was no use in making the guests feel sorry for her because it would in turn make them feel sorry for themselves, for their own helplessness.

"Laura." A worker came toward her, soaking wet. He was usually charged with third-shift gate security. "There are a bunch of people here from Pico Diablo. They're asking if there's any chance they can stay here with us to wait out the worst of the storm."

Laura remembered the edict that Miranda had reiterated during their call. They were absolutely forbidden from ever allowing anyone but their paying guests to stay at the hotel—no matter what the weather was like.

She thought of all the guests who had left in droves at the first word that there might be danger on the way, of all the rooms that would be empty all night. She thought for a moment of herself and Elena, back when they were children. Of how most of the people who were standing at the gate, seeking refuge, were likely from the families who'd refused to open their doors to her and her sister. Elena had been only four years old when it happened. They had knocked on door after door, begging for help. Her mother had fainted from the pain of her broken arms. Her father had been asleep, oblivious to the damage he'd caused.

She felt herself harden, much in the way she'd turned to steel when she'd had to claim her father's remains last summer. She'd only been able to identify her father by the missing finger on his hand. The image of children waiting out in the rain pushed itself into her consciousness. One moment, it was her and her little sister years ago. Next thing she knew, she was bombarded with images of children she'd seen around town, on the front porches of the shack houses that had likely already been blown apart by the wind; of the old people who had been too sick or infirm to make their way to the hotel. She thought about the choices of those who had risked their very lives in this weather to come here, thinking it impossible that they'd be turned away.

She thought of Dulce, who'd woken up earlier in the night. Dulce, who'd been furious once she'd realized that Laura had dosed her with sleeping pills to get her out of the way. Laura hadn't denied that she'd drugged her.

"Who have you become?" Dulce had asked her. Then she'd raged, telling her that she was calling the police, sending them the video. There would be hell to pay once the storm passed. She'd gone into the storm, had left them. Laura had decided against telling her friend about the T-shirt she'd found. She'd decided that the line had been clearly marked between her and Dulce. They were no longer on the same side of this thing.

"They can't stay in the hotel," Laura told her employee simply, thankful that her voice didn't quiver.

Ida's eyes widened. She held on to the employee's arm as he, shocked and speechless, made to walk away.

"But why?" she said. "I saw so many people check out today? There must be room to accommodate some, if not all."

Amber Vargas came over then, doing a little shimmy with her shoulders in time with the loud hip-hop that was blasting from the speakers.

"What's going on?" Amber asked happily.

"There are some locals asking for refuge," Ida said.

"Surely in a resort with thousands of acres of land, you can afford to find a place for the families to stay."

Laura heard the note of authority in Amber's voice. The sisters were used to having their way. They might have had the same color of skin as Laura, but it was clear that these women lived very differently. Laura felt bile in her throat, could taste it on her tongue. How nice it must be to live with morality and scruples. To have the freedom to choose the high ground that wealth afforded. Ida and her sister's wealth—great enough that they could afford to shut down both their hotels during peak season and spend it relaxing with their families or getting drunk by the side of the pool—meant that they had no idea what it might mean for her to let those people stay, to risk her job. Who got to be humane? Who got to be generous? She wanted to shout at them.

She wondered if her boss would handle this situation differently. If she would break the rules, show the people at the gate some mercy. But she was almost certain that Miranda would never do that. Rules were made when clearheaded, so no one forgot that they were running a business, not a charity. Her boss had made that statement many times.

"Sadly, there's nothing I can do," Laura said. "No one except registered guests are allowed on hotel premises."

The sisters both turned toward Laura and seemed to sober up immediately. She had already pivoted away from them when one of them said, "You can't be fucking serious, Laura." She had no idea who had spoken; she'd never noticed that they had the same voice.

Laura's voice was cold. "No one without a reservation can stay at this hotel."

"In a crisis like this," Amber said, "you must think of community. We're all family. A personal catastrophe becomes a communal catastrophe."

"I don't have the authority to make that decision," Laura said.

Ida took out her wallet, extracted a credit card, and pushed it at Laura with force. "We will pay for every single person who needs a room to stay," she said.

Laura nodded at them somberly, held the cold, heavy credit card in her hand. She looked at her employee and whispered that he should take the locals to the movie theater—count them and text her to let her know how many rooms they'd need. She would send someone to him with room keys. No need to further alarm the guests with an influx of people who likely looked like they'd been through hell.

When she turned back to the Vargas sisters, they were looking at her with such disappointment that Laura felt her throat close, her eyes water. The tears came then, unbidden, and she was mortified and ashamed to have them see her this way. It would be better if they thought she was heartless, a corporate robot. The world had no respect for weak people.

"Sometimes you have to lead with your heart, mi'ja," Amber said. "Not with fear. Sometimes a moment like this is what defines what we're made of."

Laura wanted to explain to them what she'd been through, explain that the people the Vargas sisters thought were kind and deserving of generosity in the face of a natural disaster were terrible human beings. When they'd had the chance to extend kindness to two little girls, they had pretended not to hear their knocks, not to hear their desperate pleas.

But she wiped her face as she looked at them, thanked them in a formal voice for their generosity. She left them. Went to process the reservations at a nearby desk. When her departed employee texted her the total, she realized that there wouldn't be enough rooms. She overrode the system. She wrote back letting him know that he could offer the movie theater to those who wanted to stay—those seats reclined—and also that if they wanted to share rooms, he should look the other way, should let them use the bathrooms in the gym to shower if they needed to, should let them each have the warm, plush bathrobes that they usually kept under lock and key for their Platinum members. He had her authority to coordinate it with room service. None of those decisions made her feel better.

She returned the credit card and the receipt for the rooms to the Vargas sisters. This time, there was no pity or even sadness in their eyes. They looked drained. After they confirmed that she had accommodated the locals, they turned from her and headed away from the lobby, making their way to their presidential suite. Their shoulders sagged. Laura wondered if they had wiped out their retirement accounts with this one act of generosity. Had they, possibly, put themselves in such a jam that they'd have to take out a loan, claim bankruptcy? She was baffled by how the women had reacted in the moment. Who knew what they'd sacrificed for people they'd never even met? In all the years they'd been visiting the Grand Paloma Resort, she'd not once seen them off the resort grounds.

Laura made her way into a bathroom stall. She lowered the lid of the toilet and sat there, dazed. There was the sound of the automatic scent spritzer, and moments later, the room filled with a rich fragrance. She called her sister. The phone rang and rang. She called again, again, again, manically, willing her sister to pick up. There was an ache inside her, a sadness that had been unleashed when she'd allowed herself to cry in front of the Vargas sisters. She thought about her sister. She wished that Elena were back here, where she could see her, where she could laugh at her silly stories about the latest mishaps in her misadventures as the self-proclaimed world's shittiest babysitter. All her stories ended the same way—the kid fine, her running around with them like she herself was nothing but a big kid. *They all love me, no matter what,* Elena would say, perplexed.

Surely there was another way she could have tried to teach her sister a lesson. If Dulce's girls were dead, it was on Laura, no one else. Her sister was hardly older than a child herself.

She thought about what tomorrow might bring. Pablo would bring that man back. She was sure of it. She hoped that the tourist man had a reasonable explanation for the exchange with her sister that had been caught on tape. She hoped that he would disclose what had happened to the girls after the point in the video where they could no longer be seen.

She invoked Elena's spirit, her kindness. She allowed herself to be activated by the way her sister moved through the world. *What if one act of mercy can inspire another?* her sister often said. Laura asked herself what she hadn't considered, hadn't thought of. The answer surfaced as if it'd been there all along, ready to be plucked out of thin air.

If she were here, Elena would have made sure that the laborers in the tent city were safe—that they had left their shabby homes and found refuge in the hotel hours ago.

CHAPTER

32

THE SUMMER BEFORE, WHEN THE DISASTER FACING LAURA had been personal, not meteorological—private and quiet, not a howling public emergency—she had been summoned to Doña Fella's dirt-floored house on the day after she had identified her father's body. It had quickly become clear that her old teacher had no idea that her father was dead. Rather, she'd called her because she'd assumed that Laura's father had decided he wasn't coming back.

Looking at Doña Fella, Laura had been struck by the deep wrinkles on her ninety-four-year-old face, by the brightness of her round eyes, by the agility with which she still handled the coal fire above which she was roasting aubergines. The woman had had a pipe hanging from her mouth, and she'd worked, spoken, and moved about without removing the pipe.

That house, that backyard, had been the place where Laura had spent nearly all the days of her childhood when she wasn't working with her mother. Here, Doña Fella taught children to read and write and educated them about their history—focusing not on what other schools around the country taught, but on an alternative Dominican history. The deepest, truest history. One in which the Taínos' traditions helped them learn to love and respect the land. Where the country acknowledged the downfall of the Haitian occupation not as a cause for celebration but as the end of the chance for communal liberation. But that morning, still bruised from the pain of her unexpected reaction to her father's death, the stunning grief that had inundated her, she'd looked at the backyard with different eyes. Laura recalled how on every Freedom Day until she was fourteen years old, Doña Fella had gone around to all the students, from toddlers to teenagers, and made them each recount the Freedom Trail. *Playa, cascadas, bosque, y Pico Diablo.* They had each had to concoct a response to the question of what they might do if they were ever in danger. *Follow the trail for food and safety,* Doña Fella would say.

The last time she had participated as a student, she remembered Pablo coming to his feet, yelling that if the enslavers came back to try to recapture his ancestors, he'd fight them. Pablo, with his skinny arms, had made a sword from an avocado tree branch, pretending to stab at the enemy. Vida, off to the side, older than Pablo by three years, had laughed at his antics. She had said she'd rather hide, wait until the danger passed before coming out to safety. When Doña Fella had turned to Laura, she'd faced her own backyard, which housed the stone profile that resembled the devil. It was this rock formation, shaped like the peak of a horn, that had given the town its name. Fresh off the death of her mother, she'd said then that she wouldn't fight, she wouldn't hide, she'd rather jump.

But that day, with the death of her remaining parent raw in her heart, more than a decade after her mother's death, she'd sat watching the old woman slowly rotate the aubergine, charring the purple skin until it blistered and turned black.

Finally, the woman had told Laura where to go in her house to recover a haphazardly constructed box made of corrugated metal that was much like that used for the roof on Doña Fella's home.

"Open it," the old woman said.

The aubergine's skin made a lot of smoke, and the wind blew it directly into her eyes as she opened the box, stinging them until they teared up. And so it happened that even before she understood the horror of the secret she'd inherited from her father, the secret she would be sworn to keep until her dying day, she was already crying. In the box, there was a series of drawings and letters—some over eighty-five years old, Fella said. Most of the early letters had been written in a language that Laura had never been taught, and she kept waiting for the old woman to explain exactly what it was that she held.

"It's Haitian Creole," the woman said, as if that explained everything. Then, irritated by how long it was taking Laura to catch on, Doña Fella threw aside the stick with which she'd stabbed the aubergine and grabbed Laura by the forearm. Inside her simple home, they sat on rocking chairs.

Doña Fella explained that the last letter was from her father, that it would help her understand everything, and that as the oldest remaining member of the Moreno family in Pico Diablo, it was now her duty to carry the secret of the town. The next part Laura remembered as if in slow motion. It had felt as if she'd fallen. As if she'd taken a step to find the ground gone and had in turn broken open.

Mi hija, her father's letter read, *you know better than anyone else how some of us keep failing, because of how often I've failed you.*

Through a blur of tears caused by either the stinging smoke or her father's words—she couldn't be sure which—Laura read that the town hadn't been founded by the freedom-seeking enslaved Americans they all thought they'd descended from. Rather, Pico Diablo had been founded by a mixed-race American couple who had taken in orphaned children—fleeing Afro-Dominican and Haitian children who'd been persecuted during the Parsley Massacre of 1937. *"We keep the secret from everyone in the town to keep them safe,"* her father had written.

"What the hell does that mean?" Laura asked, reading the last sentence aloud to Doña Fella.

"Some of us," Doña Fella said, "are descended from Haitians."

"Some of us. Who? Me and Elena?" Laura asked.

"No, you're Dominican. Dark-skin Dominicans."

"Who's Haitian? Pablo?" Laura asked.

Doña Fella nodded.

"Vida? Dulce?"

Doña Fella nodded again.

"Pasofino?"

"Everyone other than your family," Doña Fella said, exasperated. "Your family is the only family in Pico Diablo that isn't descended from Haitians. Everyone else in this town is of Haitian descendance."

Laura understood the severity of the situation. At the time, she didn't even think about the immigration raids or the loss of citizenship for the people of her hometown. She thought instead of how devastating the blow would be—to learn that instead of being Black Americans descended from freedom-seeking warriors, they'd descended from people who'd hidden and run, who'd barely survived a massacre. In the Dominican Republic, there was only one perceived underclass: the Haitians.

"When we arrived here, I was seven years old," Doña Fella said. That statement stunned Laura into stillness. She'd always thought of the massacre of 1937 as having occurred so far back in the past that anybody affected must've died long ago.

"Word had gotten around, somehow, that there was this American couple who were taking in any children who'd been orphaned by the massacre. They owned the entire mountain, were left alone by the authorities. A childless couple—the husband was a white man and the wife was a Black woman. They had left the United States because it was illegal, where they were from, for them to be together. Who knows how they ended up here? How they came to create a sanctuary place for kids. But that's what happened. They took in the kids, discreetly registered them with birth certificates, and of course, because of the way it worked back then, the man just went down to the nearest office, bribed whomever he needed to bribe, and paid the fee, and if there were any questions or hassle about it, we never heard of it. We just knew that he'd come back, and we'd each be made new—new first names and English surnames, all registered as newborns in 1937. Eventually, it wasn't just kids anymore. It was a place where survivors came and found a place to be."

"Why was my family chosen? Why do we have to be the keepers of the secret?" Laura asked.

"It is a privilege to be the keeper of the secret," Doña Fella said sternly. She went outside and returned with the now-torched aubergine, dropping it onto a nearby plate. She removed the pipe from her mouth before she sat back down on the rocking chair. She pushed herself back and forth with the strength of her feet on the dirt ground.

"The Morenos," she said, "inherited the responsibility because at a certain point, we realized that the persecution of Haitians was never going to end here. That we needed to stop teaching children Creole to protect them. We taught everyone English instead. The point is that it was also decided that it was important for someone to hold the secret, the truth, because if the worst thing was ever to happen again, we'd need a family to do what they needed to do to keep those at great risk safe. Keep the secret to keep them safe."

"Meaning what? If *what* happened again?"

"If a massacre happened again, Laura. Don't be dense. It means that while your family might be at risk because you're dark-skinned, you'd have a better chance at surviving a massacre because you're the ones who are considered real Dominicans. Your birth certificates and lineage can be traced back for as long as there has been a registry. Your birthright can never be questioned or stripped. You are safe. You would be able to house people, hide them, keep them alive."

Laura considered what the old woman was saying. It made no sense. "But everyone has birth certificates now. Pablo, Vida, Dulce, Pasofino, they all have cédulas. They work. They are Dominican citizens."

Doña Fella stopped her chair from rocking. "These days, Haitians and their children, and their children's children, those born here, are denied the right to citizenship or stripped of existing citizenship daily. It would only take someone going back in the registry to 1937 and 1938 for them to realize that hundreds of people were registered as new-borns that year even though there are no records of their births at the hospital. It would be easy for someone to pull that thread. The entire thing would come undone. The point is that your family was chosen because no one could ever strip you of your citizenship. You would be in a position to ensure people were safe, to keep people alive."

Laura handed the metal box back to Doña Fella.

"If a massacre was underway, you think I'd stick around to make sure other people were safe? I would grab my sister, my only family, and get the hell away from here."

Doña Fella shook her head. "You need to expand your definition of family," she said.

Laura had refused since then to go back to Doña Fella's house, no matter how many times the woman demanded she come visit her. If she didn't read the box's contents, if she didn't accept the charge to keep the secret, then it was almost as if she didn't know. In the weeks following her father's death and Doña Fella's revelation of the town's secret, she'd frequently woken up in a cold sweat, reeling from nightmares where she was always running through the Pico Diablo Mountain's forest, always escaping among a group of other running people from an unseen mass of murderers, holding the hand of a much-younger Elena, trying to get them both to safety. Upon waking, she would calm herself down. Remind herself that the threats were in the past.

As children, they'd never been told that, aside from running and seeking escape via the Freedom Trail, standing their ground and fighting, or jumping to their deaths by leaping from the sharpest, highest peak of the mountain, one also had the option to join the enemy, to serve them. That there was also freedom in not fighting, not running, not hiding, not dying. That maybe the sweetest freedom of all was the one gained by silently acquiescing as indispensable servants.

NOW, INSPIRED BY THE concern about her missing sister, motivated by the near certainty that Dulce's girls were dead, Laura allowed herself to be pushed by an obligation she'd willfully ignored since last year. Laura slipped out of a side entrance, headed out into the storm. The wind was powerful, unbelievably strong. The rain came down heavy, the palm trees bending dangerously close to the ground. Laura had a hard time moving against the wind. Then it changed direction, quieted down for a moment.

She moved fast, unknowingly tracing in reverse the steps her sister had taken with the unconscious tourist child in her arms a little less than two days ago. When she made it to the tent city, staggering and soaked, she found that there were no people there. The tents had been catapulted away by the wind. Stupefied, she made her way to the staff quarters. There she saw, through window after window, the Grand

Paloma workers huddled in the casitas, each housing a Haitian family from the tent city. They had not waited for permission to extend a gesture of kindness, of humanity. Confounded, she wiped at her face, surprised to find hot tears flowing down her cheeks, mixed up with the rain. She knocked hard on the door of the first house, screamed as loud as she could, but no one responded. She went to the next house, and the same thing happened. They couldn't hear her. No matter how hard she screamed. The howling wind was too much; it overpowered a human voice. Laura thought of herself as a child, leading her baby sister from door to door, screaming that they needed help. The towns-people hadn't been lying. They'd never heard her calls for help.

She came upon a casita that was unlocked and was able to open the door, shouting as the wind began to gain force again, whistling around her, that they had to head into the main building fast. These casitas weren't stormproof. It was stunning how quickly word made it from casita to casita, how people went around the structures, waving their arms until someone took notice of them, kicking in doors if no one did. Soon, everyone was running—the old and the young, dark-skinned and light-skinned bodies indistinct in the darkness of the storm. Hundreds of people moving in the direction of the main hotel.

Laura waited until the last of them had made it into the building to go inside herself. As she waited, her phone buzzed with a new text alert. Elena had written her back: I'm OK.

The rush of relief that her sister was safe brought tears to her eyes. She pressed Elena's name, called her, but there was no answer. The last few people had walked through the doors. Laura was holding the door open for no one. Her near certainty that Dulce's daughters were dead became truth in her mind. Her sister was fine. In exchange, because this was the way the cruel world always worked for people like them, Laura was certain that those two girls had been raped, killed, their bodies flung into the sea by that tourist man.

Above her, the lights blinked off, then back on. Then they blinked off again and remained that way for good. She checked her Wi-Fi. It was down. They were disconnected—in the dark, and disconnected from the rest of the world. From the lobby there came the drunken, hysterical shouts of hundreds of guests, mingling with the voices of locals who needed to be allowed refuge from the storm in rooms that other visitors had spent a fortune on.

She got up and moved as quickly as she could in the darkness, unsure what would be waiting for her around the bend of a sharp wall.

CHAPTER
33

THE VARGAS SISTERS HAD BEEN SMART TO FLEE THE LOBBY after retrieving their credit card from Laura. They'd reached their floor and sat in a hallway nook only a few steps outside their suite, in one of those living room spaces with bookshelves and big windows that no one ever sat in. The frightening views outside were holding them transfixed in awe when the lights blinked off for the first time. The wind battered the landscape—they'd be surprised if the entire island wasn't decimated—and because they hadn't been born yesterday and knew exactly what a power outage would mean in a place this vast, Ida and Amber moved with a dexterity that belied their age. Ida took out her magnetic key and tapped the lock fast so that when an additional surge of power snaked through the circuits for a few seconds on its way to puttering out, they would be able to go into their room. They showered before the heated water ran out, brushed their teeth by the illumination of their cellphones, and were in bed, cocooned in the softness of the still-cool, brilliant white blankets, and asleep before things downstairs got out of hand—which they did, fast.

The sisters didn't speak about Laura. They didn't pause to dissect what they'd witnessed or discuss the amount of money they'd spent. The sisters couldn't care less about money. The next day, they'd put their heads together to figure out what it would mean for their future plans, how they would swerve in light of what they now knew.

CHAPTER
34

THE HOTEL LOBBY'S PLUNGE INTO DARKNESS ENABLED OUR EYES to adjust. We could see just how bad things were outside. But we also gained greater clarity indoors—as if in the falling shadows, our uniforms had been cast off, and all of us—guests, locals, workers, laborers—were the same.

Outside, a sectional couch from a guest balcony flew through the air and crashed to the ground, wood splintering every which way. Later, people would say it had made a frightening sound. But the wind roared so loudly that there was no way anyone could have heard the sound of a couch breaking apart. Still, the sight of a gargantuan L-shaped projectile forced fear into our souls. Someone in the crowd screamed. It might have been one of us. Our hearts hammered as we thought about our homes, our families, our animals. It had been decades since the island had seen a storm of this magnitude. Those of us who were old enough remembered how long it had taken our island to recover last time. A sense of hopelessness and despair descended. There were still some homes that had never been restored. Some people, needing to start over with less than nothing, had decided to leave and never came back. So many were dead.

We tried not to seethe at the tourists' reaction. They were gripped with a sense of excitement—to see the danger of nature this close up while safe inside made them feel invincible, powerful, reckless. A group of them began to push against the locked doors. They were shouting that they had the right to go outside if they so wished.

We looked at Laura with a sense of anticipation, wondering

how she would handle all of this. She stepped into a rare instant of illumination—through all the darkness inside and outside, for the briefest of moments, the moon cast a spotlight through the three-story-high doors. In a loud, unwavering voice, she said, "No one is going outside."

Taveras was in his element. We knew he'd been preparing for this moment for years, maybe all his life. What a sight he was, standing next to Laura, a gun in each hand held high above his head! Like the sheep they were, the tourists allowed themselves to be herded back from the doors. Most headed back toward the bar.

From somewhere upstairs, we could hear a man shouting that the magnetic system was down—that no one could get into or out of their rooms. His voice was laced with a note of hysteria.

Again, Laura looked poised and in control, assuring everyone that of course there was a master key to let everyone into their rooms, a generator to provide power, a contingency plan well in place. She told them that there was absolutely nothing to worry about, and we could see the crowd visibly relax. Us workers, though, we knew the telltale signs that Laura was a few moments away from losing her shit. The high pitch of her voice, the useless phone clenched in her hand, the tight smile pasted on her face—they warned us to step farther away, say nothing, refrain from making eye contact, look busy.

A palm tree slammed into the huge skylight above us, the impact followed by the distinctive sound of glass cracking. The room grew silent. The rain that made it through the fractured glass was a drip before it became a stream. When hell broke loose, with a chorus of screaming people—which, if we're honest, included quite a few of us—running every which way, Laura gave up on trying to calm people down. Instead, she was the one who raised her hands as though to receive an offering and caught the rainwater in her outstretched palms.

CHAPTER
35

THE OSPREYS HAD BEEN STARVING, THEIR NUMBERS RAPIDLY dwindling, because the fish they relied on to stay alive had been dying in the warming waters of the Caribbean. As a result, the birds had begun their migration from the beaches of North Carolina, down to Georgia, past Florida, and into the Caribbean earlier and earlier over the last few years.

During the last days of his life, Pablo's father had told Vida that he remembered how, when he had been a child, the ospreys hadn't reached their beaches until late September, sometimes October. In those old days, the arcs of the ospreys' dives into the ocean to catch prey had always been a good sign for fishermen. It had meant that there would be a plentiful harvest of fish. But during those suffocating August days that had marked the end of his time on earth, the viejito had stood on the mountain to see that the birds' numbers had greatly increased. Although it had been alarming because of what it signaled to him about the changes to the planet, it had also seemed to him to be a good sign that the birds weren't so fixed on the encoded timeline of their migration that they didn't understand when it was time to move on and find food. The smarter creatures, he told Pablo and Vida, understood when their existence was at risk and it was time to move. *You have to know when to change, when to move,* he'd said. *Only the dumbest creatures stay in place, starve, thinking that what worked in the past will always be a solution in the present.*

But the change in their behavior doesn't guarantee a better chance at survival, Vida had said. Her words had dissipated in the air between the three of them, unacknowledged. Pablo had nodded at his father with vehemence, eyes fixed on his empty hands as if he'd just received a great gift.

Vida had understood that they weren't talking about birds. They had been talking about the traditions of Pico Diablo. Vida felt fiercely protective of their old ways, but she had always known that Pablo was quick to dismiss them as antiquated and, in the months following his father's death, to rush toward a coruscating modernism. Since his mother had died in childbirth, Vida worried Pablo didn't have a tensile voice to counter his father's rigid logic.

Know when to change, when to move, Pablo's father had said.

Those were the words that echoed in Vida's mind as the flapping of thousands of wings—a wet, bare-skin thrusting sound—finally brought her out of the depths of her dreamlike stupor on Saturday morning. The door through which she could access her backyard and garden was open. There was strength in her body, clarity in her mind. She had survived. She placed a hand on her stomach, knowing that the seed Pablo had planted had also survived. It was only a squirm of movement, nothing that could be considered even close to a kick. But there was the unmistakable sensation she'd long associated with her feelings for Pablo—the fluttering of butterfly wings.

She felt a profound disquiet at the thought that Pablo wouldn't be there with her when the time came for her to be a mother. How to explain it to herself? Maybe it was because she'd come this close to death, to losing the child inside her. Her near loss had made her see Pablo's mistakes with kinder, softer eyes. The fear she'd had that his immaturity and his inability to understand what most mattered in life would translate into a life of unending labor for her seemed shallow. If only he'd be willing to give her what she wanted—fidelity, loyalty, acceptance of her way of life as the way forward for them both—they could make a life together. She would forgive him. She would be willing to put in the work to help him become a better man.

The storm had passed. Fog was thick in the air, and the smell of upturned earth became overwhelming. She promised herself that when the roads were cleared, she'd find Pablo—tell him about their baby, give him a chance to come to his senses.

Vida stood on shaky legs. She'd take a shower with her cistern water. She would head down the road to check on the elders of Pico Diablo and find ways to give back as thanks for her own gift of abundant life.

CHAPTER
36

AURA HADN'T STOPPED MOVING FOR THE BETTER PART OF three days. Neither had her team. Toiling as one, workers and laborers cleared up the debris, repaired what they could of the damaged grounds. They hung the more festive, aqua-colored fabrics used for special occasions. By the time the guests came outside early on Saturday afternoon, they could hardly believe there had been a hurricane. The workers had been that thorough, that efficient. Of course, it took only moments for the guests to pinch their noses. The smell from the ocean caused instant nausea for anyone not used to it—putrid, pungent. Laura explained to perturbed guests that the rancid stench was completely normal. That it had to do with the storm surge, bacteria that had risen from the undisturbed seabed would be swept back out to sea within a day. Maybe less. Some guests ran back indoors and called about flights out, asked for early checkout. It was announced the roads wouldn't be cleared until later in the day. They had to stay put. Those who were petulant were told that management was sourcing another method of transport.

Pablo called to tell Laura that there was no way through. They'd have to wait until the next day, Sunday. Laura considered that tourist man, wondered aloud if he was scared about what would be waiting for him when he returned. But Pablo said he'd not been troubled about the fact that he'd have to be questioned by the police. The wife and the husband both agreed to fully cooperate. The wife said her husband had been by her side for the entire trip. Pablo and Laura shared a moment of silence at the obvious lie. It was clear that the couple's priority was to go home as quickly as possible.

Miranda called a meeting of the senior members of the team. Those of Laura's colleagues who'd fled during the storm seemed unmoved by the disaster, by how the land had been battered. They were Monday-morning quarterbacking Laura's handling of the disaster and waxing poetic about their retrospective concerns about the hotel and the unacceptable power outage, insisting on the importance of finding transport for the folks who wanted to leave. Astrid, the Colombiana who'd remained behind, was calling in from the suite she occupied, eating a croissant and sipping on coffee inside her video box. Laura hadn't had breakfast, couldn't remember the last time she'd had a glass of water.

"It would be good to get as many guests out of the Grand Paloma as possible," Miranda said. She walked through the gates of Bordeaux Airport. It was bright blue behind her and the glare of fluorescent lights made Laura's eyes hurt. Laura didn't have the energy to ask her where she was headed next. Even Miranda had neglected to thank her for her efforts.

Dulce had been calling and texting her nonstop. Laura had eventually responded that Pablo was attempting to make his way back. She'd told Dulce that they would take the tourist man directly to the police station. She would be in touch. *Nothing is going to happen today,* she'd told Dulce. *They won't be here until tomorrow morning.* Then she'd blocked Dulce's number. She needed a break from the frantic mother.

She gazed through the immaculate glass of her office building, exhausted. As the águilas pescadoras arrived, gliding over the surface of that eerily gray ocean, then dipping under the surface to get their food, Laura felt a jolt of hope. If nature found a way, so could they. Once they had captured their fill, the birds lounged on the beach—unmoving, idle. Within a few minutes, there were thousands of ospreys lining the shore. Laura had a strange feeling that this was the way it had been long ago. Maybe there hadn't been so many deaths; maybe homes hadn't been destroyed. Maybe they wouldn't have to deal with a resurgence of dengue, Zika, or chikungunya. Maybe the hurricane had come to balance out the month's long drought, to give the land what it needed.

"Laura," Miranda said. "Did you hear me?"

Laura snapped back to attention. "Can you repeat the last part?"

Miranda nodded empathetically. "I know it's been endless. I just need you to stay with me for a few more hours, then you can take a long, big rest. Can you help Astrid? She's trying to work with the local police to leverage their helicopters to transport the guests to the airport. The roads won't be cleared for a day or two."

Laura nodded. She wrote to Astrid in the conference call's private chat that she'd be around for whatever she needed.

Don't worry, Astrid wrote back. I got this. Take a rest. You look like shit.

SUNDAY

CHAPTER
37

ON SUNDAY, THE DAY AFTER THE HURRICANE, THE STENCH from the beach had intensified to such an extent that many of the guests who had persevered through the storm finally began making arrangements to leave. The fetidness spread through the vents of the Grand Paloma Resort, mixed with the aroma from the diffusers that sprayed the lobby, hallways, and all other public spaces at ten-minute intervals, resulting in an odor that was simply revolting. Laura attempted to hold her breath as she moved through the lobby but made it only halfway before she had to take a big gulping breath. Onions, boiled eggs, rotten meat, stinky feet—all of it swirled into her nostrils and rested in the cavity of her mouth.

Most guests, especially those with a sensitivity to smells, had gone. Those who'd persisted past the opening of the airports hadn't lasted long once they'd seen the brown water coming out of the faucets and showers. Even though the front-desk staff had assured them that it would only be a matter of a few hours before their water was restored to its former clarity, few were willing to take the risk. Among those who remained, many had been complaining of headaches. They locked themselves in their suites and bedrooms, which were somewhat more bearable if you didn't step out onto a balcony, didn't open a door to let in any of the air from the hotel's interior. Meanwhile, Patrick, the VP for interiors (Laura's regretted, once-upon-a-time-booty call), refused to turn off the diffusers. He claimed that turning them off would make a bad situation worse. No surprise there. He was also of the mind that applying deodorant was just as good as taking a shower.

By Sunday morning, the resort was at an all-time low occupancy of 20 percent. Judging by the long lines of people waiting at checkout as Laura happened by reception, it would soon be even lower.

The engineers and contractors had finished their walk-through that morning. When Laura had set up a video conference with Miranda to review the storm's impact on the hotel, they'd found that the tally for a complete restoration was in the tens of millions of dollars. Considering the labor shortage caused by the mass deportations, they might've been looking at a price far upward of that. The casitas where the employees lived had been pummeled, were uninhabitable. The tents had all been blown away. The all-glass wellness center had been battered and would require a complete overhaul. Likewise, the business center and the spa—which included the multilevel gym—would need to be repaired, projects that would take many months to complete. The stunning skylight had been cracked and would require custom-made glass from Mexico. The only good news was that the aggressive seaweed, which had been a problem for many months, had vanished. After the initial cleanup, the beach, which was by far the worst place to stand because of the intensity of the funk, had the most pristine, beautifully clear sand anyone had ever seen.

"I can't believe this," Miranda said from the screen of Laura's computer. "That storm wasn't even supposed to touch the DR."

There was a question bouncing between the most-senior members of management that Laura was unaware of because of her pay grade. Was it worth the investment to get the hotel back to its full capacity, or did it make more sense to shut it down altogether—to sell it off to the interested party? Paloma Enterprises had already established itself as the biggest provider of commoditized rest in the Caribbean. In the last five years, they'd driven most of the competition out of business. Now it was clear that they could shift to a smaller footprint, provide fewer options to their guests on the islands. This would mean less employment for the locals, sure. But it made business sense, from a strategic standpoint, to know when it was time to cut losses. Already, newly arriving guests had been shifted to the Yellow Paloma, and the

cunning sales team had even convinced some to upgrade to better accommodations. It was the agility with which they were able to move
things around within hours that made the option a no-brainer.

Decisions would be made in a matter of days. Truth was, in a post-
pandemic world, resources were limited, contractors were in high demand, and the prices of construction materials were rocketing higher
and higher. And even without knowing that the fate of the entire hotel
rested in the hands of people who were currently off on vacation themselves, enjoying the one time of the year when they'd committed to real
family time, Laura didn't know that the senior leaders were one es-
cándalo away from calling it quits on the Grand Paloma Resort.

That ignorance meant that as soon as they finished discussing the
grounds, Laura briefed her boss about the developing situation with
Dulce's daughters. She explained that the father of the children was
supposed to arrive in the coming day or two. He was a powerful,
wealthy businessman. And though he'd have to use discretion because
the affected children were a product of an extramarital affair, there was
no doubt that he would wield the influence available to someone of his
status to get shit done. A man like that wouldn't accept the idea that
his children had been missing for nearly seventy-two hours and that
the police had decided there were more pressing issues than making a
real attempt to find them. That they hadn't so much as sent a single
patrol car out on their behalf. Their main hope, which was now dimin-
ishing hour by hour until it seemed heartbreakingly impossible, was
that the girls would be found alive.

Miranda almost choked on her coffee. "And you're sure this man in
the footage is one of our guests?"

"Positive," Laura said. "The police will question him today."

"Let the police do their jobs," Miranda said. "Let's just hope that
there's been some mistake. That this situation doesn't implicate us."

THE STAFF AT THE resort were relieved to see the guests leaving. It
meant that Laura's denial of their anxious requests to go home were

unjustified. Laura had told them that their jobs might not be waiting for them when they wanted to return. Most had gritted their teeth, cursed her out, turned their backs, and left anyway.

There was no way she could tell them that management had decided that since revenue would decrease by 70 to 80 percent, she would need to cut the staff ahead of September. They'd likely only keep a quarter of the people who worked there. In the coming days, she'd have to deliver the bad news to those who'd made their way back thinking their jobs would be waiting for them and watch as it dawned on them that in addition to coping with the devastation of having lost homes, livestock, and even family members—losses from which it would likely take months, if not years, to recover—they would also need to search for new jobs.

Laura was glad when she was able to make it out the front doors, climb into one of the resort's SUVs, and get the hell off the resort grounds. She was less glad about the task ahead. She'd timed it so that when Pablo reached the police station, she would already be there. Today, they would get to the bottom of what the guests of PH7 had to do with Dulce's daughters' disappearance.

Laura was a woman of her word. But she wasn't a dummy. She needed to understand what this man would say about her sister's involvement. Elena would need to be protected at all costs. She'd texted Pablo, who'd confirmed that he and the tourist family had left the Yellow Paloma hours earlier. It was slow going due to the debris and flooding on the road. The family had decided that they were ready to head home, he said. It had ended up being easier than he'd anticipated. There had been no resistance whatsoever once it started raining in Jarabacoa, too.

When she finished the exchange with Pablo, she considered what to do next. She knew it would be risky to call Dulce, but chances were that she'd find out the tourist man was back in town the minute he checked back in to the hotel. She had to attempt to at least not rile her up further. She called Dulce and told her that she was heading to the police station, that the tourist from the video would be there.

"I'll meet you there," Dulce said.

"It's not a good idea for you to go," Laura said. "Pablo and I will be there. We'll advocate. We'll make sure that we get the information to you as quickly as possible."

Dulce didn't respond. Then she said, "You can't expect me to sit at home while the only person who knows what happened to my girls is a couple of miles away."

"Nothing good will come of you being there, Dulce," Laura insisted. "I can come over to your house as soon as we learn what happened. I will pick you up."

Dulce grumbled something unintelligible. Then she said, "I don't want you anywhere near me or my house. You're a fucking snake."

"The police will not take anything you say seriously," Laura said, knowing that she had to be tougher than she wanted to be with her friend. "They wouldn't even go out and search for your girls, for shit's sake. Stay home and let me at least try to use some of the hotel's influence to get us real information."

"I don't trust anything you say," Dulce said, then hung up on her.

Laura regretted the call. Making her way toward Ciudad Paloma Falls, she swerved around a large tree that was in the middle of the road. That made her put the phone down. The last thing she needed was to get into an accident on the way to the police station. The asphalt road was still flooded in certain places, and where it wasn't flooded, there were gradations of sand and pebbles that had washed onto the road from the beach. She was relieved that the hurricane hadn't felled as many trees as she'd feared. Ahead, a swarm of those ugly ospreys that had been eerily present on the beach yesterday moved from one side of the forest to the other. They had taken refuge among the trees, and as she drove along the main road that cut the land in half, she lowered her window. The birds had a jarring, disturbing cry. It matched her current mood.

IN CIUDAD PALOMA FALLS, she found Pablo pacing up and down the cobblestone street. The high-end designer stores were still boarded up. They would likely stay closed for several weeks. There were a lot of locals about, which was unusual, coming in and out of the police station with worried expressions darkening their features. According to the bits and pieces of conversations she caught, they needed help reaching their families who were stranded in the parts of the mountain that were still inaccessible. The police kept saying that there was no access to the helicopters. She thought of the scene she'd just left back at the hotel, of the orderly way in which her staff were triaging the needs of the foreigners—of course they'd call to make arrangements for flights, for transportation to the airports. The police helicopters were in use at the Grand Paloma Resort to get wealthy folks to the airports. Here, based on the hopeless looks of those who left the station, Laura knew that the answer they were receiving was much the same as the one Dulce had gotten on Friday. *Tough luck. Get out of our face.*

She was relieved to see Pablo waiting for her. He looked a little pale, a little tired, but no worse for wear.

Pablo told her that it had all been so civilized. When he'd told the tourist man that they'd been asked to go directly to the police station, he had nodded, unbothered. The wife had also been unconcerned, pretending not to hear the exchange, watching the landscape blur past. When they'd arrived, the chief of police had shaken hands with the tourist man, then ushered him to a back room. Pablo said that all this had happened in the span of the last ten minutes.

"Did you follow them?" Laura asked.

"Of course," Pablo said.

"And?" Laura asked impatiently.

Pablo shifted his weight from one foot to the other. "They played the video. He said it wasn't him."

"But it obviously is him," she said.

"I know that. The police chief said I had to go while they spoke. Last I heard, he said there were sufficient grounds to hold him and so he had to answer some questions, make a statement."

Laura felt her blood pressure rise. She motioned for Pablo to follow her, and they wove their way through the many bodies that had amassed in the small waiting room. A few people yelled at her to wait her turn. Laura ignored them. She wasn't about to wait. The AC wasn't on, even though the electricity was working. The air became ever more stifling as she forced her way to the back. With an ease that she didn't quite feel, she pushed all the way through to an office space that was meant for personnel only. No one stopped her.

Her eyes lingered on the wall with the Dominican flag. Dominicans often boasted that DR was the only country with the Bible on its national flag, in the heart of its coat of arms. Open to the Gospel of John 8:32: *And you will know the truth, and the truth shall set you free.* Laura focused on the way a tourist invitation had been overwritten on the blue ribbon above the coat of arms. *God* a shadow of *Please, Homeland* a shadow of *Come, Freedom* a shadow of *Again.* Doña Fella had taught every child in Pico Diablo to reject the idea of the sacredness of the history as portrayed in that flag. The colors themselves were suspect, she said: Blue to symbolize freedom for whom? Red the blood spilled by what heroes? White as salvation, really?

Laura had dealt with the policemen in this station many times. And because she knew that the tourist man had already been arrested a few times for hard partying the week before, she felt that she and Dulce were at a disadvantage. The tourist man probably understood how things moved here. He didn't have to look at the flag to understand the historic significance and dismiss it. To know that the only color that mattered here was the green of his dollars.

"Where are the wife and the kid?" Laura asked. She wondered if they could recruit the wife to talk some sense into the man. Maybe if she knew what was at stake, knew that these girls—so close to her own daughter in age—had been now missing for three days, she'd help them.

"They're waiting in the car," Pablo said. "The husband told her he would let her know if they needed her statement as an alibi." He shifted away from her uncomfortably. He seemed to be hiding something from her. She wondered if he had spoken to Elena.

"You made quite an impression at the Yellow Paloma," Laura said. "One of their managers called me this morning. Pilar? Asked me to tell you there's a job for you there, if you want it."

She wasn't sure Pablo had heard her. He seemed distracted, far away.

"Humph," she said. "Have you gotten in touch with Elena? Did she call you again?"

He shook his head.

"Coño, Pablo," she said, exasperated. "What's wrong with you?"

Laura felt the heat of the room on her scalp. It itched in a spot that she couldn't quite reach. She wished she could rip the extensions clean off her head. She worried that she might faint, might scream.

"Listen," he said. "I know we've got other things to worry about, but have you heard from Vida? I've been texting her and calling since the storm hit but can't get through."

Laura sighed. She remembered Dulce saying that Pablo didn't know Vida was pregnant and felt herself soften toward him, then become pragmatic. She couldn't tell him that now. He would rush away, and no one she trusted would be around to help her.

"I haven't heard from her," Laura said. "I'm sure if she wanted to be found, she would be. There is no power in Pico Diablo. Telephone and cell towers are scheduled to be repaired late next week, maybe the week after, depending on how much work has to be done to restore power here."

She pointed outside, through the crowds of people and the walls that blocked their view of the fancy stores.

"There's no Wi-Fi or electricity at the hotel?" Pablo asked, shocked.

Laura looked at him like he was dense.

"Claro que hay," she said. "That was the power company's first stop. They'll come here next. Once they restore power here, then they'll get to the rural areas. The mountain isn't a priority for anyone."

Pablo considered what it would mean for Vida to be stranded without water, electricity, Wi-Fi, or access to groceries for more than a day. He shook his head. He hoped that she had bunked up with someone in town instead of going to the mountain to wait out the storm. Everyone in Paloma Falls knew how treacherous it was up there during and after even a little bit of rain. He had a nagging feeling that something wasn't right. That he should go up to the mountain. It was an instinct he'd learned to trust from his father. Sometimes while he was out on the water on a cold morning, he'd have a sense that he needed to go that way or the other, and his father always told him to trust it. *There are things our bodies know that our minds can't quite comprehend.* With that, Pablo decided that he would go, right after this. He wasn't going to ask for permission. He would drop off these guests back at the hotel and make his way to Vida.

When the chief and the tourist man emerged from the back, Laura couldn't believe her eyes. The police chief was attempting to look serious, but there was a jolly pep to his step that told Laura all she needed to know. The tourist man was off the hook. How much money had it taken this time? she wondered. She tried to slow her rapid heartbeat, knew her breathing sounded labored. She felt repulsion at herself because she was a bit relieved that this was the outcome. She wasn't sure that there was any way this tourist could go down without bringing her sister with him.

"I can fill you in, licenciada," the police chief said to Laura, extending his hand to the tourist. Laura watched in stunned disbelief as the two men shook hands.

"All clear," the tourist said. Laura stepped in front of him to block his way. He walked around her and stood in front of Pablo.

"What did you learn about the girls?" Laura asked. "What did he have to say?"

"Unfortunately, this man isn't who we're looking for," the police chief said. After walking her a bit farther away, he continued in a lower tone. "But I had to write a warrant for your sister's arrest for alleged human trafficking."

Laura tried to make sense of what the police chief was saying. He was letting the man from the video go. And the arrest warrant was for her sister, who was on camera accepting money from this man, but had walked away and left after the girls used the bathroom, after the girls could be seen running around on the beach. It made no sense.

"We can lift the warrant once she comes and gives us a full statement. She's really the only one who can tell us who is in that video."

If there was one thing Laura was sure of, it was that it wouldn't matter what Elena said. The video was clear as day. It was unmistakably this man.

"All clear?" the tourist man asked and took a step in the direction of the exit.

"Not quite," the police chief said, as if the man wasn't playing the part they'd rehearsed. "Remember that you can't leave the country for any reason just yet. We'll hopefully wrap up the investigation in the next day or so."

"We're planning to leave tomorrow," the tourist said with finality.

"You can get your sister to come in today, yes?" the chief asked Laura. Laura was surprised that no one had told the police chief that her sister was abroad.

"She's out of the country," Laura said. "I'm not sure when she'll be back."

"Have her call me," he said. "You have my phone number."

Just as Laura considered whether she should get her sister a lawyer before she spoke to this man, Dulce ran toward them, followed by the same flat-assed police cadet who had ushered Laura to a room to claim the remains of her father. Dulce's eyes were bloodshot, her manner desperate. What had Laura been thinking, telling Dulce they'd be here? How could Laura have expected her to not show up?

"Where are my daughters?" she shouted at the tourist.

The man shot a look at the police chief. Everyone in the station grew quiet.

"Fabien will be here by tomorrow," Dulce said to the chief. "There will be hell to pay if you let this man get away."

"We have no grounds to keep this man," the chief said in a reasonable tone. Laura suspected that he was hedging his bets. He didn't think a wealthy and powerful man like Fabien would trouble himself with this woman or her children. If he did, he would have done something by now.

"Where are they?" Dulce yelled again.

"I'm sorry about your situation," the tourist said to Dulce. He was very calm. "I'm sure you must be worried sick. But that isn't me in that video. I've never met your daughters."

"It *is* you in that video," she said desperately. She searched Laura's face for agreement. Laura meant to grab at her, to offer Dulce some comfort, but she found herself frozen in place. She looked helplessly toward Pablo, trying to wordlessly tell him to hold Dulce. But his eyes were fixed on the tourist.

"Sir," Laura managed to say. "If there's any chance you have an inkling of an idea of where these girls are ..."

"How would I know where they are," the man said sharply, "if I've never seen them?" Then he turned to Pablo. "Let's go."

Dulce lunged at the man. She was ferocious, slapping and kicking at him, screaming that he needed to tell her what happened.

"Did you hurt them? If you hurt my girls, I will kill you."

She bit into his face. The pimply cadet, who was closest to her, tried to get at her, but he was slammed in the chest by an errant kick. It took the police chief and two additional policemen to get Dulce off the tourist. They quickly put handcuffs on her and dragged her, sobbing, away.

The tourist man covered his bleeding cheek with the palm of his hand. The gash bled through his fingers. Laura remembered the way she'd scratched her sister's face with her bracelet. That had been in the same spot where Dulce had bitten this man. Laura closed her eyes, willing the chaos to end.

The cadet was asking the tourist if he wanted to press charges. The man looked at his bloody hands, nodded. Pablo snapped into action then, begging for mercy, explaining that the girls had been missing since Thursday. It had been three days. This woman had been a dear friend of his since they were children. The tourist seemed stunned and didn't acknowledge anything Pablo had said. He followed the cadet, who led him to the appropriate forms.

Dulce: arrested for assaulting a police officer and a civilian.

Elena: would be arrested the minute she set foot in this country for alleged human trafficking.

The tourist stepped out of the police station, bleeding but free. The policemen who had witnessed the attack felt sympathy for his ordeal. After all, he'd come to the island for a restful vacation and had ended up surviving a category-five hurricane, only to be attacked by a neglectful mother who everyone knew ran a prostitution ring.

———

WHEN LAURA REACHED THE hotel, she immediately went to her office. But there were too many of her colleagues there, those who'd finally made it back after leaving them. Many ongoing emergencies had to be dealt with in the aftermath of a hurricane. There was the issue of the non-potable water. There was the issue of the tons and tons of food that had to be discarded because the power had been out for over twelve hours. They couldn't risk any kind of illness outbreak. She wove in and out of cubicles, in and out of conference rooms. Then it dawned on her. There was one room that was free. The Wall Street bros who'd insisted on the stunning, all-glass ocean-facing conference room that could accommodate up to one hundred people had instead ended up holding every single "business" discussion on the golf course. It would be free. They had all left, speedily, as soon as the storm had changed course.

She made her way to the conference room, which she was shocked to find had neither glass damage nor the bad smell. It must've been the way the glass was sealed. She sat in the room, knowing how important it was that she make this next call. But looking at the ocean, at its serene movement, at the foam rippling on the surface here and there, she thought of her father. Her mother had always said that her father was the ocean. He left, but he'd always come back—just as the waves always retreated and came back.

Laura understood that there were those who never paid for mistakes. Who didn't even need to acknowledge harm or attempt repair. Did it even matter whether those who had caused the most harm felt remorse? She didn't think she'd ever forgive herself for what she was about to do. Laura had heard, a thousand times, that the road to freedom began with a step: forgiveness. That the ones shackled were those who held on to rage, hurt, sadness. Every time she thought of her dead father, she felt the searing imprint of fury. She was glad he was dead. His desire to leave, to forge a life consistently out of his reach, had led to the worst thing that had ever happened to him. But before that, it had led to the worst thing that had ever happened to their family.

She'd never heard him express remorse for her mother's death. It had been as if he'd thought that if he ran away, progressed past it, all would be forgiven, forgotten. Before the last trip her father had taken to seek asylum in the United States, the trip that had ultimately claimed his life, she had refused to say goodbye. Maybe this would be the time when he'd make it and be out of their lives forever, she'd hoped. As the days had turned into weeks that turned into months, she'd replaced the worry that often visited her when he went missing with vivid memories of how he used to beat her mother. She'd felt sympathetic toward Elena; she was more lenient and indulged her youthful impulses to spare her from knowing the worst about their father, which was also the worst about their lives. Even now, she felt fiercely protective of Elena's innocence. If only one of them would get to live a good life, overflowing with autonomy, abundance, and joy, it would be her sister.

The tourist was lying, and since the girls were missing and might remain missing forever, he was the only one who could solve the mystery of what had happened. Her sister had left while the girls were alive. He had been upstairs, away from them and away from Elena. Laura also understood that when Fabien came to town, there would be hell to pay, and the police would quickly pivot to pin this on her sister. There was no way she'd have Elena make any kind of statement. Fuck that.

Laura wiped at her wet cheeks. She needed to keep a clear head. She placed her hands on her hips à la Superman, the way an article had once advised her to do anytime she needed to feel powerful. She reminded herself that in this same conference room she'd been taught—by the sharpest minds in global leadership—all she needed to know to land on top, no matter how bleak the outlook. But there was no surge of invincibility, only a sense of duty.

It was time. She video-called her boss. Miranda was surrounded by sheer curtains, seated on a bouclé couch. It was the familiar Paloma Resort suite. She was dressed up, didn't have a lot of time to talk. Laura explained what had happened at the police station.

"So the police said he was cleared," her boss said.

"Not quite," Laura responded. She tried to think of the best way to explain that it was likely the police chief had been bribed. There was no question that the man in the video was the guest who was purporting complete innocence. That it was the fact he didn't admit to the truth of having been there, that his wife was willing to lie for him, that convinced Laura he had in fact done something criminal. Otherwise, why lie?

"The last thing we need is a scandal," Miranda said.

Miranda explained to Laura what was happening at the most senior level of Paloma Enterprises. The bosses were considering shutting down their location. The Yellow Paloma could swallow the overflow and quickly be put into rotation.

"It would serve the greater good if this mess went away quietly," Miranda said.

Laura nodded.

"Solve the issue, Laura," her boss urged. "I'm giving you authority to do what needs to be done to clean it up. You know the code for the safe in my office. There should be plenty of petty cash for any fines."

Laura nodded. She would go back to the police station. It would be her turn to spend some time in the back room to discover and remove any passport restrictions they may have placed on the tourist's record. She would take the petty cash and get the tourist cleared of all wrongdoing—after all, the video showing him giving money to her sister proved nothing; the man couldn't realistically be charged with anything. Pablo told her the last time her sister had seen the girls, they'd been swimming in the sea. No fault there, either. If she was lucky, she'd have these people to the airport by the end of the day and would never have to deal with them again for the remainder of her life. She wanted them off her island for good.

She thought about how easily the police chief had believed the tourist when he'd claimed it wasn't him. It had been near-effortless, truly, how he'd gotten away with whatever it was he'd done. She felt a loss such as her father must have felt each time he'd returned, defeated and injured. The second-to-last attempt had cost him his pinky before the last time, when he'd lost everything. The amputation that Laura experienced now, as she took the first step toward ensuring the freedom of a person who didn't deserve it, would be invisible to others. But as she gave her back to the tumultuous views of the sun and sea, she felt as if, with this last decision, she'd mutilated the last part of her that made her human. From this day forth, she'd be walking around with half a heart. Even now, she felt its earlier gallop slow to an imperceptible trot. Soon enough, it would stop beating altogether, leaving every vein hollow, dusty.

CHAPTER
38

LATER IN THE DAY ON SUNDAY, PABLO DISMISSED THE STENCH on the resort grounds the way one might ignore human waste on the side of the road. He hurried to move past it and put it out of his mind, even as it persisted and intensified. There was no escaping it. In his garden-view room, the odor had been imperceptible. It was most prominent on the balconies of the oceanfront presidential suites, and so the few guests who had dug in their heels to push through, hoping that the infernal funk would pass within a few hours, found themselves in the strange position of considering downgrades—rooms that were as far away as possible from the ocean they'd paid tens of thousands of dollars to gaze at. Pablo had been asked to move his living quarters to the twelfth floor and now had one of the most expensive views on the entire island.

A pretty brown baby waddled onto the expansive balcony next to his. An older Asian woman with cropped hair soon followed the toddler and made a series of gagging sounds as she reached for him. The baby was much faster than she was and ran in zigzags.

"No, baby," she said in English. "This air is terrible for you; Mommy will be mad-mad-mad that you are breathing this terrible air." She grabbed the speedy tot and hurried back indoors, closing the glass doors with such force that the frame on Pablo's suite rattled. She hadn't even noticed Pablo. He wondered if, on seeing him in his pristine white robe, she might've thought that he belonged here—if she'd mistaken him for a paying guest instead of hired staff like her. Though he'd been resentful when Laura had first told him not to set one foot off the resort grounds until they'd sorted out what was happening with the tourist man, he now felt flushed with happiness that he'd made it to the top floor. Laura had chosen him to receive this upgrade during the rush of the last round of departures.

The only time he'd been in this suite had been to give a massage and finish it with a satisfying fuck. But this time, he was here because he'd earned it. This room was his.

Twelve floors beneath him, the white sand glittered, the sun and wind creating a mesmerizing illusion of motion on its surface. Backward and forward, side to side. The hurricane had swept away the pebbles that management had deposited on the beach in an attempt to get rid of the aggressive seaweed. The beach was gorgeous—if you didn't mind the smell. He almost laughed at the thought that this was what senior management had so long desired—pristine, seaweed-free shores. The pummeled coconut trees had already been replaced with new ones. Where had those come from? Pablo had no idea. While Pablo had been driving the tourists from the Yellow Paloma to the police station, naïvely hoping that the police would finally get to the bottom of what had happened to Dulce's girls, his colleagues had been mobilized on this beach, and they had done such an absolute job of removing debris that by the time the first few guests had decided to wander onto the shore, there had been no sign a hurricane had ever struck the resort.

Well, unless you had a nose. And happened to see the buildings that had been flattened by the storm, or venture beyond the resort grounds to the community that had been devastated by the losses— where Pablo knew, because of all the storms he'd survived, that it would take so long to recover. Some people would never recover.

Pablo understood that he would need to vacate the premises the nanosecond the bad air drifted away from the Grand Paloma Resort, but in this moment, as the sky turned a chalky gray, he felt his yearning for Vida pierce him as if he'd been harpooned through the chest. Vida would make a joke about all the mierda he'd eaten to get to this floor. She'd have no idea how real that statement would be.

Vida had often spoken about the easy relationship she had with decay. She never seemed bothered by the way her patients smelled. Here, Pablo was reminded of his father's last few days. He'd smelled like death way before his heart had stopped beating. But Vida had leaned over his body, gently wiping at his brow with cold compresses, lowering her ear to catch his feverish mumblings. In the evenings, when she'd gone home, Pablo would get water from the backyard well and try his best to clean his father's skeletal body. So often, he'd sullied himself with piss, shit, vomit. So often, Pablo had to step away from his father in disgust, thinking of the indignities that came not only with bad health but with poverty. He was certain that a bit of disposable income would have given his father the dignity he deserved.

Months after his father had died, when he'd made a comment to Vida saying so, she had disagreed with him. The pain would have been managed better, she agreed. But no matter how much money you earned, when it came time to die, there was little dignity for anyone. *Death,* she'd said, *isn't about dignity. It's all spit, shit, blood, and piss. We go out exactly the way we came in. What truly mattered,* she insisted, *was who held your hand at the end. Whose love would carry your memory forward.* Pablo saw her statements as a kindness. She was just trying to lessen his guilt about not doing better by his father, holding on to the limited traditions of the fisherman in his family, and living a life so small that his father had had no option but to fit his dissipation within its confines.

Now he allowed himself to sit with all he'd broken. Pablo, the first in many generations who no longer needed to go out in the morning to fish.

He'd tried to help bring that tourist man to justice. Once he'd left the man at the infirmary, he'd gone back to the police station. Pablo had told the police chief that he'd been at the bar the night the girls had gone missing, that he'd seen with his own eyes the passport that identified the tourist they'd just let go. The police chief had nodded and scribbled some notes in a raggedy-looking spiral notebook, not once making a record on the computer. When Pablo had asked the chief if he was going to arrest the tourist, he'd curtly thanked Pablo for his statement, not bothering to respond to his question.

When the suite's landline rang, he ignored it, sure it was for the paying residents of the room. He thought about Vida—how she hadn't called or responded to a text in so long. He'd thought that everything that came after a hurricane—the illness brought on by bad water and insects—might necessitate her to seek him out, even if it was just for a place to stay temporarily. What if she was calling? But when he made it to the phone, it had stopped ringing.

The doorbell to the suite rang. A wireless speaker that he hadn't noticed pulsed with a soft blue light. "*There's someone at the door,*" an electronic voice said, speaking English in an elegant French accent.

Pablo tightened the belt of the plush white robe.

When he opened the door, Laura stepped inside.

"You wasted no time making yourself at home, huh?" she said.

"It *is* home," he said, standing at attention, scared she would say that they'd demoted him, that they had taken away his Platinum Member Companion status.

"Can you get dressed? I need you to come with me," she said.

"What happened to my day off?"

"Never mind that," she said. "Just hurry up."

Pablo consented without another question. He went into the bedroom and changed into his second-shift light-blue uniform. The bloodstained one had been replaced. His thoughts of Vida and what he would do next were suspended to be retrieved later, or forgotten.

WHEN THEY EXITED THE guest elevators on the ground floor, Laura stared at the strange shadows across the floor. She searched around her until she understood what they were. Up above them, on the cracked skylight, were the lifeless carcasses of hundreds of ospreys, splayed across the fractured glass. Aside from the expected stench from the oceanfront, which had diminished by now, the dead birds were part of the reason the hotel smelled so bad. She noticed all her workers scurrying about, not once pausing to notice the shadows at their feet. She used her walkie-talkie to call the head of grounds staff. Gustavo needed to get someone up there fast.

When she focused on the hallway ahead, she noticed a camera crew interviewing the VP for guest services and media relations about the hotel's generosity in housing those who'd been left destitute by the storm. Laura came to a full stop and stood aghast, watching Astrid answer questions. Astrid, who had disappeared the night of the storm, who'd been nowhere to be found. Astrid, who now grabbed the microphone from her interviewer so the BBC logo was centered a few inches from her mouth—this was a shot she'd practiced for, a shot that would become her profile picture on LinkedIn by the end of the day.

"Bueno," Astrid said. "That was truly done because of the generosity of a couple of anonymous guests. We would have housed those affected by the storm. Our hotel's policy is to be a shelter of safety in uncertain times—that goes for the guests and for our local family. You know, we in the hospitality business have a habit of giving tourists a bad rap, especially here in DR. We have this love-hate thing going. But as the climate crisis makes these storms ever more powerful and destructive, our communities' ability to survive will be ever more dependent on international aid. Everyone knows that the future is a frightening place when we consider natural disasters. It isn't just homes, businesses, and crops that are destroyed. Everything that keeps us safe—from sewage systems to water filtration—all of it is affected when we lose power. We will not recover our infrastructure unless we galvanize our international community to be as generous as possible. There is an intersection between natural disasters, infrastructure resiliency, and social justice. We at Paloma Enterprises understand how these intersections affect people in reality and not just in the abstract. The members of our society who are most affected are often those who are also the most vulnerable, who have the least ability to advocate for themselves."

Then, as if on cue, a group of workers and tourists wearing Paloma T-shirts, caps, and gloves made their way through the lobby with shovels. The Vargas sisters led the charge.

"We aren't here to exploit the natural beauty of the island," Astrid finished, glowing at the timing of the group's entrance. "We're here to leave it better than we found it. We want to remind those watching that only a handful of us will ever be positioned to affect the world. We can choose to do it for the good of humanity."

Laura closed her eyes momentarily, a vein throbbing on her forehead, then sped out of the lobby.

CHAPTER
39

FOR THE THIRD TIME ON SUNDAY, PABLO DROVE THE RESORT SUV in the direction of Paloma Falls. Laura had explained that they were on their way to the police station. She told him what she needed him to do. She avoided making eye contact and had wisely insisted he drive so that his ability to take his eyes off the road would be limited.

"Laura," he said, when he finally found his voice. "You can't be serious."

"I already made the change in the computer. You just have to say that you were with them every day since they checked in."

"To the police," Pablo said. "You want me to lie to the police and say I was with the family, with that man, the entire day the girls went missing?"

"Yes," Laura said.

"You removed the paper trail that linked Elena to them as their babysitter?" he asked.

Laura turned her face away so that only the enormous bun at the nape of her neck was in his view. Not her stinging eyes, not her tight lips, not her constricted throat.

"The police aren't going to do shit. We already know that. And there's nothing anyone can do with the disaster of the hurricane's aftermath. The earlier we can get this man off this island, the better."

Pablo gripped the steering wheel. He hadn't told Laura that he'd doubled back to the police station. Laura was probably right; he'd been amazed at how corrupt the police chief had been. But he also believed that the truth would come out, that the girls were alive, and that their father, with his own money and power, would out-bribe this tourist. If the tourist was gone, it would be impossible for them to get to the truth.

"But if he's responsible for something terrible," he said, "he will never pay for it. Fabien is supposed to land in the next few hours. Maybe with his influence, he can get the police to focus. Laura, you have to leave the man grounded. You gotta keep him at the resort. At least until we can find out what happened."

"The girls are dead," Laura said. "That's what happened."

Pablo winced. "What do you mean? Did they find them?"

Laura shook her head. "No," she said. "But I found one of their T-shirts at the beach. It had been in the water for days, ripped apart. There is no way those girls survived."

"Why didn't you tell the police?"

"We just need to focus on damage control, Pablo. Those girls may never be found."

"You don't know that," Pablo said. "There's a million reasons why the T-shirt could've been in the water. The girls could be somewhere, right now, alive."

"Where are they? If they were alive, don't you think someone would have found them by now?"

Laura's voice broke. She brought her hand to her mouth, her eyes glistening with unshed tears.

"The police will absolve that tourist of any fault no matter what," she said, gaining control over her voice. "Men like him never pay."

"That isn't true," he said. "There's some corruption here, but if we have solid proof that he did something wrong, God forbid, something terrible, he will be arrested. He will pay. But I have a good feeling that the girls are alive. That they're unharmed."

"Por el amor de Dios, Pablo. They took his word. They chose to believe him. Those girls are gone. How could they have survived the storm? Three days, Pablo. It's been three days!"

Laura met his gaze. Pablo could see that her eyes were bloodshot, tiny veins visible. She might have cried before she came to get him. There was something manic about her blinking. When was the last time she'd slept? Eaten?

"Horrible people get away with terrible things all the time," Laura said, irritated. "This way, at least you and I get to keep our jobs. Elena keeps her record clean."

Pablo pulled the car over. "You can't possibly mean that," he said, getting out of the car. "Consider for just one moment that the girls may be alive. These are vital moments when we need to find them. If he goes, he takes the secret of where they are with him."

"Keep living in the clouds," Laura said. "You need a villain? Someone to tell you what you have to do so you don't feel bad later?"

She threw her hands in the air.

"You either help me or you're fired," she said, not leaving the car. She folded her hands over her chest. "We might *all* get fired, Pablo. They are considering selling the hotel. If we don't make this mess go away, if it turns into a scandal, they will do just that. Hundreds of people will lose their jobs. Can you live with that? And all for what? To try to bring to justice someone who will never pay for what he's done? Nothing we do will bring the girls back."

It took a few moments for Pablo to realize that they'd arrived at the place where Don Quito's sugarcane stand had been. The wooden shack had been lifted and swept far away—it was only because of the peculiar placement of the coconut trees behind it, the way they bent toward each other in the shape of a heart, that he understood where they were. He felt it was a miracle that the trees had survived the storm.

"You're right," Pablo said, trying to change tactics. "It's possible that he will get away with whatever it is he did. But the difference is complicity. You don't want to be the one who made it easy for him to go."

Pablo spoke about the legacy of Pico Diablo, of their ancestors. About the pride and strength it had taken for people who had been in chains, who had been forced to labor relentlessly, to escape enslavement. He told her that both of them had this pride and strength running through their veins.

"All of it is a lie," Laura said. "None of that is true. That's not the real history of this town."

Pablo stared, waiting for her to go on. She almost told him then that the town had been founded by Haitians and Dominicans who had been fleeing a massacre. Somehow, the obligation she felt to the secret, to her dead father, kept her from it.

"Never mind that," she said. "Vida is pregnant, Pablo. She's about to have your baby. And what are you going to offer her if you lose this job?"

There had been a time, months ago, when he had let the love of his life walk away with the fear that it might be forever, that he would have done anything for the job. Even on Thursday afternoon, when she'd paused by his station as he descaled the fish, roping her arm around her waist, he'd had this feeling—a certainty that if he begged her to take him back, assured her that he was done with everyone else, she would say yes. It had scared him, the knowledge that the thing he wanted was within his reach, if only he could make the right choice. But what was the right choice? Laura's revelation had an unintended impact. Instead of thinking about work, or about stability, or about money, he thought instead about the way Vida's body had been pulling at his since the breakup. It was what—*who*—their love had made that had beckoned. He turned to look at the forest, up at the mountain where they'd both grown up. Pablo felt a sadness he'd never let enter his heart, not since his father died. What did it mean to live a life of dignity? He wished his father was around to help him understand how he could be a better man. He seemed to always get it wrong. Was he supposed to stay or go?

He'd kept his mouth shut about what he knew. He had ignored the pleas of his friends to help search for the girls, thinking he might be of more help if he had a bit more status, a bit more power. He'd allowed himself to use his body to forget, to push away the love he had for everyone he'd ever cared about—and this job always required more. He'd let the tourist do painful, unspeakable things to him. Then he'd turned over and let the wife ride him. *I can't believe this is your job,* she had said. Which should have made him feel big, proud, but had instead brought to his chest the weight of shame.

Vida's house was six miles up the mountain. If he cut through the forest, he could make it four. He'd have to pass the shack where he'd grown up, where he'd never returned since he'd buried his father and wandered into the resort, asking for help from his old school friend, who'd once shown up at their door soaking wet in the middle of a hurricane with her little sister, asking for help for their injured mom. Laura had cried with relief when his father had opened the door, shouting that no one else in their entire village had helped. He remembered how on the way to the hospital, as Laura had looked distraught and he'd attempted to help her care for a sleepy Elena, he'd tried to distract her. *Did you know that if you walked to the moon at a rate of three miles every hour without ever stopping, it would take you nine and a half years to reach it?* Laura had emerged from the place where she'd been until then, a place he'd intuited was one of despair and horror, and said to him, *Pablo, you're a real idiot. Who would walk? Who could? The only amazing thing about the moon is that it doesn't have its own light. It gets its illumination from the sun.*

Thirteen years later, he wasn't sure whether that was true. But when he'd knocked on her office door, asking if she could hook him up with a job, she had said yes without thinking twice. There had been something about the way Laura—a woman who was known to take her job way too seriously, who was rumored to refuse to do favors, who wouldn't provide employment in exchange for bribes—had caved in. She'd seemed relieved, as if she'd finally been able to settle a debt she'd been waiting her entire life to be rid of. At the time, he'd thought that Laura was the illumination that lit their town. Everyone else the moon, she the invisible sun. Sure, people disliked her, but she had risen. Now, as she stood in front of him, he hardly recognized her. Was it the resort that had ruined her? The loss of her mother? Her father? The need to care for another person when she herself should have been the one who was cared for, tended to?

"I'm not going with you to the police station," he said simply. He handed her the keys.

He made his way into the thick forest while Laura shouted demands for him to return immediately. He climbed over some smaller fallen trees and a ridged zinc roof that had landed in this spot from God knew where. On the drive back from the Yellow Paloma, they'd heard that the hurricane had had the fastest winds ever recorded in the

Caribbean. He felt a sharp, stabbing pain in the heel of his left foot—and a gush of blood soon followed. He stopped, squatted, looked at the wound. It was an ugly cut. He was off to a rough start.

When he glanced behind him, Laura had folded her arms, as if she was waiting for him to come to his senses. He turned away from her for the second time, knowing that he was also turning away from the shiny, mud-free SUV with the Grand Paloma Resort logo emblazoned on both front doors. He was turning away from the presidential suite, the garden-view room, the warm meals, and the nice uniforms. But instead of being scared, he had the sensation that he was being enveloped in a warm embrace—that maybe, just this once, he was headed in the right direction.

He distracted himself from the throbbing injury on his foot and the trail of blood behind him by considering how he might be able to make a living. Truthfully, he hadn't felt quite like himself since he'd been away from the boat, from the ocean, from his job catching marvels beneath the surface of the sea.

A swarm of mosquitoes went about making Pablo their next meal. He glanced around, sure that there were plants that acted as natural repellents, but whatever knowledge he'd once had was gone. Instead, he was surprised to find that miles away from the resort, the peonies that had been growing in the greenhouse were sprinkled all around this land. It was as if a giant hand had picked them up and dropped them, roots and all, right where the dirt was moist. Pablo didn't notice that just ten feet from him, beyond the peonies, there were eucalyptus, lavender, and peppermint plants growing by the bucketful, any of which would have kept the pests away. But Pablo missed them altogether.

He made his way slowly, thinking about Vida. *It isn't that difficult to choose to live a good life,* she had said. *What you call small is as big as the entire earth to me.* She had been right. He had been obsessed with puras tonterías.

CHAPTER

40

WHEN LAURA'S PHONE RANG, AND SHE SAW A PLUS SIGN followed by too many zeros to count, she sighed with relief. First, because it meant that cellphone service had been restored outside the footprint of the Grand Paloma Resort and extended to Paloma Falls. Second, because she'd been keeping all her worries about her sister's refusal to be in touch at bay. As the phone rang, Pablo disappeared into the forest ahead. Laura had been considering following in his footsteps, reminding him of all that he owed her. The ringing phone halted that plan.

On the other side of her *hello* was her sister's voice, choked with emotion. It had been three days since they'd spoken, but it felt as if it had been so much longer than that.

"Sis," Elena said. "Are you okay? After the storm."

"I'm good," Laura said. "Everyone here is good."

"And Dulce's girls, have they been found?"

"No, there's no sign. The hurricane made everything slow."

"They'd just finished swimming when I left. They were happy. Laughing. It feels like I lost everything."

Elena sounded so young.

"I'm still here," Laura said.

"I'm coming back home," Elena said, throat locking, nearly in tears.

"What do you mean?" Laura asked. "Are you all right?"

"La Gata robbed me. When I confronted her, she gave me my passport and my clothes and pretended there was no money in my bag."

"Are you all right? Are you okay?" Laura repeated her questions, her eyes stinging with worry.

"I need to come back."

"Do you understand how much trouble you're in?" Laura said. "The tourist man will be gone tomorrow. It's not safe for you here."

Silence fell between them. Laura waited for Elena to tell her that this was all her fault. That it was her original lie that had gotten them into this predicament. But Elena only cried and cried. Laura leaned against the car, relieved that at least this sound was familiar. Elena followed instructions when she was sad. She was less likely to be impulsive.

The warmth of the sun had made the surface of the car unbelievably hot. Laura twisted her body around to push herself off. The palm that touched the surface jolted away instantly. She allowed the pain in her hand to act as an accelerant.

"I know someone who works at the Paloma in London. She'll help you. Let me just get that sorted out for you. Just stay put."

On the other end of the line, Elena continued to sob. "How is the world supposed to become a better place if no one takes responsibility for their mistakes?"

Laura's heart hurt as she listened to her.

"Some people do pay. People like us. Listen to me: Stay where you are. It isn't safe here."

"It isn't safe anywhere," Elena said. Then, sounding defeated, she went on: "I just wish Daddy would come back. He would be able to help."

"He would be able to help?" Laura was momentarily blinded by her sister's words. "When has our father done anything except make life more difficult for us? Listen to me: Daddy is never coming back home." Laura spoke slowly, allowing each word to take on the appropriate weight inside her sister's consciousness. She needed Elena to stay away from here. If that meant breaking her heart, so be it. "He died. A year ago. He's buried deep in our property. Papi would want you to be safe. He would want you to remain free."

"You're lying," Elena said. "Just like you lied about the little tourist girl."

"I'm not lying," Laura said. "Not this time."

Elena went completely silent on the other end of the line. When she spoke, her voice sounded so different. "I didn't have a chance to say goodbye. To kiss him on the cheek one last time."

Laura couldn't allow herself the cruelty of telling her sister how little of their father had been left. There hadn't been a face to kiss.

"I've gotten a lot of things wrong with you, Elena. I know that. I'm doing all I can to make sure you remain free. This isn't a lie."

All that Laura had done on Thursday to force Elena to grow up had backfired. She sounded younger than ever.

"I'm done running," Elena said, then hung up the phone. Laura called her back. Tried again, again. Laura understood that Elena would ignore her. Helplessly, she realized that her sister might turn around, despite her warnings, and come back home.

She got into the SUV, made her way to the Paloma Falls police station.

FIRST, LAURA MANAGED TO get Dulce out on bail.

When Dulce emerged from the back, she'd been held there for several hours, enough time for her anger to boil over, but no fury erupted. There were no hard slaps to Laura's face, no shouts about how she'd drugged her and stood by as the police let the man responsible for her daughters' disappearance go free. She sat down next to Laura on those hard plastic chairs.

"What if they're dead?" Dulce said. She seemed broken.

"They're not dead," Laura said, hoping she sounded convincing. "The girls are alive. We just have to find them."

A loud sob ripped out of Dulce's chest. "It's Sunday," she said. "They've been gone since Thursday. If I've lost them, I don't know what I'm going to do."

Laura felt the same way about Elena. But she was careful not to say her name. She needed Dulce to focus on her sorrow, on search and rescue. Hopelessness would lead to despair, despair to resignation, resignation to acceptance. Acceptance was half a step away from fury.

"Have you heard from Fabien?" Laura asked.

"Yes," Dulce said. "We finally spoke this morning. He lands to-night."

Fabien's arrival wouldn't be good news for Elena.

They listened to the residents of Pico Diablo begging the police to have someone make their way up the mountain. They had elderly parents who needed to be cared for, who needed their medicine refrigerated. The police explained that they were working as furiously as possible to get help up the mountain. They would be turning the helicopters over to the Red Cross to help in just another day. There would be nothing much they could do until Monday morning, the police said.

"They won't ignore him," Laura said. "Just focus on that."

"You're right," Dulce said. She stood up. "Whatever I need to do to find my girls, I'm going to do. You should pray to God they're not dead."

Dulce didn't sound broken anymore. There was a determination in her voice that forced Laura to clench her fists. She nodded somberly, watching Dulce leave the station.

She stood up with her bag full of money and made her way to the back of the station. Dulce must have forgotten that Laura wasn't one to pray to God.

CHAPTER
41

I N VIDA'S BACKYARD, THE AIR WAS CLEAR, CRISP. THE GROUND was saturated with moisture. Soon, the plants strong enough to survive the storm would fasten to the dirt, stand erect.

Vida ventured out to the road and cautiously journeyed a few hundred meters through the thicket. When she'd tried earlier, she'd realized that she was too weak to make it even the short distance to Doña Fella's house. The mahogany trees had been downed by the storm, impossible to climb over. At least in her condition. She placed a hand on her belly, speaking to the baby about the trees, how they'd managed to stand for hundreds of years, how maybe they'd been there during the Taíno times.

It was impossible that they'd see trees like that again in her lifetime. But she'd plant some trees, charge her baby with their care. And then maybe her baby, if they decided to have children, could charge their future descendants with caring for the trees.

Would you like that? she asked the seed in her belly. In response came a stirring of butterflies, a sensation that started in her belly but ended as vibration on her eardrums.

She walked patiently around the fallen trees, sometimes finding smaller branches that she could climb over. By the time she made it to the street where Doña Fella lived, she could hear that everyone who'd been unable to make their way down the mountain had gathered at the safe harbor that was Doña Fella's house. The wooden shack had miraculously been left untouched. There, the older members of Pico Diablo, who took care of children whose mothers had traveled abroad, and those who'd been too infirm or injured to make the treacherous walk down during the storm waited. There were viejitas Vida had grown up with cooking on wood-burning stoves and children playing a game of jacks, giggling, while another group ran around playing tag. They all wore the simple clothes that had been passed down from older siblings to younger siblings, from neighbor to neighbor, mended and repaired for years. Their boisterous energy invigorated her. Among them, she noticed two golden-skinned girls with the biggest hair puffs and threaded hair ribbons she'd made by hand. The ribbons were now limp, but the girls had kept them clipped to their hair. One of them had only one of the ribbons—the one that had the most pronounced red fabric. In profile, this little girl looked exactly like Niña, Dulce's oldest. Vida recalled her dream, where she'd imagined she'd seen one of the girls, had heard their feet on the muddy ground as the storm intensified. Had she been hallucinating? Was she hallucinating now?

A girl was playing jacks with rigid fingers that were unable to sweep the ground well enough, to gather the metal pieces fast enough, or to fling the plastic ball with enough expertise to play a good winning game. The other kids mocked her good-naturedly, then showed her how it was done. As if sensing her burning gaze, the children turned toward Vida at the same time.

Vida gasped in surprise. She saw Niña and Perfecta among those kids. Dulce's daughters. The girls rose off the ground, came rushing toward her. What in the world were the girls doing all the way up here? They reached her, hugged her.

"What are you doing here?" Vida shouted at them. She knew there was no way in hell that Dulce would have allowed the girls to spend the weekend up here during a storm. Niña sported a dark shadow on her cheekbone. Perfecta had bruising around her slender neck. Both girls had many scratches on their arms, their legs.

"What are *you* doing here?" Doña Fella asked Vida. "I thought for sure you were down in the resort, staying with Pablo, or waiting out the storm with Dulce."

Vida shook her head. It had taken days for her body to repair itself. But she was focused on the girls. Their bodies showed signs that they'd been assaulted.

"What happened?" she asked the girls, lightly touching their faces, their necks. "Who did this to you?"

"A man tried to hurt us," Niña, the older of the two, said. "We fought hard, the way Toqui taught us."

"We ran away from him," Perfecta cut in. "We followed the Freedom Trail."

"They only came over when the storm got bad," Doña Fella said. "Can you believe that? They've been away from home since Thursday!"

Vida imagined the hell her friend had been through. Dulce must've been losing her mind.

"Jesus," Vida said. "Is your phone working? Does anyone have cellphone service?"

Doña Fella, the oldest member of the community, shook her head. They'd been trying to reach people down the mountain to no avail. She was putting on a strong face but didn't look good at all. The elders said that they were almost out of water, almost out of food. Vida mentioned Fella's pallor.

"Don't you worry about me," Doña Fella said.

She pointedly looked at Vida's belly. Her stomach had popped—it was obvious that she was pregnant. Vida split some water with the old woman because by the sight of her, she needed medical help. Then she left the girls in the care of the community. She went foraging outside, found a few helpful herbs, and got to work making tinctures that would help those who weren't looking too good. Doña Fella thanked her as she drank some tea. A few moments later, she went inside to get away from the heat of the day, to rest.

As night began to fall, Vida bid everyone good night and prayed with them that help would be on its way soon. Off in the distance, they could hear the sound of helicopters, but none of them came their way. She thanked the older women for caring for Dulce's girls, but told them that she would take the girls with her, to her home.

WHEN THEY ARRIVED AT her house, stars were glittering in the rich dark-blue night sky. They seemed close enough to touch. And right there, on her couch, Pablo waited for them, asleep. By the looks of it, he'd only just arrived. She took note of his arms and legs—so many bug bites. On his stomach, chest, and face, there were so many scratches, some of which he was still bleeding from. His feet were swollen, looked raw. Even asleep, he grimaced. Rest was no relief from the pain. She moved closer to him, ran her hand across his forehead, down his jaw, let it rest right above his heart. He seemed like an apparition, another hallucination. She was overcome by love for him, brought on by the fact that he'd come after she and the girls seemed to have been forgotten by others.

Pablo came out of sleep slowly. The sound of the girls giggling was the first thing his consciousness grasped. He tried to shake his sleepiness away. When he finally was awake enough to understand the sight before him—the girls, alive! Looking at him with coy smiles!—he tried to sit up, but was shot through to stillness by an awareness of how much his body ached, how swollen his extremities were. Vida leaned over him, held his hand.

"Don't move," she said.

"How is this possible? Have they been here all along?"

"I just found them. They were hiding out."

"I have to go back, get help. Tell everyone the girls are alive. Dulce has been so worried."

"He came such a long way," Perfecta was saying to her older sister. "Like a prince to rescue his princess."

"He's no prince," Vida said, holding up a cloth that was now stained with his blood and the mud he'd traveled over, as well as bits of branches and leaves. They both stared at all the filth that had come off his body.

"I'm so sorry, Vida," he said. "For everything."

"I know," she said.

"I need to tell you," he started to say.

She shushed him. "Not now. We'll talk later." Vida raised an eyebrow, her face fixed in an expression that said that if he thought risking his health and limbs, his very life, would be enough to get her to forgive him, it was not. But she turned her attention back to his injuries with pronounced gentleness, and there was deep relief in her eyes, a tenderness for him that washed over them both like the biggest wave, submerging them in hope.

He placed his palm over hers, bringing her to stillness. He placed both their hands on her stomach. His eyes filled and spilled, and she understood that he knew—that what had brought him here was the impulse to safeguard their future.

She sent the girls to sleep in her bed, but every few minutes they kept coming out, curiosity making their pretty green eyes wide. Vida retrieved a balm from a closet and began to apply it to his cuts. How she had missed his body. How she had missed his face.

He didn't have the words to say what he needed to say. He would spend most of his life being grateful for the last few days—for the way the most horrible decisions of his life had led to this. This life, this love that was bigger than the moon shining bright into the falling darkness. How close he'd come to missing out on it.

After he ate some food, they spoke about what they should do next. Pablo insisted that he needed to head back now, try to get help as soon as possible, and let Dulce know that her girls were alive and well. It was a six-mile trip that could be cut substantially if he was willing to fling himself into the ocean by jumping off the Pico Diablo stone formation in Elena and Laura's backyard.

"You don't look like you're in any shape to make it," Vida said. "If you miscalculate, you'll crash into the rocks."

"I'll be in worse shape tomorrow," he said, standing up. "I won't miss. I promise you."

Vida tried again to dissuade him. She grabbed her cellphone, tried to call Dulce, but there was still no cellphone service in Pico Diablo. She knew deep down that he was right. The people at the top of the mountain in Pico Diablo were often at the bottom of the list. They stood together, watching the darkening night and the silvery reflection of the ocean in the distance.

"I'll be back before you know it," he said.

He leaned over and kissed her softly. Then, together, Pablo, Vida, and Dulce's girls walked the short distance to Laura and Elena's backyard. Vida prayed softly for his well-being, entrusted him to the wind, the trees, the ocean. But as she looked at the insane descent, the many sharp rocks that bordered the crashing ocean waves, she remembered Doña Fella's lessons. You jumped to your death. That was the reason why the rock formation had been made an option. Not as an escape, but as an end.

She called out Pablo's name.

"You have to go the way you came," she said. "I can't risk losing you."

"So, you forgive me? You'll give me another chance?"

She shook her head at him. Smiled. "I'm not sure about all of that. Just keep yourself alive so we can find out if there's anything worth saving."

CHAPTER
42

LAURA FELT HER COMPOSURE WANING, FEARED SHE WOULDN'T be able to hold on. But for the first time since Thursday, she didn't want to hurt someone else. She wanted to hurt only herself. She'd spent most of the day at the police station, speaking to official after official about what needed to be done to remove the stay from the tourist record so he could leave that same day. She'd accomplished what she needed to do in time for him to catch the last flight out. She had gotten her sister's name removed from the investigation—at least for now.

Her phone buzzed. Elena had texted her to say that she had boarded her connecting flight at JFK in New York. She would land in Punta Cana in four hours. She sent the flight number. It was the same aircraft that would transport the tourist family back to New York City.

In the resort SUV, she drove through the night with the tourist man, the adorable daughter, and the wife to the Punta Cana airport. When they arrived, she pushed their enormous luggage in a baggage cart with a stuck wheel that kept turning the wrong way. Finally, she gave up the effort and called over a couple of maleteros, who quickly gave her a hand. Without consulting the couple, she directed them all to the curbside check-in and nodded at the father to do what he needed to do. He raised no objections.

Laura had enough connections at the airport that there was no issue with her getting through security without a ticket, without her passport.

Laura stood by with the family at the fancy lounge—which, admittedly, wasn't that fancy—and watched the couple drink champagne that they didn't have to pay for. Tourists left half-full bottles of water on the tables that Dominican workers gathered and threw in the trash. The little tourist girl made friends with some other kids, and they all sat on the carpeted floor. Someone brought out a game of jacks, but because of the carpet, the ball wouldn't bounce. Still, the kids had Wi-Fi and electricity. They played next to each other on their own electronic devices, separate and together.

The father told her that she could go, but she refused.

The mother told her that they were fine now, but she told them it was no bother.

She had to make sure that they got on the plane—that they left her island for good.

But of course, she heard the couple speaking about how much they'd loved it here, despite all they'd been through. The tourist man's face looked raw and inflamed with the stitches. The bite mark now clearly looked like a hook. Despite his injury, he said they would be back. But not for some time. There was Medellín, which he'd wanted to visit for years. There were the islands they'd yet to visit: Trinidad and Tobago, Puerto Rico, Martinique, St. Martin. They wouldn't stop until they'd visited every island in the Caribbean, he said.

Off to the side, some businessmen were talking loudly, obviously drunk. They wanted to make more investments in the region. They were talking about building villas that overlooked the sea. They were frustrated that the locals in Pico Diablo had refused to talk to them, that the storm had halted their plans to leave this place as landowners.

"Sometimes," one of the men said, "I think that this country would be better off without Dominicans. What a greedy, dumb, sorry lot."

"Only good things about it," his friend said, "are the good rum and the cheap whores."

Laura swallowed against the soreness in her throat. She forced herself to remain silent.

She hovered as the flight departure was announced. She felt a surge of adrenaline as the people who'd just arrived made their way past the gate. But as dozens of people walked through, there was no sign of Elena. Finally, when the crew made their way out of the plane, she knew that the plane was empty. Elena had lied. She hadn't been on this flight.

She shadowed the family to the runway, her body feeling as if it were made of fog. Anyone could step right through her. Because of the storm, passengers had to make their way to the planes on foot. She followed them at a distance, catching the curious glances that the couple exchanged when they noticed her looming—a sentinel faithful to the task at hand until the very end. She refused to think deeply about what she was doing, about what she had become—refused to linger on the look of disappointment and repulsion that she'd received from Pablo as he made his way into the forest. It shouldn't bother her so much, that she'd lost his respect. He would be back, begging her for his job.

The wife walked back toward her and discreetly handed her an envelope thick with cash.

"For all your help," she said.

Laura refused the envelope. "We're a no-gratuity hotel, ma'am," she said.

The woman insisted. Her face was golden, rosy from the sun. Her lips shone a natural pink. "It's very important to my family to support the local people," she said. "Everywhere we go."

Laura folded her arms across her chest. She left the conversation for a moment, unfurled to yesterday, which felt so long ago, to this woman's decision to stay in the car as her husband was questioned at the police station. Maybe she had imagined disorderly conduct— maybe she'd remembered when he'd been too aggressive with one of the cueros they'd seen at the start of their trip. But it was more likely that this woman had made a life out of looking the other way, of protecting her innocence by refusing to acknowledge things that would disrupt it. Could Laura blame her? The less she knew, the less she'd be forced to contend with, forgive. Would it matter to her, to learn what they all thought this man had done? She felt a perverse impulse to shatter this pretty woman's perfect life.

"Please, take it," Sophie said, sounding perturbed. It was as if she couldn't grasp why anyone in the history of the world would ever refuse free money. Laura wanted to slap this woman hard across the face. She told herself that she needed to calm down.

As Laura opened her mouth to tell this woman that everyone wasn't for sale, the tourist girl with her blond curls came out of nowhere, face flushed, yanking on Laura's hand. The bruise that had previously bloomed on her chest was now gone, leaving no sign that it had ever been there. She tugged and pulled until Laura understood that she wanted to whisper something in her ear. Laura turned away from the mother and gave her full attention to the little girl.

"Tell your sister I'll miss her the most," the girl whispered with cotton-candy-ice-cream-flavored breath. Earlier, when the girl had rushed to get some ice cream in the dining room, two other girls had crowded around her. Those girls had been around the same age, with light-brown skin and big hair puffs. They could have been Dulce's girls. Laura had considered what it might mean if Dulce's girls were safe, free to also get some ice cream out of the soft-serve machine.

The woman seemed to have given up on trying to convince her to take the money. The envelope was nowhere in sight.

"We're going to send a letter telling everyone what a star employee you are," the wife said as they moved to go toward the plane. She held her daughter's hand and met her husband, who waited for them a few paces away. Once they started walking in tandem, his arm moved protectively around his wife. They climbed a movable stairway that led them into their plane, headed back to New York City. The hotel had happily covered their ticket-change fees, as well as their ride to the airport and their transportation home once they landed, all to ensure that they left early. She imagined them reclining in their first-class seats, the little girl touching the scab through her hair, the parents clinking glasses and saying cheers to the other rich people around them. They would each ask in turn, *How was your trip, where did you stay?* And the couple would say, *We stayed at the Grand Paloma Resort. No place like it. They treated us like kings.* Then, upon reaching home, they would put the entire ordeal out of their minds.

Elena called her just as the plane taxied onto the runway. Laura found the clasp on her purse undone, and next to her phone, inside her purse, was the white envelope full of dollars. She had been for sale, whether she'd wanted to admit it or not.

"Where are you?" Laura asked.

"They pulled me off the plane as soon as it landed. I'm being held by airport security. They said I'm under arrest."

Laura was flabbergasted. She'd spent so much money, bribing all those men at the police station. They had assured her that there would be no record, no warrant, no investigation, so long as the girls' family didn't raise a big stink. Did this mean that Fabien had arrived early? Had Dulce pressed charges against Elena? Laura saw the plane with the tourist family pick up speed. She saw its nose ascend, the wheels disappearing into the plane's belly. In a matter of moments, they mounted the air, disappeared into the darkness, free.

MONDAY

CHAPTER
43

AURA ARRIVED AT THE HOTEL AFTER MIDNIGHT, FEELING A weariness she'd never known before. She held Elena's hand in hers, softly tugging at her sister. It had taken hours to get things sorted out, to get her released. But she'd done it. Elena had slept the entire way back to the Grand Paloma Resort. Now she was slow-moving, drowsy.

When they passed through the front of the lobby, she saw Ida and Amber Vargas holding court over by the balcony. The lights that illuminated the infinity pool created a mesmerizing effect; the ocean and sky beyond were made of the deepest black, as if the world stopped at the hotel's edge. There were no guests other than the Vargas sisters on the balcony. Again, they were sipping on expensive champagne. Pasofino sat on a low stool, massaging Amber's feet. The women were still wearing the hotel logo T-shirts from that morning, and based on the way they both had their eyes closed, she imagined it had been a tough day. She stopped herself from walking over there. She couldn't face the women, though of course, they had no idea what she'd just done. Pasofino nodded stiffly, acknowledging her. His movement must have drawn the sisters' attention because they both opened their eyes and turned their necks to look at her, and she was grateful that in their countenances there was no trace of judgment or disapproval. But neither beckoned for her to join them.

WHEN THEY REACHED THE presidential suite that would be their room, she called downstairs and asked for them to bring up some food.

"What would you like, boss?" one of her workers asked.

"Whatever is easy and fast," she responded.

When she turned around, Elena was facing her, alert.

"I want to go to our old house in the morning, to say goodbye to Papi. And then I want to go see Dulce."

Her sister's big eyes were swollen. It wasn't just from sleeping in the car. She had likely been crying nonstop over the loss of their father since Laura had told her that morning. She nodded at her sister.

"Whatever you want," Laura said. "Why don't you go shower? When the food arrives, I'll grab you."

Elena didn't argue, didn't talk back. She went down the hallway in the direction of the second bedroom.

Laura contemplated loss. She thought about how close she'd come to telling Pablo about the truth of their town's origin—and how she'd ultimately been unable to do it. She'd felt protective of Pablo, of the community at large. As if the silence around the existence of pain was the same as pretending it didn't exist. She knew that the impulse to keep it all quiet was connected somehow to the impulse to do whatever she could to get that white man out of her country. There was a leap there, an important revelation waiting for her that might very well change her life if she managed to think it through, understand it. But Laura was too tired to examine the tenuous connection between the horrors of the past, her own actions in the present, and the questionable ability she might have to control Elena's and her own future.

She sat on the beautiful white couch, intending only to rest her eyes until the food came but quickly fell asleep.

CHAPTER
44

PABLO STEPPED INTO THE LOBBY OF THE GRAND PALOMA Resort, limping and ragged, minutes before sunrise on Monday with Dulce and Fabien. When he'd told Dulce that the girls were alive, she'd been stunned into silence. Fabien was the one who'd been able to speak, who'd asked, "They're alive? Unharmed?"

Pablo had remembered the bruises on Perfecta's neck. The dark shadow on Niña's cheek. He'd wanted to know exactly what had happened to the girls, but hadn't wanted to ask, worried that making the girls relive the experience might re-traumatize them. The details were for their parents to learn.

"I don't know about unharmed," he'd said. "But they are alive."

Pablo hobbled over to the front desk. Astrid, the executive in charge of guest services, extended her hand to Fabien.

"The helicopter is ready, sir," she said. She escorted them to a golf cart and drove all three of them to the appropriate landing place.

Pablo watched the ease with which Fabien stepped up to the helipad, extending a hand to Dulce to help her climb in first. It had taken one phone call for Fabien to gain access to the helicopter, a call he'd made on the drive here.

Pablo watched Dulce and Fabien through the glass as the rotor blades sped up, rotating furiously until the helicopter lifted off the pad. He was glad they would reach the mountain in minutes as opposed to the many hours it'd taken him to travel up and then down. Slowly, he headed in the direction of the infirmary.

CHAPTER
45

FROM THE HELICOPTER, DULCE WITNESSED THE MAGNIFICENT sunrise casting its purple and orange rays on an ocean so expansive that it pained her to take it in. The blue of the sea turned turquoise toward the shore, waves foaming into white as they touched the sand. They flew above the Grand Paloma Resort, and she saw that many of the hotel's outlying structures had been flattened. As they ascended toward the mountain, she saw the lush green of the forest but also the many trees that had been toppled. In a matter of minutes, they had summited the Pico Diablo Mountain. Up there, she saw the devastation caused by the storm. So many of the homes had been ruined. As they reached a small clearing in the back of Doña Fella's backyard, Dulce worried that it was all a lie. That her daughters hadn't been found. That her worst fear had come true, and her girls weren't alive. That she would get off the helicopter only to learn it had been a cruel joke. But just as the helicopter touched the ground, her daughters, Niña and Perfecta, rushed out of the house. They were smiling, so happy to see her and Fabien.

Dulce felt tears sting her eyes. She couldn't remember the last time she had felt this overwhelming sense of relief, of overflowing love. Fabien, next to her, was crying also. He reached the girls first, embracing them and kissing them like crazy. Dulce got off the helicopter and opened her arms, receiving both her daughters at once. They were strong, and the force of their hugs pushed her to the ground. The girls fell on top of her, laughing and crying, yelling about how much they'd missed her. Then Niña, the older girl, began to shiver. Perfecta stepped back in surprise as her sister began to sob, and tears rolled seemingly endlessly down her face. Since they'd left, run away from the bad man, her older sister hadn't once cried. Dulce, sensing that her older daughter had kept her fear and hurt hidden until now, hugged her tighter, kissing her tears away. She pulled Perfecta close so her arms clasped both her daughters tightly to her heart and whispered to them, "You're safe now, no one can hurt you."

In the last day, she'd spent so many hours researching how many girls and women had gone missing in the Caribbean. She had learned that so often, crimes connected to the tourism industry were never solved. No one was charged, no one was convicted. On the rare occasions when someone was apprehended, it was easy for a perpetrator to bribe their way to freedom. She had seen so many pictures of the bodies of girls, some much younger than her daughters, brutalized by the often-unspoken danger of tourism. She'd shed so many tears, imagining the pain those girls had suffered in their last living moments. She hadn't been able to avoid the image of her own daughters brutalized by that man. Now, as she folded her daughters in her arms, feeling their sweaty skin, she thanked God that her daughters hadn't met such a terrible fate. She felt an overwhelming sense of gratitude. But she also felt a renewed sense of purpose. Just because her daughters were fine didn't mean she would allow herself to forget the horror of the experience. It didn't mean she would allow those who'd conspired to harm them to get away scot-free.

Vida looked worse for wear, and Dulce insisted that she should ride back with them. But Vida declined, saying that Doña Fella was the one who needed immediate medical help.

"Take Fella and the girls back, get them a doctor," Vida said. "I can wait to ride back on the next go. Just please make sure the helicopters come back. We have to get all these kids and old people off the mountain."

Dulce gathered the old woman and her girls and climbed into the helicopter alongside Fabien, hurling into the air and heading down to the Grand Paloma Resort. As soon as she had her girls checked out, she would ask them exactly what that man had done to them. And she would make sure that Elena and her monster of a sister paid for all their sins.

CHAPTER
46

WAKING UP TO THE INSISTENT BUZZING OF HER PHONE, IN what felt like mere seconds after she'd fallen asleep, Laura wondered what kind of awful human she'd been in a past life to deserve this inability to get any rest. All she wanted was to be off the grounds of this resort, to rest without worrying about the needy people all around her. The phone call was coming from one of the offices in the main hotel.

She noticed that the tray of food had been brought inside the suite. The workers had likely decided that she needed the rest more than she needed food. She checked her phone's clock. It was 8 A.M. on Monday morning.

"Laura speaking," she said, trying to keep the exhaustion out of her voice.

"I need you to come to the conference room in thirty minutes," Miranda said. "We're going to make some announcements to the senior leadership team."

When had Miranda arrived? Why hadn't anyone in Laura's team told her that she was here?

She managed to wash her face hurriedly, moisturize it so she smelled fresh. Her hair, in its bun, had held up, though the roots were rebelling, kinking up. She applied an obscene amount of gel to tamp it down, make it flat and straight. But her hair kinked right back up. She hoped that everyone's eyes would be trained on Miranda and her announcements.

She checked on Elena, found her soundly asleep. She touched her forehead and bent her head to kiss her. On Elena's head, the tiniest of hair growths pricked at her lips. Laura wasn't sure what they'd have to face on this day. She allowed herself to acknowledge how happy she was to have her sister nearby, the relief that even if hell was ahead, it'd be better for having her sister close.

Elena opened her eyes, reached over to the bedside table for a box of tissues, and blew her nose.

"What's going on?" she asked.

"Miranda called a meeting," Laura said. "I'm going downstairs. I'll order you some breakfast. Mangú con los tres golpes?"

"No," Elena said, sitting up. "I'm a vegan now. I'll come down with you. I want to find out what I can do to help with the search."

They reached the lobby and saw that Pasofino had switched over to his first shift as the lobby bartender, remaining faithful to his duties even in a nearly empty hotel. Next to him, there was Pablo, bandaged up and leaning against the bar, wincing in pain. He looked like he'd been through hell. But both men sported smiles, seemed relaxed in a way no one had been in days. When Pablo saw Elena, he gave a loud shout, received her with open arms. "I'm glad you're back home," he said, even as some passing thought clouded his features.

"What the hell happened to you?" Laura asked him.

"I found the girls," he said. "They were up in Pico Diablo with Vida."

"Alive?" Elena asked.

"Alive," Pablo said. He fixed his gaze on Laura. "They are very much alive."

Laura was flushed with relief. Momentarily, everything came to a stop.

"Where are they now?" Elena asked.

Pablo explained that they were now back at Dulce's. Fabien had exercised his influence. The helicopters were making trips to bring the remaining people down from the mountain. Vida hadn't made it yet, so Pablo was waiting for her.

"I wish you'd come to me first," Laura said. She considered how much better things would have gone for Elena if Laura had been involved in the girls' rescue.

"Why would I do that?" Pablo said. "You're a terrible person."

Miranda walked over then and gave her a warm hug. Laura hoped that her boss hadn't heard the last bit from Pablo.

"Congratulations on your promotion," Miranda said, extending a hand to Pablo.

Pablo nodded but didn't respond. Miranda made no mention of his various injuries. Instead, she smiled kindly at Elena, pausing to take her presence in before patting Laura's shoulder. "Good work," she said. Laura wasn't sure if the praise was for the hurricane response or getting the tourist man and his family off the island. Together, they moved away from her sister and Pablo. They didn't speak until they reached the conference room.

There, all of her colleagues sat around the big glass table, most wringing their hands nervously.

"Well, now that everyone is here, I'll get right to it. Most of you knew that the C-suite has been considering a restructure. It became obvious that we don't need two hotels in the same location. The decision was further cemented after this one was hammered by the storm and the other remained untouched. There is no appetite for further investment in a restoration project. We'd been having conversations with an interested party, and they happened to be here during the storm. The deal was finalized over the weekend."

There was mumbling as everyone looked at the person next to them—fast minds at work, wondering how this change would affect them. If the hotel was a stepping stone, they'd now have to go back to being stepped on or stepping on others. Laura placed both her palms on the glass table. She felt disoriented. She'd done much of what she'd done to ensure stability here, to make this place inviolable.

"Our buyers are here," Miranda said. She made a show of walking to the doors and opening them wide, but no one walked through. Miranda took a step outside and laughed, saying, "Take your time. No one will rush you today."

Laura's gaze fell on the glass table. Around her own fingers, there were so many other fingerprints. No one had been here to clean. Then she remembered that these were likely *her* prints—she had been in this room, sitting in this same chair, just a day ago, when her boss had told her to get rid of the problem. She was already tuned out of the conversation, couldn't care less who took over the hotel, when the Vargas sisters walked in. Laura's jaw fell, but not nearly as far as those of the rest of the people around the conference table. But it wasn't possible. Could Amber and Ida Vargas be the new owners of the Grand Paloma Resort?

"Yes," Amber said, with a smile that said she was used to those stares, to always being underestimated. "We are the new owners of the Grand Paloma Resort."

AFTER THE MEETING, the Vargas sisters asked Laura to walk out to the beach with them. There, all of them barefoot, they took in the glittering ocean. It would be a bright, beautiful day.

"We had high hopes for you, Laura," Ida said. "Actually, we debated letting you in on our surprise. But we noticed that you were under tremendous pressure and didn't want this to add to it."

Had she known, would she have made different decisions? She wasn't sure.

"We love you very much, but you, mi'ja, have lost your way. You have lost your soul."

Would explaining what had happened help her?

"This is a special place. It's a magical place. We love it very much. Maybe because this is the exact spot where our husbands brought us so many years ago. It holds such sentimental value for us. There are many vultures about, ready to take over this land."

Laura thought of the businessmen at the airport lounge. The way they'd seemed annoyed that local landowners had dared to say no. How they'd called those landowners greedy, thinking it was a higher price they were waiting for.

"There's no place for you here," Amber said. "We harbored some hopes that maybe, under different circumstances, you could run this place for us. That girl you were a decade ago had such a strong ethic, had such tenderness and fire but now . . ."

Who had she been? Did she even want to go back to being that person?

"We have an offer for you," Ida cut in. "If you help us transition the hotel to another management team, we'll transfer you to our Mallorca hotel. You can work there for the next couple of years and see if there's a way for you to heal. We can also offer your sister a place there, so you can be together again. We have many connections. Elena needs to go to school, get a college degree. She's been working here since she was a teenager. Gosh, she's still a teenager, isn't she? Maybe she can go to college while you work, figure out what it is you want to do next? We think this can be a kind of—what did you call it?"

"Probationary period," Amber said.

Laura thought about it. A chance for them to start over. For her sister to go to school. What a gift.

"I really appreciate your offer. I do. But I have built something with this company. They've invested a lot in me, I have invested a lot in them. I believe in my place here."

The women looked at each other. Amber let out a frustrated sigh.

"Think it over," Ida said. "No need to say yes or no."

There was something going on between the sisters—a kind of unspoken communication that should have raised an alarm. Surely, Laura thought, they couldn't know what had happened with the tourist, his wife, the child, Elena, Dulce's girls. Surely they had no idea that she had lied and schemed, all to keep the resort they now owned smudge-free—to maintain a safe haven for people from all over the world to visit. To keep her sister free. But there was something about the way they let the silence linger between them that made Laura aware they knew more than they let on.

"Your loyalty to this company is admirable," Ida said, voice laced with something Laura didn't grasp.

"No one knows the inner workings of this hotel the way you do," Amber said. "Even if you decide to move on with Paloma Enterprises, we'd love for you to help us for a couple of months. Our plan is to shrink the footprint of the hotel. The lands here are sacred—as I'm sure you know. We have traced the journeys of persecuted people here and beyond ... Brazil, Panama. Our hope is to employ as many local people as possible to make it a nature reserve, the way some cities are doing with the Land Back movement. We're trying to figure out what might be the best way to return the land to local people. But also, we hope to create a place for rest and meditation, where, through a love of nature, we can celebrate the heritage of those who journeyed for survival, freedom, liberation—whose backbreaking labor contributed to our own family's wealth, to all wealth. Capitalism is built on human blood and sweat. This will take a very long time, probably longer than what we have left. But our commitment starts now, to not put brick and mortar on sacred land. Eventually, we hope to find someone who can help carry this mission forward."

Laura noticed that the women hadn't once mentioned the United States. The way they spoke about persecuted people made Laura feel as though they might know the true origins of Pico Diablo. Her concerns turned to her sister. To how much she loved this land. How much she'd always loved the people. Laura realized that without the nonsense of the last year, Elena could've been someone who was grounded in caring for this place so she could gently offer it to someone else. She and Vida would be great—tree-hugging and barefoot-dancing about the sanctity of life.

All her daydreaming came to an abrupt halt. Who knew where Elena would be in a few months? Elena wanted to go to Dulce. She wanted to face her mistakes. She might end up in prison. Laura knew that no matter how hard she tried to convince her sister to run away, she wouldn't do it.

"We're going to transition the staff to the new VP of nature reserve, so we hope you'll also consider helping us with the logistics. There is a system that needs to be built where donations by those who visit the nature reserve will allow it to become self-sustainable. We'll figure out what to name it. We've been talking about maybe building a monument to honor our husbands. Subtle but, you know, splendid. A way for us to honor our love stories."

These women who had, for the last ten years, been the queens of talking shit, delightful in their personalities because they were down-to-earth despite their wealth, were speaking a completely new language. To honor the dead by putting something beautiful in the world—wasn't that what her sister wanted to do? Honor their father by being honest, by facing her mistakes in a way that E.Z. never had?

"Have you already chosen someone for VP?" Laura tried to keep her voice level, but there was a shaky quality to it.

"Yes, we love Pasofino, as you know. We're going to give him a shot. If he can't handle it, bah. We'll find someone else. But he has worked here, been committed, knows how to talk to people, knows when to walk away from this place. What's most important to us is that our employees have a real sense of balance. It's the only way to make it the long way. Take it from us."

"And you're calling him a VP because there's going to be a president above the job?"

"Well, we want there to be a connection between the nature reserves so there will be some slight management oversight. Mainly so that visitors have some kind of common experience. We love the bracelets, too. We're thinking of coming up with our own, maybe necklaces instead that would link into each other, as a way for visitors to showcase all the places they've visited and learned from."

Laura thought of gold chains linked to each other, locking endlessly in place, around a bunch of white necks.

"That sounds lovely," Laura said. "I'll be sure to circle back with you in the next day. I have a meeting with my boss in just a couple of hours. I should know all I need to know then."

CHAPTER

47

MIRANDA KEPT PUSHING LAURA'S MEETING FURTHER BACK. By the time Laura was summoned to meet with her, it was early evening.

Miranda had moved the remainder of her meetings to her place. Before now, Miranda had been strict with her boundaries, never blurring the lines between her private space and her professional life. Laura had never been to her house, and she'd been under the assumption that no one else in the leadership team had been there, either. She found the front door unlocked and was surprised by how beautiful the space was. It was a pool house with a kidney-shaped pool and a cute casita set apart from the main building, which was sturdy enough that it'd withstood the storm. Her colleagues—all four of them—sat in the outdoor space, and someone had started a fire in the propane stone firepit. Although it was probably a bad idea to sit outdoors after a big storm, it was obvious, from the lack of any insect sounds, that the yard had been fumigated with some powerful insecticides.

"Laura," her ex–booty call Patrick called out. All her colleagues shouted greetings. Everyone was drunk.

The fire danced in the humid air, illuminating the animated faces of people she'd worked with for many years. There was Astrid, la Colombiana, who seemed high and happy with whatever deal she'd been offered. James, the VP for business outreach, turned his attention away after greeting her. He was also in high spirits, and she heard him talk about how tough it would be to get used to the winters in New York City again, how afraid he was about the rat infestation that was dominating the headlines. There was Michael, the head of finance and accounting, whom she'd never even seen outside a meeting room or a video conference. David, the head of legal, had bloodshot eyes and seemed to be completely smashed. There were so many empty glasses everywhere. She understood that as people finished their meetings with Miranda, they would just come to the backyard and stay, drinking and talking.

Whatever unease and fear had permeated the group earlier at the announcement of the upcoming changes had dissipated like foam above crashing waves. There was a feeling of merriment, of *lo que sera, sera* among these fuckers. These were people who knew they would be fine, no matter what. Laura wondered how different she might be if she'd grown up with half this certainty.

"It's a pretty sweet deal," James was saying to Astrid, handing Laura some Paloma Palomas in a clean glass someone had brought from inside. "You'll be in charge of all Latin American media relations for Paloma Enterprises. That's a hell of a promotion."

Laura raised an eyebrow while allowing herself a full gulp. The tequila set her throat aflame—the fresh pulp of grapefruits and limes released a tartness that caused little explosions on her tongue.

Astrid was saying that she would prefer a location other than the soon-to-be-constructed Pura Vida Paloma, which would be nestled in Arenal, Costa Rica. She wouldn't be caught dead near an active volcano.

"Have you seen what has been happening in Iceland the last couple of years?" Michael said, laughing. "The whole world is on fire. Isn't it always? Each day feels like we're on the brink of extinction. Dios me libre."

But based on the way Astrid spoke, twirling her fingers around her hair, it seemed as though she wasn't pressed. Laura understood that Astrid's BBC interview had been her audition for her next job, positioning herself to win. All while Laura had been running around like a chicken without a head, helping criminals flee justice.

She finished her drink and got another. Then, quickly, another. She had a bad feeling as to why Miranda had left her for last. She had learned during one of those leadership summits that when it came to calibration and work performance, bosses were supposed to leave the most difficult conversation for last. She didn't talk much, just laughed along as Astrid told a story of a video that had been uploaded to Insta. One of those extreme athletes had decided to go surfing during the hurricane, right on their beach. There was a poor bastard staff member who'd been forced to go out there, to help bring them to shore.

"They don't pay us enough for that," Patrick said.

Laura recalled the pride she'd always taken in her work ethic. As everyone laughed, she felt a burning shame that she'd been so naïve, giving this job her all. She laughed along, too. She didn't once let on that she had been that idiot bastard.

A FEW HOURS LATER, only she and Miranda were left by the fire. Astrid and a few others had transitioned inside the house, complaining of the rising humidity. Miranda had yet to mention to Laura what the plan was for her future with the company. Laura had this deadening feeling that by not saying anything, she'd already spoken. But she wasn't going to let Miranda off the hook. She told her what the Vargas sisters had offered her, waiting to see if this would push her to tell her what was going on.

"There are worse places to end up than Mallorca," Miranda said. "Have you ever been?"

Laura shook her head. Miranda would never understand the kind of hatred Laura's father had felt for the colonizing country of Spain—it was rivaled only by his love of all things American. Laura was sure that her father would turn in his grave if he knew this was the latest path her life seemed to be set toward.

"I'd much prefer staying with Paloma Enterprises," Laura felt forced to say. She attempted to sit up, to give her words more weight, but her body was in lounge mode. Horrified, she noticed her bare feet. When had she removed her shoes? "I'd much prefer to run the Platinum Member Companion Program globally, as we discussed."

There. She'd gotten it out. Miranda looked at her with the same expression that she'd had more than a year ago when Laura had explained that her staff's tendency to think every Black person was poor wasn't rooted in racism.

"We're not going to expand the program, Laura. It doesn't make any financial sense. The benefits to the employees far outweigh any benefit to the business, beyond the initial burst of productivity and competition. It was a good idea, but without your genius way of dangling the carrot and the employees' unusual gullibility here, it doesn't work."

They'd spoken a few days ago. Miranda had said things were marching forward. The bafflement must have shown on her features.

"I know," Miranda said. "Things change direction so quickly that it's hard not to get nauseous and throw up."

"What's left for me at Paloma Enterprises?" The words were heavy on Laura's tongue.

"We haven't been able to find a spot for you as of yet," Miranda said.

As it dawned on Laura that there would be no place for her at all, she felt a sense of embarrassment. Even now, with Miranda's faraway gaze, she waited, hoping for good news. But Laura's boss didn't speak. She didn't explain.

"I don't understand," Laura said. "We spoke yesterday. You said to make the scandal go away. I did it."

"Fabien is so closely connected to our CEO. I didn't know that. These allegiances, they go back far longer than you've been alive. I didn't realize that the businessman with a double life and a secret family was Fabien, a person who has founded hundreds of luxury shopping centers next to our resorts. You've made a lot of bad decisions since this fucking nightmare started. Why didn't you tell me this involved your sister?"

Laura remembered Astrid's talking points about interdependency and generosity. About the resort being like a family, ready to step up when the need was most dire.

"Please help me," Laura said, face hovering over the fire between them at a dangerous angle. It was her mother's voice that came out of her throat. Begging for mercy from someone who seemed hell-bent on hurting her.

"I can help you get another job," Miranda said. "That won't be hard. I just don't get why you won't take the Vargas sisters' offer. Having powerful people in your corner who know you and care as much as they do, that's how careers are made."

"I've given ten years of my life to this company. I don't understand how you can't find a place for me. There are hundreds of Palomas around the globe! And what power? They are two retired widows. How do they even have enough money to buy this hotel?"

Miranda got up, and she stumbled a little as she sat next to Laura. Her sharp-angled face, with its short hair, turned softer.

"Have you not looked them up?"

"Of course I looked them up," she said. "The Vargas sisters have a Facebook account featuring their grandkids. Most of their posts are about olive trees."

Miranda fumbled on her phone, typed a few words, and brought up a website that featured the older women, looking properly suited up and years younger. "Vargas is their maiden name, obviously. Ida was married to oil and Amber was the principal and CEO of a billion-dollar hedge fund before she retired. With a *B*."

Laura laughed bitterly. All she'd done had come to this. She excused herself, made her way to the bathroom. In the bright room, she splashed her face with cold water, commanding herself to sober up. But the room was spinning and spinning. It wouldn't stop, no matter how hard she held on to the basin. There was a soft knock on the door. When she opened it, Astrid was standing there. Of all the people that Laura least wanted to see, Astrid ranked in the top five.

"You okay?" Astrid asked.

Laura nodded. Her eyes stung with humiliation. Astrid knew. Everyone knew that Laura hadn't been asked to stay. She'd be damned if she cried in front of Astrid. Now there was a woman who knew how to play the game.

"You did the best you could with that shitty hand you got dealt,"

Astrid said. She applied a bright-red lipstick with a steady hand. Laura could see that she wasn't drunk like everyone else. She faced Laura, used her lipstick to apply color to Laura's lips. "The complaint Fabien asked me to file against you and your sister has been lost in the post-hurricane madness. There won't be any formal paper trail linking you to any of it, unless he asks again. You can come with me to Costa Rica. I will hire you. We'll be the ones surfing in bad weather, shouting *pura vida*. Fuck these people."

Laura realized that this entire time, as she'd been thinking that Astrid had abandoned her, Astrid had merely stepped out of Laura's way to do what she had to do.

"Thank you," Laura said.

Astrid put some of the lipstick stain on her index fingertip, applied it to Laura's cheeks. "Say it after me," she said. "Fuck. These. People."

Laura said it, and that single act of solidarity made her feel stronger. She hadn't made it this far to give up now. Fortified, she made her way back to Miranda.

"Did you end up with a promotion from this entire deal?" she asked, her voice strong. "Is that the reason you had to come back early? On the heels of a hurricane? To be closer on the deal with the Vargas sisters?"

"No," Miranda said. She looked at Laura with more respect. "I didn't have anything to do with the sale of the property. Don't be absurd. I advocated for you, every chance I got. I know how hard you work. All that you deserve. Jesus, I've never met anyone willing to do more for a job. This will pass, Laura. I know. It must feel like the world is ending for you, but it's not. Just tread water for a bit. We have to wait to see what happens with Fabien, if he decides to take legal action against your sister, the hotel, you. The girls are alive. They're unharmed. In a few days, Fabien and his baby momma might decide to forget the bad experience. Just like how people get so mad about lost luggage and then go home and don't even lodge the complaint. Everyone is busy. Everyone has better things to do."

"And if they don't forget it? If they decide to sue or come after us?"

"We'll all be royally screwed. The hotel has to think about self-preservation, you get that? But we'd pay for your legal obligations. In this way, being a director-slash-officer makes all the difference. You will be protected. But not your sister. In these situations, there are winners and losers. Your sister, my friend, happened to end up at the bottom this go."

Not just this go. Every go.

"My sister is seventeen," Laura said. "She's a child."

"She hasn't behaved like a child."

Miranda fixed her gaze on Laura, didn't waver as she made her judgment clear. But her boss didn't realize that there was no difference between Laura and her sister. Whatever happened to her sister, happened to her. And this wasn't the first time that they'd ended up screwed.

On her phone was a text alert. Dulce was demanding that Elena and Laura come to her house the next morning.

Be here by 11am If you don't turn yourselves in, the police will pick you up, she'd written.

CHAPTER

48

IDA AND AMBER VARGAS HUNG THEIR HEADS IN DISAPPOINT-
ment. Pasofino and his boyfriend Rio were sitting with them in the
gallery, watching as the dark night deepened.

"And there's nothing we can do to change your minds?" Ida asked.

Pasofino reached for Rio's hand, tugged at it a little.

"Bae," he said. "This is such a good deal. Take care of some plants.
Be on vacation forever."

Rio sighed in frustration, kicked the case of his violin. He had put
his entire career on hold for love. Now that his place of employment
no longer existed, it was time for him to call the shots. But he was worried. He wasn't sure that New York City would be a good place for
Pasofino. But he knew that if they didn't take this chance to go, they
would never leave.

"If you want to stay, you should stay," Rio said, sadness elongating
his pronunciation of each word.

"Get out of here," Pasofino said. *As if I would ever pick any job over
you,* he thought. Turning to the Vargas sisters, he shook his head. "I'm
really sorry that I can't take the job. We're going to live in America for
a while. We're going to give it a shot."

The sisters nodded, tilting their heads back in identical gestures as
they downed the last of their Paloma Palomas. Before they'd placed
their empty glasses on the table, a new pitcher had materialized.

"This is sad news," Amber said. "But you're doing it right. Successful relationships are all about taking turns doing exactly what you don't
want to do for the person you love."

The two young men laughed. Rio leaned over to Pasofino, kissed him lightly on the mouth. "You might be surprised. You might love it."

Pasofino rolled his eyes. "Don't be delusional."

"A little song?" Rio said, taking his violin out of its case.

The sisters nodded enthusiastically.

Rio began to play "Bésame Mucho," and Pasofino joined in, singing the original arrangement as it had been written by Consuelo Velázquez in the 1940s. The two women clapped their hands, enchanted. They joined Pasofino's strong, beautiful song with their off-key, pitchy voices.

Quiero tenerte muy cerca, mirarme en tus ojos, verte junto a mi,
piensa que tal vez mañana yo ya estaré muy lejos, muy lejos de ti

When Rio finished playing, the women clapped and clapped. "Bravo," they said.

"Now what?" Amber asked.

"I've no idea who we can pick," Ida responded.

"I know someone willing to do anything for this place," Pasofino said.

"We already decided that Laura isn't the right choice," Amber said.

Pasofino nodded. "I meant Pablo," he said. "Now there's a guy who loves this land like no one else I've ever met."

The sisters smiled, nodding.

"Pablo makes perfect sense," the sisters said in unison.

TUESDAY

CHAPTER
49

N THE BACKYARD OF THEIR OLD HOUSE IN PICO DIABLO, LAURA
stood a few paces behind her little sister as she sat cross-legged on
the dirt atop their father's grave. Laura and Pablo had marked it with
a small aloe plant. After the storm, Laura had been certain that all
their plants would be destroyed, but when they'd reached the plot of
land, they'd found that the aloe plant had multiplied. As if their father
had nourished the soil.

Elena cried in deep, heart-wrenching sobs. She was crying about her
father being gone and about the girls being alive. For the last five days,
she'd gone back and forth, one day certain that they were dead and the
next sure that they had to be alive. Learning that the girls were alive had
filled her with a sense of hope and optimism and shame and guilt. She'd
been given a second chance, one that she wasn't sure she deserved. Niña
and Perfecta each became two different girls, and they multiplied time
and time again, but this time they were not in her drugged imagination.
It was Elena's sober mind that forced her to consider the multitudes,
including the ones who'd faced the fate that another Elena somewhere
else had abandoned them to and they had ended up dead. The sorrow
she felt came from a place where there was no pretense. She couldn't
blame her dead mother or her dead father or her misguided sister. She
couldn't blame the writers she loved, who hadn't prepared her for how
difficult it was to make a real difference in the world. She couldn't blame
systems or governments because how futile would that be, anyway? She
had to face the truth that she was the one who'd made the decision,
centered on her own safety and survival. When she'd driven off and left

the girls on the beach, she'd told herself that they'd be fine, but had she truly believed it? It didn't matter. She'd left them anyway.

Laura felt helpless as she saw her sister shaking. She wanted to alleviate Elena's torment. She wanted to fold her up in her arms and turn her face in to her neck so that she'd never see anything ugly or harmful. So she would never feel any pain. But she held back. Elena needed this time alone. Elena had refused to tell Laura what had happened to her in London beyond Socorro robbing her. What it was that had made her turn around and come back so quickly. Laura feared that she'd been assaulted, hurt. But Elena had shaken her head. *Nothing like that,* she'd said. Still, she'd kept this from her, which she'd never done before with any significant experience. As Elena caressed the ground, those big, heavy tears indented the soil with tiny craters.

Laura worried about the upcoming meeting with Dulce. She kept turning it in her mind, trying to decide what the last move she could play was, how she could maneuver them both to safety, but she kept coming up blank. The only move left was to run. But she wanted to see the girls. She wanted to make sure that they were unharmed. Maybe then what she'd done to facilitate the tourist man's exit wouldn't feel so heartless. The girls weren't dead. As far as she could tell, they hadn't been raped. They were home with two parents who loved them, in a mansion where they had anything they could desire at their fingertips. They had a life ahead of them full of ease and joy and love. Should anyone have to pay for the *possibility* that something terrible could have happened if it *hadn't*?

Laura took in the way that nature had been battered. There was a lesson that the land offered them about endurance and resilience, because this land had been battered, abused, by people, by weather, time and time again, and yet it came back. Laura felt within herself a burgeoning power of persistence, with a toughness in her heart as hard as the storm-resistant tempered glass of the hotel. Impenetrable. Unshakable.

When her sister began speaking about their parents, Laura was surprised. There had been something about the crying that'd made her think that she was considering what she'd done to the girls. But she was focused on the past, a past that had so little relevance to their current crisis that Laura wanted to shake her once again, to tell her to focus on what they had to deal with here and now. But when her sister rose and stood in front of her, Laura was forced to pay attention.

"What I'm telling you is that you didn't know our parents, Laura. They lived in Santo Domingo for many years before you came along. Papi told me that they used to live with all these people, Dominicans, Haitians, people who had come from poverty, like us, and found a way to make a good life. He told me that there were doctors and lawyers and business owners among them. He told me that you and me, we could be anything we wanted to be. That if we took the steps to create the conditions to make ourselves free, we could help others in small and big ways. He regretted so much. He used to say, *If the past doesn't push, let the future pull.*"

Laura had never heard these stories. She wasn't sure if they made any difference, but Laura was certain that her sister needed to believe these things about their father. How could you be hopeful about the world if you accepted that the person you'd come from was worthless? It was possible that she was speaking the truth. That their father had changed. But that didn't change what he'd done. What he was responsible for. Her sister, with her youth and optimism, didn't understand that they hadn't inherited anything from their parents except the ability to make bad choices.

"We have to go," Laura said.

Her sister shook her head. "You're the one who is a prisoner to your pain. To your resentment. He's gone."

Laura looked away. Could she let go? Forgive him? If she forgave her father, what would be left?

The sisters climbed into the resort SUV. Laura was grateful for Fabien's influence, for his money. Over the last day, they had cleared a path down the mountain. Ahead of them, there was the movement of big trucks removing fallen trees. Those who wanted to rebuild their homes would have funds available thanks to Fabien's promise to finance Pico Diablo's reconstruction. The sisters made their way easily down the mountain. They'd be on the road, out of Paloma Falls, in a matter of minutes.

CHAPTER
50

A S THEY DROVE PAST THE RESORT, PAST THE FANCY, MADE-UP little town of Ciudad Paloma Falls, the beach zipping by in a blur as her sister picked up speed, Elena felt a sense of relief. She was glad that she would be able to face Dulce. She needed to ask for forgiveness. But when they reached the fork in the road that would take them to Dulce's beachfront mansion, her sister sped past it.

"You missed the turn," Elena said, thinking for a moment that her sister was so distracted she'd forgotten where to go.

"You really think we're going to surrender?" Laura said, incredulous.

"Where are you going?" Elena asked.

"To the airport," she said. "I have contacts. I've set it up. We'll be out of the country in a few hours."

"You can't be serious," Elena said.

"We need to go into hiding," Laura said, digging into her hairline, trying to get at an itch. "I have some associates willing to help us in Costa Rica. We can make our way there. Figure out what's next when things calm down."

"Stop it," Elena said. "Stop!"

Laura pulled the SUV over. Faced her sister.

"Take me to Dulce's," Elena said. "I want to see the girls."

"You don't know what's good for you," Laura said, speaking to Elena in her slow, condescending tone. "You don't understand the severity of what's about to happen. They will charge you with attempted human trafficking, Elena. They will accuse me of complicity, of aiding a suspect, of bribery. This will mean real prison, for a very long time.

You lost your shit over airport security. You think you can handle facing your mistakes? You will not be treated as a child because you haven't behaved like a child. You will be treated as an adult. They will not be lenient with you. Not with either of us."

"You don't get to say," Elena said. "This is my life. I made the decision to leave the girls with that terrible man. I left knowing they were in danger. I'm not running away this time."

"You didn't mean to do anything bad," Laura said, biting at her lips. Why did she need to convince her sister that a mistake, no matter how big or small, shouldn't cost her life? "You were thoughtless and immature and very stupid, but you never meant for harm to come to those girls."

"You're right," Elena said. "I trusted that someone else would come. That someone else would take care of it! Don't you see? I turned *my* back." Elena was transported to those moments when she'd been in the tourist man's car, right before she'd pressed hard on the gas with all her might. Hadn't that original mistake been rooted in the trust that someone else would do what was right? That somehow the world would tilt toward goodness without her involvement? "People don't just show up to do what's right."

Elena felt herself be lifted by a cool breeze. On their right, past the car windows, the shimmer on the sea intensified. It was a diamond necklace around the throat of this land. Next to her, her sister gawked at her, uncomprehending and scared.

"This is my life," Elena added with determination. "I get to decide what happens next."

"But it isn't just your life," Laura murmured. "This is my life, too. You don't understand what I've done since you left. To keep you safe and free."

"What have you done?" Elena asked, thinking that maybe if she could get her sister to tell the truth, to hear herself say it, she might understand how the past corroded the present, how Laura had been blinded by everything they'd been through. Elena hoped she could see what she'd never been able to see before.

But Laura's eyes fell on her lap. She couldn't say any of it aloud.

"I'm a freedom-seeking warrior," Elena chanted. "In the face of in-justice and greed, I stand tall, like my ancestors."

"Shut up, shut up," Laura said, gripping the steering wheel until her knuckles turned white. She opened the door, left the car. She kicked off her shoes, walked the short distance from the road to the beach. The sun was burning, burning. The sand torched her feet. Elena rushed after her, stood next to her—both sisters facing the ocean so deep and blue.

"It's all lies, Elena. All of it. We aren't descended from freedom-seeking warriors."

Elena's eyebrows knitted. "What are you talking about?"

"Pico Diablo was founded by people who were running away from the Parsley Massacre. That's the genesis of this place. People who were scared, who knew that the best way to survive was to hide."

"You would say anything to convince me to do what you want," Elena said.

"No, Elena," Laura said, forcing calm that she didn't feel into her tone. "Doña Fella told me the truth a year ago. She was worried that our father would never come back because he'd been gone for months. This is our truth. Our family, we're the ones who are supposed to create a sanctuary for those in danger. It is meant to be our job, being the secret-keepers, the guardians who provide a safe haven if danger comes. It has been passed down from generation to generation."

Elena's eyes widened. Her mind reeled. It was as if things were fi-nally falling into place. She remembered the many times her father had told her that he felt unable to rise to his real purpose in life. He used to say that one day, Elena and her sister would be the ones to do what he couldn't. How many times had Elena heard him say that true safety was only possible with money and power? He must have meant sanctuary for themselves and others. It was the reason he'd kept trying to make it to the United States. He had been sure he would attain there the class mobility that had been denied to him here. And the world back home would be a better place for it. This revelation made Elena realize how flawed her father's way of looking at the world had been. He, too, had thought that things would be better if he turned his back. She ached for him.

"Laura," Elena said, turning her entire body toward her sister, "you know what? It's all the same. The only thing that matters more than our roots is our community. Facing the people who are the only family we know. We wronged them. We face them."

"No," Laura said. Out of nowhere, she began to weep. She felt her lips tremble. What was happening to her? "I promised Mami I would do my job. I would take care of you. I wouldn't let anything bad happen to you."

Elena leaned over, wiped the tears. "Mami is dead. The dead have no expectations. What we do, we do for the living."

The dead feel no shame, she had said to Carmen. *They have no expectations,* her sister was saying to her. It was hearing her sister say those words with such resignation that helped Laura understand that she didn't believe either statement to be true. Laura felt a sob come from somewhere deep. She'd had only one job that truly mattered. She had failed at it, disastrously. She had failed at every level.

"You aren't my mother," Elena said. "You are my sister. I don't need you to mother me. Smother me. I don't need you to try to fix things. Always acting like you know what's best for me. I know the kind of person I want to be. You have your life, and I have mine. It's not one life. There are two lives. And I'm telling you right now, unless you drug me like you did Dulce, I will make my way back here."

Laura turned away from her sister, ashamed. Elena had spoken to Dulce. Dulce had told her what she'd done. Or maybe Pablo had told her.

"It's so exhausting, dealing with you," Elena said. "You make the wrong decisions all the time. You pretend you're doing it to keep me safe, but it isn't true. You're a coward. All the grown-ups are, my God. So complicit in harm. You leave it to us, always passing the responsibility of attempting to repair things to young people."

"You're so ungrateful," Laura spat out, feeling a fire burning in her stomach. "Do you have any idea where you would have ended up without me? Do you?"

"Not worse off than where I stand right now," Elena said.

Laura took a step back, as if she'd been wounded. Elena closed the gap between them. She raised her hand to her sister's face. She wiped away the tears that kept falling, even as Laura pretended to be so tough. Her anger was so often a façade that hid pain. "I know I owe you my life. I'm not ungrateful. I'm asking you to see *me*. Not the little girl who needed protecting. The person who's telling you that we'll be worse off if we run away."

It was true, what Elena was saying. The only way they'd be worse off would be if they ran away. It had happened. In a matter of a few days, her sister had grown up. Then, as Laura began walking toward the car, it occurred to her that maybe it wasn't that her sister had magically matured, but that Laura herself had been unable to see her sister for who she truly was all along.

"Have it your way," Laura shouted over her shoulder. "Let's go see Dulce."

CHAPTER
51

THEY ARRIVED AT DULCE'S MANSION, BUT THERE WERE NO police cars. Instead, they found Vida, Pablo, Rio, and Pasofino clinking champagne glasses with Dulce on her outdoor balcony that overlooked the sea. Dulce's house had suffered no damage during the hurricane. If anything, it looked even more resilient now amid the battered landscape. Down below, Fabien was at the beach, swimming with Niña and Perfecta, who giggled and splashed each other as if nothing terrible had happened to them, either.

When Elena and Laura stepped onto the balcony, an awkward silence fell.

"What's the celebration for?" Laura asked, feigning joviality even as her heart hammered.

"The Vargas sisters offered Pablo the job," Vida said proudly. "He's going to become the caretaker of the new sanctuary."

"Congrats," Laura said. "That's great!" She meant it. Pablo deserved the job. He was the best person for it.

"Will you both come with me?" Dulce asked, standing up and heading inside the massive house before either of the sisters could respond.

On the third floor, water lapped over the edge of the infinity pool. They could see Vida and Pablo holding hands two floors beneath them. Rio and Pasofino must've been saying something funny, based on the way they all laughed.

"You're both lucky that you have people who love you," Dulce said.

Laura hung back while Elena rushed over to Dulce. She fell on her knees. The tears were instant. She sobbed about how sorry she was, how she'd never meant for any of it to happen.

"Stop it," Dulce said coldly. "You don't get to come here and cry. You don't get to apologize. The girls—they look fine, you know. Almost as if nothing awful happened to them. But you know, they couldn't sleep all night. They kept waking up with night terrors. That man, he punched Niña. He choked Perfecta. He ripped their clothes off. If they hadn't fought back, he would have raped them. It might seem like the girls walked away unscathed, but this trauma will follow them for their entire lives."

Laura stumbled, sat on a nearby stool. Off to the side, down on the ground floor where the rest of the group continued to drink and chat happily, window curtains parted. Laura saw Doña Fella moving slowly to allow the sunlight into the room. When she noticed the women by the pool up above, she abruptly moved out of Laura's view.

Elena's gaze was glued to Dulce. She was pale.

"Vida, Pablo, Rio, Pasofino," Dulce went on. "They came here, early, to beg on your behalf. They kept talking about everything I already knew, about what you both have been through. The cruelty that seems to follow you no matter what. I didn't realize that your father had died."

Dulce's eyes clouded over.

"I'm not going to press charges," she said.

Laura's hand flew to her mouth.

Elena stood up and held on to Dulce's hands. "Thank you," she said in a small voice.

"You have to leave this country," Dulce said. "I don't want you to ever come back, not as long as my daughters and I are here."

Elena took a step back, her eyebrows knitted. "You can't mean that."

"Leave and never come back or stay locked up for a long time. You choose."

"We have obligations here," Elena said. "We can't just walk away."

"Whatever you need to do, figure out how to do it far away."

Laura found the strength to stand up. She faced Dulce for the first time. She didn't know what to say. How could she explain that most of the decisions she'd made had been motivated by the assumption that the situation was hopeless, that Dulce's daughters were dead? What could she possibly say that wouldn't make things worse?

"I never meant for any harm to come to your children."

Dulce let out a bitter laugh. "You never meant any harm? That's rich, Laura. Is that what you're telling yourself? That everything you did was to keep your sister safe? The worst calamities are rooted in love. Leave my house. You have twenty-four hours to get the hell off this island."

Elena and Laura were stepping away when Dulce called Laura back.

"There is one other thing I'm going to need you to do," she said.

Laura nodded. "Anything," she said. "Wait for me in the car," she commanded Elena.

CHAPTER
52

Elena didn't wait in the car. As she made her way down to the ground floor, the door to one of the bedroom suites opened and Doña Fella stepped through the doorway. She waved Elena over. Elena moved into the room, following Doña Fella to a spacious seating area.

"Did you move in with Dulce?" Elena asked after giving her old teacher a kiss on the cheek, asking for her blessing.

"Just until things up in Pico Diablo are back to normal," Doña Fella said. They still had no electricity or running water, no cellphone service. Doña Fella pointed to the corrugated metal box that sat in the middle of the large glass coffee table.

"Is this the box?" Elena asked, awed.

Doña Fella nodded. She extended her hand in a gesture that said, *Feel free to open, touch.* During the short drive after their confrontation by the beach, Laura had filled Elena in on the rest of the conversation with Doña Fella from a year ago, the details she'd learned about the past. The day Laura had found out that everyone in Pico Diablo except their own family was of Haitian descent had also been the day that she had refused the obligation to be the keeper of the secret. She had handed this old tin box back to Doña Fella and refused to accept her duty to the past.

Elena opened the box. Tenderly and with great care, she touched the fragile documents, noticing the pictures that had been drawn; the poems that she couldn't yet read but would one day be able to; the letters that had been written to prepare those in the future for what it would mean to exist despite hatred, pain, separation, loss. Elena could clearly see that these documents were an archive of love.

"Why didn't you ask me?" Elena said.

"The tradition says we ask the eldest," Doña Fella said. "But I can see that I chose wrong. Sometimes we must break the tradition. I kept giving chances to people who didn't deserve a second chance at all."

Elena didn't think that was fair. Even those who faltered and seemed hopeless deserved a second chance.

"I hope to honor the duty for my family," Elena said, placing the objects carefully back inside the box. "Will you let me?"

"Not yet. You'll have to work fast and prove yourself," Doña Fella said. "I won't be around forever."

Elena noticed her old teacher's expression. Doña Fella quickly covered it with a stern look of disapproval, but Elena had caught the soft smile that had played on her features. It was as if she finally had some reason to feel hopeful for the sorry Moreno lot. Elena couldn't wait to sit with her, to learn as much as she could about the past. To do something practical and consequential. Doña Fella motioned for Elena to help her up, and together, through the glass, they gazed at the group outside.

"So how does it work with *your* job?" Elena asked. "Who becomes the keeper of the history?"

"You mean, who becomes the new me?" Doña Fella said.

Elena nodded.

"We will need someone who is part of the town to safeguard the history and work with the secret-keeper." She fixed her eyes on Pablo. "I'm waiting for him to earn his place, too."

Elena nodded, understanding. She knew exactly what to do to help Pablo earn his position.

PASOFINO AND RIO WERE at the other end of the balcony, dancing to a fast-paced bachata. They had the fancy footwork that Pasofino had been nicknamed for, and every other move was a flourish of hand gestures and dramatic turns.

Elena knew that she didn't have much time. Any moment now, her sister would come downstairs with Dulce, and they'd have to leave.

Sitting between Pablo and Vida, Elena asked, "Do you think you could set up some time for me to speak to Amber and Ida? Today?"

Pablo raised an eyebrow. "About what?"

"I think the sanctuary shouldn't just be a place that safeguards the plants, the ocean, and the wildlife. We should try to convince the Vargas sisters to use all that money and influence to do something for the people who are most vulnerable in this country."

Pablo remembered the drive through the country with that tourist family, how he'd had to pretend not to notice the many times they'd passed Haitians who were being subjected to raids, forced into vans, and assaulted; some, it was murmured, were killed out of eyesight. The dangers to those poor people were real. It wouldn't hurt to help Elena. Maybe this was the way in which she'd try to make amends. He'd come to believe that if you gave someone enough responsibility and provided support along the way, they truly could become the best version of themselves.

"We're meeting later today at the gallery to watch the sunset at the Grand Paloma," he said. "Come join us. I'll do what I can to help."

Laura and Dulce joined the group just as Pablo finished speaking. Laura motioned for Elena to follow her, preferring to leave hurriedly, without saying goodbye. Elena lingered for a few moments, giving everyone hugs. She noticed that Fabien stayed away from the group. The girls hadn't been allowed to come close to either Elena or Laura.

When they entered the car, Laura handed Elena a red-label bottle of Beyond Proof rum.

"Isn't this the poison rum?" Elena asked. "Why did she give it to you? She wants us to poison ourselves?"

"No, it's not for us. It's a way for me to earn our way back."

"By doing what?"

Laura shrugged, made a dismissive gesture. But her features were clouded over with concern, a new heavy obligation for her to bear. This time Laura wasn't sure she'd be able to ignore it the way she had chosen to disregard the secret of Pico Diablo.

WEDNESDAY

CHAPTER
53

IN THE END, SAYING GOODBYE TO PICO DIABLO AND TO Ciudad Paloma Falls ended up being easier than either Elena or Laura had imagined. After all, they had both been daydreaming about this day for many years. Ida and Amber Vargas were happy to fast-track the trip once Laura assured them that she'd be able to manage all transitions virtually, since she and Pablo already had a good working relationship. The last of the paying guests had departed the Grand Paloma Resort to head home or to finish their vacations at the Yellow Paloma, and so now it would be simpler to officially shut down operations. It would be easy to start anew.

Packing the few belongings Laura and Elena each had left took no time at all. Laura wrapped the poisoned rum in a few of her old uniforms and told herself that if it wasn't seized by authorities as they made their way into Spain, then she'd have to take it as a sign that God himself wanted the tourist man dead. They headed up to the mountain to spend their last night in the home where they had grown up.

VIDA AND PABLO CAME over that evening, bringing a pot full of pollo guisado and another small container with oxtail stew. They made vegan yellow rice with okra, corn, peppers, cilantro, garlic, and onions so that Elena could enjoy their last meal together. The various pots filled the wooden home with their aromas instantly, much more delicious than the fragrance that was spritzed back in the luxurious lobby of the Grand Paloma Resort.

"So, you two are back together?" Laura asked. "You forgave him?"

"Let's leave the mistakes of the past in the past," Pablo said.

Vida laughed. "I'm forcing Pablo to be celibate until the baby comes. I need to see that he truly has changed. That he's able to create a life founded on what's important to us, our own values. If he can do that, then yes, I'm going to agree to marry him."

"I asked," Pablo said. "She said no."

"I said, *not yet,*" Vida said, rubbing her cute belly.

Laura stuck a finger through her extensions, trying to reach a terrible itch that was driving her crazy.

"Are you gonna let me take out those ridiculous tracks?" Elena said.

"You look like shit," Pablo said. Pablo spoke to her the way he used to speak to her before she became his boss. He was no longer scared of her.

Laura rose off the old rocking chair and looked at herself in the mirror. Nobody cared what she looked like anymore, including herself, so she was ready to give in. Her sister carefully cut away the thread that sutured the fake hair extensions to her own sparse, kinky hair. Moments into the process, the lightness she felt on her head became overpowering. When it was finished, she stepped back in front of the mirror. The tears came by themselves. There were so many bald spots from the constant pressure on her scalp. Vida used an electric shaver to get rid of the little patches of hair that remained. She rubbed coconut oil on Laura's bruised scalp. She mumbled some words—a song, it sounded like—that Laura couldn't make out. But soon after, she felt flushed with hope. Over the next few hours and days, optimism about the future would bloom.

"Who would have thought you'd look better bald?" Elena said, gazing in wonder. "You look crazy young."

THURSDAY

CHAPTER
54

THE HOTEL THAT WOULD BECOME THEIR HOME WAS LOCATED in Platja de Alcúdia, Mallorca. Since it was closed for the month of August, that meant that the Moreno sisters would be on vacation, for the first time in their lives, for an entire week. They arrived on Thursday in the late afternoon, right before sunset. The caretaker greeted them and showed them around their new home, and Laura and Elena were stupefied by the beauty of this place. It was a three-bedroom apartment with a courtyard that had views of the ocean and the sky. The waning sunlight flooded through all the tall windows, warming the space with so much illumination.

"Let's go to the beach," Elena said. "Come on! Before it gets dark."

Laura nodded. Made her way to the bedroom and unzipped the bag. The poison rum bottle had made it through. She patted it and placed it inside the hotel safe that was nestled on a crowded bookshelf with many well-loved books. She figured that in order to use it, if she ever were to even attempt it, she'd have to make it through another set of airports on the way to New York. If it actually made it through the last two legs of its journey, then the decision had been made by God.

She put on some shorts, and they headed out the door.

When they reached the shore, they were surprised at how crowded the beach was. They'd never seen so many beachgoers in the same place. They walked around, trying to find some free beach lounge chairs, but couldn't. When Laura went up to a nearby restaurant and said her full name, an older man with kind eyes who was manning the host stand introduced himself as Eduardo, the owner.

"Ida and Amber said to take good care of you," he said. "Welcome to Mallorca! My wife and I have been to the Dominican Republic so many times. We love it there! Son hermosas las dos!"

Eduardo spoke in rich Castilian Spanish. Within moments, he'd ushered the sisters to a reserved lounging space and they were reclining in the comfiest beach chairs. Drinks and more food than either of them could possibly eat in one sitting followed shortly thereafter. Every few moments, servers came by to check on them, asking them if they needed anything.

"I could get used to this," Laura said.

"Look at us," Elena said, switching her phone camera on. She sat up, took a selfie with her sister. She posted it right away. *Tourists in Mallorca!* her caption read.

A short distance away, there was a group of teenagers laughing and joking. In the other direction was a rocky ledge from which young kids were taking big, acrobatic leaps.

"Wow," Elena said. "It's amazing here."

Laura almost laughed, hearing that reverence in her sister's voice. But when she took it all in, she couldn't deny it. She was equally moved. The sky here had a different texture. It seemed more expansive. The enormous golden sun hid behind bulbous clouds which, right before their very eyes, revolved. It made the world seem to be moving slowly in a surreal dream. The seawater ahead of them was impossibly clear. A short distance away was a tiny little island, which made her instantly homesick. Who would have thought that she would miss that miserable place where she'd been born? There was an ache inside of her, the part of her that recognized they were in a faraway place. The future was full of so many unknown possibilities.

"I wanna jump," Elena said.

"Go," Laura said. "I'm going to relax."

She turned her attention to her sister as she ran away from her with such a strong, athletic stride. Elena reached the summit and laughed with the kids, who made room for her. Laura saw her sister take a huge leap off the rocky ledge into the air, a swan dive that was all grace and fierce courage. After she broke the surface of the water, she didn't come up right away. Laura stood up, waiting. Many long moments passed, and still, no Elena.

Laura rushed toward the water. She dove in. Swam with hard strokes toward her sister. By the time she reached the place where she'd gone through, Elena had emerged. She thrust her arms up triumphantly.

"I did it!" she said.

"Did what?" Laura asked, relieved her sister was fine. *No need to worry,* she reminded herself. Elena was a strong swimmer. She was okay on her own.

"I touched the bottom! I did it."

Laura was moved by her sister's giddiness. She was acting like a proud kid.

"You wanna try?" Elena asked.

Laura looked at the rocky ledge, so high off the surface of the beach. Up close, she noticed it wasn't a natural rock formation. It was man-made, created for the merriment of visitors, like them.

"Sure," she said. "Let's jump again, together."

Moments later, Elena and Laura held hands as they leaped off the rocks, bathed in golden sunlight.

EPILOGUE

Six Months Later

THE GREEN-EYED MAN CAME INTO THE ROOFTOP BAR AT NEW York City's Grand Liberty Paloma every evening at seven o'clock. Sometimes with colleagues, sometimes alone. Laura wasn't surprised that each night he'd struck up a conversation with her, staring her straight in the face, with no recognition of who she was. She sported her hair in a low-cut afro. She was often told that she looked like a teenager, what with all the sleep she got these nights and with her newfound ability to laugh more often. She had told him the truth. She had been invited to participate in a weeklong leadership training course by Paloma Enterprises; she had traveled from Spain thanks to her mentor, Miranda, who had generously sponsored her participation even though she wasn't an employee of the company. She gave him a false name. Just in case he ended up not-dead.

It must be said that Laura had given up on the idea of acting on Dulce's command to seek retribution, to stop this man permanently. But months ago, Dulce had forwarded her a post from BELatina's Insta: "The Dark Side of Tourism in Latin America: Medellín Cracks Down on Its Safety Measures After a Tourist Abuses Two Underaged Girls." This time, the girls had been twelve and thirteen. Just as before, the man had been in police custody, yet was able to walk away despite compelling evidence. *Who did he bribe this time?* Dulce had asked. *How many more times will this man keep doing this to our girls?* Laura had responded right away, saying that this was horrible but that they had no clue if it was the same man. Dulce had sent her a deluge of local newspaper articles. In one, an unnamed local had mentioned the green-eyed man with a scar on his cheek that resembled a fishing hook. In an NBC news piece, the mayor of the city had said, "It's sad to see how many people believe they can come to Medellín and do whatever they want."

They can go anywhere in the world and do whatever they want, Dulce had written.

Laura had sat with the weight of her responsibility. Had been unable to stop thinking about it.

On the first night he'd bought her a drink, he'd blurted out something about his last trip to Medellín. She sensed how close he was to confiding in her about what he'd done. There was an impulse to boast about how he'd managed to get away with his crimes time and time again. But he was a smart person. The closest he'd come had been on the fifth night, when she'd made a comment about sex exploitation in the Caribbean.

"If someone is for sale," he said, "you can't blame the consumer for buying."

Tonight, the sixth night, Laura finally agreed to let him join her upstairs in her room.

"You sure your wife won't mind?" she said, eyeing his wedding ring.

"She'd probably join us if she could," he said. "But our sitter is down with Covid this week. Who knows? Maybe next time you're in town she can join us."

He leaned back on the bed, watched her pull the bottle of red-label Beyond Proof rum out of her bag.

"I've seen that rum before," he said.

"I bet you haven't," she said. "It's illegal to take this rum out of DR. Hell, it's illegal to consume it there."

"So, you're an outlaw," he chuckled.

They did one shot, then another. Finally, a third. Laura put the bottle away.

"You can't drink more than three shots of this, it'll make you sick," Laura said.

The sensation of the special alcohol hadn't been exaggerated. The feeling of euphoria was instant. He laughed and, just as she'd planned, took the bottle out of her bag without asking. Served himself a water glass full of rum. He offered her some and she shook her head.

"I've got a lot more living to do," she said.

"You can't possibly believe rum will kill you," he said.

She turned away from him, facing the window. At night, Manhattan was as glorious and majestic as people said—the blinking lights made her feel a sense of awe and possibility. But the glass was reflective. She had to put much effort to see beyond her own body and the tourist man's as he raised the glass to his lips. There was no way she could let him go through with it. She turned back and ran to him, slapped the glass out of his hands before he could swallow it. "You can't have any more. It'll make you very sick. It will kill you."

"You fucking bitch," he said. And as if it was the most natural thing for him to do, he slapped her across the face, hard enough she fell to the ground. From down on the floor, she saw him looming above her. She didn't rise. The tourist man didn't apologize, didn't make an excuse for his violence. He went back to the bottle, poured himself a larger glass of rum than the one she'd spilled. Laura watched him drink it. Watched his eyes glaze over with desire. He kissed her, roughly fondled her breasts.

"I don't even feel drunk," he said, slurring his words.

"You have to get the hell out of my room," she said. "Or I will call the police."

He slapped her ass. "Too bad," he said. "I thought you would be a good time. I can tell you like it rough. Maybe tomorrow? I'll come back. Don't tell anybody I was here."

He brought a finger to his lips, loudly said, *Shhhh*. It would take somewhere between twenty-four and forty-eight hours for the rum to do its work. He'd start feeling nauseous; would develop severe vomiting; would heave, growing more breathless, until his heart gave out. By then, Laura would be in Mallorca, cheering on Elena as she learned that she'd gotten accepted to her first-choice college in sunny California. She was ready to study social justice. Ready to take on the cruelty of the world.

They would lovingly say hello to Pablo and Vida on a video call just a few days later. Their new baby girl would be screaming her head off, a head full of so much hair. Vida would say something about her mother getting the gender wrong, which they would think had to do with the loss of blood. The wedding, scheduled for early June, would take place in the new sanctuary with Niña and Perfecta as flower girls, and the couple would insist the sisters had to come back for it.

BACK AT PALOMA FALLS Sanctuary on Vida and Pablo's wedding day, Laura and Elena found the Grand Paloma's glass-and-metal hotel structure gone. Once word had gotten around that the sanctuary was a haven that housed all Dominican people regardless of descendance, offering legal refuge to all persecuted people, the number of residents had increased dramatically. The people who walked along the cobblestone path spoke Creole and Spanish; on occasion the sisters heard French or English. But all these people were Dominicans and Haitians. The buildings that had once housed the business center, the wellness center and spa, and even the multilevel gym had been demolished, and in their place were neat rows of spacious homes, built by those who would live in them. These homes were made of concrete and bamboo, materials meant to aid in cooling the planet, with indoor plumbing and electricity and built-in air-conditioning powered by wind and solar sources.

The amount of donations that had poured into the Vargas sisters' foundation had been so astonishing that they'd been able to form a new superfund. Unsurprisingly, many politicians had been persuaded to join. It seemed corrupt people could just as easily be coaxed to accept bribes for humanitarian causes. E.Z. had been right about some things, Elena mused on her way up to Pico Diablo. It turned out that having money and power really did make a difference when it came to refuge. Foreigners were no longer welcome at the sanctuary. There were no longer any tourists to be found in Paloma Falls.

True to his word, Fabien had rerouted some of the profit from Ciudad Paloma Falls to help rebuild homes up on Pico Diablo Mountain. He'd simply written people checks, no fuss, no muss, and Elena saw the way those funds had been used. The homes were now made of concrete, with strong foundations that would help the area's oldest inhabitants to fare better as more severe storms made their way through the region in the years to come.

When Doña Fella handed Elena the corrugated box that confirmed she was now the keeper of the secret, she had been rocking herself in a home that would survive her, that would shelter the many generations that would come after her. Doña Fella was glad that Elena had proven to be such an agile and smart person. Already, the weariness in her own bones had transformed into a useful impulse to teach the girl more of what she needed to know. Would there be enough time? There was never enough time to prepare for a world in which the cycles of the past insisted on overtaking the present.

"Look," Doña Fella said, while Elena was transfixed by the papers in the box. In the sky, hovering above the ocean, was a single dark cloud. It moved rapidly away from their area, traveling fast, heading west toward the capital. "We honor the past by remaining vigilant in the present," Doña Fella said.

Elena nodded somberly.

The wedding reception took place on a clear, bright night on the pebble-free beach. The family and neighbors who'd attended feasted on fish that Pablo had caught himself and on food they'd grown on Pico Diablo's new self-sustaining farms. Niña and Perfecta's giant hair puffs were decorated with beautiful flower crowns made from the peonies that had ended up growing and thriving all over the Pico Diablo Mountain after the hurricane, flourishing in the cooler mountain air despite the daytime Caribbean heat. Vida had made the crowns herself. They matched Vida's and her baby's crowns. It was easy to pretend that the Grand Paloma Resort had never existed, but the land bore the evidence. Nadine swiped the crown away every time someone placed it on her head. And each of them tried to put it back as they held her: first Dulce, then Elena, then Laura, each in turn thinking, *We'll do what we can to make a better world for you, baby girl.*

ACKNOWLEDGMENTS

'M IMMENSELY THANKFUL TO THE WORKERS AND LABORERS who were willing to speak to me about their experiences in the resort industry of the Dominican Republic. Those interviews were truly a moving and enlightening experience. I walked away with a very different perspective on what it means to claim a place as home when that place is hostile and dangerous, especially after speaking to Dominicans of Haitian descent. I'm also grateful to the scholars whose extensive work on Dominican history helped animate Pico Diablo's lore. Among those whose work most impacted this narrative are Dr. Edward Paulino, Soraya Aracena, and Matthew Alexander Randolph. Edwidge Danticat's *The Farming of Bones* and Julia Alvarez's *In the Time of the Butterflies* were instrumental points of inspiration for this novel.

My deep gratitude goes to the editors of the literary journals that published sections of this novel, first conceived of as short stories: Nicole Terez Dutton published "Curandera" at the *Kenyon Review;* Morgan Frank published "The Odd Difficulty of Sinking" at *Memorious: A Journal of New Verse and Fiction;* and Dawnie Walton, Deesha Philyaw, and Mark Armstrong published "Fog" at *Ursa.*

I had the privilege of working with three exceptional editors whose questions and insights transformed this book. I'm immensely grateful to Chelcee Johns, Rita Jaramillo, and Jennifer Hershey. Thank you to Erika Morillo for the wonderful work in translating this novel to

Spanish. I'm grateful to the team at Ballantine Books for their hard work and dedication: Kate Gomer, Sydney Collins, Anusha Khan, Abdi Omer, Kara Welsh, Kathleen Quinlan, Sophie Normil, Kimberly Hovey, Taylor Noel, Jennifer Rodriguez, Stephany Diaz, Pamela Alders, Nathalie Mairena, Barbara M. Bachman, and Taylor McGowan. For anyone whose labor is invisible to me and aided in getting this book into the hands of readers: thank you from the bottom of my heart.

My deepest gratitude to the world's best literary agent. Te adoro, PJ Mark! Thanks to Madeline Ticknor, the extended team at Janklow & Nesbit Associates, as well as Kerry-Ann Bentley.

This novel was completed with the gift of time from the Hermitage Artist Retreat, the Vermont Studio Center, the Virginia Center for the Creative Arts, Rowland Writers Retreat, and the Butternut Farm Writer Retreat.

The people and organizations whose missions center on supporting writers have done so much to uplift my work. Thank you to Laura Pegram of Kweli; Angela Abreu of Dominican Writers Association; Marsha Massiah, Mellany Paynter, and Melissa Harper of the Brooklyn Caribbean Literary Festival; Nicholas Laughlin and Shivanee Ramlochan at the Bocas Lit Fest; Lee Clay Johnson of The Writer's Foundry MFA program at St. Joseph's University; Nicole Terez Dutton and Elizabeth Dark of the Kenyon Review; David Simpson of the Fine Arts Work Center; Jennifer Grotz and Lauren Francis-Sharma of the Bread Loaf Writers' Conference; Noy Holland, Betsy Wheeler, Saffron Turner, and Jeff Parker of the Juniper Summer Writing Institute; Lance Cleland and A.L. Major of Tin House Workshop; Elizabeth Knapp of the Low-Residency MFA Program at Hood College; Lisa Locascio Nighthawk and Alistair McCartney of the Antioch low-residency MFA in Creative Writing program; Ken Chen at Barnard College; Helen Schulman and John Reed of The New School creative writing MFA program; Jeremy Lopez, Peter Kingstone, Leslie Wilson, David Galef, Mark Rotella, Marta López-Luaces, and Johnny Lorez of Montclair State University; Amelia Possanza of Lavender Public Relations.

I'm astonished by the generosity and love of my writing community. Thank you Angie Cruz, Sofija Stefanovic, Xochitl Gonzalez, Peggy Bourjaily, Carrie Cooperider, Joanne Ramos, Lupita Aquino, Justine Van de Leun, Leila Mottley, Mitchell S. Jackson, Caleb Gayle, Kimberly King Parsons, Diana Marie Delgado, Nicole Treska, Robb Todd, Tracy O'Neill, Joseph Riippi, Yahdon Israel, Porsalin Israel, Alejandro Varela, Paul Tran, Dawnie Walton, Deesha Philyaw, Robert Jones, Jr., Kiese Laymon, Lupita Aquino, Naima Coster, Nadia Owusu, Mateo Askaripour, Caits Meissner, Nafissa Thompson-Spires, Suleika Jaouad, Maurice Carlos Ruffin, Dionne Ford, Kim Coleman Foote, Christine Pride, Maisy Card, Emillio Mesa, Lorraine Avila, Deirdre Sugiuchi, Carmen Tanner Slaughter, Sidik Fofana, Shaunna Edwards, Tanya Shirazi, Amanda Tien, Shivanee Ramlochan, Charmaine Wilkerson, Nelly Rosario, Myriam J. A. Chancy, Jennifer Baker, Mahogany L. Browne, and Nicole Dennis-Benn. I'm thankful for the artists and writers whose lectures informed this book: Elizabeth Flood, Samantha Hunt, Marie Helene Bertino, and Adriana Corral.

And thank you to my teachers and mentors, who have given me so much, especially Julia Alvarez, Tayari Jones, Steven Millhauser, Cristina García, Robert Eversz, and Mat Johnson.

My family and dear friends continue to be an endless source of support and encouragement. Thank you Nicolasa Lucas, Josephine Tucker, Mary Lucas, Jacqueline Lucas, Nuris, Cristian, and Evelyn Natera, Cheryl and Kyle Tucker, Harry Marte, Katie Sciurba-Jenkins, Angel B. Pérez, Rhonda Buege, Kristen Lepore, Tory Neff, Judy Guzman, Evelyn Vasquez, Wendy Soto, Judy Francisco King, Elizabeth Francisco Calenda, Juana Trejo-Reyes, Rachelle Lahens Harris, Natasha Friedrichs, Amanda Perez Leder, Jean M. Reich, Wendy Allred, Amanda Goldman, Diane Tehranian, Madeline Rowan, Jamie Smith, Erin Gladney, Ashlee Wolf, and Karen Ermler.

To Penelope and Julian: All I do is for you. To Kevin: I couldn't do any of it without you. I love you.

CLEYVIS NATERA is the author of *Neruda on the Park*. She was born in the Dominican Republic, migrated to the United States at ten years old, and grew up in New York City. She holds a BA from Skidmore College and an MFA from New York University. Her writing has won awards and fellowships from the International Latino Book Awards, PEN America, the Bread Loaf Writers' Conference, *The Kenyon Review*'s Writers Workshops, the Vermont Studio Center, the Hermitage Artist Retreat, Rowland Writers Retreat, and the Virginia Center for the Creative Arts. She is currently a Fulbright Specialist. She lives with her husband and two young children in Montclair, New Jersey. *The Grand Paloma Resort* is her second novel.

cleyvisnatera.com